The Collected
Supernatural and Weird
Fiction of
Mary Shelley
Volume 1

The Collected Supernatural and Weird Fiction of Mary Shelley Volume 1

Including One Novel "Frankenstein or
The Modern Prometheus"
and Fourteen Short Stories
of the Strange and Unusual

Mary Shelley

LEONAUR

The Collected
Supernatural and Weird
Fiction of
Mary Shelley
Volume 1
Including One Novel "Frankenstein or
The Modern Prometheus"
and Fourteen Short Stories
of the Strange and Unusual
by Mary Shelley

FIRST EDITION

Leonaur is an imprint
of Oakpast Ltd

Copyright in this form © 2010 Oakpast Ltd

ISBN: 978-0-85706-058-7 (hardcover)
ISBN: 978-0-85706-057-0 (softcover)

http://www.leonaur.com

Contents

Frankenstein

Letter 1

To Mrs. Saville, England

St. Petersburgh, Dec. 11th, 17—

You will rejoice to hear that no disaster has accompanied the commencement of an enterprise which you have regarded with such evil forebodings. I arrived here yesterday, and my first task is to assure my dear sister of my welfare and increasing confidence in the success of my undertaking.

I am already far north of London, and as I walk in the streets of Petersburgh, I feel a cold northern breeze play upon my cheeks, which braces my nerves and fills me with delight. Do you understand this feeling? This breeze, which has travelled from the regions towards which I am advancing, gives me a foretaste of those icy climes. Inspirited by this wind of promise, my daydreams become more fervent and vivid. I try in vain to be persuaded that the pole is the seat of frost and desolation; it ever presents itself to my imagination as the region of beauty and delight.

There, Margaret, the sun is forever visible, its broad disk just skirting the horizon and diffusing a perpetual splendour. There—for with your leave, my sister, I will put some trust in preceding navigators—there snow and frost are banished; and, sailing over a calm sea, we may be wafted to a land surpassing in wonders and in beauty every region hitherto discovered on the habitable globe. Its productions and features may be without example, as the phenomena of the heavenly bodies undoubtedly are in those undiscovered solitudes. What may not be expected in a country of eternal light?

I may there discover the wondrous power which attracts the needle and may regulate a thousand celestial observations that require only this voyage to render their seeming eccentricities consistent forever. I shall satiate my ardent curiosity with the sight of a part of the world never before visited, and may tread a land never before imprinted by the foot of man. These are my enticements, and they are sufficient to conquer all fear of danger or death and to induce me to commence this laborious voyage with the joy a child feels when he embarks in a little boat, with his holiday mates, on an expedition of discovery up his native river. But supposing all these conjectures to be false, you cannot contest the inestimable benefit which I shall confer on all mankind, to the last generation, by discovering a passage near the pole to those countries, to reach which at present so many months are requisite; or by ascertaining the secret of the magnet, which, if at all possible, can only be effected by an undertaking such as mine.

These reflections have dispelled the agitation with which I began my letter, and I feel my heart glow with an enthusiasm which elevates me to heaven, for nothing contributes so much to tranquillize the mind as a steady purpose—a point on which the soul may fix its intellectual eye. This expedition has been the favourite dream of my early years. I have read with ardour the accounts of the various voyages which have been made in the prospect of arriving at the North Pacific Ocean through the seas which surround the pole.

You may remember that a history of all the voyages made for purposes of discovery composed the whole of our good Uncle Thomas' library. My education was neglected, yet I was passionately fond of reading. These volumes were my study day and night, and my familiarity with them increased that regret which I had felt, as a child, on learning that my father's dying injunction had forbidden my uncle to allow me to embark in a seafaring life.

These visions faded when I perused, for the first time, those poets whose effusions entranced my soul and lifted it to heaven. I also became a poet and for one year lived in a paradise of my own creation; I imagined that I also might obtain a niche in the temple where the names of Homer and Shakespeare are consecrated. You are well acquainted with my failure and how heavily I bore the disappointment. But just at that time I inherited the fortune of my cousin, and my thoughts were turned into the channel of their earlier bent.

Six years have passed since I resolved on my present undertaking. I can, even now, remember the hour from which I dedicated myself to this great enterprise. I commenced by inuring my body to hardship. I accompanied the whale-fishers on several expeditions to the North Sea; I voluntarily endured cold, famine, thirst, and want of sleep; I often worked harder than the common sailors during the day and devoted my nights to the study of mathematics, the theory of medicine, and those branches of physical science from which a naval adventurer might derive the greatest practical advantage.

Twice I actually hired myself as an under-mate in a Greenland whaler, and acquitted myself to admiration. I must own I felt a little proud when my captain offered me the second dignity in the vessel and entreated me to remain with the greatest earnestness, so valuable did he consider my services. And now, dear Margaret, do I not deserve to accomplish some great purpose? My life might have been passed in ease and luxury, but I preferred glory to every enticement that wealth placed in my path.

Oh, that some encouraging voice would answer in the affirmative! My courage and my resolution is firm; but my hopes fluctuate, and my spirits are often depressed. I am about to proceed on a long and difficult voyage, the emergencies of which will demand all my fortitude: I am required not only to raise the spirits of others, but sometimes to sustain my own, when theirs are failing.

This is the most favourable period for travelling in Russia. They fly quickly over the snow in their sledges; the motion is pleasant, and, in my opinion, far more agreeable than that of an English stagecoach. The cold is not excessive, if you are wrapped in furs—a dress which I have already adopted, for there is a great difference between walking the deck and remaining seated motionless for hours, when no exercise prevents the blood from actually freezing in your veins. I have no ambition to lose my life on the post-road between St. Petersburgh and Archangel. I shall depart for the latter town in a fortnight or three weeks; and my intention is to hire a ship there, which can easily be done by paying the insurance for the owner, and to engage as many sailors as I think necessary among those who are accustomed to the whale-fishing. I do not intend to sail until the month of June; and when shall I return? Ah, dear sister, how can I answer this question? If I succeed, many, many months, perhaps years, will pass before you and I may meet. If I fail, you will see me again soon, or never. Farewell, my dear, excellent Margaret. Heaven shower down blessings on you, and save me, that I may again and again testify my gratitude for all your love and kindness.

Your affectionate brother,
R. Walton

LETTER 2

To Mrs. Saville, England

Archangel, 28th March, 17—

How slowly the time passes here, encompassed as I am by frost and snow! Yet a second step is taken towards my enterprise. I have hired a vessel and am occupied in collecting my sailors; those whom I have already engaged appear to be men on whom I can depend and are certainly possessed of dauntless courage.

But I have one want which I have never yet been able to satisfy, and the absence of the object of which I now feel as a most severe evil, I have no friend, Margaret: when I am glowing with the enthusiasm of success, there will be none to participate my joy; if I am assailed by disappointment, no one will endeavour to sustain me in dejection. I shall commit my thoughts to paper, it is true; but that is a poor medium for the communication of feeling. I desire the company of a man who could sympathize with me, whose eyes would reply to mine.

You may deem me romantic, my dear sister, but I bitterly feel the want of a friend. I have no one near me, gentle yet courageous, possessed of a cultivated as well as of a capacious mind, whose tastes are like my own, to approve or amend my plans. How would such a friend repair the faults of your poor brother! I am too ardent in execution and too impatient of difficulties. But it is a still greater evil to me that I am self-educated: for the first fourteen years of my life I ran wild on a common and read nothing but our Uncle Thomas' books of voyages. At that age I became acquainted with the celebrated poets of our own country; but it was only when it had ceased to be in my power to derive its most important benefits from such a conviction that I perceived the necessity of becoming acquainted with more languages than that of my native country.

Now I am twenty-eight and am in reality more illiterate than many schoolboys of fifteen. It is true that I have thought more and that my daydreams are more extended and magnificent, but they want (as the painters call it) KEEPING; and I greatly need a friend who would have sense enough not to despise me as romantic, and affection enough for me to endeavour to regulate my mind.

Well, these are useless complaints; I shall certainly find no friend on the wide ocean, nor even here in Archangel, among merchants and seamen. Yet some feelings, unallied to the dross of human nature, beat even in these rugged bosoms.

My lieutenant, for instance, is a man of wonderful courage and enterprise; he is madly desirous of glory, or rather, to word my phrase more characteristically, of advancement in his profession. He is an Englishman, and in the midst of national and professional prejudices, unsoftened by cultivation, retains some of the noblest endowments of humanity. I first became acquainted with him on board a whale vessel; finding that he was unemployed in this city, I easily engaged him to assist in my enterprise. The master is a person of an excellent disposition and is remarkable in the ship for his gentleness and the mildness of his discipline.

This circumstance, added to his well-known integrity and dauntless courage, made me very desirous to engage him. A youth passed in solitude, my best years spent under your gentle and feminine fosterage, has so refined the groundwork of my character that I cannot overcome an intense distaste to the usual brutality exercised on board ship: I have never believed it to be necessary, and when I heard of a mariner equally noted for his kindliness of heart and the respect and obedience paid to him by his crew, I felt myself peculiarly fortunate in being able to secure his services. I heard of him first in rather a romantic manner, from a lady who owes to him the happiness of her life. This, briefly, is his story.

Some years ago he loved a young Russian lady of moderate fortune, and having amassed a considerable sum in prize-money, the father of the girl consented to the match. He saw his mistress once before the destined ceremony; but she was bathed in tears, and throwing herself at his feet, entreated him to spare her, confessing at the same time that she loved another, but that he was poor, and that her father would never consent to the union. My generous friend reassured the suppliant, and on being informed of the name of her lover, instantly abandoned his pursuit. He had already bought a farm with his money, on which he had designed to pass the remainder of his life; but he bestowed the whole on his rival, together with the remains of his prize-money to purchase stock, and then himself solicited the young woman's father to consent to her marriage with her lover.

But the old man decidedly refused, thinking himself bound in honour to my friend, who, when he found the father inexorable, quitted his country, nor returned until he heard that his former mistress was married according to her inclinations. "What a noble fellow!" you will exclaim. He is so; but then he is wholly uneducated: he is as silent as a Turk, and a kind of ignorant carelessness attends him, which, while it renders his conduct the more astonishing, detracts from the interest and sympathy which otherwise he would command.

Yet do not suppose, because I complain a little or because I can conceive a consolation for my toils which I may never know, that I am wavering in my resolutions. Those are as fixed as fate, and my voyage is only now delayed until the weather shall permit my embarkation. The winter has been dreadfully severe, but the spring promises well, and it is considered as a remarkably early season, so that perhaps I may sail sooner than I expected. I shall do nothing rashly: you know me sufficiently to confide in my prudence and considerateness whenever the safety of others is committed to my care.

I cannot describe to you my sensations on the near prospect of my undertaking. It is impossible to communicate to you a conception of the trembling sensation, half pleasurable and half fearful, with which I am preparing to depart. I am going to unexplored regions, to "the land of mist and snow," but I shall kill no albatross; therefore do not be alarmed for my safety or if I should come back to you as worn and woeful as the "Ancient Mariner." You will smile at my allusion, but I will disclose a secret. I have often attributed my attachment to, my passionate enthusiasm for, the dangerous mysteries of ocean to that production of the most imaginative of modern poets.

There is something at work in my soul which I do not understand. I am practically industrious—painstaking, a workman to execute with perseverance and labour—but besides this there is a love for the marvellous, a belief in the marvellous, intertwined in all my projects, which hurries me out of the common pathways of men, even to the wild sea and unvisited regions I am about to explore. But to return to dearer considerations. Shall I meet you again, after having traversed immense seas, and returned by the most southern cape of Africa or America? I dare not expect such success, yet I cannot bear to look on the reverse of the picture. Continue for the present to write to me by every opportunity: I may receive your letters on some occasions when I need them most to support my spirits. I love you very tenderly. Remember me with affection, should you never hear from me again.

Your affectionate brother,
Robert Walton

Letter 3

To Mrs. Saville, England

July 7th, 17—

My dear Sister,

I write a few lines in haste to say that I am safe—and well advanced on my voyage. This letter will reach England by a merchantman now on its homeward voyage from Archangel; more fortunate than I, who may not see my native land, perhaps, for many years. I am, however, in good spirits: my men are bold and apparently firm of purpose, nor do the floating sheets of ice that continually pass us, indicating the dangers of the region towards which we are advancing, appear to dismay them. We have already reached a very high latitude; but it is the height of summer, and although not so warm as in England, the southern gales, which blow us speedily towards those shores which I so ardently desire to attain, breathe a degree of renovating warmth which I had not expected.

No incidents have hitherto befallen us that would make a figure in a letter. One or two stiff gales and the springing of a leak are accidents which experienced navigators scarcely remember to record, and I shall be well content if nothing worse happen to us during our voyage.

Adieu, my dear Margaret. Be assured that for my own sake, as well as yours, I will not rashly encounter danger. I will be cool, persevering, and prudent.

But success SHALL crown my endeavours. Wherefore not? Thus far I have gone, tracing a secure way over the pathless seas, the very stars themselves being witnesses and testimonies of my triumph. Why not still proceed over the untamed yet obedient element? What can stop the determined heart and resolved will of man?

My swelling heart involuntarily pours itself out thus. But must finish. Heaven bless my beloved sister!

R.W.

LETTER 4

To Mrs. Saville, England

August 5th, 17—

So strange an accident has happened to us that I cannot forbear recording it, although it is very probable that you will see me before these papers can come into your possession.

Last Monday (July 31st) we were nearly surrounded by ice, which closed in the ship on all sides, scarcely leaving her the sea-room in which she floated. Our situation was somewhat dangerous, especially as we were compassed round by a very thick fog. We accordingly lay to, hoping that some change would take place in the atmosphere and weather.

About two o'clock the mist cleared away, and we beheld, stretched out in every direction, vast and irregular plains of ice, which seemed to have no end. Some of my comrades groaned, and my own mind began to grow watchful with anxious thoughts, when a strange sight suddenly attracted our attention and diverted our solicitude from our own situation. We perceived a low carriage, fixed on a sledge and drawn by dogs, pass on towards the north, at the distance of half a mile; a being which had the shape of a man, but apparently of gigantic stature, sat in the sledge and guided the dogs. We watched the rapid progress of the traveller with our telescopes until he was lost among the distant inequalities of the ice. This appearance excited our unqualified wonder.

We were, as we believed, many hundred miles from any land; but this apparition seemed to denote that it was not, in reality, so distant as we had supposed. Shut in, however, by ice, it was impossible to follow his track, which we had observed with the greatest attention. About two hours after this occurrence we heard the ground sea, and before night the ice broke and freed our ship. We, however, lay to until the morning, fearing to encounter in the dark those large loose masses which float about after the breaking up of the ice. I profited of this time to rest for a few hours.

In the morning, however, as soon as it was light, I went upon deck and found all the sailors busy on one side of the vessel, apparently talking to someone in the sea. It was, in fact, a sledge, like that we had seen before, which had drifted towards us in the night on a large fragment of ice. Only one dog remained alive; but there was a human being within it whom the sailors were persuading to enter the vessel. He was not, as the other traveller seemed to be, a savage inhabitant of some undiscovered island, but a European. When I appeared on deck the master said, "Here is our captain, and he will not allow you to perish on the open sea."

On perceiving me, the stranger addressed me in English, although with a foreign accent. "Before I come on board your vessel," said he, "will you have the kindness to inform me whither you are bound?"

You may conceive my astonishment on hearing such a question addressed to me from a man on the brink of destruction and to whom I should have supposed that my vessel would have been a resource which he would not have exchanged for the most precious wealth the earth can afford. I replied, however, that we were on a voyage of discovery towards the northern pole.

Upon hearing this he appeared satisfied and consented to come on board. Good God! Margaret, if you had seen the man who thus capitulated for his safety, your surprise would have been boundless. His limbs were nearly frozen, and his body dreadfully emaciated by fatigue and suffering. I never saw a man in so wretched a condition. We attempted to carry him into the cabin, but as soon as he had quitted the fresh air he fainted. We accordingly brought him back to the deck and restored him to animation by rubbing him with brandy and forcing him to swallow a small quantity. As soon as he showed signs of life we wrapped him up in blankets and placed him near the chimney of the kitchen stove. By slow degrees he recovered and ate a little soup, which restored him wonderfully.

Two days passed in this manner before he was able to speak, and I often feared that his sufferings had deprived him of understanding. When he had in some measure recovered, I removed him to my own cabin and attended on him as much as my duty would permit. I never saw a more interesting creature: his eyes have generally an expression of wildness, and even madness, but there are moments when, if anyone performs an act of kindness towards him or does him the most trifling service, his whole countenance is lighted up, as it were, with a beam of benevolence and sweetness that I never saw equalled. But he is generally melancholy and despairing, and sometimes he gnashes his teeth, as if impatient of the weight of woes that oppresses him.

When my guest was a little recovered I had great trouble to keep off the men, who wished to ask him a thousand questions; but I would not allow him to be tormented by their idle curiosity, in a state of body and mind whose restoration evidently depended upon entire repose. Once, however, the lieutenant asked why he had come so far upon the ice in so strange a vehicle.

His countenance instantly assumed an aspect of the deepest gloom, and he replied, "To seek one who fled from me."

"And did the man whom you pursued travel in the same fashion?"

"Yes."

"Then I fancy we have seen him, for the day before we picked you up we saw some dogs drawing a sledge, with a man in it, across the ice."

This aroused the stranger's attention, and he asked a multitude of questions concerning the route which the demon, as he called him, had pursued. Soon after, when he was alone with me, he said, "I have, doubtless, excited your curiosity, as well as that of these good people; but you are too considerate to make inquiries."

"Certainly; it would indeed be very impertinent and inhuman in me to trouble you with any inquisitiveness of mine."

"And yet you rescued me from a strange and perilous situation; you have benevolently restored me to life."

Soon after this he inquired if I thought that the breaking up of the ice had destroyed the other sledge. I replied that

I could not answer with any degree of certainty, for the ice had not broken until near midnight, and the traveller might have arrived at a place of safety before that time; but of this I could not judge. From this time a new spirit of life animated the decaying frame of the stranger. He manifested the greatest eagerness to be upon deck to watch for the sledge which had before appeared; but I have persuaded him to remain in the cabin, for he is far too weak to sustain the rawness of the atmosphere. I have promised that someone should watch for him and give him instant notice if any new object should appear in sight.

Such is my journal of what relates to this strange occurrence up to the present day. The stranger has gradually improved in health but is very silent and appears uneasy when anyone except myself enters his cabin. Yet his manners are so conciliating and gentle that the sailors are all interested in him, although they have had very little communication with him. For my own part, I begin to love him as a brother, and his constant and deep grief fills me with sympathy and compassion. He must have been a noble creature in his better days, being even now in wreck so attractive and amiable. I said in one of my letters, my dear Margaret, that I should find no friend on the wide ocean; yet I have found a man who, before his spirit had been broken by misery, I should have been happy to have possessed as the brother of my heart.

I shall continue my journal concerning the stranger at intervals, should I have any fresh incidents to record.

August 13th, 17—

My affection for my guest increases every day. He excites at once my admiration and my pity to an astonishing degree. How can I see so noble a creature destroyed by misery without feeling the most poignant grief? He is so gentle, yet so wise; his mind is so cultivated, and when he speaks, although his words are culled with the choicest art, yet they flow with rapidity and unparalleled eloquence.

He is now much recovered from his illness and is continually on the deck, apparently watching for the sledge that preceded his own. Yet, although unhappy, he is not so utterly occupied by his own misery but that he interests himself deeply in the projects of others. He has frequently conversed with me on mine, which I have communicated to him without disguise. He entered attentively into all my arguments in favour of my eventual success and into every minute detail of the measures I had taken to secure it. I was easily led by the sympathy which he evinced to use the language of my heart, to give utterance to the burning ardour of my soul and to say, with all the fervour that warmed me, how gladly I would sacrifice my fortune, my existence, my every hope, to the furtherance of my enterprise.

One man's life or death were but a small price to pay for the acquirement of the knowledge which I sought, for the dominion I should acquire and transmit over the elemental foes of our race. As I spoke, a dark gloom spread over my listener's countenance. At first I perceived that he tried to suppress his emotion; he placed his hands before his eyes, and my voice quivered and failed me as I beheld tears trickle fast from between his fingers; a groan burst from his heaving breast. I paused; at length he spoke, in broken accents: "Unhappy man! Do you share my madness? Have you drunk also of the intoxicating draught? Hear me; let me reveal my tale, and you will dash the cup from your lips!"

Such words, you may imagine, strongly excited my curiosity; but the paroxysm of grief that had seized the stranger overcame his weakened powers, and many hours of repose and tranquil conversation were necessary to restore his composure. Having conquered the violence of his feelings, he appeared to despise himself for being the slave of passion; and quelling the dark tyranny of despair, he led me again to converse concerning myself personally. He asked me the history of my earlier years.

The tale was quickly told, but it awakened various trains of reflection. I spoke of my desire of finding a friend, of my thirst for a more intimate sympathy with a fellow mind than had ever fallen to my lot, and expressed my conviction that a man could boast of little happiness who did not enjoy this blessing. "I agree with you," replied the stranger; "we are unfashioned creatures, but half made up, if one wiser, better, dearer than ourselves—such a friend ought to be—do not lend his aid to perfectionate our weak and faulty natures. I once had a friend, the most noble of human creatures, and am entitled, therefore, to judge respecting friendship. You have hope, and the world before you, and have no cause for despair. But I—I have lost everything and cannot begin life anew."

As he said this his countenance became expressive of a calm, settled grief that touched me to the heart. But he was silent and presently retired to his cabin.

Even broken in spirit as he is, no one can feel more deeply than he does the beauties of nature. The starry sky, the sea, and every sight afforded by these wonderful regions seem still to have the power of elevating his soul from earth. Such a man has a double existence: he may suffer misery and be overwhelmed by disappointments, yet when he has retired into himself, he will be like a celestial spirit that has a halo around him, within whose circle no grief or folly ventures.

Will you smile at the enthusiasm I express concerning this divine wanderer? You would not if you saw him. You have been tutored and refined by books and retirement from the world, and you are therefore somewhat fastidious; but this only renders you the more fit to appreciate the extraordinary merits of this wonderful man. Sometimes I have endeavoured to discover what quality it is which he possesses that elevates him so immeasurably above any other person I ever knew. I believe it to be an intuitive discernment, a quick but never-failing power of judgment, a penetration into the causes of things, unequalled for clearness and precision; add to this a facility of expression and a voice whose varied intonations are soul-subduing music.

August 19, 17—

Yesterday the stranger said to me, "You may easily perceive, Captain Walton, that I have suffered great and unparalleled misfortunes. I had determined at one time that the memory of these evils should die with me, but you have won me to alter my determination. You seek for knowledge and wisdom, as I once did; and I ardently hope that the gratification of your wishes may not be a serpent to sting you, as mine has been. I do not know that the relation of my disasters will be useful to you; yet, when I reflect that you are pursuing the same course, exposing yourself to the same dangers which have rendered me what I am, I imagine that you may deduce an apt moral from my tale, one that may direct you if you succeed in your undertaking and console you in case of failure.

Prepare to hear of occurrences which are usually deemed marvellous. Were we among the tamer scenes of nature I might fear to encounter your unbelief, perhaps your ridicule; but many things will appear possible in these wild and mysterious regions which would provoke the laughter of those unacquainted with the ever-varied powers of nature; nor can I doubt but that my tale conveys in its series internal evidence of the truth of the events of which it is composed."

You may easily imagine that I was much gratified by the offered communication, yet I could not endure that he should renew his grief by a recital of his misfortunes. I felt the greatest eagerness to hear the promised narrative, partly from curiosity and partly from a strong desire to ameliorate his fate if it were in my power. I expressed these feelings in my answer.

"I thank you," he replied, "for your sympathy, but it is

useless; my fate is nearly fulfilled. I wait but for one event, and then I shall repose in peace. I understand your feeling," continued he, perceiving that I wished to interrupt him; "but you are mistaken, my friend, if thus you will allow me to name you; nothing can alter my destiny; listen to my history, and you will perceive how irrevocably it is determined."

He then told me that he would commence his narrative the next day when I should be at leisure. This promise drew from me the warmest thanks. I have resolved every night, when I am not imperatively occupied by my duties, to record, as nearly as possible in his own words, what he has related during the day. If I should be engaged, I will at least make notes. This manuscript will doubtless afford you the greatest pleasure; but to me, who know him, and who hear it from his own lips—with what interest and sympathy shall I read it in some future day! Even now, as I commence my task, his full-toned voice swells in my ears; his lustrous eyes dwell on me with all their melancholy sweetness; I see his thin hand raised in animation, while the lineaments of his face are irradiated by the soul within.

Strange and harrowing must be his story, frightful the storm which embraced the gallant vessel on its course and wrecked it—thus!

CHAPTER 1

I am by birth a Genevese, and my family is one of the most distinguished of that republic. My ancestors had been for many years counsellors and syndics, and my father had filled several public situations with honour and reputation. He was respected by all who knew him for his integrity and indefatigable attention to public business. He passed his younger days perpetually occupied by the affairs of his country; a variety of circumstances had prevented his marrying early, nor was it until the decline of life that he became a husband and the father of a family.

As the circumstances of his marriage illustrate his character, I cannot refrain from relating them. One of his most intimate friends was a merchant who, from a flourishing state, fell, through numerous mischances, into poverty. This man, whose name was Beaufort, was of a proud and unbending disposition and could not bear to live in poverty and oblivion in the same country where he had formerly been distinguished for his rank and magnificence. Having paid his debts, therefore, in the most honourable manner, he retreated with his daughter to the town of Lucerne, where he lived unknown and in wretchedness.

My father loved Beaufort with the truest friendship and was deeply grieved by his retreat in these unfortunate circumstances. He bitterly deplored the false pride which led his friend to a conduct so little worthy of the affection that united them. He lost no time in endeavouring to seek him out, with the hope of persuading him to begin the world again through his credit and assistance. Beaufort had taken effectual measures to conceal himself, and it was ten months before my father discovered his abode.

Overjoyed at this discovery, he hastened to the house, which was situated in a mean street near the Reuss. But when he entered, misery and despair alone welcomed him. Beaufort had saved but a very small sum of money from the wreck of his fortunes, but it was sufficient to provide him with sustenance for some months, and in the meantime he hoped to procure some respectable employment in a merchant's house. The interval was, consequently, spent in inaction; his grief only became more deep and rankling when he had leisure for reflection, and at length it took so fast hold of his mind that at the end of three months he lay on a bed of sickness, incapable of any exertion.

His daughter attended him with the greatest tenderness, but she saw with despair that their little fund was rapidly decreasing and that there was no other prospect of support. But Caroline Beaufort possessed a mind of an uncommon mould, and her courage rose to support her in her adversity. She procured plain work; she plaited straw and by various means contrived to earn a pittance scarcely sufficient to support life.

Several months passed in this manner. Her father grew worse; her time was more entirely occupied in attending him; her means of subsistence decreased; and in the tenth month her father died in her arms, leaving her an orphan and a beggar. This last blow overcame her, and she knelt by Beaufort's coffin weeping bitterly, when my father entered the chamber. He came like a protecting spirit to the poor girl, who committed herself to his care; and after the interment of his friend he conducted her to Geneva and placed her under the protection of a relation. Two years after this event Caroline became his wife.

There was a considerable difference between the ages of my parents, but this circumstance seemed to unite them only closer in bonds of devoted affection. There was a sense of justice in my father's upright mind which rendered it necessary that he should approve highly to love strongly. Perhaps during former years he had suffered from the late-discovered unworthiness of one beloved and so was disposed to set a greater value on tried worth. There was a show of gratitude and worship in his attachment to my mother, differing wholly from the doting fondness of age, for it was inspired by reverence for her virtues and a desire to be the means of, in some degree, recompensing her for the sorrows she had endured, but which gave inexpressible grace to his behaviour to her.

Everything was made to yield to her wishes and her convenience. He strove to shelter her, as a fair exotic is sheltered by the gardener, from every rougher wind and to surround her with all that could tend to excite pleasurable emotion in her soft and benevolent mind. Her health, and even the tranquillity of her hitherto constant spirit, had been shaken by what she had gone through. During the two years that had elapsed previous to their marriage my father had gradually relinquished all his public functions; and immediately after their union they sought the pleasant climate of Italy, and the change of scene and interest attendant on a tour through that land of wonders, as a restorative for her weakened frame.

From Italy they visited Germany and France. I, their eldest child, was born at Naples, and as an infant accompanied them in their rambles. I remained for several years their only child. Much as they were attached to each other, they seemed to draw inexhaustible stores of affection from a very mine of love to bestow them upon me. My mother's tender caresses and my father's smile of benevolent pleasure while regarding me are my first recollections. I was their plaything and their idol, and something better—their child, the innocent and helpless creature bestowed on them by heaven, whom to bring up to good, and whose future lot it was in their hands to direct to happiness or misery, according as they fulfilled their duties towards me.

With this deep consciousness of what they owed towards the being to which they had given life, added to the active spirit of tenderness that animated both, it may be imagined that while during every hour of my infant life I received a lesson of patience, of charity, and of self-control, I was so guided by a silken cord that all seemed but one train of enjoyment to me. For a long time I was their only care. My mother had much desired to have a daughter, but I continued their single offspring.

When I was about five years old, while making an excursion beyond the frontiers of Italy, they passed a week on the shores of the Lake of Como. Their benevolent disposition often made them enter the cottages of the poor. This, to my mother, was more than a duty; it was a necessity, a passion—remembering what she had suffered, and how she had been relieved—for her to act in her turn the guardian angel to the afflicted. During one of their walks a poor cot in the foldings of a vale attracted their notice as being singularly disconsolate, while the number of half-clothed children gathered about it spoke of penury in its worst shape.

One day, when my father had gone by himself to Milan, my mother, accompanied by me, visited this abode. She found a peasant and his wife, hard working, bent down by care and labour, distributing a scanty meal to five hungry babes. Among these there was one which attracted my mother far above all the rest. She appeared of a different stock. The four others were dark-eyed, hardy little vagrants; this child was thin and very fair. Her hair was the brightest living gold, and despite the poverty of her clothing, seemed to set a crown of distinction on her head. Her brow was clear and ample, her blue eyes cloudless, and her lips and the moulding of her face so expressive of sensibility and sweetness that none could behold her without looking on her as of a distinct species, a being heaven-sent, and bearing a celestial stamp in all her features.

The peasant woman, perceiving that my mother fixed eyes of wonder and admiration on this lovely girl, eagerly communicated her history. She was not her child, but the daughter of a Milanese nobleman. Her mother was a German and had died on giving her birth. The infant had been placed with these good people to nurse: they were better off then. They had not been long married, and their eldest child was but just born. The father of their charge was one of those Italians nursed in the memory of the antique glory of Italy—one among the *schiavi ognor fre-menti*, who exerted himself to obtain the liberty of his country. He became the victim of its weakness.

Whether he had died or still lingered in the dungeons of Austria was not known. His property was confiscated; his child became an orphan and a beggar. She continued with her foster parents and bloomed in their rude abode, fairer than a garden rose among dark-leaved brambles. When my father returned from Milan, he found playing with me in the hall of our villa a child fairer than pictured cherub—a creature who seemed to shed radiance from her looks and whose form and motions were lighter than the chamois of the hills. The apparition was soon explained. With his permission my mother prevailed on her rustic guardians to yield their charge to her.

They were fond of the sweet orphan. Her presence had seemed a blessing to them, but it would be unfair to her to keep her in poverty and want when Providence afforded her such powerful protection. They consulted their village priest, and the result was that Elizabeth Lavenza became the inmate of my parents' house—my more than sister—the beautiful and adored companion of all my occupations and my pleasures.

Everyone loved Elizabeth. The passionate and almost reverential attachment with which all regarded her became, while I shared it, my pride and my delight. On the evening previous to her being brought to my home, my mother had said playfully, "I have a pretty present for my Victor—tomorrow he shall have it." And when, on the morrow, she presented Elizabeth to me as her promised gift, I, with childish seriousness, interpreted her words literally and looked upon Elizabeth as mine—mine to protect, love, and cherish. All praises bestowed on her I received as made to a possession of my own. We called each other familiarly by the name of cousin. No word, no expression could body forth the kind of relation in which she stood to me—my more than sister, since till death she was to be mine only.

Chapter 2

We were brought up together; there was not quite a year difference in our ages. I need not say that we were strangers to any species of disunion or dispute. Harmony was the soul of our companionship, and the diversity and contrast that subsisted in our characters drew us nearer together. Elizabeth was of a calmer and more concentrated disposition; but, with all my ardour, I was capable of a more intense application and was more deeply smitten with the thirst for knowledge. She busied herself with following the aerial creations of the poets; and in the majestic and wondrous scenes which surrounded our Swiss home—the sublime shapes of the mountains, the changes of the seasons, tempest and calm, the silence of winter, and the life and turbulence of our Alpine summers—she found ample scope for admiration and delight.

While my companion contemplated with a serious and satisfied spirit the magnificent appearances of things, I delighted in investigating their causes. The world was to me a secret which I desired to divine. Curiosity, earnest research to learn the hidden laws of nature, gladness akin to rapture, as they were unfolded to me, are among the earliest sensations I can remember.

On the birth of a second son, my junior by seven years, my parents gave up entirely their wandering life and fixed themselves in their native country. We possessed a house in Geneva, and a *campagne* on Belrive, the eastern shore of the lake, at the distance of rather more than a league from the city. We resided principally in the latter, and the lives of my parents were passed in considerable seclusion. It was my temper to avoid a crowd and to attach myself fervently to a few. I was indifferent, therefore, to my school-fellows in general; but I united myself in the bonds of the closest friendship to one among them.

Henry Clerval was the son of a merchant of Geneva. He was a boy of singular talent and fancy. He loved enterprise, hardship, and even danger for its own sake. He was deeply read in books of chivalry and romance. He composed heroic songs and began to write many a tale of enchantment and knightly adventure. He tried to make us act plays and to enter into masquerades, in which the characters were drawn from the heroes of Roncesvalles, of the Round Table of King Arthur, and the chivalrous train who shed their blood to redeem the holy sepulchre from the hands of the infidels.

No human being could have passed a happier childhood than myself. My parents were possessed by the very spirit of kindness and indulgence. We felt that they were not the tyrants to rule our lot according to their caprice, but the agents and creators of all the many delights which we enjoyed. When I mingled with other families I distinctly discerned how peculiarly fortunate my lot was, and gratitude assisted the development of filial love.

My temper was sometimes violent, and my passions vehement; but by some law in my temperature they were turned not towards childish pursuits but to an eager desire to learn, and not to learn all things indiscriminately. I confess that neither the structure of languages, nor the code of governments, nor the politics of various states possessed attractions for me. It was the secrets of heaven and earth that I desired to learn; and whether it was the outward substance of things or the inner spirit of nature and the mysterious soul of man that occupied me, still my inquiries were directed to the metaphysical, or in it highest sense, the physical secrets of the world.

Meanwhile Clerval occupied himself, so to speak, with the moral relations of things. The busy stage of life, the virtues of heroes, and the actions of men were his theme; and his hope and his dream was to become one among those whose names are recorded in story as the gallant and adventurous benefactors of our species. The saintly soul of Elizabeth shone like a shrine-dedicated lamp in our peaceful home. Her sympathy was ours; her smile, her soft voice, the sweet glance of her celestial eyes, were ever there to bless and animate us. She was the living spirit of love to soften and attract; I might have become sullen in my study, through the ardour of my nature, but that she was there to subdue me to a semblance of her own gentleness. And Clerval— could aught ill entrench on the noble spirit of Clerval? Yet he might not have been so perfectly humane, so thoughtful in his generosity, so full of kindness and tenderness amidst his passion for adventurous exploit, had she not unfolded to him the real loveliness of beneficence and made the doing good the end and aim of his soaring ambition.

I feel exquisite pleasure in dwelling on the recollections of childhood, before misfortune had tainted my mind and changed its bright visions of extensive usefulness into gloomy and narrow reflections upon self. Besides, in drawing the picture of my early days, I also record those events which led, by insensible steps, to my after tale of misery, for when I would account to myself for the birth of that passion which afterwards ruled my destiny I find it arise, like a mountain river, from ignoble and almost forgotten sources; but, swelling as it proceeded, it became the torrent which, in its course, has swept away all my hopes and joys.

Natural philosophy is the genius that has regulated my fate; I desire, therefore, in this narration, to state those facts which led to my predilection for that science. When I was thirteen years of age we all went on a party of pleasure to the baths near

Thonon; the inclemency of the weather obliged us to remain a day confined to the inn. In this house I chanced to find a volume of the works of Cornelius Agrippa. I opened it with apathy; the theory which he attempts to demonstrate and the wonderful facts which he relates soon changed this feeling into enthusiasm. A new light seemed to dawn upon my mind, and bounding with joy, I communicated my discovery to my father. My father looked carelessly at the title page of my book and said, "Ah! Cornelius Agrippa! My dear Victor, do not waste your time upon this; it is sad trash."

If, instead of this remark, my father had taken the pains to explain to me that the principles of Agrippa had been entirely exploded and that a modern system of science had been introduced which possessed much greater powers than the ancient, because the powers of the latter were chimerical, while those of the former were real and practical, under such circumstances I should certainty have thrown Agrippa aside and have contented my imagination, warmed as it was, by returning with greater ardour to my former studies. It is even possible that the train of my ideas would never have received the fatal impulse that led to my ruin. But the cursory glance my father had taken of my volume by no means assured me that he was acquainted with its contents, and I continued to read with the greatest avidity.

When I returned home my first care was to procure the whole works of this author, and afterwards of Paracelsus and Albertus Magnus. I read and studied the wild fancies of these writers with delight; they appeared to me treasures known to few besides myself. I have described myself as always having been imbued with a fervent longing to penetrate the secrets of nature. In spite of the intense labour and wonderful discoveries of modern philosophers, I always came from my studies discontented and unsatisfied. Sir Isaac Newton is said to have avowed that he felt like a child picking up shells beside the great and unexplored ocean of truth. Those of his successors in each branch of natural philosophy with whom I was acquainted appeared even to my boy's apprehensions as tyros engaged in the same pursuit.

The untaught peasant beheld the elements around him and was acquainted with their practical uses. The most learned philosopher knew little more. He had partially unveiled the face of Nature, but her immortal lineaments were still a wonder and a mystery. He might dissect, anatomize, and give names; but, not to speak of a final cause, causes in their secondary and tertiary grades were utterly unknown to him. I had gazed upon the fortifications and impediments that seemed to keep human beings from entering the citadel of nature, and rashly and ignorantly I had repined.

But here were books, and here were men who had penetrated deeper and knew more. I took their word for all that they averred, and I became their disciple. It may appear strange that such should arise in the eighteenth century; but while I followed the routine of education in the schools of Geneva, I was, to a great degree, self-taught with regard to my favourite studies. My father was not scientific, and I was left to struggle with a child's blindness, added to a student's thirst for knowledge. Under the guidance of my new preceptors I entered with the greatest diligence into the search of the philosopher's stone and the elixir of life; but the latter soon obtained my undivided attention.

Wealth was an inferior object, but what glory would attend the discovery if I could banish disease from the human frame and render man invulnerable to any but a violent death! Nor were these my only visions. The raising of ghosts or devils was a promise liberally accorded by my favourite authors, the fulfilment of which I most eagerly sought; and if my incantations were always unsuccessful, I attributed the failure rather to my own inexperience and mistake than to a want of skill or fidelity in my instructors. And thus for a time I was occupied by exploded systems, mingling, like an unadept, a thousand contradictory theories and floundering desperately in a very slough of multifarious knowledge, guided by an ardent imagination and childish reasoning, till an accident again changed the current of my ideas.

When I was about fifteen years old we had retired to our

house near Belrive, when we witnessed a most violent and terrible thunderstorm. It advanced from behind the mountains of Jura, and the thunder burst at once with frightful loudness from various quarters of the heavens. I remained, while the storm lasted, watching its progress with curiosity and delight. As I stood at the door, on a sudden I beheld a stream of fire issue from an old and beautiful oak which stood about twenty yards from our house; and so soon as the dazzling light vanished, the oak had disappeared, and nothing remained but a blasted stump. When we visited it the next morning, we found the tree shattered in a singular manner. It was not splintered by the shock, but entirely reduced to thin ribbons of wood. I never beheld anything so utterly destroyed.

Before this I was not unacquainted with the more obvious laws of electricity. On this occasion a man of great research in natural philosophy was with us, and excited by this catastrophe, he entered on the explanation of a theory which he had formed on the subject of electricity and galvanism, which was at once new and astonishing to me. All that he said threw greatly into the shade Cornelius Agrippa, Albertus Magnus, and Paracelsus, the lords of my imagination; but by some fatality the overthrow of these men disinclined me to pursue my accustomed studies. It seemed to me as if nothing would or could ever be known.

All that had so long engaged my attention suddenly grew despicable. By one of those caprices of the mind which we are perhaps most subject to in early youth, I at once gave up my former occupations, set down natural history and all its progeny as a deformed and abortive creation, and entertained the greatest disdain for a would-be science which could never even step within the threshold of real knowledge. In this mood of mind I betook myself to the mathematics and the branches of study appertaining to that science as being built upon secure foundations, and so worthy of my consideration.

Thus strangely are our souls constructed, and by such slight ligaments are we bound to prosperity or ruin. When I look back, it seems to me as if this almost miraculous change of inclination and will was the immediate suggestion of the guardian angel of my life—the last effort made by the spirit of preservation to avert the storm that was even then hanging in the stars and ready to envelop me. Her victory was announced by an unusual tranquillity and gladness of soul which followed the relinquishing of my ancient and latterly tormenting studies. It was thus that I was to be taught to associate evil with their prosecution, happiness with their disregard.

It was a strong effort of the spirit of good, but it was ineffectual. Destiny was too potent, and her immutable laws had decreed my utter and terrible destruction.

CHAPTER 3

When I had attained the age of seventeen my parents resolved that I should become a student at the university of Ingolstadt. I had hitherto attended the schools of Geneva, but my father thought it necessary for the completion of my education that I should be made acquainted with other customs than those of my native country. My departure was therefore fixed at an early date, but before the day resolved upon could arrive, the first misfortune of my life occurred—an omen, as it were, of my future misery. Elizabeth had caught the scarlet fever; her illness was severe, and she was in the greatest danger.

During her illness many arguments had been urged to persuade my mother to refrain from attending upon her. She had at first yielded to our entreaties, but when she heard that the life of her favourite was menaced, she could no longer control her anxiety. She attended her sickbed; her watchful attentions triumphed over the malignity of the distemper—Elizabeth was saved, but the consequences of this imprudence were fatal to her preserver. On the third day my mother sickened; her fever was accompanied by the most alarming symptoms, and the looks of her medical attendants prognosticated the worst event.

On her deathbed the fortitude and benignity of this best of women did not desert her. She joined the hands of Elizabeth and myself. "My children," she said, "my firmest hopes of future happiness were placed on the prospect of your union. This expectation will now be the consolation of your father. Elizabeth, my love, you must supply my place to my younger children. Alas! I regret that I am taken from you; and, happy and beloved as I have been, is it not hard to quit you all? But these are not thoughts befitting me; I will endeavour to resign myself cheerfully to death and will indulge a hope of meeting you in another world."

She died calmly, and her countenance expressed affection even in death. I need not describe the feelings of those whose dearest ties are rent by that most irreparable evil, the void that presents itself to the soul, and the despair that is exhibited on the countenance. It is so long before the mind can persuade itself that she whom we saw every day and whose very existence appeared a part of our own can have departed forever—that the brightness of a beloved eye can have been extinguished and the sound of a voice so familiar and dear to the ear can be hushed, never more to be heard. These are the reflections of the first days; but when the lapse of time proves the reality of the evil, then the actual bitterness of grief commences.

Yet from whom has not that rude hand rent away some dear connection? And why should I describe a sorrow which all have felt, and must feel? The time at length arrives when grief is rather an indulgence than a necessity; and the smile that plays upon the lips, although it may be deemed a sacrilege, is not banished. My mother was dead, but we had still duties which we ought to perform; we must continue our course with the rest and learn to think ourselves fortunate whilst one remains whom the spoiler has not seized.

My departure for Ingolstadt, which had been deferred by these events, was now again determined upon. I obtained from my father a respite of some weeks. It appeared to me sacrilege so soon to leave the repose, akin to death, of the house of mourning and to rush into the thick of life. I was new to sorrow, but it did not the less alarm me. I was unwilling to quit the sight of those that remained to me, and above all, I desired to see my sweet Elizabeth in some degree consoled.

She indeed veiled her grief and strove to act the comforter to us all. She looked steadily on life and assumed its duties with courage and zeal. She devoted herself to those whom she had been taught to call her uncle and cousins. Never was she so enchanting as at this time, when she recalled the sunshine of her smiles and spent them upon us. She forgot even her own regret in her endeavours to make us forget.

The day of my departure at length arrived. Clerval spent the last evening with us. He had endeavoured to persuade his father to permit him to accompany me and to become my fellow student, but in vain. His father was a narrow-minded trader and saw idleness and ruin in the aspirations and ambition of his son. Henry deeply felt the misfortune of being debarred from a liberal education. He said little, but when he spoke I read in his kindling eye and in his animated glance a restrained but firm resolve not to be chained to the miserable details of commerce.

We sat late. We could not tear ourselves away from each other nor persuade ourselves to say the word "Farewell!" It was said, and we retired under the pretence of seeking repose, each fancying that the other was deceived; but when at morning's dawn I descended to the carriage which was to convey me away, they were all there—my father again to bless me, Clerval to press my hand once more, my Elizabeth to renew her entreaties that I would write often and to bestow the last feminine attentions on her playmate and friend.

I threw myself into the chaise that was to convey me away and indulged in the most melancholy reflections. I, who had ever been surrounded by amiable companions, continually engaged in endeavouring to bestow mutual pleasure—I was now alone. In the university whither I was going I must form my own friends and be my own protector. My life had hitherto been remarkably secluded and domestic, and this had given me invincible repugnance to new countenances. I loved my brothers, Elizabeth, and Clerval; these were "old familiar faces," but I believed myself totally unfitted for the company of strangers.

Such were my reflections as I commenced my journey; but as I proceeded, my spirits and hopes rose. I ardently desired the acquisition of knowledge. I had often, when at home, thought it hard to remain during my youth cooped up in one place and had longed to enter the world and take my station among other human beings. Now my desires were complied with, and it would, indeed, have been folly to repent.

I had sufficient leisure for these and many other reflections during my journey to Ingolstadt, which was long and fatiguing. At length the high white steeple of the town met my eyes. I alighted and was conducted to my solitary apartment to spend the evening as I pleased.

The next morning I delivered my letters of introduction and paid a visit to some of the principal professors. Chance-or rather the evil influence, the Angel of Destruction, which asserted omnipotent sway over me from the moment I turned my reluctant steps from my father's door—led me first to M. Krempe, professor of natural philosophy. He was an uncouth man, but deeply imbued in the secrets of his science. He asked me several questions concerning my progress in the different branches of science appertaining to natural philosophy. I replied carelessly, and partly in contempt, mentioned the names of my alchemists as the principal authors I had studied. The professor stared. "Have you," he said, "really spent your time in studying such nonsense?"

I replied in the affirmative. "Every minute," continued M. Krempe with warmth, "every instant that you have wasted on those books is utterly and entirely lost. You have burdened your memory with exploded systems and useless names. Good God! In what desert land have you lived, where no one was kind enough to inform you that these fancies which you have so greedily imbibed are a thousand years old and as musty as they are ancient? I little expected, in this enlightened and scientific age, to find a disciple of Albertus Magnus and Paracelsus. My dear sir, you must begin your studies entirely anew."

So saying, he stepped aside and wrote down a list of several books treating of natural philosophy which he desired me to procure, and dismissed me after mentioning that in the beginning of the following week he intended to commence a course of lectures upon natural philosophy in its general relations, and that M. Waldman, a fellow professor, would lecture upon chemistry the alternate days that he omitted.

I returned home not disappointed, for I have said that I had long considered those authors useless whom the professor reprobated; but I returned not at all the more inclined to recur to these studies in any shape. M. Krempe was a little squat man with a gruff voice and a repulsive countenance; the teacher, therefore, did not prepossess me in favour of his pursuits. In rather a too philosophical and connected a strain, perhaps, I have given an account of the conclusions I had come to concerning them in my early years. As a child I had not been content with the results promised by the modern professors of natural science. With a confusion of ideas only to be accounted for by my extreme youth and my want of a guide on such matters, I had retrod the steps of knowledge along the paths of time and exchanged the discoveries of recent inquirers for the dreams of forgotten alchemists. Besides, I had a contempt for the uses of modern natural philosophy. It was very different when the masters of the science sought immortality and power; such views, although futile, were grand; but now the scene was changed. The ambition of the inquirer seemed to limit itself to the annihilation of those visions on which my interest in science was chiefly founded. I was required to exchange chimeras of boundless grandeur for realities of little worth.

Such were my reflections during the first two or three days of my residence at Ingolstadt, which were chiefly spent in becoming acquainted with the localities and the principal residents in my new abode. But as the ensuing week commenced, I thought of the information which M. Krempe had given me concerning the lectures. And although I could not consent to go and hear that little conceited fellow deliver sentences out of a pulpit, I recollected what he had said of M. Waldman, whom I had never seen, as he had hitherto been out of town.

Partly from curiosity and partly from idleness, I went into the lecturing room, which M. Waldman entered shortly after. This professor was very unlike his colleague. He appeared about fifty years of age, but with an aspect expressive of the greatest benevolence; a few grey hairs covered his temples, but those at the back of his head were nearly black. His person was short but remarkably erect and his voice the sweetest I had ever heard. He began his lecture by a recapitulation of the history of chemistry and the various improvements made by different men of learning, pronouncing with fervour the names of the most distinguished discoverers. He then took a cursory view of the present state of the science and explained many of its elementary terms. After having made a few preparatory experiments, he concluded with a panegyric upon modern chemistry, the terms of which I shall never forget: "The ancient teachers of this science," said he, "promised impossibilities and performed nothing.

The modern masters promise very little; they know that metals cannot be transmuted and that the elixir of life is a chimera but these philosophers, whose hands seem only made to dabble in dirt, and their eyes to pore over the microscope or crucible, have indeed performed miracles. They penetrate into the recesses of nature and show how she works in her hiding-places. They ascend into the heavens; they have discovered how the blood circulates, and the nature of the air we breathe. They have acquired new and almost unlimited powers; they can command the thunders of heaven, mimic the earthquake, and even mock the invisible world with its own shadows."

Such were the professor's words—rather let me say such the words of the fate—enounced to destroy me. As he went on I felt as if my soul were grappling with a palpable enemy; one by one the various keys were touched which formed the mechanism of my being; chord after chord was sounded, and soon my mind was filled with one thought, one conception, one purpose. So much has been done, exclaimed the soul of Frankenstein—more, far more, will I achieve; treading in the steps already marked, I will pioneer a new way, explore unknown powers, and unfold to the world the deepest mysteries of creation.

I closed not my eyes that night. My internal being was in a state of insurrection and turmoil; I felt that order would thence arise, but I had no power to produce it. By degrees, after the morning's dawn, sleep came. I awoke, and my yesternight's thoughts were as a dream. There only remained a resolution to return to my ancient studies and to devote myself to a science for which I believed myself to possess a natural talent. On the same day I paid M. Waldman a visit. His manners in private were even more mild and attractive than in public, for there was a certain dignity in his mien during his lecture which in his own house was replaced by the greatest affability and kindness.

I gave him pretty nearly the same account of my former pursuits as I had given to his fellow professor. He heard with attention the little narration concerning my studies and smiled at the names of Cornelius Agrippa and Paracelsus, but without the contempt that M. Krempe had exhibited. He said that "These were men to whose indefatigable zeal modern philosophers were indebted for most of the foundations of their knowledge. They had left to us, as an easier task, to give new names and arrange in connected classifications the facts which they in a great degree had been the instruments of bringing to light. The labours of men of genius, however erroneously directed, scarcely ever fail in ultimately turning to the solid advantage of mankind."

I listened to his statement, which was delivered without any presumption or affectation, and then added that his lecture had removed my prejudices against modern chemists; I expressed myself in measured terms, with the modesty and deference due from a youth to his instructor, without letting escape (inexperience in life would have made me ashamed) any of the enthusiasm which stimulated my intended labours. I requested his advice concerning the books I ought to procure.

"I am happy," said M. Waldman, "to have gained a disciple; and if your application equals your ability, I have no doubt of your success. Chemistry is that branch of natural philosophy in which the greatest improvements have been and may be made; it is on that account that I have made it my peculiar study; but at the same time, I have not neglected the other branches of science. A man would make but a very sorry chemist if he attended to that department of human knowledge alone. If your wish is to become really a man of science and not merely a petty experimentalist, I should advise you to apply to every branch of natural philosophy, including mathematics."

He then took me into his laboratory and explained to me the uses of his various machines, instructing me as to what I ought to procure and promising me the use of his own when I should have advanced far enough in the science not to derange their mechanism. He also gave me the list of books which I had requested, and I took my leave.

Thus ended a day memorable to me; it decided my future destiny.

CHAPTER 4

From this day natural philosophy, and particularly chemistry, in the most comprehensive sense of the term, became nearly my sole occupation. I read with ardour those works, so full of genius and discrimination, which modern inquirers have written on these subjects. I attended the lectures and cultivated the acquaintance of the men of science of the university, and I found even in M. Krempe a great deal of sound sense and real information, combined, it is true, with a repulsive physiognomy and manners, but not on that account the less valuable. In M. Waldman I found a true friend. His gentleness was never tinged by dogmatism, and his instructions were given with an air of frankness and good nature that banished every idea of pedantry.

In a thousand ways he smoothed for me the path of knowledge and made the most abstruse inquiries clear and facile to my apprehension. My application was at first fluctuating and uncertain; it gained strength as I proceeded and soon became so ardent and eager that the stars often disappeared in the light of morning whilst I was yet engaged in my laboratory.

As I applied so closely, it may be easily conceived that my progress was rapid. My ardour was indeed the astonishment of the students, and my proficiency that of the masters. Professor Krempe often asked me, with a sly smile, how Cornelius Agrippa went on, whilst M. Waldman expressed the most heartfelt exultation in my progress. Two years passed in this manner, during which I paid no visit to Geneva, but was engaged, heart and soul, in the pursuit of some discoveries which I hoped to make. None but those who have experienced them can conceive of the enticements of science. In other studies you go as far as others have gone before you, and there is nothing more to know; but in a scientific pursuit there is continual food for discovery and wonder.

A mind of moderate capacity which closely pursues one study must infallibly arrive at great proficiency in that study; and I, who continually sought the attainment of one object of pursuit and was solely wrapped up in this, improved so rapidly that at the end of two years I made some discoveries in the improvement of some chemical instruments, which procured me great esteem and admiration at the university. When I had arrived at this point and had become as well acquainted with the theory and practice of natural philosophy as depended on the lessons of any of the professors at Ingolstadt, my residence there being no longer conducive to my improvements, I thought of returning to my friends and my native town, when an incident happened that protracted my stay.

One of the phenomena which had peculiarly attracted my attention was the structure of the human frame, and, indeed, any animal endued with life. Whence, I often asked myself, did the principle of life proceed? It was a bold question, and one which has ever been considered as a mystery; yet with how many things are we upon the brink of becoming acquainted, if cowardice or carelessness did not restrain our inquiries. I revolved these circumstances in my mind and determined thenceforth to apply myself more particularly to those branches of natural philosophy which relate to physiology. Unless I had been animated by an almost supernatural enthusiasm, my application to this study would have been irksome and almost intolerable.

To examine the causes of life, we must first have recourse to death. I became acquainted with the science of anatomy, but this was not sufficient; I must also observe the natural decay and corruption of the human body. In my education my father had taken the greatest precautions that my mind should be impressed with no supernatural horrors. I do not ever remember to have trembled at a tale of superstition or to have feared the apparition of a spirit. Darkness had no effect upon my fancy, and a churchyard was to me merely the receptacle of bodies deprived of life, which, from being the seat of beauty and strength, had become food for the worm. Now I was led to examine the cause and progress of this decay and forced to spend days and nights in vaults and charnel-houses.

My attention was fixed upon every object the most insupportable to the delicacy of the human feelings. I saw how the fine form of man was degraded and wasted; I beheld the corruption of death succeed to the blooming cheek of life; I saw how the worm inherited the wonders of the eye and brain. I paused, examining and analysing all the minutiae of causation, as exemplified in the change from life to death, and death to life, until from the midst of this darkness a sudden light broke in upon me—a light so brilliant and wondrous, yet so simple, that while I became dizzy with the immensity of the prospect which it illustrated, I was surprised that among so many men of genius who had directed their inquiries towards the same science, that I alone should be reserved to discover so astonishing a secret.

Remember, I am not recording the vision of a madman. The sun does not more certainly shine in the heavens than that which I now affirm is true. Some miracle might have produced it, yet the stages of the discovery were distinct and probable. After days and nights of incredible labour and fatigue, I succeeded in discovering the cause of generation and life; nay, more, I became myself capable of bestowing animation upon lifeless matter.

The astonishment which I had at first experienced on this

discovery soon gave place to delight and rapture. After so much time spent in painful labour, to arrive at once at the summit of my desires was the most gratifying consummation of my toils. But this discovery was so great and overwhelming that all the steps by which I had been progressively led to it were obliterated, and I beheld only the result. What had been the study and desire of the wisest men since the creation of the world was now within my grasp. Not that, like a magic scene, it all opened upon me at once: the information I had obtained was of a nature rather to direct my endeavours so soon as I should point them towards the object of my search than to exhibit that object already accomplished. I was like the Arabian who had been buried with the dead and found a passage to life, aided only by one glimmering and seemingly ineffectual light.

I see by your eagerness and the wonder and hope which your eyes express, my friend, that you expect to be informed of the secret with which I am acquainted; that cannot be; listen patiently until the end of my story, and you will easily perceive why I am reserved upon that subject. I will not lead you on, unguarded and ardent as I then was, to your destruction and infallible misery. Learn from me, if not by my precepts, at least by my example, how dangerous is the acquirement of knowledge and how much happier that man is who believes his native town to be the world, than he who aspires to become greater than his nature will allow.

When I found so astonishing a power placed within my hands, I hesitated a long time concerning the manner in which I should employ it. Although I possessed the capacity of bestowing animation, yet to prepare a frame for the reception of it, with all its intricacies of fibres, muscles, and veins, still remained a work of inconceivable difficulty and labour. I doubted at first whether I should attempt the creation of a being like myself, or one of simpler organization; but my imagination was too much exalted by my first success to permit me to doubt of my ability to give life to an animal as complete and wonderful as man.

The materials at present within my command hardly appeared adequate to so arduous an undertaking, but I doubted not that I should ultimately succeed. I prepared myself for a multitude of reverses; my operations might be incessantly baffled, and at last my work be imperfect, yet when I considered the improvement which every day takes place in science and mechanics, I was encouraged to hope my present attempts would at least lay the foundations of future success. Nor could I consider the magnitude and complexity of my plan as any argument of its impracticability. It was with these feelings that I began the creation of a human being.

As the minuteness of the parts formed a great hindrance to my speed, I resolved, contrary to my first intention, to make the being of a gigantic stature, that is to say, about eight feet in height, and proportionably large. After having formed this determination and having spent some months in successfully collecting and arranging my materials, I began.

No one can conceive the variety of feelings which bore me onwards, like a hurricane, in the first enthusiasm of success. Life and death appeared to me ideal bounds, which I should first break through, and pour a torrent of light into our dark world. A new species would bless me as its creator and source; many happy and excellent natures would owe their being to me. No father could claim the gratitude of his child so completely as I should deserve theirs. Pursuing these reflections, I thought that if I could bestow animation upon lifeless matter, I might in process of time (although I now found it impossible) renew life where death had apparently devoted the body to corruption.

These thoughts supported my spirits, while I pursued my undertaking with unremitting ardour. My cheek had grown pale with study, and my person had become emaciated with confinement. Sometimes, on the very brink of certainty, I failed; yet still I clung to the hope which the next day or the next hour might realize. One secret which I alone possessed was the hope to which I had dedicated myself; and the moon gazed on my midnight labours, while, with unrelaxed and breathless eagerness, I pursued nature to her hiding-places. Who shall conceive the horrors of my secret toil as I dabbled among the unhallowed damps of the grave or tortured the living animal to animate the lifeless clay?

My limbs now tremble, and my eyes swim with the remembrance; but then a resistless and almost frantic impulse urged me forward; I seemed to have lost all soul or sensation but for this one pursuit. It was indeed but a passing trance, that only made me feel with renewed acuteness so soon as, the unnatural stimulus ceasing to operate, I had returned to my old habits. I collected bones from charnelhouses and disturbed, with profane fingers, the tremendous secrets of the human frame. In a solitary chamber, or rather cell, at the top of the house, and separated from all the other apartments by a gallery and staircase, I kept my workshop of filthy creation; my eyeballs were starting from their sockets in attending to the details of my employment. The dissecting room and the slaughterhouse furnished many of my materials; and often did my human nature turn with loathing from my occupation, whilst, still urged on by an eagerness which perpetually increased, I brought my work near to a conclusion.

The summer months passed while I was thus engaged, heart and soul, in one pursuit. It was a most beautiful season; never did the fields bestow a more plentiful harvest or the vines yield a more luxuriant vintage, but my eyes were insensible to the charms of nature. And the same feelings which made me neglect the scenes around me caused me also to forget those friends who were so many miles absent, and whom I had not seen for so long a time. I knew my silence disquieted them, and I well remembered the words of my father: "I know that while you are pleased with yourself you will think of us with affection, and we shall hear regularly from you. You must pardon me if I regard any interruption in your correspondence as a proof that your other duties are equally neglected."

I knew well therefore what would be my father's feelings, but I could not tear my thoughts from my employment, loathsome in itself, but which had taken an irresistible hold of my imagination. I wished, as it were, to procrastinate all that related to my feelings of affection until the great object, which swallowed up every habit of my nature, should be completed.

I then thought that my father would be unjust if he ascribed my neglect to vice or faultiness on my part, but I am now convinced that he was justified in conceiving that I should not be altogether free from blame. A human being in perfection ought always to preserve a calm and peaceful mind and never to allow passion or a transitory desire to disturb his tranquillity. I do not think that the pursuit of knowledge is an exception to this rule. If the study to which you apply yourself has a tendency to weaken your affections and to destroy your taste for those simple pleasures in which no alloy can possibly mix, then that study is certainly unlawful, that is to say, not befitting the human mind. If this rule were always observed; if no man allowed any pursuit whatsoever to interfere with the tranquillity of his domestic affections, Greece had not been enslaved, Caesar would have spared his country, America would have been discovered more gradually, and the empires of Mexico and Peru had not been destroyed.

But I forget that I am moralizing in the most interesting part of my tale, and your looks remind me to proceed. My father made no reproach in his letters and only took notice of my science by inquiring into my occupations more particularly than before. Winter, spring, and summer passed away during my labours; but I did not watch the blossom or the expanding leaves—sights which before always yielded me supreme delight—so deeply was I engrossed in my occupation. The leaves of that year had withered before my work drew near to a close, and now every day showed me more plainly how well I had succeeded. But my enthusiasm was checked by my anxiety, and I appeared rather like one doomed by slavery to toil in the mines, or any other unwholesome trade than an artist occupied by his favourite employment.

Every night I was oppressed by a slow fever, and I became nervous to a most painful degree; the fall of a leaf startled me, and I shunned my fellow creatures as if I had been guilty of a crime. Sometimes I grew alarmed at the wreck I perceived that I had become; the energy of my purpose alone sustained me: my labours would soon end, and I believed that exercise and amusement would then drive away incipient disease; and I promised myself both of these when my creation should be complete.

CHAPTER 5

It was on a dreary night of November that I beheld the accomplishment of my toils. With an anxiety that almost amounted to agony, I collected the instruments of life around me, that I might infuse a spark of being into the lifeless thing that lay at my feet. It was already one in the morning; the rain pattered dismally against the panes, and my candle was nearly burnt out, when, by the glimmer of the half-extinguished light, I saw the dull yellow eye of the creature open; it breathed hard, and a convulsive motion agitated its limbs.

How can I describe my emotions at this catastrophe, or how delineate the wretch whom with such infinite pains and care I had endeavoured to form? His limbs were in proportion, and I had selected his features as beautiful. Beautiful! Great God! His yellow skin scarcely covered the work of muscles and arteries beneath; his hair was of a lustrous black, and flowing; his teeth of a pearly whiteness; but these luxuriances only formed a more horrid contrast with his watery eyes, that seemed almost of the same colour as the dun-white sockets in which they were set, his shrivelled complexion and straight black lips.

The different accidents of life are not so changeable as the feelings of human nature. I had worked hard for nearly two years, for the sole purpose of infusing life into an inanimate body. For this I had deprived myself of rest and health. I had desired it with an ardour that far exceeded moderation; but now that I had finished, the beauty of the dream vanished, and breathless horror and disgust filled my heart. Unable to endure the aspect of the being I had created, I rushed out of the room and continued a long time traversing my bedchamber, unable to compose my mind to sleep. At length lassitude succeeded to the tumult I had before endured, and I threw myself on the bed in my clothes, endeavouring to seek a few moments of forgetfulness.

But it was in vain; I slept, indeed, but I was disturbed by the wildest dreams. I thought I saw Elizabeth, in the bloom of health, walking in the streets of Ingolstadt. Delighted and surprised, I embraced her, but as I imprinted the first kiss on her lips, they became livid with the hue of death; her features appeared to change, and I thought that I held the corpse of my dead mother in my arms; a shroud enveloped her form, and I saw the grave-worms crawling in the folds of the flannel. I started from my sleep with horror; a cold dew covered my forehead, my teeth chattered, and every limb became convulsed; when, by the dim and yellow light of the moon, as it forced its way through the window shutters, I beheld the wretch—the miserable monster whom I had created.

He held up the curtain of the bed; and his eyes, if eyes they may be called, were fixed on me. His jaws opened, and he muttered some inarticulate sounds, while a grin wrinkled his cheeks. He might have spoken, but I did not hear; one hand was stretched out, seemingly to detain me, but I escaped and rushed downstairs. I took refuge in the courtyard belonging to the house which I inhabited, where I remained during the rest of the night, walking up and down in the greatest agitation, listening attentively, catching and fearing each sound as if it were to announce the approach of the demoniacal corpse to which I had so miserably given life.

Oh! No mortal could support the horror of that countenance. A mummy again endued with animation could not be so hideous as that wretch. I had gazed on him while unfinished; he was ugly then, but when those muscles and joints were rendered capable of motion, it became a thing such as even Dante could not have conceived.

I passed the night wretchedly. Sometimes my pulse beat so quickly and hardly that I felt the palpitation of every artery; at others, I nearly sank to the ground through languor and extreme weakness. Mingled with this horror, I felt the bitterness of disappointment; dreams that had been my food and pleasant rest for so long a space were now become a hell to me; and the change was so rapid, the overthrow so complete!

Morning, dismal and wet, at length dawned and discovered to my sleepless and aching eyes the church of Ingolstadt, its white steeple and clock, which indicated the sixth hour. The porter opened the gates of the court, which had that night been my asylum, and I issued into the streets, pacing them with quick steps, as if I sought to avoid the wretch whom I feared every turning of the street would present to my view. I did not dare return to the apartment which I inhabited, but felt impelled to hurry on, although drenched by the rain which poured from a black and comfortless sky.

I continued walking in this manner for some time, endeavouring by bodily exercise to ease the load that weighed upon my mind. I traversed the streets without any clear conception of where I was or what I was doing. My heart palpitated in the sickness of fear, and I hurried on with irregular steps, not daring to look about me:

> *Like one who, on a lonely road,*
> *Doth walk in fear and dread,*
> *And, having once turned round, walks on,*
> *And turns no more his head;*
> *Because he knows a frightful fiend*
> *Doth close behind him tread.*
>
> [Coleridge's *Ancient Mariner.*]

Continuing thus, I came at length opposite to the inn at which the various diligences and carriages usually stopped. Here I paused, I knew not why; but I remained some minutes with my eyes fixed on a coach that was coming towards me from the other end of the street. As it drew nearer I observed that it was the Swiss diligence; it stopped just where I was standing, and on the door being opened, I perceived Henry Clerval, who, on seeing me, instantly sprung out. "My dear Frankenstein," exclaimed he, "how glad I am to see you! How fortunate that you should be here at the very moment of my alighting!"

Nothing could equal my delight on seeing Clerval; his presence brought back to my thoughts my father, Elizabeth, and all those scenes of home so dear to my recollection. I grasped his hand, and in a moment forgot my horror and misfortune; I felt suddenly, and for the first time during many months, calm and serene joy. I welcomed my friend, therefore, in the most cordial manner, and we walked towards my college. Clerval continued talking for some time about our mutual friends and his own good fortune in being permitted to come to Ingolstadt.

"You may easily believe," said he, "how great was the difficulty to persuade my father that all necessary knowledge was not comprised in the noble art of bookkeeping; and, indeed, I believe I left him incredulous to the last, for his constant answer to my unwearied entreaties was the same as that of the Dutch schoolmaster in The Vicar of Wakefield: 'I have ten thousand florins a year without Greek, I eat heartily without Greek.' But his affection for me at length overcame his dislike of learning, and he has permitted me to undertake a voyage of discovery to the land of knowledge."

"It gives me the greatest delight to see you; but tell me how you left my father, brothers, and Elizabeth."

"Very well, and very happy, only a little uneasy that they hear from you so seldom. By the by, I mean to lecture you a little upon their account myself. But, my dear Frankenstein," continued he, stopping short and gazing full in my face, "I did not before remark how very ill you appear; so thin and pale; you look as if you had been watching for several nights."

"You have guessed right; I have lately been so deeply engaged in one occupation that I have not allowed myself sufficient rest, as you see; but I hope, I sincerely hope, that all these employments are now at an end and that I am at length free."

I trembled excessively; I could not endure to think of, and far less to allude to, the occurrences of the preceding night. I walked with a quick pace, and we soon arrived at my college. I then reflected, and the thought made me shiver, that the creature whom I had left in my apartment might still be there, alive and walking about. I dreaded to behold this monster, but I feared still more that Henry should see him. Entreating him, therefore, to remain a few minutes at the bottom of the stairs, I darted up towards my own room.

My hand was already on the lock of the door before I recollected myself. I then paused, and a cold shivering came over me. I threw the door forcibly open, as children are accustomed to do when they expect a spectre to stand in waiting for them on the other side; but nothing appeared. I stepped fearfully in: the apartment was empty, and my bedroom was also freed from its hideous guest. I could hardly believe that so great a good fortune could have befallen me, but when I became assured that my enemy had indeed fled, I clapped my hands for joy and ran down to Clerval.

We ascended into my room, and the servant presently brought breakfast; but I was unable to contain myself. It was not joy only that possessed me; I felt my flesh tingle with excess of sensitiveness, and my pulse beat rapidly. I was unable to remain for a single instant in the same place; I jumped over the chairs, clapped my hands, and laughed aloud. Clerval at first attributed my unusual spirits to joy on his arrival, but when he observed me more attentively, he saw a wildness in my eyes for which he could not account, and my loud, unrestrained, heartless laughter frightened and astonished him.

"My dear Victor," cried he, "what, for God's sake, is the matter? Do not laugh in that manner. How ill you are! What is the cause of all this?"

"Do not ask me," cried I, putting my hands before my eyes, for I thought I saw the dreaded spectre glide into the room; "HE can tell. Oh, save me! Save me!" I imagined that the monster seized me; I struggled furiously and fell down in a fit.

Poor Clerval! What must have been his feelings? A meeting, which he anticipated with such joy, so strangely turned to bitterness. But I was not the witness of his grief, for I was lifeless and did not recover my senses for a long, long time.

This was the commencement of a nervous fever which confined me for several months. During all that time Henry was my only nurse. I afterwards learned that, knowing my father's advanced age and unfitness for so long a journey, and how wretched my sickness would make Elizabeth, he spared them this grief by concealing the extent of my disorder. He knew that I could not have a more kind and attentive nurse than himself; and, firm in the hope he felt of my recovery, he did not doubt that, instead of doing harm, he performed the kindest action that he could towards them.

But I was in reality very ill, and surely nothing but the unbounded and unremitting attentions of my friend could have restored me to life. The form of the monster on whom I had bestowed existence was forever before my eyes, and I raved incessantly concerning him. Doubtless my words surprised Henry; he at first believed them to be the wanderings of my disturbed imagination, but the pertinacity with which I continually recurred to the same subject persuaded him that my disorder indeed owed its origin to some uncommon and terrible event.

By very slow degrees, and with frequent relapses that alarmed and grieved my friend, I recovered. I remember the first time I became capable of observing outward objects with any kind of pleasure, I perceived that the fallen leaves had disappeared and that the young buds were shooting forth from the trees that shaded my window. It was a divine spring, and the season contributed greatly to my convalescence. I felt also sentiments of joy and affection revive in my bosom; my gloom disappeared, and in a short time I became as cheerful as before I was attacked by the fatal passion.

"Dearest Clerval," exclaimed I, "how kind, how very good you are to me. This whole winter, instead of being spent in study, as you promised yourself, has been consumed in my sick room. How shall I ever repay you? I feel the greatest remorse for the disappointment of which I have been the occasion, but you will forgive me."

"You will repay me entirely if you do not discompose yourself, but get well as fast as you can; and since you appear in such good spirits, I may speak to you on one subject, may I not?"

I trembled. One subject! What could it be? Could he allude to an object on whom I dared not even think? "Compose yourself," said Clerval, who observed my change of colour, "I will not mention it if it agitates you; but your father and cousin would be very happy if they received a letter from you in your own handwriting. They hardly know how ill you have been and are uneasy at your long silence."

"Is that all, my dear Henry? How could you suppose that my first thought would not fly towards those dear, dear friends whom I love and who are so deserving of my love?"

"If this is your present temper, my friend, you will perhaps be glad to see a letter that has been lying here some days for you; it is from your cousin, I believe."

CHAPTER 6

Clerval then put the following letter into my hands. It was from my own Elizabeth:

My dearest Cousin,
You have been ill, very ill, and even the constant letters of dear kind Henry are not sufficient to reassure me on your account. You are forbidden to write—to hold a pen; yet one word from you, dear Victor, is necessary to calm our apprehensions. For a long time I have thought that each post would bring this line, and my persuasions have restrained my uncle from undertaking a journey to Ingolstadt. I have prevented his encountering the inconveniences and perhaps dangers of so long a journey, yet how often have I regretted not being able to perform it myself! I figure to myself that the task of attending on your sickbed has devolved on some mercenary old nurse, who could never guess your wishes nor minister to them with the care and affection of your poor cousin. Yet that is over now: Clerval writes that indeed you are getting better. I eagerly hope that you will confirm this intelligence soon

in your own handwriting.

Get well—and return to us. You will find a happy, cheerful home and friends who love you dearly. Your father's health is vigorous, and he asks but to see you, but to be assured that you are well; and not a care will ever cloud his benevolent countenance. How pleased you would be to remark the improvement of our Ernest! He is now sixteen and full of activity and spirit. He is desirous to be a true Swiss and to enter into foreign service, but we cannot part with him, at least until his elder brother returns to us. My uncle is not pleased with the idea of a military career in a distant country, but Ernest never had your powers of application. He looks upon study as an odious fetter; his time is spent in the open air, climbing the hills or rowing on the lake. I fear that he will become an idler unless we yield the point and permit him to enter on the profession which he has selected.

Little alteration, except the growth of our dear children, has taken place since you left us. The blue lake and snow-clad mountains—they never change; and I think our placid home and our contented hearts are regulated by the same immutable laws. My trifling occupations take up my time and amuse me, and I am rewarded for any exertions by seeing none but happy, kind faces around me. Since you left us, but one change has taken place in our little household. Do you remember on what occasion Justine Moritz entered our family? Probably you do not; I will relate her history, therefore in a few words.

Madame Moritz, her mother, was a widow with four children, of whom Justine was the third. This girl had always been the favourite of her father, but through a strange perversity, her mother could not endure her, and after the death of M. Moritz, treated her very ill. My aunt observed this, and when Justine was twelve years of age, prevailed on her mother to allow her to live at our house. The republican institutions of our country have produced simpler and happier manners than those which prevail in the great monarchies that surround it. Hence there is less distinction between the several classes of its inhabitants; and the lower orders, being neither so poor nor so despised, their manners are more refined and moral. A servant in Geneva does not mean the same thing as a servant in France and England. Justine, thus received in our family, learned the duties of a servant, a condition which, in our fortunate country, does not include the idea of ignorance and a sacrifice of the dignity of a human being.

Justine, you may remember, was a great favourite of yours; and I recollect you once remarked that if you were in an ill humour, one glance from Justine could dissipate it, for the same reason that Ariosto gives concerning the beauty of Angelica—she looked so frank-hearted and happy. My aunt conceived a great attachment for her, by which she was induced to give her an education superior to that which she had at first intended. This benefit was fully repaid; Justine was the most grateful little creature in the world: I do not mean that she made any professions I never heard one pass her lips, but you could see by her eyes that she almost adored her protectress. Although her disposition was gay and in many respects inconsiderate, yet she paid the greatest attention to every gesture of my aunt. She thought her the model of all excellence and endeavoured to imitate her phraseology and manners, so that even now she often reminds me of her.

When my dearest aunt died everyone was too much occupied in their own grief to notice poor Justine, who had attended her during her illness with the most anxious affection. Poor Justine was very ill; but other trials were reserved for her.

One by one, her brothers and sister died; and her mother, with the exception of her neglected daughter, was left childless. The conscience of the woman was troubled; she began to think that the deaths of her favourites was a judgement from heaven to chastise her partiality. She was a Roman Catholic; and I believe her confessor confirmed the idea which she had conceived. Accordingly, a few months after your departure for Ingolstadt, Justine was called home by her repentant mother. Poor girl! She wept when she quitted our house; she was much altered since the death of my aunt; grief had given softness and a winning mildness to her manners, which had before been remarkable for vivacity.

Nor was her residence at her mother's house of a nature to restore her gaiety. The poor woman was very vacillating in her repentance. She sometimes begged Justine to forgive her unkindness, but much oftener accused her of having caused the deaths of her brothers and sister. Perpetual fretting at length threw Madame Moritz into a decline, which at first increased her irritability, but she is now at peace for ever. She died on the first approach of cold weather, at the beginning of this last winter. Justine has just returned to us; and I assure you I love her tenderly. She is very clever and gentle, and extremely pretty; as I mentioned before, her mein and her expression continually remind me of my dear aunt.

I must say also a few words to you, my dear cousin, of little darling William. I wish you could see him; he is very tall of his age, with sweet laughing blue eyes, dark eyelashes, and curling hair. When he smiles, two little dimples appear on each cheek, which are rosy with health. He has already had one or two little WIVES, but Louisa Biron is his favourite, a pretty little girl of five years of age.

Now, dear Victor, I dare say you wish to be indulged in a little gossip concerning the good people of Geneva. The pretty Miss Mansfield has already received the congratulatory visits on her approaching marriage with a young Englishman, John Melbourne, Esq. Her ugly sister, Manon, married M. Duvillard, the rich banker, last autumn. Your favourite schoolfellow, Louis Manoir, has suffered several misfortunes since the departure of Clerval from Geneva. But he has already recovered his spirits, and is reported to be on the point of marrying a lively pretty Frenchwoman, Madame Tavernier. She is a widow, and much older than Manoir; but she is very much admired, and a favourite with everybody.

I have written myself into better spirits, dear cousin; but my anxiety returns upon me as I conclude. Write, dearest Victor, one line—one word will be a blessing to us. Ten thousand thanks to Henry for his kindness, his affection, and his many letters; we are sincerely grateful. *Adieu!* my cousin; take care of yourself; and, I entreat you, write!

Elizabeth Lavenza.

Geneva, March 18, 17—,

"Dear, dear Elizabeth!" I exclaimed, when I had read her letter: "I will write instantly and relieve them from the anxiety they must feel." I wrote, and this exertion greatly fatigued me; but my convalescence had commenced, and proceeded regularly. In another fortnight I was able to leave my chamber.

One of my first duties on my recovery was to introduce Clerval to the several professors of the university. In doing this, I underwent a kind of rough usage, ill befitting the wounds that my mind had sustained. Ever since the fatal night, the end of my labours, and the beginning of my misfortunes, I had conceived a violent antipathy even to the name of natural philosophy.

When I was otherwise quite restored to health, the sight of a chemical instrument would renew all the agony of my nervous symptoms. Henry saw this, and had removed all my apparatus from my view. He had also changed my apartment; for he perceived that I had acquired a dislike for the room which had previously been my laboratory. But these cares of Clerval were made of no avail when I visited the professors.

M. Waldman inflicted torture when he praised, with kindness and warmth, the astonishing progress I had made in the sciences. He soon perceived that I disliked the subject; but not guessing the real cause, he attributed my feelings to modesty, and changed the subject from my improvement, to the science itself, with a desire, as I evidently saw, of drawing me out. What could I do? He meant to please, and he tormented me. I felt as if he had placed carefully, one by one, in my five those instruments which were to be afterwards used in putting me to a slow and cruel death. I writhed under his words, yet dared not exhibit the pain I felt.

Clerval, whose eyes and feelings were always quick in discerning the sensations of others, declined the subject, alleging, in excuse, his total ignorance; and the conversation took a more general turn. I thanked my friend from my heart, but I did not speak. I saw plainly that he was surprised, but he never attempted to draw my secret from me; and although I loved him with a mixture of affection and reverence that knew no bounds, yet I could never persuade myself to confide in him that event which was so often present to my recollection, but which I feared the detail to another would only impress more deeply.

M. Krempe was not equally docile; and in my condition at that time, of almost insupportable sensitiveness, his harsh blunt encomiums gave me even more pain than the benevolent approbation of M. Waldman. "D—n the fellow!" cried he; "why, M. Clerval, I assure you he has outstript us all. Ay, stare if you please; but it is nevertheless true. A youngster who, but a few years ago, believed in Cornelius Agrippa as firmly as in the gospel, has now set himself at the head of the university; and if he is not soon pulled down, we shall all be out of countenance.—Ay, ay," continued he, observing my face expressive of suffering, "M. Frankenstein is modest; an excellent quality in a young man. Young men should be diffident of themselves, you know, M. Clerval: I was myself when young; but that wears out in a very short time."

M. Krempe had now commenced an eulogy on himself, which happily turned the conversation from a subject that was so annoying to me.

Clerval had never sympathized in my tastes for natural science; and his literary pursuits differed wholly from those which had occupied me. He came to the university with the design of making himself complete master of the oriental languages, and thus he should open a field for the plan of life he had marked out for himself. Resolved to pursue no inglorious career, he turned his eyes toward the East, as affording scope for his spirit of enterprise. The Persian, Arabic, and Sanscrit languages engaged his attention, and I was easily induced to enter on the same studies. Idleness had ever been irksome to me, and now that I wished to fly from reflection, and hated my former studies, I felt great relief in being the fellow-pupil with my friend, and found not only instruction but consolation in the works of the orientalists.

I did not, like him, attempt a critical knowledge of their dialects, for I did not contemplate making any other use of them than temporary amusement. I read merely to understand their meaning, and they well repaid my labours. Their melancholy is soothing, and their joy elevating, to a degree I never experienced in studying the authors of any other country. When you read their writings, life appears to consist in a warm sun and a garden of roses,—in the smiles and frowns of a fair enemy, and the fire that consumes your own heart. How different from the manly and heroical poetry of Greece and Rome!

Summer passed away in these occupations, and my return to Geneva was fixed for the latter end of autumn; but being delayed by several accidents, winter and snow arrived, the roads were deemed impassable, and my journey was retarded until the ensuing spring. I felt this delay very bitterly; for I longed to see my native town and my beloved friends. My return had only been delayed so long, from an unwillingness to leave Clerval in a strange place, before he had become acquainted with any of its inhabitants. The winter, however, was spent cheerfully; and although the spring was uncommonly late, when it came its beauty compensated for its dilatoriness.

The month of May had already commenced, and I expected the letter daily which was to fix the date of my departure, when Henry proposed a pedestrian tour in the environs of Ingolstadt, that I might bid a personal farewell to the country I had so long inhabited. I acceded with pleasure to this proposition: I was fond of exercise, and Clerval had always been my favourite companion in the ramble of this nature that I had taken among the scenes of my native country.

We passed a fortnight in these perambulations: my health and spirits had long been restored, and they gained additional strength from the salubrious air I breathed, the natural incidents of our progress, and the conversation of my friend. Study had before secluded me from the intercourse of my fellowcreatures, and rendered me unsocial; but Clerval called forth the better feelings of my heart; he again taught me to love the aspect of nature, and the cheerful faces of children. Excellent friend! how sincerely you did love me, and endeavour to elevate my mind until it was on a level with your own.

A selfish pursuit had cramped and narrowed me, until your gentleness and affection warmed and opened my senses; I became the same happy creature who, a few years ago, loved and beloved by all, had no sorrow or care. When happy, inanimate nature had the power of bestowing on me the most delightful sensations. A serene sky and verdant fields filled me with ecstasy. The present season was indeed divine; the flowers of spring bloomed in the hedges, while those of summer were already in bud. I was undisturbed by thoughts which during the preceding year had pressed upon me, notwithstanding my endeavours to throw them off, with an invincible burden.

Henry rejoiced in my gaiety, and sincerely sympathised in my feelings: he exerted himself to amuse me, while he expressed the sensations that filled his soul. The resources of his mind on this occasion were truly astonishing: his conversation was full of imagination; and very often, in imitation of the Persian and Arabic writers, he invented tales of wonderful fancy and passion. At other times he repeated my favourite poems, or drew me out into arguments, which he supported with great ingenuity.

We returned to our college on a Sunday afternoon: the peasants were dancing, and every one we met appeared gay and happy. My own spirits were high, and I bounded along with feelings of unbridled joy and hilarity.

CHAPTER 7

On my return, I found the following letter from my father:

My dear Victor,

You have probably waited impatiently for a letter to fix the date of your return to us; and I was at first tempted to write only a few lines, merely mentioning the day on which I should expect you. But that would be a cruel kindness, and I dare not do it. What would be your surprise, my son, when you expected a happy and glad welcome, to behold, on the contrary, tears and wretchedness? And how, Victor, can I relate our misfortune? Absence cannot have rendered you callous to our joys and griefs; and how shall I inflict pain on my long absent son? I wish to prepare you for the woeful news, but I know it is impossible; even now your eye skims over the page to seek the words which are to convey to you the horrible tidings.

William is dead!—that sweet child, whose smiles delighted and warmed my heart, who was so gentle, yet so gay! Victor, he is murdered!

I will not attempt to console you; but will simply relate the circumstances of the transaction.

Last Thursday (May 7th), I, my niece, and your two brothers, went to walk in Plainpalais. The evening was warm and serene, and we prolonged our walk farther than usual. It was already dusk before we thought of returning; and then we discovered that William and Ernest, who had gone on before, were not to be found. We accordingly rested on a seat until they should return. Presently Ernest came, and enquired if we had seen his brother; he said, that he had been playing with him, that William had run away to hide himself, and that he vainly sought for him, and afterwards waited for a long time, but that he did not return.

This account rather alarmed us, and we continued to search for him until night fell, when Elizabeth conjectured that he might have returned to the house. He was not there. We returned again, with torches; for I could not rest, when I thought that my sweet boy had lost himself, and was exposed to all the damps and dews of night; Elizabeth also suffered extreme anguish. About five in the morning I discovered my lovely boy, whom the night before I had seen blooming and active in health, stretched on the grass livid and motionless; the print of the murder's finger was on his neck.

He was conveyed home, and the anguish that was visible in my countenance betrayed the secret to Elizabeth. She was very earnest to see the corpse. At first I attempted to prevent her but she persisted, and entering the room where it lay, hastily examined the neck of the victim, and clasping her hands exclaimed, 'O God! I have murdered my darling child!'

She fainted, and was restored with extreme difficulty. When she again lived, it was only to weep and sigh. She told me, that that same evening William had teased her to let him wear a very valuable miniature that she possessed of your mother. This picture is gone, and was doubtless the temptation which urged the murderer to the deed. We have no trace of him at present, although our exertions to discover him are unremitted; but they will not restore my beloved William!

Come, dearest Victor; you alone can console Elizabeth. She weeps continually, and accuses herself unjustly as the cause of his death; her words pierce my heart. We are all unhappy; but will not that be an additional motive for you, my son, to return and be our comforter? Your dear mother! Alas, Victor! I now say, Thank God she did not live to witness the cruel, miserable death of her youngest darling!

Come, Victor; not brooding thoughts of vengeance against the assassin, but with feelings of peace and gentleness, that will heal, instead of festering, the wounds of our minds.

Enter the house of mourning, my friend, but with kindness and affection for those who love you, and not with hatred for your enemies.

Your affectionate and afflicted father,

Alphonse Frankenstein.

Geneva, May 12th, 17—.

Clerval, who had watched my countenance as I read this letter, was surprised to observe the despair that succeeded the joy I at first expressed on receiving new from my friends. I threw the letter on the table, and covered my face with my hands.

"My dear Frankenstein," exclaimed Henry, when he perceived me weep with bitterness, "are you always to be unhappy? My dear friend, what has happened?"

I motioned him to take up the letter, while I walked up and down the room in the extremest agitation. Tears also gushed from the eyes of Clerval, as he read the account of my misfortune.

"I can offer you no consolation, my friend," said he; "your disaster is irreparable. What do you intend to do?"

"To go instantly to Geneva: come with my, Henry, to order the horses."

During our walk, Clerval endeavoured to say a few words of consolation; he could only express his heartfelt sympathy. "Poor William!" said he, dear lovely child, he now sleeps with his angel mother! Who that had seen him bright and joyous in his young beauty, but must weep over his untimely loss! To die so miserably; to feel the murderer's grasp! How much more a murdered that could destroy radiant innocence! Poor little fellow! one only consolation have we; his friends mourn and weep, but he is at rest. The pang is over, his sufferings are at an end forever. A sod covers his gentle form, and he knows no pain. He can no longer be a subject for pity; we must reserve that for his miserable survivors."

Clerval spoke thus as we hurried through the streets; the words impressed themselves on my mind and I remembered them afterwards in solitude. But now, as soon as the horses arrived, I hurried into a *cabriolet*, and bade farewell to my friend.

My journey was very melancholy. At first I wished to hurry on, for I longed to console and sympathise with my loved and sorrowing friends; but when I drew near my native town, I slackened my progress. I could hardly sustain the multitude of feelings that crowded into my mind. I passed through scenes familiar to my youth, but which I had not seen for nearly six years. How altered everything might be during that time! One sudden and desolating change had taken place; but a thousand little circumstances might have by degrees worked other alterations, which, although they were done more tranquilly, might not be the less decisive.

Fear overcame me; I dared no advance, dreading a thousand nameless evils that made me tremble, although I was unable to define them. I remained two days at Lausanne, in this painful state of mind. I contemplated the lake: the waters were placid; all around was calm; and the snowy mountains, 'the palaces of nature,' were not changed. By degrees the calm and heavenly scene restored me, and I continued my journey towards Geneva.

The road ran by the side of the lake, which became narrower as I approached my native town. I discovered more distinctly the black sides of Jura, and the bright summit of Mont Blanc. I wept like a child. "Dear mountains! my own beautiful lake! how do you welcome your wanderer? Your summits are clear; the sky and lake are blue and placid. Is this to prognosticate peace, or to mock at my unhappiness?"

I fear, my friend, that I shall render myself tedious by dwelling on these preliminary circumstances; but they were days of comparative happiness, and I think of them with pleasure. My country, my beloved country! who but a native can tell the delight I took in again beholding thy streams, thy mountains, and, more than all, thy lovely lake!

Yet, as I drew nearer home, grief and fear again overcame me. Night also closed around; and when I could hardly see the dark mountains, I felt still more gloomily. The picture appeared a vast and dim scene of evil, and I foresaw obscurely that I was destined to become the most wretched of human beings. Alas! I prophesied truly, and failed only in one single circumstance, that in all the misery I imagined and dreaded, I did not conceive the hundredth part of the anguish I was destined to endure. It was completely dark when I arrived in the environs of Geneva; the gates of the town were already shut; and I was obliged to pass the night at Secheron, a village at the distance of half a league from the city.

The sky was serene; and, as I was unable to rest, I resolved to visit the spot where my poor William had been murdered. As I could not pass through the town, I was obliged to cross the lake in a boat to arrive at Plainpalais. During this short voyage I saw the lightning playing on the summit of Mont Blanc in the most beautiful figures. The storm appeared to approach rapidly, and, on landing, I ascended a low hill, that I might observe its progress. It advanced; the heavens were clouded, and I soon felt the rain coming slowly in large drops, but its violence quickly increased.

I quitted my seat, and walked on, although the darkness and storm increased every minute, and the thunder burst with a terrific crash over my head. It was echoed from Saleve, the Juras, and the Alps of Savoy; vivid flashes of lightning dazzled my eyes, illuminating the lake, making it appear like a vast sheet of fire; then for an instant everything seemed of a pitchy darkness, until the eye recovered itself from the preceding flash. The storm, as is often the case in Switzerland, appeared at once in various parts of the heavens. The most violent storm hung exactly north of the town, over the part of the lake which lies between the promontory of Belrive and the village of Copet. Another storm enlightened Jura with faint flashes; and another darkened and sometimes disclosed the Mole, a peaked mountain to the east of the lake.

While I watched the tempest, so beautiful yet terrific, I wandered on with a hasty step. This noble war in the sky elevated my spirits; I clasped my hands, and exclaimed aloud, "William, dear angel! this is thy funeral, this thy dirge!" As I said these words,

I perceived in the gloom a figure which stole from behind a clump of trees near me; I stood fixed, gazing intently: I could not be mistaken. A flash of lightning illuminated the object, and discovered its shape plainly to me; its gigantic stature, and the deformity of its aspect more hideous than belongs to humanity, instantly informed me that it was the wretch, the filthy daemon, to whom I had given life. What did he there? Could he be (I shuddered at the conception) the murderer of my brother? No sooner did that idea cross my imagination, than I became convinced of its truth; my teeth chattered, and I was forced to lean against a tree for support. The figure passed me quickly, and I lost it in the gloom.

Nothing in human shape could have destroyed the fair child. HE was the murderer! I could not doubt it. The mere presence of the idea was an irresistible proof of the fact. I thought of pursuing the devil; but it would have been in vain, for another flash discovered him to me hanging among the rocks of the nearly perpendicular ascent of Mont Saleve, a hill that bounds Plainpalais on the south. He soon reached the summit, and disappeared.

I remained motionless. The thunder ceased; but the rain still continued, and the scene was enveloped in an impenetrable darkness. I revolved in my mind the events which I had until now sought to forget: the whole train of my progress toward the creation; the appearance of the works of my own hands at my bedside; its departure. Two years had now nearly elapsed since the night on which he first received life; and was this his first crime? Alas! I had turned loose into the world a depraved wretch, whose delight was in carnage and misery; had he not murdered my brother?

No one can conceive the anguish I suffered during the remainder of the night, which I spent, cold and wet, in the open air. But I did not feel the inconvenience of the weather; my imagination was busy in scenes of evil and despair. I considered the being whom I had cast among mankind, and endowed with the will and power to effect purposes of horror, such as the deed which he had now done, nearly in the light of my own vampire, my own spirit let loose from the grave, and forced to destroy all that was dear to me.

Day dawned; and I directed my steps towards the town. The gates were open, and I hastened to my father's house. My first thought was to discover what I knew of the murderer, and cause instant pursuit to be made. But I paused when I reflected on the story that I had to tell. A being whom I myself had formed, and endued with life, had met me at midnight among the precipices of an inaccessible mountain. I remembered also the nervous fever with which I had been seized just at the time that I dated my creation, and which would give an air of delirium to a tale otherwise so utterly improbable. I well knew that if any other had communicated such a relation to me, I should have looked upon it as the ravings of insanity. Besides, the strange nature of the animal would elude all pursuit, even if I were so far credited as to persuade my relatives to commence it. And then of what use would be pursuit? Who could arrest a creature capable of scaling the overhanging sides of Mont Salève? These reflections determined me, and I resolved to remain silent.

It was about five in the morning when I entered my father's house. I told the servants not to disturb the family, and went into the library to attend their usual hour of rising.

Six years had elapsed, passed in a dream but for one indelible trace, and I stood in the same place where I had last embraced my father before my departure for Ingolstadt. Beloved and venerable parent! He still remained to me. I gazed on the picture of my mother, which stood over the mantel-piece. It was an historical subject, painted at my father's desire, and represented Caroline Beaufort in an agony of despair, kneeling by the coffin of her dead father. Her garb was rustic, and her cheek pale; but there was an air of dignity and beauty, that hardly permitted the sentiment of pity.

Below this picture was a miniature of William; and my tears flowed when I looked upon it. While I was thus engaged, Ernest entered: he had heard me arrive, and hastened to welcome me: "Welcome, my dearest Victor," said he. "Ah! I wish you had come three months ago, and then you would have found us all joyous and delighted. You come to us now to share a misery which nothing can alleviate; yet you presence will, I hope, revive our father, who seems sinking under his misfortune; and your persuasions will induce poor Elizabeth to cease her vain and tormenting self-accusations.—Poor William! he was our darling and our pride!"

Tears, unrestrained, fell from my brother's eyes; a sense of mortal agony crept over my frame. Before, I had only imagined the wretchedness of my desolated home; the reality came on me as a new, and a not less terrible, disaster. I tried to calm Ernest; I enquired more minutely concerning my father, and her I named my cousin.

"She most of all," said Ernest, "requires consolation; she accused herself of having caused the death of my brother, and that made her very wretched. But since the murderer has been discovered—"

"The murderer discovered! Good God! how can that be? who could attempt to pursue him? It is impossible; one might as well try to overtake the winds, or confine a mountain-stream with a straw. I saw him too; he was free last night!"

"I do not know what you mean," replied my brother, in accents of wonder, "but to us the discovery we have made completes our misery. No one would believe it at first; and even now Elizabeth will not be convinced, notwithstanding all the evidence. Indeed, who would credit that Justine Moritz, who was so amiable, and fond of all the family, could suddenly become so capable of so frightful, so appalling a crime?"

"Justine Moritz! Poor, poor girl, is she the accused? But it is wrongfully; everyone knows that; no one believes it, surely, Ernest?"

"No one did at first; but several circumstances came out, that have almost forced conviction upon us; and her own behaviour has been so confused, as to add to the evidence of facts a weight that, I fear, leaves no hope for doubt. But she will be tried today, and you will then hear all."

He then related that, the morning on which the murder of poor William had been discovered, Justine had been taken ill, and confined to her bed for several days. During this interval, one of the servants, happening to examine the apparel she had worn on the night of the murder, had discovered in her pocket the picture of my mother, which had been judged to be the temptation of the murderer. The servant instantly showed it to one of the others, who, without saying a word to any of the family, went to a magistrate; and, upon their deposition, Justine was apprehended. On being charged with the fact, the poor girl confirmed the suspicion in a great measure by her extreme confusion of manner.

This was a strange tale, but it did not shake my faith; and I replied earnestly, "You are all mistaken; I know the murderer. Justine, poor, good Justine, is innocent."

At that instant my father entered. I saw unhappiness deeply impressed on his countenance, but he endeavoured to welcome me cheerfully; and, after we had exchanged our mournful greeting, would have introduced some other topic than that of our disaster, had not Ernest exclaimed, "Good God, papa! Victor says that he knows who was the murderer of poor William."

"We do also, unfortunately," replied my father, "for indeed I had rather have been for ever ignorant than have discovered so much depravity and ungratitude in one I valued so highly."

"My dear father, you are mistaken; Justine is innocent."

"If she is, God forbid that she should suffer as guilty. She is to be tried today, and I hope, I sincerely hope, that she will be acquitted."

This speech calmed me. I was firmly convinced in my own mind that Justine, and indeed every human being, was guiltless of this murder. I had no fear, therefore, that any circumstantial evidence could be brought forward strong enough to convict her. My tale was not one to announce publicly; its astounding horror would be looked upon as madness by the vulgar. Did any one indeed exist, except I, the creator, who would believe, unless his senses convinced him, in the existence of the living monument of presumption and rash ignorance which I had let loose upon the world?

We were soon joined by Elizabeth. Time had altered her since I last beheld her; it had endowed her with loveliness surpassing the beauty of her childish years. There was the same candour, the same vivacity, but it was allied to an expression more full of sensibility and intellect. She welcomed me with the greatest affection. "Your arrival, my dear cousin," said she, "fills me with hope. You perhaps will find some means to justify my poor guiltless Justine. Alas! who is safe, if she be convicted of crime? I rely on her innocence as certainly as I do upon my own. Our misfortune is doubly hard to us; we have not only lost that lovely darling boy, but this poor girl, whom I sincerely love, is to be torn away by even a worse fate. If she is condemned, I never shall know joy more. But she will not, I am sure she will not; and then I shall be happy again, even after the sad death of my little William."

"She is innocent, my Elizabeth," said I, "and that shall be proved; fear nothing, but let your spirits be cheered by the assurance of her acquittal."

"How kind and generous you are! everyone else believes in her guilt, and that made me wretched, for I knew that it was impossible: and to see every one else prejudiced in so deadly a manner rendered me hopeless and despairing." She wept.

"Dearest niece," said my father, "dry your tears. If she is, as you believe, innocent, rely on the justice of our laws, and the activity with which I shall prevent the slightest shadow of partiality."

CHAPTER 8

We passed a few sad hours until eleven o'clock, when the trial was to commence. My father and the rest of the family being obliged to attend as witnesses, I accompanied them to the court. During the whole of this wretched mockery of justice I suffered living torture. It was to be decided whether the result of my curiosity and lawless devices would cause the death of two of my fellow beings: one a smiling babe full of innocence and joy, the other far more dreadfully murdered, with every aggravation of infamy that could make the murder memorable in horror. Justine also was a girl of merit and possessed qualities which promised to render her life happy; now all was to be obliterated in an ignominious grave, and I the cause! A thousand times rather would I have confessed myself guilty of the crime ascribed to Justine, but I was absent when it was committed, and such a declaration would have been considered as the ravings of a madman and would not have exculpated her who suffered through me.

The appearance of Justine was calm. She was dressed in mourning, and her countenance, always engaging, was rendered, by the solemnity of her feelings, exquisitely beautiful. Yet she appeared confident in innocence and did not tremble, although gazed on and execrated by thousands, for all the kindness which her beauty might otherwise have excited was obliterated in the minds of the spectators by the imagination of the enormity she was supposed to have committed. She was tranquil, yet her tranquillity was evidently constrained; and as her confusion had before been adduced as a proof of her guilt, she worked up her mind to an appearance of courage. When she entered the court she threw her eyes round it and quickly discovered where we were seated. A tear seemed to dim her eye when she saw us, but she quickly recovered herself, and a look of sorrowful affection seemed to attest her utter guiltlessness.

The trial began, and after the advocate against her had stated the charge, several witnesses were called. Several strange facts combined against her, which might have staggered anyone who had not such proof of her innocence as I had. She had been out the whole of the night on which the murder had been committed and towards morning had been perceived by a marketwoman not far from the spot where the body of the murdered child had been afterwards found. The woman asked her what she did there, but she looked very strangely and only returned a confused and unintelligible answer.

She returned to the house about eight o'clock, and when one inquired where she had passed the night, she replied that she had been looking for the child and demanded earnestly if anything had been heard concerning him. When shown the body, she fell into violent hysterics and kept her bed for several days. The picture was then produced which the servant had found in her pocket; and when Elizabeth, in a faltering voice, proved that it was the same which, an hour before the child had been missed, she had placed round his neck, a murmur of horror and indignation filled the court.

Justine was called on for her defence. As the trial had proceeded, her countenance had altered. Surprise, horror, and misery were strongly expressed. Sometimes she struggled with her tears, but when she was desired to plead, she collected her powers and spoke in an audible although variable voice.

"God knows," she said, "how entirely I am innocent. But I do not pretend that my protestations should acquit me; I rest my innocence on a plain and simple explanation of the facts which have been adduced against me, and I hope the character I have always borne will incline my judges to a favourable interpretation where any circumstance appears doubtful or suspicious."

She then related that, by the permission of Elizabeth, she had passed the evening of the night on which the murder had been committed at the house of an aunt at Chene, a village situated at about a league from Geneva. On her return, at about nine o'clock, she met a man who asked her if she had seen anything of the child who was lost. She was alarmed by this account and passed several hours in looking for him, when the gates of Geneva were shut, and she was forced to remain several hours of the night in a barn belonging to a cottage, being unwilling to call up the inhabitants, to whom she was well known.

Most of the night she spent here watching; towards morning she believed that she slept for a few minutes; some steps disturbed her, and she awoke. It was dawn, and she quitted her asylum, that she might again endeavour to find my brother. If she had gone near the spot where his body lay, it was without her knowledge. That she had been bewildered when questioned by the market-woman was not surprising, since she had passed a sleepless night and the fate of poor William was yet uncertain. Concerning the picture she could give no account.

"I know," continued the unhappy victim, "how heavily and fatally this one circumstance weighs against me, but I have no power of explaining it; and when I have expressed my utter ignorance, I am only left to conjecture concerning the probabilities by which it might have been placed in my pocket. But here also I am checked. I believe that I have no enemy on earth, and none surely would have been so wicked as to destroy me wantonly. Did the murderer place it there? I know of no opportunity afforded him for so doing; or, if I had, why should he have stolen the jewel, to part with it again so soon?

"I commit my cause to the justice of my judges, yet I see no room for hope. I beg permission to have a few witnesses examined concerning my character, and if their testimony shall not overweigh my supposed guilt, I must be condemned, although I would pledge my salvation on my innocence."

Several witnesses were called who had known her for many years, and they spoke well of her; but fear and hatred of the crime of which they supposed her guilty rendered them timorous and unwilling to come forward. Elizabeth saw even this last resource, her excellent dispositions and irreproachable conduct, about to fail the accused, when, although violently agitated, she desired permission to address the court.

"I am," said she, "the cousin of the unhappy child who was murdered, or rather his sister, for I was educated by and have lived with his parents ever since and even long before his birth. It may therefore be judged indecent in me to come forward on this occasion, but when I see a fellow creature about to perish through the cowardice of her pretended friends, I wish to be allowed to speak, that I may say what I know of her character. I am well acquainted with the accused. I have lived in the same house with her, at one time for five and at another for nearly two years. During all that period she appeared to me the most amiable and benevolent of human creatures.

She nursed Madame Frankenstein, my aunt, in her last illness, with the greatest affection and care and afterwards attended her own mother during a tedious illness, in a manner that excited the admiration of all who knew her, after which she again lived in my uncle's house, where she was beloved by all the family. She was warmly attached to the child who is now dead and acted towards him like a most affectionate mother. For my own part, I do not hesitate to say that, notwithstanding all the evidence produced against her, I believe and rely on her perfect innocence. She had no temptation for such an action; as to the bauble on which the chief proof rests, if she had earnestly desired it, I should have willingly given it to her, so much do I esteem and value her."

A murmur of approbation followed Elizabeth's simple and powerful appeal, but it was excited by her generous interference, and not in favour of poor Justine, on whom the public indignation was turned with renewed violence, charging her with the blackest ingratitude. She herself wept as Elizabeth spoke, but she did not answer. My own agitation and anguish was extreme during the whole trial. I believed in her innocence; I knew it. Could the demon who had (I did not for a minute doubt) murdered my brother also in his hellish sport have betrayed the innocent to death and ignominy? I could not sustain the horror of my situation, and when I perceived that the popular voice and the countenances of the judges had already condemned my unhappy victim, I rushed out of the court in agony. The tortures of the accused did not equal mine; she was sustained by innocence, but the fangs of remorse tore my bosom and would not forgo their hold.

I passed a night of unmingled wretchedness. In the morning I went to the court; my lips and throat were parched. I dared not ask the fatal question, but I was known, and the officer guessed the cause of my visit. The ballots had been thrown; they were all black, and Justine was condemned.

I cannot pretend to describe what I then felt. I had before

experienced sensations of horror, and I have endeavoured to bestow upon them adequate expressions, but words cannot convey an idea of the heart-sickening despair that I then endured. The person to whom I addressed myself added that Justine had already confessed her guilt. "That evidence," he observed, "was hardly required in so glaring a case, but I am glad of it, and, indeed, none of our judges like to condemn a criminal upon circumstantial evidence, be it ever so decisive."

This was strange and unexpected intelligence; what could it mean? Had my eyes deceived me? And was I really as mad as the whole world would believe me to be if I disclosed the object of my suspicions? I hastened to return home, and Elizabeth eagerly demanded the result.

"My cousin," replied I, "it is decided as you may have expected; all judges had rather that ten innocent should suffer than that one guilty should escape. But she has confessed."

This was a dire blow to poor Elizabeth, who had relied with firmness upon Justine's innocence. "Alas!" said she. "How shall I ever again believe in human goodness? Justine, whom I loved and esteemed as my sister, how could she put on those smiles of innocence only to betray? Her mild eyes seemed incapable of any severity or guile, and yet she has committed a murder."

Soon after we heard that the poor victim had expressed a desire to see my cousin. My father wished her not to go but said that he left it to her own judgment and feelings to decide. "Yes," said Elizabeth, "I will go, although she is guilty; and you, Victor, shall accompany me; I cannot go alone." The idea of this visit was torture to me, yet I could not refuse. We entered the gloomy prison chamber and beheld Justine sitting on some straw at the farther end; her hands were manacled, and her head rested on her knees. She rose on seeing us enter, and when we were left alone with her, she threw herself at the feet of Elizabeth, weeping bitterly. My cousin wept also.

"Oh, Justine!" said she. "Why did you rob me of my last consolation? I relied on your innocence, and although I was then very wretched, I was not so miserable as I am now."

"And do you also believe that I am so very, very wicked? Do you also join with my enemies to crush me, to condemn me as a murderer?" Her voice was suffocated with sobs.

"Rise, my poor girl," said Elizabeth; "why do you kneel, if you are innocent? I am not one of your enemies, I believed you guiltless, notwithstanding every evidence, until I heard that you had yourself declared your guilt. That report, you say, is false; and be assured, dear Justine, that nothing can shake my confidence in you for a moment, but your own confession."

"I did confess, but I confessed a lie. I confessed, that I might obtain absolution; but now that falsehood lies heavier at my heart than all my other sins. The God of heaven forgive me! Ever since I was condemned, my confessor has besieged me; he threatened and menaced, until I almost began to think that I was the monster that he said I was. He threatened excommunication and hell fire in my last moments if I continued obdurate. Dear lady, I had none to support me; all looked on me as a wretch doomed to ignominy and perdition. What could I do? In an evil hour I subscribed to a lie; and now only am I truly miserable."

She paused, weeping, and then continued, "I thought with horror, my sweet lady, that you should believe your Justine, whom your blessed aunt had so highly honoured, and whom you loved, was a creature capable of a crime which none but the devil himself could have perpetrated. Dear William! dearest blessed child! I soon shall see you again in heaven, where we shall all be happy; and that consoles me, going as I am to suffer ignominy and death."

"Oh, Justine! Forgive me for having for one moment distrusted you. Why did you confess? But do not mourn, dear girl. Do not fear. I will proclaim, I will prove your innocence. I will melt the stony hearts of your enemies by my tears and prayers. You shall not die! You, my playfellow, my companion, my sister, perish on the scaffold! No! No! I never could survive so horrible a misfortune."

Justine shook her head mournfully. "I do not fear to die," she said; "that pang is past. God raises my weakness and gives me courage to endure the worst. I leave a sad and bitter world; and if you remember me and think of me as of one unjustly condemned, I am resigned to the fate awaiting me. Learn from me, dear lady, to submit in patience to the will of heaven!"

During this conversation I had retired to a corner of the prison room, where I could conceal the horrid anguish that possessed me. Despair! Who dared talk of that? The poor victim, who on the morrow was to pass the awful boundary between life and death, felt not, as I did, such deep and bitter agony. I gnashed my teeth and ground them together, uttering a groan that came from my inmost soul. Justine started. When she saw who it was, she approached me and said, "Dear sir, you are very kind to visit me; you, I hope, do not believe that I am guilty?"

I could not answer. "No, Justine," said Elizabeth; "he is more convinced of your innocence than I was, for even when he heard that you had confessed, he did not credit it."

"I truly thank him. In these last moments I feel the sincerest gratitude towards those who think of me with kindness. How sweet is the affection of others to such a wretch as I am! It removes more than half my misfortune, and I feel as if I could die in peace now that my innocence is acknowledged by you, dear lady, and your cousin."

Thus the poor sufferer tried to comfort others and herself. She indeed gained the resignation she desired. But I, the true murderer, felt the never-dying worm alive in my bosom, which allowed of no hope or consolation. Elizabeth also wept and was unhappy, but hers also was the misery of innocence, which, like a cloud that passes over the fair moon, for a while hides but cannot tarnish its brightness. Anguish and despair had penetrated into the core of my heart; I bore a hell within me which nothing could extinguish. We stayed several hours with Justine, and it was with great difficulty that Elizabeth could tear herself away. "I wish," cried she, "that I were to die with you; I cannot live in this world of misery."

Justine assumed an air of cheerfulness, while she with difficulty repressed her bitter tears. She embraced Elizabeth and said in a voice of half-suppressed emotion, "Farewell, sweet lady, dearest Elizabeth, my beloved and only friend; may heaven, in its bounty, bless and preserve you; may this be the last misfortune that you will ever suffer! Live, and be happy, and make others so."

And on the morrow Justine died. Elizabeth's heart-rending eloquence failed to move the judges from their settled conviction in the criminality of the saintly sufferer. My passionate and indignant appeals were lost upon them. And when I received their cold answers and heard the harsh, unfeeling reasoning of these men, my purposed avowal died away on my lips. Thus I might proclaim myself a madman, but not revoke the sentence passed upon my wretched victim. She perished on the scaffold as a murderess!

From the tortures of my own heart, I turned to contemplate the deep and voiceless grief of my Elizabeth. This also was my doing! And my father's woe, and the desolation of that late so smiling home all was the work of my thrice-accursed hands! Ye weep, unhappy ones, but these are not your last tears! Again shall you raise the funeral wail, and the sound of your lamentations shall again and again be heard! Frankenstein, your son, your kinsman, your early, much-loved friend; he who would spend each vital drop of blood for your sakes, who has no thought nor sense of joy except as it is mirrored also in your dear countenances, who would fill the air with blessings and spend his life in serving you—he bids you weep, to shed countless tears; happy beyond his hopes, if thus inexorable fate be satisfied, and if the destruction pause before the peace of the grave have succeeded to your sad torments!

Thus spoke my prophetic soul, as, torn by remorse, horror, and despair, I beheld those I loved spend vain sorrow upon the graves of William and Justine, the first hapless victims to my unhallowed arts.

CHAPTER 9

Nothing is more painful to the human mind than, after the

feelings have been worked up by a quick succession of events, the dead calmness of inaction and certainty which follows and deprives the soul both of hope and fear. Justine died, she rested, and I was alive. The blood flowed freely in my veins, but a weight of despair and remorse pressed on my heart which nothing could remove. Sleep fled from my eyes; I wandered like an evil spirit, for I had committed deeds of mischief beyond description horrible, and more, much more (I persuaded myself) was yet behind. Yet my heart overflowed with kindness and the love of virtue. I had begun life with benevolent intentions and thirsted for the moment when I should put them in practice and make myself useful to my fellow beings. Now all was blasted; instead of that serenity of conscience which allowed me to look back upon the past with self-satisfaction, and from thence to gather promise of new hopes, I was seized by remorse and the sense of guilt, which hurried me away to a hell of intense tortures such as no language can describe.

This state of mind preyed upon my health, which had perhaps never entirely recovered from the first shock it had sustained. I shunned the face of man; all sound of joy or complacency was torture to me; solitude was my only consolation—deep, dark, deathlike solitude.

My father observed with pain the alteration perceptible in my disposition and habits and endeavoured by arguments deduced from the feelings of his serene conscience and guiltless life to inspire me with fortitude and awaken in me the courage to dispel the dark cloud which brooded over me. "Do you think, Victor," said he, "that I do not suffer also? No one could love a child more than I loved your brother"—tears came into his eyes as he spoke—"but is it not a duty to the survivors that we should refrain from augmenting their unhappiness by an appearance of immoderate grief? It is also a duty owed to yourself, for excessive sorrow prevents improvement or enjoyment, or even the discharge of daily usefulness, without which no man is fit for society."

This advice, although good, was totally inapplicable to my

case; I should have been the first to hide my grief and console my friends if remorse had not mingled its bitterness, and terror its alarm, with my other sensations. Now I could only answer my father with a look of despair and endeavour to hide myself from his view.

About this time we retired to our house at Belrive. This change was particularly agreeable to me. The shutting of the gates regularly at ten o'clock and the impossibility of remaining on the lake after that hour had rendered our residence within the walls of Geneva very irksome to me. I was now free. Often, after the rest of the family had retired for the night, I took the boat and passed many hours upon the water. Sometimes, with my sails set, I was carried by the wind; and sometimes, after rowing into the middle of the lake, I left the boat to pursue its own course and gave way to my own miserable reflections.

I was often tempted, when all was at peace around me, and I the only unquiet thing that wandered restless in a scene so beautiful and heavenly—if I except some bat, or the frogs, whose harsh and interrupted croaking was heard only when I approached the shore—often, I say, I was tempted to plunge into the silent lake, that the waters might close over me and my calamities forever. But I was restrained, when I thought of the heroic and suffering Elizabeth, whom I tenderly loved, and whose existence was bound up in mine. I thought also of my father and surviving brother; should I by my base desertion leave them exposed and unprotected to the malice of the fiend whom I had let loose among them?

At these moments I wept bitterly and wished that peace would revisit my mind only that I might afford them consolation and happiness. But that could not be. Remorse extinguished every hope. I had been the author of unalterable evils, and I lived in daily fear lest the monster whom I had created should perpetrate some new wickedness. I had an obscure feeling that all was not over and that he would still commit some signal crime, which by its enormity should almost efface the recollection of the past. There was always scope for fear so long as anything I loved remained behind. My abhorrence of this fiend cannot be conceived. When I thought of him I gnashed my teeth, my eyes became inflamed, and I ardently wished to extinguish that life which I had so thoughtlessly bestowed.

When I reflected on his crimes and malice, my hatred and revenge burst all bounds of moderation. I would have made a pilgrimage to the highest peak of the Andes, could I when there have precipitated him to their base. I wished to see him again, that I might wreak the utmost extent of abhorrence on his head and avenge the deaths of William and Justine. Our house was the house of mourning. My father's health was deeply shaken by the horror of the recent events.

Elizabeth was sad and desponding; she no longer took delight in her ordinary occupations; all pleasure seemed to her sacrilege toward the dead; eternal woe and tears she then thought was the just tribute she should pay to innocence so blasted and destroyed. She was no longer that happy creature who in earlier youth wandered with me on the banks of the lake and talked with ecstasy of our future prospects. The first of those sorrows which are sent to wean us from the earth had visited her, and its dimming influence quenched her dearest smiles.

"When I reflect, my dear cousin," said she, "on the miserable death of Justine Moritz, I no longer see the world and its works as they before appeared to me. Before, I looked upon the accounts of vice and injustice that I read in books or heard from others as tales of ancient days or imaginary evils; at least they were remote and more familiar to reason than to the imagination; but now misery has come home, and men appear to me as monsters thirsting for each other's blood. Yet I am certainly unjust.

Everybody believed that poor girl to be guilty; and if she could have committed the crime for which she suffered, assuredly she would have been the most depraved of human creatures. For the sake of a few jewels, to have murdered the son of her benefactor and friend, a child whom she had nursed from its birth, and appeared to love as if it had been her own! I could not consent to the death of any human being, but certainly I should have thought such a creature unfit to remain in the society of men. But she was innocent. I know, I feel she was innocent; you are of the same opinion, and that confirms me.

Alas! Victor, when falsehood can look so like the truth, who can assure themselves of certain happiness? I feel as if I were walking on the edge of a precipice, towards which thousands are crowding and endeavouring to plunge me into the abyss. William and Justine were assassinated, and the murderer escapes; he walks about the world free, and perhaps respected. But even if I were condemned to suffer on the scaffold for the same crimes, I would not change places with such a wretch."

I listened to this discourse with the extremest agony. I, not in deed, but in effect, was the true murderer. Elizabeth read my anguish in my countenance, and kindly taking my hand, said, "My dearest friend, you must calm yourself. These events have affected me, God knows how deeply; but I am not so wretched as you are. There is an expression of despair, and sometimes of revenge, in your countenance that makes me tremble. Dear Victor, banish these dark passions. Remember the friends around you, who centre all their hopes in you. Have we lost the power of rendering you happy? Ah! While we love, while we are true to each other, here in this land of peace and beauty, your native country, we may reap every tranquil blessing—what can disturb our peace?"

And could not such words from her whom I fondly prized before every other gift of fortune suffice to chase away the fiend that lurked in my heart? Even as she spoke I drew near to her, as if in terror, lest at that very moment the destroyer had been near to rob me of her.

Thus not the tenderness of friendship, nor the beauty of earth, nor of heaven, could redeem my soul from woe; the very accents of love were ineffectual. I was encompassed by a cloud which no beneficial influence could penetrate. The wounded deer dragging its fainting limbs to some untrodden brake, there to gaze upon the arrow which had pierced it, and to die, was but a type of me.

Sometimes I could cope with the sullen despair that overwhelmed me, but sometimes the whirlwind passions of my soul drove me to seek, by bodily exercise and by change of place, some relief from my intolerable sensations. It was during an access of this kind that I suddenly left my home, and bending my steps towards the near Alpine valleys, sought in the magnificence, the eternity of such scenes, to forget myself and my ephemeral, because human, sorrows. My wanderings were directed towards the valley of Chamounix. I had visited it frequently during my boyhood. Six years had passed since then: *I* was a wreck, but nought had changed in those savage and enduring scenes.

I performed the first part of my journey on horseback. I afterwards hired a mule, as the more sure-footed and least liable to receive injury on these rugged roads. The weather was fine; it was about the middle of the month of August, nearly two months after the death of Justine, that miserable epoch from which I dated all my woe. The weight upon my spirit was sensibly lightened as I plunged yet deeper in the ravine of Arve. The immense mountains and precipices that overhung me on every side, the sound of the river raging among the rocks, and the dashing of the waterfalls around spoke of a power mighty as Omnipotence—and I ceased to fear or to bend before any being less almighty than that which had created and ruled the elements, here displayed in their most terrific guise.

Still, as I ascended higher, the valley assumed a more magnificent and astonishing character. Ruined castles hanging on the precipices of piny mountains, the impetuous Arve, and cottages every here and there peeping forth from among the trees formed a scene of singular beauty. But it was augmented and rendered sublime by the mighty Alps, whose white and shining pyramids and domes towered above all, as belonging to another earth, the habitations of another race of beings.

I passed the bridge of Pelissier, where the ravine, which the river forms, opened before me, and I began to ascend the mountain that overhangs it. Soon after, I entered the valley of

Chamounix. This valley is more wonderful and sublime, but not so beautiful and picturesque as that of Servox, through which I had just passed. The high and snowy mountains were its immediate boundaries, but I saw no more ruined castles and fertile fields. Immense glaciers approached the road; I heard the rumbling thunder of the falling avalanche and marked the smoke of its passage. Mont Blanc, the supreme and magnificent Mont Blanc, raised itself from the surrounding aiguilles, and its tremendous dome overlooked the valley.

A tingling long-lost sense of pleasure often came across me during this journey. Some turn in the road, some new object suddenly perceived and recognized, reminded me of days gone by, and were associated with the lighthearted gaiety of boyhood. The very winds whispered in soothing accents, and maternal Nature bade me weep no more. Then again the kindly influence ceased to act—I found myself fettered again to grief and indulging in all the misery of reflection. Then I spurred on my animal, striving so to forget the world, my fears, and more than all, myself—or, in a more desperate fashion, I alighted and threw myself on the grass, weighed down by horror and despair.

At length I arrived at the village of Chamounix. Exhaustion succeeded to the extreme fatigue both of body and of mind which I had endured. For a short space of time I remained at the window watching the pallid lightnings that played above Mont Blanc and listening to the rushing of the Arve, which pursued its noisy way beneath. The same lulling sounds acted as a lullaby to my too keen sensations; when I placed my head upon my pillow, sleep crept over me; I felt it as it came and blessed the giver of oblivion.

CHAPTER 10

I spent the following day roaming through the valley. I stood beside the sources of the Arveiron, which take their rise in a glacier, that with slow pace is advancing down from the summit of the hills to barricade the valley. The abrupt sides of vast mountains were before me; the icy wall of the glacier overhung me; a few shattered pines were scattered around; and the solemn silence of this glorious presence-chamber of imperial nature was broken only by the brawling waves or the fall of some vast fragment, the thunder sound of the avalanche or the cracking, reverberated along the mountains, of the accumulated ice, which, through the silent working of immutable laws, was ever and anon rent and torn, as if it had been but a plaything in their hands. These sublime and magnificent scenes afforded me the greatest consolation that I was capable of receiving.

They elevated me from all littleness of feeling, and although they did not remove my grief, they subdued and tranquillized it. In some degree, also, they diverted my mind from the thoughts over which it had brooded for the last month. I retired to rest at night; my slumbers, as it were, waited on and ministered to by the assemblance of grand shapes which I had contemplated during the day. They congregated round me; the unstained snowy mountaintop, the glittering pinnacle, the pine woods, and ragged bare ravine, the eagle, soaring amidst the clouds—they all gathered round me and bade me be at peace.

Where had they fled when the next morning I awoke? All of soulinspiriting fled with sleep, and dark melancholy clouded every thought. The rain was pouring in torrents, and thick mists hid the summits of the mountains, so that I even saw not the faces of those mighty friends. Still I would penetrate their misty veil and seek them in their cloudy retreats. What were rain and storm to me? My mule was brought to the door, and I resolved to ascend to the summit of Montanvert. I remembered the effect that the view of the tremendous and ever-moving glacier had produced upon my mind when I first saw it.

It had then filled me with a sublime ecstasy that gave wings to the soul and allowed it to soar from the obscure world to light and joy. The sight of the awful and majestic in nature had indeed always the effect of solemnizing my mind and causing me to forget the passing cares of life. I determined to go without a guide, for I was well acquainted with the path, and the presence of another would destroy the solitary grandeur of the scene.

The ascent is precipitous, but the path is cut into continual and short windings, which enable you to surmount the perpendicularity of the mountain. It is a scene terrifically desolate. In a thousand spots the traces of the winter avalanche may be perceived, where trees lie broken and strewed on the ground, some entirely destroyed, others bent, leaning upon the jutting rocks of the mountain or transversely upon other trees. The path, as you ascend nigher, is intersected by ravines of snow, down which stones continually roll from above; one of them is particularly dangerous, as the slightest sound, such as even speaking in a loud voice, produces a concussion of air sufficient to draw destruction upon the head of the speaker. The pines are not tall or luxuriant, but they are sombre and add an air of severity to the scene.

I looked on the valley beneath; vast mists were rising from the rivers which ran through it and curling in thick wreaths around the opposite mountains, whose summits were hid in the uniform clouds, while rain poured from the dark sky and added to the melancholy impression I received from the objects around me. Alas! Why does man boast of sensibilities superior to those apparent in the brute; it only renders them more necessary beings. If our impulses were confined to hunger, thirst, and desire, we might be nearly free; but now we are moved by every wind that blows and a chance word or scene that that word may convey to us.

> We rest; a dream has power to poison sleep.
> We rise; one wand'ring thought pollutes the day.
> We feel, conceive, or reason; laugh or weep,
> Embrace fond woe, or cast our cares away;
> It is the same: for, be it joy or sorrow,
> The path of its departure still is free.
> Man's yesterday may ne'er be like his morrow;
> Nought may endure but mutability!

It was nearly noon when I arrived at the top of the ascent. For some time I sat upon the rock that overlooks the sea of ice. A mist covered both that and the surrounding mountains. Presently a breeze dissipated the cloud, and I descended upon the glacier. The surface is very uneven, rising like the waves of a troubled sea, descending low, and interspersed by rifts that sink deep. The field of ice is almost a league in width, but I spent nearly two hours in crossing it. The opposite mountain is a bare perpendicular rock. From the side where I now stood Montanvert was exactly opposite, at the distance of a league; and above it rose Mont Blanc, in awful majesty.

I remained in a recess of the rock, gazing on this wonderful and stupendous scene. The sea, or rather the vast river of ice, wound among its dependent mountains, whose aerial summits hung over its recesses. Their icy and glittering peaks shone in the sunlight over the clouds. My heart, which was before sorrowful, now swelled with something like joy; I exclaimed, "Wandering spirits, if indeed ye wander, and do not rest in your narrow beds, allow me this faint happiness, or take me, as your companion, away from the joys of life."

As I said this I suddenly beheld the figure of a man, at some distance, advancing towards me with superhuman speed. He bounded over the crevices in the ice, among which I had walked with caution; his stature, also, as he approached, seemed to exceed that of man. I was troubled; a mist came over my eyes, and I felt a faintness seize me, but I was quickly restored by the cold gale of the mountains. I perceived, as the shape came nearer (sight tremendous and abhorred!) that it was the wretch whom I had created. I trembled with rage and horror, resolving to wait his approach and then close with him in mortal combat. He approached; his countenance bespoke bitter anguish, combined with disdain and malignity, while its unearthly ugliness rendered it almost too horrible for human eyes. But I scarcely observed this; rage and hatred had at first deprived me of utterance, and I recovered only to overwhelm him with words expressive of furious detestation and contempt.

"Devil," I exclaimed, "do you dare approach me? And do not you fear the fierce vengeance of my arm wreaked on your miserable head? Begone, vile insect! Or rather, stay, that I may trample you to dust! And, oh! That I could, with the extinction of your miserable existence, restore those victims whom you have so diabolically murdered!"

"I expected this reception," said the daemon. "All men hate the wretched; how, then, must I be hated, who am miserable beyond all living things! Yet you, my creator, detest and spurn me, thy creature, to whom thou art bound by ties only dissoluble by the annihilation of one of us. You purpose to kill me. How dare you sport thus with life? Do your duty towards me, and I will do mine towards you and the rest of mankind. If you will comply with my conditions, I will leave them and you at peace; but if you refuse, I will glut the maw of death, until it be satiated with the blood of your remaining friends."

"Abhorred monster! Fiend that thou art! The tortures of hell are too mild a vengeance for thy crimes. Wretched devil! You reproach me with your creation, come on, then, that I may extinguish the spark which I so negligently bestowed."

My rage was without bounds; I sprang on him, impelled by all the feelings which can arm one being against the existence of another.

He easily eluded me and said,

"Be calm! I entreat you to hear me before you give vent to your hatred on my devoted head. Have I not suffered enough, that you seek to increase my misery? Life, although it may only be an accumulation of anguish, is dear to me, and I will defend it. Remember, thou hast made me more powerful than thyself; my height is superior to thine, my joints more supple. But I will not be tempted to set myself in opposition to thee. I am thy creature, and I will be even mild and docile to my natural lord and king if thou wilt also perform thy part, the which thou owest me.

"Oh, Frankenstein, be not equitable to every other and trample upon me alone, to whom thy justice, and even thy clemency and affection, is most due. Remember that I am thy creature; I ought to be thy Adam, but I am rather the fallen angel, whom thou drivest from joy for no misdeed. Everywhere I see bliss, from which I alone am irrevocably excluded. I was benevolent and good; misery made me a fiend. Make me happy, and I shall again be virtuous."

"Begone! I will not hear you. There can be no community between you and me; we are enemies. Begone, or let us try our strength in a fight, in which one must fall."

"How can I move thee? Will no entreaties cause thee to turn a favourable eye upon thy creature, who implores thy goodness and compassion? Believe me, Frankenstein, I was benevolent; my soul glowed with love and humanity; but am I not alone, miserably alone? You, my creator, abhor me; what hope can I gather from your fellow creatures, who owe me nothing? They spurn and hate me. The desert mountains and dreary glaciers are my refuge. I have wandered here many days; the caves of ice, which I only do not fear, are a dwelling to me, and the only one which man does not grudge. These bleak skies I hail, for they are kinder to me than your fellow beings. If the multitude of mankind knew of my existence, they would do as you do, and arm themselves for my destruction.

"Shall I not then hate them who abhor me? I will keep no terms with my enemies. I am miserable, and they shall share my wretchedness. Yet it is in your power to recompense me, and deliver them from an evil which it only remains for you to make so great, that not only you and your family, but thousands of others, shall be swallowed up in the whirlwinds of its rage. Let your compassion be moved, and do not disdain me. Listen to my tale; when you have heard that, abandon or commiserate me, as you shall judge that I deserve. But hear me. The guilty are allowed, by human laws, bloody as they are, to speak in their own defence before they are condemned. Listen to me, Frankenstein. You accuse me of murder, and yet you would, with a satisfied conscience, destroy your own creature. Oh, praise the eternal justice of man! Yet I ask you not to spare me; listen to me, and then, if you can, and if you will, destroy the work of your hands."

"Why do you call to my remembrance," I rejoined, "circumstances of which I shudder to reflect, that I have been the miserable origin and author? Cursed be the day, abhorred devil, in which you first saw light! Cursed (although I curse myself) be the hands that formed you! You have made me wretched beyond expression. You have left me no power to consider whether I am just to you or not. Begone! Relieve me from the sight of your detested form."

"Thus I relieve thee, my creator," he said, and placed his hated hands before my eyes, which I flung from me with violence; "thus I take from thee a sight which you abhor. Still thou canst listen to me and grant me thy compassion. By the virtues that I once possessed, I demand this from you. Hear my tale; it is long and strange, and the temperature of this place is not fitting to your fine sensations; come to the hut upon the mountain. The sun is yet high in the heavens; before it descends to hide itself behind your snowy precipices and illuminate another world, you will have heard my story and can decide. On you it rests, whether I quit forever the neighbourhood of man and lead a harmless life, or become the scourge of your fellow creatures and the author of your own speedy ruin."

As he said this he led the way across the ice; I followed. My heart was full, and I did not answer him, but as I proceeded, I weighed the various arguments that he had used and determined at least to listen to his tale. I was partly urged by curiosity, and compassion confirmed my resolution. I had hitherto supposed him to be the murderer of my brother, and I eagerly sought a confirmation or denial of this opinion. For the first time, also, I felt what the duties of a creator towards his creature were, and that I ought to render him happy before I complained of his wickedness.

These motives urged me to comply with his demand. We crossed the ice, therefore, and ascended the opposite rock. The air was cold, and the rain again began to descend; we entered the hut, the fiend with an air of exultation, I with a heavy heart and depressed spirits. But I consented to listen, and seating myself by the fire which my odious companion had lighted, he thus began his tale.

Chapter 11

"It is with considerable difficulty that I remember the original era of my being; all the events of that period appear confused and indistinct. A strange multiplicity of sensations seized me, and I saw, felt, heard, and smelt at the same time; and it was, indeed, a long time before I learned to distinguish between the operations of my various senses. By degrees, I remember, a stronger light pressed upon my nerves, so that I was obliged to shut my eyes. Darkness then came over me and troubled me, but hardly had I felt this when, by opening my eyes, as I now suppose, the light poured in upon me again. I walked and, I believe, descended, but I presently found a great alteration in my sensations.

"Before, dark and opaque bodies had surrounded me, impervious to my touch or sight; but I now found that I could wander on at liberty, with no obstacles which I could not either surmount or avoid. The light became more and more oppressive to me, and the heat wearying me as I walked, I sought a place where I could receive shade. This was the forest near Ingolstadt; and here I lay by the side of a brook resting from my fatigue, until I felt tormented by hunger and thirst. This roused me from my nearly dormant state, and I ate some berries which I found hanging on the trees or lying on the ground. I slaked my thirst at the brook, and then lying down, was overcome by sleep.

"It was dark when I awoke; I felt cold also, and half frightened, as it were, instinctively, finding myself so desolate. Before I had quitted your apartment, on a sensation of cold, I had covered myself with some clothes, but these were insufficient to secure me from the dews of night. I was a poor, helpless, miserable wretch; I knew, and could distinguish, nothing; but feeling pain invade me on all sides, I sat down and wept.

"Soon a gentle light stole over the heavens and gave me a sensation of pleasure. I started up and beheld a radiant form rise from among the trees. [The moon] I gazed with a kind of wonder. It moved slowly, but it enlightened my path, and I again went out in search of berries. I was still cold when under one of the trees I found a huge cloak, with which I covered myself, and sat down upon the ground. No distinct ideas occupied my mind; all was confused. I felt light, and hunger, and thirst, and darkness; innumerable sounds rang in my ears, and on all sides various scents saluted me; the only object that I could distinguish was the bright moon, and I fixed my eyes on that with pleasure.

"Several changes of day and night passed, and the orb of night had greatly lessened, when I began to distinguish my sensations from each other. I gradually saw plainly the clear stream that supplied me with drink and the trees that shaded me with their foliage. I was delighted when I first discovered that a pleasant sound, which often saluted my ears, proceeded from the throats of the little winged animals who had often intercepted the light from my eyes. I began also to observe, with greater accuracy, the forms that surrounded me and to perceive the boundaries of the radiant roof of light which canopied me. Sometimes I tried to imitate the pleasant songs of the birds but was unable. Sometimes I wished to express my sensations in my own mode, but the uncouth and inarticulate sounds which broke from me frightened me into silence again.

"The moon had disappeared from the night, and again, with a lessened form, showed itself, while I still remained in the forest. My sensations had by this time become distinct, and my mind received every day additional ideas. My eyes became accustomed to the light and to perceive objects in their right forms; I distinguished the insect from the herb, and by degrees, one herb from another. I found that the sparrow uttered none but harsh notes, whilst those of the blackbird and thrush were sweet and enticing.

"One day, when I was oppressed by cold, I found a fire which had been left by some wandering beggars, and was overcome with delight at the warmth I experienced from it. In my joy I thrust my hand into the live embers, but quickly drew it out again with a cry of pain. How strange, I thought, that the same cause should produce such opposite effects! I examined the materials of the fire, and to my joy found it to be composed of wood. I quickly collected some branches, but they were wet and would not burn. I was pained at this and sat still watching the operation of the fire.

"The wet wood which I had placed near the heat dried and itself became inflamed. I reflected on this, and by touching the various branches, I discovered the cause and busied myself in collecting a great quantity of wood, that I might dry it and have a plentiful supply of fire. When night came on and brought sleep with it, I was in the greatest fear lest my fire should be extinguished. I covered it carefully with dry wood and leaves and placed wet branches upon it; and then, spreading my cloak, I lay on the ground and sank into sleep.

"It was morning when I awoke, and my first care was to visit the fire. I uncovered it, and a gentle breeze quickly fanned it into a flame. I observed this also and contrived a fan of branches, which roused the embers when they were nearly extinguished. When night came again I found, with pleasure, that the fire gave light as well as heat and that the discovery of this element was useful to me in my food, for I found some of the offals that the travellers had left had been roasted, and tasted much more savoury than the berries I gathered from the trees. I tried, therefore, to dress my food in the same manner, placing it on the live embers. I found that the berries were spoiled by this operation, and the nuts and roots much improved.

"Food, however, became scarce, and I often spent the whole day searching in vain for a few acorns to assuage the pangs of hunger. When I found this, I resolved to quit the place that I had hitherto inhabited, to seek for one where the few wants I experienced would be more easily satisfied. In this emigration I exceedingly lamented the loss of the fire which I had obtained through accident and knew not how to reproduce it. I gave several hours to the serious consideration of this difficulty, but I was obliged to relinquish all attempt to supply it, and wrapping myself up in my cloak, I struck across the wood towards the setting sun. I passed three days in these rambles and at length discovered the open country. A great fall of snow had taken place the night before, and the fields were of one uniform white; the appearance was disconsolate, and I found my feet chilled by the cold damp substance that covered the ground.

"It was about seven in the morning, and I longed to obtain food and shelter; at length I perceived a small hut, on a rising ground, which had doubtless been built for the convenience of some shepherd. This was a new sight to me, and I examined the structure with great curiosity. Finding the door open, I entered. An old man sat in it, near a fire, over which he was preparing his breakfast. He turned on hearing a noise, and perceiving me, shrieked loudly, and quitting the hut, ran across the fields with a speed of which his debilitated form hardly appeared capable. His appearance, different from any I had ever before seen, and his flight somewhat surprised me.

"But I was enchanted by the appearance of the hut; here the snow and rain could not penetrate; the ground was dry; and it presented to me then as exquisite and divine a retreat as Pandemonium appeared to the demons of hell after their sufferings in the lake of fire. I greedily devoured the remnants of the shepherd's breakfast, which consisted of bread, cheese, milk, and wine; the latter, however, I did not like. Then, overcome by fatigue, I lay down among some straw and fell asleep.

"It was noon when I awoke, and allured by the warmth of the sun, which shone brightly on the white ground, I determined to recommence my travels; and, depositing the remains of the peasant's breakfast in a wallet I found, I proceeded across the fields for several hours, until at sunset I arrived at a village. How miraculous did this appear! The huts, the neater cottages, and stately houses engaged my admiration by turns. The vegetables in the gardens, the milk and cheese that I saw placed at the windows of some of the cottages, allured my appetite.

"One of the best of these I entered, but I had hardly placed my foot within the door before the children shrieked, and one of the women fainted. The whole village was roused; some fled, some attacked me, until, grievously bruised by stones and many other kinds of missile weapons, I escaped to the open country and fearfully took refuge in a low hovel, quite bare, and making a wretched appearance after the palaces I had beheld in the village. This hovel however, joined a cottage of a neat and pleasant appearance, but after my late dearly bought experience, I dared not enter it. My place of refuge was constructed of wood, but so low that I could with difficulty sit upright in it. No wood, however, was placed on the earth, which formed the floor, but it was dry; and although the wind entered it by innumerable chinks, I found it an agreeable asylum from the snow and rain.

"Here, then, I retreated and lay down happy to have found a shelter, however miserable, from the inclemency of the season, and still more from the barbarity of man. As soon as morning dawned I crept from my kennel, that I might view the adjacent cottage and discover if I could remain in the habitation I had found. It was situated against the back of the cottage and surrounded on the sides which were exposed by a pig sty and a clear pool of water. One part was open, and by that I had crept in; but now I covered every crevice by which I might be perceived with stones and wood, yet in such a manner that I might move them on occasion to pass out; all the light I enjoyed came through the sty, and that was sufficient for me.

"Having thus arranged my dwelling and carpeted it with clean straw, I retired, for I saw the figure of a man at a distance, and I remembered too well my treatment the night before to trust myself in his power. I had first, however, provided for my sustenance for that day by a loaf of coarse bread, which I purloined, and a cup with which I could drink more conveniently than from my hand of the pure water which flowed by my retreat. The floor was a little raised, so that it was kept perfectly dry, and by its vicinity to the chimney of the cottage it was tolerably warm.

"Being thus provided, I resolved to reside in this hovel until something should occur which might alter my determination. It was indeed a paradise compared to the bleak forest, my former residence, the rain-dropping branches, and dank earth. I ate my breakfast with pleasure and was about to remove a plank to procure myself a little water when I heard a step, and looking through a small chink, I beheld a young creature, with a pail on her head, passing before my hovel. The girl was young and of gentle demeanour, unlike what I have since found cottagers and farmhouse servants to be. Yet she was meanly dressed, a coarse blue petticoat and a linen jacket being her only garb; her fair hair was plaited but not adorned: she looked patient yet sad.

"I lost sight of her, and in about a quarter of an hour she returned bearing the pail, which was now partly filled with milk. As she walked along, seemingly incommoded by the burden, a young man met her, whose countenance expressed a deeper despondence. Uttering a few sounds with an air of melancholy, he took the pail from her head and bore it to the cottage himself. She followed, and they disappeared. Presently I saw the young man again, with some tools in his hand, cross the field behind the cottage; and the girl was also busied, sometimes in the house and sometimes in the yard.

"On examining my dwelling, I found that one of the windows of the cottage had formerly occupied a part of it, but the panes had been filled up with wood. In one of these was a small and almost imperceptible chink through which the eye could just penetrate. Through this crevice a small room was visible, whitewashed and clean but very bare of furniture. In one corner, near a small fire, sat an old man, leaning his head on his hands in a disconsolate attitude. The young girl was occupied in arranging the cottage; but presently she took something out of a drawer, which employed her hands, and she sat down beside the old man, who, taking up an instrument, began to play and to produce sounds sweeter than the voice of the thrush or the nightingale.

"It was a lovely sight, even to me, poor wretch who had never beheld aught beautiful before. The silver hair and benevolent countenance of the aged cottager won my reverence, while the gentle manners of the girl enticed my love. He played a sweet mournful air which I perceived drew tears from the eyes of his amiable companion, of which the old man took no notice, until she sobbed audibly; he then pronounced a few sounds, and the fair creature, leaving her work, knelt at his feet. He raised her and smiled with such kindness and affection that I felt sensations of a peculiar and overpowering nature; they were a mixture of pain and pleasure, such as I had never before experienced, either from hunger or cold, warmth or food; and I withdrew from the window, unable to bear these emotions.

"Soon after this the young man returned, bearing on his shoulders a load of wood. The girl met him at the door, helped to relieve him of his burden, and taking some of the fuel into the cottage, placed it on the fire; then she and the youth went apart into a nook of the cottage, and he showed her a large loaf and a piece of cheese. She seemed pleased and went into the garden for some roots and plants, which she placed in water, and then upon the fire. She afterwards continued her work, whilst the young man went into the garden and appeared busily employed in digging and pulling up roots. After he had been employed thus about an hour, the young woman joined him and they entered the cottage together.

"The old man had, in the meantime, been pensive, but on the appearance of his companions he assumed a more cheerful air, and they sat down to eat. The meal was quickly dispatched. The young woman was again occupied in arranging the cottage, the old man walked before the cottage in the sun for a few minutes, leaning on the arm of the youth. Nothing could exceed in beauty the contrast between these two excellent creatures. One was old, with silver hairs and a countenance beaming with benevolence and love; the younger was slight and graceful in his figure, and his features were moulded with the finest symmetry, yet his eyes and attitude expressed the utmost sadness and despondency. The old man returned to the cottage, and the youth, with tools different from those he had used in the morning, directed his steps across the fields.

"Night quickly shut in, but to my extreme wonder, I found that the cottagers had a means of prolonging light by the use of tapers, and was delighted to find that the setting of the sun did not put an end to the pleasure I experienced in watching my human neighbours. In the evening the young girl and her companion were employed in various occupations which I did not understand; and the old man again took up the instrument which produced the divine sounds that had enchanted me in the morning. So soon as he had finished, the youth began, not to play, but to utter sounds that were monotonous, and neither resembling the harmony of the old man's instrument nor the songs of the birds; I since found that he read aloud, but at that time I knew nothing of the science of words or letters.

"The family, after having been thus occupied for a short time, extinguished their lights and retired, as I conjectured, to rest."

CHAPTER 12

"I lay on my straw, but I could not sleep. I thought of the occurrences of the day. What chiefly struck me was the gentle manners of these people, and I longed to join them, but dared not. I remembered too well the treatment I had suffered the night before from the barbarous villagers, and resolved, whatever course of conduct I might hereafter think it right to pursue, that for the present I would remain quietly in my hovel, watching and endeavouring to discover the motives which influenced their actions.

"The cottagers arose the next morning before the sun. The young woman arranged the cottage and prepared the food, and the youth departed after the first meal.

"This day was passed in the same routine as that which preceded it. The young man was constantly employed out of doors, and the girl in various laborious occupations within. The old man, whom I soon perceived to be blind, employed his leisure hours on his instrument or in contemplation. Nothing could exceed the love and respect which the younger cottagers exhibited towards their venerable companion. They performed towards him every little office of affection and duty with gentleness, and he rewarded them by his benevolent smiles.

"They were not entirely happy. The young man and his companion often went apart and appeared to weep. I saw no cause for their unhappiness, but I was deeply affected by it. If such lovely creatures were miserable, it was less strange that I, an imperfect and solitary being, should be wretched. Yet why were these gentle beings unhappy? They possessed a delightful house (for such it was in my eyes) and every luxury; they had a fire to warm them when chill and delicious viands when hungry; they were dressed in excellent clothes; and, still more, they enjoyed one another's company and speech, interchanging each day looks of affection and kindness. What did their tears imply? Did they really express pain? I was at first unable to solve these questions, but perpetual attention and time explained to me many appearances which were at first enigmatic.

"A considerable period elapsed before I discovered one of the causes of the uneasiness of this amiable family: it was poverty, and they suffered that evil in a very distressing degree. Their nourishment consisted entirely of the vegetables of their garden and the milk of one cow, which gave very little during the winter, when its masters could scarcely procure food to support it. They often, I believe, suffered the pangs of hunger very poignantly, especially the two younger cottagers, for several times they placed food before the old man when they reserved none for themselves.

"This trait of kindness moved me sensibly. I had been accustomed, during the night, to steal a part of their store for my own consumption, but when I found that in doing this I inflicted pain on the cottagers, I abstained and satisfied myself with berries, nuts, and roots which I gathered from a neighbouring wood.

"I discovered also another means through which I was enabled to assist their labours. I found that the youth spent a great part of each day in collecting wood for the family fire, and during the night I often took his tools, the use of which I quickly discovered, and brought home firing sufficient for the consumption of several days.

"I remember, the first time that I did this, the young woman, when she opened the door in the morning, appeared greatly astonished on seeing a great pile of wood on the outside. She uttered some words in a loud voice, and the youth joined her, who also expressed surprise. I observed, with pleasure, that he did not go to the forest that day, but spent it in repairing the cottage and cultivating the garden.

"By degrees I made a discovery of still greater moment. I found that these people possessed a method of communicating their experience and feelings to one another by articulate sounds. I perceived that the words they spoke sometimes produced pleasure or pain, smiles or sadness, in the minds and countenances of the hearers. This was indeed a godlike science, and I ardently desired to become acquainted with it. But I was baffled in every attempt I made for this purpose. Their pronunciation was quick, and the words they uttered, not having any apparent connection with visible objects, I was unable to discover any clue by which I could unravel the mystery of their reference.

"By great application, however, and after having remained during the space of several revolutions of the moon in my hovel, I discovered the names that were given to some of the most familiar objects of discourse; I learned and applied the words, 'fire,' 'milk,' 'bread,' and 'wood.' I learned also the names of the cottagers themselves. The youth and his companion had each of them several names, but the old man had only one, which was 'father.' The girl was called 'sister' or 'Agatha,' and the youth 'Felix,' 'brother,' or 'son.' I cannot describe the delight I felt when I learned the ideas appropriated to each of these sounds and was able to pronounce them. I distinguished several other words without being able as yet to understand or apply them, such as 'good,' 'dearest,' 'unhappy.'

"I spent the winter in this manner. The gentle manners and beauty of the cottagers greatly endeared them to me; when they were unhappy, I felt depressed; when they rejoiced, I sympathized in their joys. I saw few human beings besides them, and if any other happened to enter the cottage, their harsh manners and rude gait only enhanced to me the superior accomplishments of my friends. The old man, I could perceive, often endeavoured to encourage his children, as sometimes I found that he called them, to cast off their melancholy. He would talk in a cheerful accent, with an expression of goodness that bestowed pleasure even upon me.

"Agatha listened with respect, her eyes sometimes filled with tears, which she endeavoured to wipe away unperceived; but I generally found that her countenance and tone were more cheerful after having listened to the exhortations of her father. It was not thus with Felix. He was always the saddest of the group, and even to my unpractised senses, he appeared to have suffered more deeply than his friends. But if his countenance was more sorrowful, his voice was more cheerful than that of his sister, especially when he addressed the old man.

"I could mention innumerable instances which, although slight, marked the dispositions of these amiable cottagers. In the midst of poverty and want, Felix carried with pleasure to his sister the first little white flower that peeped out from beneath the snowy ground. Early in the morning, before she had risen, he cleared away the snow that obstructed her path to the milk-house, drew water from the well, and brought the wood from the outhouse, where, to his perpetual astonishment, he found his store always replenished by an invisible hand. In the day, I believe, he worked sometimes for a neighbouring farmer, because he often went forth and did not return until dinner, yet brought no wood with him. At other times he worked in the garden, but as there was little to do in the frosty season, he read to the old man and Agatha.

"This reading had puzzled me extremely at first, but by degrees I discovered that he uttered many of the same sounds when he read as when he talked. I conjectured, therefore, that he found on the paper signs for speech which he understood, and I ardently longed to comprehend these also; but how was that possible when I did not even understand the sounds for which they stood as signs? I improved, however, sensibly in this science, but not sufficiently to follow up any kind of conversation, although I applied my whole mind to the endeavour, for I easily perceived that, although I eagerly longed to discover myself to the cottagers, I ought not to make the attempt until I had first become master of their language, which knowledge might enable me to make them overlook the deformity of my figure, for with this also the contrast perpetually presented to my eyes had made me acquainted.

"I had admired the perfect forms of my cottagers—their grace, beauty, and delicate complexions; but how was I terrified when I viewed myself in a transparent pool! At first I started back, unable to believe that it was indeed I who was reflected in the mirror; and when I became fully convinced that I was in reality the monster that I am, I was filled with the bitterest sensations of despondence and mortification. Alas! I did not yet entirely know the fatal effects of this miserable deformity.

"As the sun became warmer and the light of day longer, the snow vanished, and I beheld the bare trees and the black earth. From this time Felix was more employed, and the heart-moving indications of impending famine disappeared. Their food, as I afterwards found, was coarse, but it was wholesome; and they procured a sufficiency of it. Several new kinds of plants sprang up in the garden, which they dressed; and these signs of comfort increased daily as the season advanced.

"The old man, leaning on his son, walked each day at noon, when it did not rain, as I found it was called when the heavens poured forth its waters. This frequently took place, but a high wind quickly dried the earth, and the season became far more pleasant than it had been.

"My mode of life in my hovel was uniform. During the morning I attended the motions of the cottagers, and when they were dispersed in various occupations, I slept; the remainder of the day was spent in observing my friends. When they had retired to rest, if there was any moon or the night was star-light, I went into the woods and collected my own food and fuel for the cottage. When I returned, as often as it was necessary, I cleared their path from the snow and performed those offices that I had seen done by Felix. I afterwards found that these labours, performed by an invisible hand, greatly astonished them; and once or twice I heard them, on these occasions, utter the words 'good spirit,' 'wonderful'; but I did not then understand the signification of these terms.

"My thoughts now became more active, and I longed to discover the motives and feelings of these lovely creatures; I was inquisitive to know why Felix appeared so miserable and Agatha so sad. I thought (foolish wretch!) that it might be in my power to restore happiness to these deserving people. When I slept or was absent, the forms of the venerable blind father, the gentle Agatha, and the excellent Felix flitted before me. I looked upon them as superior beings who would be the arbiters of my future destiny. I formed in my imagination a thousand pictures of presenting myself to them, and their reception of me. I imagined that they would be disgusted, until, by my gentle demeanour and conciliating words, I should first win their favour and afterwards their love.

"These thoughts exhilarated me and led me to apply with fresh ardour to the acquiring the art of language. My organs were indeed harsh, but supple; and although my voice was very unlike the soft music of their tones, yet I pronounced such words as I understood with tolerable ease. It was as the ass and the lapdog; yet surely the gentle ass whose intentions were affectionate, although his manners were rude, deserved better treatment than blows and execration.

"The pleasant showers and genial warmth of spring greatly altered the aspect of the earth. Men who before this change seemed to have been hid in caves dispersed themselves and were employed in various arts of cultivation. The birds sang in more cheerful notes, and the leaves began to bud forth on the trees. Happy, happy earth! Fit habitation for gods, which, so short a time before, was bleak, damp, and unwholesome. My spirits were elevated by the enchanting appearance of nature; the past was blotted from my memory, the present was tranquil, and the future gilded by bright rays of hope and anticipations of joy."

Chapter 13

"I now hasten to the more moving part of my story. I shall relate events that impressed me with feelings which, from what I had been, have made me what I am.

"Spring advanced rapidly; the weather became fine and the skies cloudless. It surprised me that what before was desert and gloomy should now bloom with the most beautiful flowers and verdure. My senses were gratified and refreshed by a thousand scents of delight and a thousand sights of beauty.

"It was on one of these days, when my cottagers periodically rested from labour—the old man played on his guitar, and the children listened to him—that I observed the countenance of Felix was melancholy beyond expression; he sighed frequently, and once his father paused in his music, and I conjectured by his manner that he inquired the cause of his son's sorrow. Felix replied in a cheerful accent, and the old man was recommencing his music when someone tapped at the door.

"It was a lady on horseback, accompanied by a country-man as a guide. The lady was dressed in a dark suit and covered with a thick black veil. Agatha asked a question, to which the stranger only replied by pronouncing, in a sweet accent, the name of Felix. Her voice was musical but unlike that of either of my friends. On hearing this word, Felix came up hastily to the lady, who, when she saw him, threw up her veil, and I beheld a countenance of angelic beauty and expression. Her hair of a shining raven black, and curiously braided; her eyes were dark, but gentle, although animated; her features of a regular proportion, and her complexion wondrously fair, each cheek tinged with a lovely pink.

"Felix seemed ravished with delight when he saw her, every trait of sorrow vanished from his face, and it instantly expressed a degree of ecstatic joy, of which I could hardly have believed it capable; his eyes sparkled, as his cheek flushed with pleasure; and at that moment I thought him as beautiful as the stranger. She appeared affected by different feelings; wiping a few tears from her lovely eyes, she held out her hand to Felix, who kissed it rapturously and called her, as well as I could distinguish, his sweet Arabian. She did not appear to understand him, but smiled. He assisted her to dismount, and dismissing her guide, conducted her into the cottage. Some conversation took place between him and his father, and the young stranger knelt at the old man's feet and would have kissed his hand, but he raised her and embraced her affectionately.

"I soon perceived that although the stranger uttered articulate sounds and appeared to have a language of her own, she was neither understood by nor herself understood the cottagers. They made many signs which I did not comprehend, but I saw that her presence diffused gladness through the cottage, dispelling their sorrow as the sun dissipates the morning mists. Felix seemed peculiarly happy and with smiles of delight welcomed his Arabian. Agatha, the ever-gentle Agatha, kissed the hands of the lovely stranger, and pointing to her brother, made signs which appeared to me to mean that he had been sorrowful until she came. Some hours passed thus, while they, by their countenances, expressed joy, the cause of which I did not comprehend.

"Presently I found, by the frequent recurrence of some sound which the stranger repeated after them, that she was endeavouring to learn their language; and the idea instantly occurred to me that I should make use of the same instructions to the same end. The stranger learned about twenty words at the first lesson; most of them, indeed, were those which I had before understood, but I profited by the others.

"As night came on, Agatha and the Arabian retired early. When they separated Felix kissed the hand of the stranger and said, 'Good night sweet Safie.' He sat up much longer, conversing with his father, and by the frequent repetition of her name I conjectured that their lovely guest was the subject of their conversation. I ardently desired to understand them, and bent every faculty towards that purpose, but found it utterly impossible.

"The next morning Felix went out to his work, and after the usual occupations of Agatha were finished, the Arabian sat at the feet of the old man, and taking his guitar, played some airs so entrancingly beautiful that they at once drew tears of sorrow and delight from my eyes. She sang, and her voice flowed in a rich cadence, swelling or dying away like a nightingale of the woods.

"When she had finished, she gave the guitar to Agatha, who at first declined it. She played a simple air, and her voice accompanied it in sweet accents, but unlike the wondrous strain of the stranger. The old man appeared enraptured and said some words which Agatha endeavoured to explain to Safie, and by which he appeared to wish to express that she bestowed on him the greatest delight by her music.

"The days now passed as peaceably as before, with the sole alteration that joy had taken place of sadness in the countenances of my friends. Safie was always gay and happy; she and I improved rapidly in the knowledge of language, so that in two months I began to comprehend most of the words uttered by my protectors.

"In the meanwhile also the black ground was covered with herbage, and the green banks interspersed with innumerable flowers, sweet to the scent and the eyes, stars of pale radiance among the moonlight woods; the sun became warmer, the nights clear and balmy; and my nocturnal rambles were an extreme pleasure to me, although they were considerably shortened by the late setting and early rising of the sun, for I never ventured abroad during daylight, fearful of meeting with the same treatment I had formerly endured in the first village which I entered.

"My days were spent in close attention, that I might more speedily master the language; and I may boast that I improved more rapidly than the Arabian, who understood very little and conversed in broken accents, whilst I comprehended and could imitate almost every word that was spoken.

"While I improved in speech, I also learned the science of letters as it was taught to the stranger, and this opened before me a wide field for wonder and delight.

"The book from which Felix instructed Safie was Volney's *Ruins of Empires*. I should not have understood the purport of this book had not Felix, in reading it, given very minute explanations. He had chosen this work, he said, because the declamatory style was framed in imitation of the Eastern authors. Through this work I obtained a cursory knowledge of history and a view of the several empires at present existing in the world; it gave me an insight into the manners, governments, and religions of the different nations of the earth. I heard of the slothful Asiatics, of the stupendous genius and mental activity of the Grecians, of the wars and wonderful virtue of the early Romans—of their subsequent degenerating—of the decline of that mighty empire, of chivalry, Christianity, and kings. I heard of the discovery of the American hemisphere and wept with Safie over the hapless fate of its original inhabitants.

"These wonderful narrations inspired me with strange feelings. Was man, indeed, at once so powerful, so virtuous and magnificent, yet so vicious and base? He appeared at one time a mere scion of the evil principle and at another as all that can be conceived of noble and godlike. To be a great and virtuous man appeared the highest honour that can befall a sensitive being; to be base and vicious, as many on record have been, appeared the lowest degradation, a condition more abject than that of the blind mole or harmless worm. For a long time I could not conceive how one man could go forth to murder his fellow, or even why there were laws and governments; but when I heard details of vice and bloodshed, my wonder ceased and I turned away with disgust and loathing.

"Every conversation of the cottagers now opened new wonders to me. While I listened to the instructions which Felix bestowed upon the Arabian, the strange system of human society was explained to me. I heard of the division of property, of immense wealth and squalid poverty, of rank, descent, and noble blood.

"The words induced me to turn towards myself. I learned that the possessions most esteemed by your fellow creatures were high and unsullied descent united with riches. A man might be respected with only one of these advantages, but without either he was considered, except in very rare instances, as a vagabond and a slave, doomed to waste his powers for the profits of the chosen few! And what was I? Of my creation and creator I was absolutely ignorant, but I knew that I possessed no money, no friends, no kind of property.

"I was, besides, endued with a figure hideously deformed and loathsome; I was not even of the same nature as man. I was more agile than they and could subsist upon coarser diet; I bore the extremes of heat and cold with less injury to my frame; my stature far exceeded theirs. When I looked around I saw and heard of none like me. Was I, then, a monster, a blot upon the earth, from which all men fled and whom all men disowned?

"I cannot describe to you the agony that these reflections inflicted upon me; I tried to dispel them, but sorrow only increased with knowledge. Oh, that I had forever remained in my native wood, nor known nor felt beyond the sensations of hunger, thirst, and heat!

"Of what a strange nature is knowledge! It clings to the mind when it has once seized on it like a lichen on the rock. I wished sometimes to shake off all thought and feeling, but I learned that there was but one means to overcome the sensation of pain, and that was death—a state which I feared yet did not understand. I admired virtue and good feelings and loved the gentle manners and amiable qualities of my cottagers, but I was shut out from intercourse with them, except through means which I obtained by stealth, when I was unseen and unknown, and which rather increased than satisfied the desire I had of becoming one among my fellows. The gentle words of Agatha and the animated smiles of the charming Arabian were not for me. The mild exhortations of the old man and the lively conversation of the loved Felix were not for me. Miserable, unhappy wretch!

"Other lessons were impressed upon me even more deeply. I heard of the difference of sexes, and the birth and growth of children, how the father doted on the smiles of the infant, and the lively sallies of the older child, how all the life and cares of the mother were wrapped up in the precious charge, how the mind of youth expanded and gained knowledge, of brother, sister, and all the various relationships which bind one human being to another in mutual bonds.

"But where were my friends and relations? No father had watched my infant days, no mother had blessed me with smiles and caresses; or if they had, all my past life was now a blot, a blind vacancy in which I distinguished nothing. From my earliest remembrance I had been as I then was in height and proportion. I had never yet seen a being resembling me or who claimed any intercourse with me. What was I? The question again recurred, to be answered only with groans.

"I will soon explain to what these feelings tended, but allow me now to return to the cottagers, whose story excited in me such various feelings of indignation, delight, and wonder, but which all terminated in additional love and reverence for my protectors (for so I loved, in an innocent, half-painful self-deceit, to call them)."

CHAPTER 14

"Some time elapsed before I learned the history of my friends. It was one which could not fail to impress itself deeply on my mind, unfolding as it did a number of circumstances, each interesting and wonderful to one so utterly inexperienced as I was.

"The name of the old man was De Lacey. He was descended from a good family in France, where he had lived for many years in affluence, respected by his superiors and beloved by his equals. His son was bred in the service of his country, and Agatha had ranked with ladies of the highest distinction. A few months before my arrival they had lived in a large and luxurious city called Paris, surrounded by friends and possessed of every enjoyment which virtue, refinement of intellect, or taste, accompanied by a moderate fortune, could afford.

"The father of Safie had been the cause of their ruin. He was a Turkish merchant and had inhabited Paris for many years, when, for some reason which I could not learn, he became obnoxious to the government. He was seized and cast into prison the very day that Safie arrived from Constantinople to join him. He was tried and condemned to death. The injustice of his sentence was very flagrant; all Paris was indignant; and it was judged that his religion and wealth rather than the crime alleged against him had been the cause of his condemnation.

"Felix had accidentally been present at the trial; his horror and indignation were uncontrollable when he heard the decision of the court. He made, at that moment, a solemn vow to deliver him and then looked around for the means. After many fruitless attempts to gain admittance to the prison, he found a strongly grated window in an unguarded part of the building, which lighted the dungeon of the unfortunate Muhammadan, who, loaded with chains, waited in despair the execution of the barbarous sentence.

"Felix visited the grate at night and made known to the prisoner his intentions in his favour. "The Turk, amazed and delighted, endeavoured to kindle the zeal of his deliverer by promises of reward and wealth. Felix rejected his offers with contempt, yet when he saw the lovely Safie, who was allowed to visit her father and who by her gestures expressed her lively gratitude, the youth could not help owning to his own mind that the captive possessed a treasure which would fully reward his toil and hazard.

"The Turk quickly perceived the impression that his daughter had made on the heart of Felix and endeavoured to secure him more entirely in his interests by the promise of her hand in marriage so soon as he should be conveyed to a place of safety. Felix was too delicate to accept this offer, yet he looked forward to the probability of the event as to the consummation of his happiness.

"During the ensuing days, while the preparations were going forward for the escape of the merchant, the zeal of Felix was warmed by several letters that he received from this lovely girl, who found means to express her thoughts in the language of her lover by the aid of an old man, a servant of her father who understood French. She thanked him in the most ardent terms for his intended services towards her parent, and at the same time she gently deplored her own fate.

"I have copies of these letters, for I found means, during my residence in the hovel, to procure the implements of writing; and the letters were often in the hands of Felix or Agatha. Before I depart I will give them to you; they will prove the truth of my tale; but at present, as the sun is already far declined, I shall only have time to repeat the substance of them to you.

"Safie related that her mother was a Christian Arab, seized and made a slave by the Turks; recommended by her beauty, she had won the heart of the father of Safie, who married her. The young girl spoke in high and enthusiastic terms of her mother, who, born in freedom, spurned the bondage to which she was now reduced. She instructed her daughter in the tenets of her religion and taught her to aspire to higher powers of intellect and an independence of spirit forbidden to the female followers of Muhammad.

"This lady died, but her lessons were indelibly impressed on the mind of Safie, who sickened at the prospect of again returning to Asia and being immured within the walls of a harem, allowed only to occupy herself with infantile amusements, ill-suited to the temper of her soul, now accustomed to grand ideas and a noble emulation for virtue. The prospect of marrying a Christian and remaining in a country where women were allowed to take a rank in society was enchanting to her.

"The day for the execution of the Turk was fixed, but on the night previous to it he quitted his prison and before morning was distant many leagues from Paris. Felix had procured passports in the name of his father, sister, and himself. He had previously communicated his plan to the former, who aided the deceit by quitting his house, under the pretence of a journey and concealed himself, with his daughter, in an obscure part of Paris.

"Felix conducted the fugitives through France to Lyons and

across Mont Cenis to Leghorn, where the merchant had decided to wait a favourable opportunity of passing into some part of the Turkish dominions.

"Safie resolved to remain with her father until the moment of his departure, before which time the Turk renewed his promise that she should be united to his deliverer; and Felix remained with them in expectation of that event; and in the meantime he enjoyed the society of the Arabian, who exhibited towards him the simplest and tenderest affection. They conversed with one another through the means of an interpreter, and sometimes with the interpretation of looks; and Safie sang to him the divine airs of her native country.

"The Turk allowed this intimacy to take place and encouraged the hopes of the youthful lovers, while in his heart he had formed far other plans. He loathed the idea that his daughter should be united to a Christian, but he feared the resentment of Felix if he should appear lukewarm, for he knew that he was still in the power of his deliverer if he should choose to betray him to the Italian state which they inhabited. He revolved a thousand plans by which he should be enabled to prolong the deceit until it might be no longer necessary, and secretly to take his daughter with him when he departed. His plans were facilitated by the news which arrived from Paris.

"The government of France were greatly enraged at the escape of their victim and spared no pains to detect and punish his deliverer. The plot of Felix was quickly discovered, and De Lacey and Agatha were thrown into prison. The news reached Felix and roused him from his dream of pleasure. His blind and aged father and his gentle sister lay in a noisome dungeon while he enjoyed the free air and the society of her whom he loved. This idea was torture to him. He quickly arranged with the Turk that if the latter should find a favourable opportunity for escape before Felix could return to Italy, Safie should remain as a boarder at a convent at Leghorn; and then, quitting the lovely Arabian, he hastened to Paris and delivered himself up to the vengeance of the law, hoping to free De Lacey and Agatha by this proceeding. "He did not succeed. They remained confined for five months before the trial took place, the result of which deprived them of their fortune and condemned them to a perpetual exile from their native country.

"They found a miserable asylum in the cottage in Germany, where I discovered them. Felix soon learned that the treacherous Turk, for whom he and his family endured such unheard-of oppression, on discovering that his deliverer was thus reduced to poverty and ruin, became a traitor to good feeling and honour and had quitted Italy with his daughter, insultingly sending Felix a pittance of money to aid him, as he said, in some plan of future maintenance.

"Such were the events that preyed on the heart of Felix and rendered him, when I first saw him, the most miserable of his family. He could have endured poverty, and while this distress had been the meed of his virtue, he gloried in it; but the ingratitude of the Turk and the loss of his beloved Safie were misfortunes more bitter and irreparable. The arrival of the Arabian now infused new life into his soul.

"When the news reached Leghorn that Felix was deprived of his wealth and rank, the merchant commanded his daughter to think no more of her lover, but to prepare to return to her native country. The generous nature of Safie was outraged by this command; she attempted to expostulate with her father, but he left her angrily, reiterating his tyrannical mandate.

"A few days after, the Turk entered his daughter's apartment and told her hastily that he had reason to believe that his residence at Leghorn had been divulged and that he should speedily be delivered up to the French government; he had consequently hired a vessel to convey him to Constantinople, for which city he should sail in a few hours. He intended to leave his daughter under the care of a confidential servant, to follow at her leisure with the greater part of his property, which had not yet arrived at Leghorn.

"When alone, Safie resolved in her own mind the plan of conduct that it would become her to pursue in this emergency.

A residence in Turkey was abhorrent to her; her religion and her feelings were alike averse to it. By some papers of her father which fell into her hands she heard of the exile of her lover and learnt the name of the spot where he then resided. She hesitated some time, but at length she formed her determination. Taking with her some jewels that belonged to her and a sum of money, she quitted Italy with an attendant, a native of Leghorn, but who understood the common language of Turkey, and departed for Germany.

"She arrived in safety at a town about twenty leagues from the cottage of De Lacey, when her attendant fell dangerously ill. Safie nursed her with the most devoted affection, but the poor girl died, and the Arabian was left alone, unacquainted with the language of the country and utterly ignorant of the customs of the world. She fell, however, into good hands. The Italian had mentioned the name of the spot for which they were bound, and after her death the woman of the house in which they had lived took care that Safie should arrive in safety at the cottage of her lover."

CHAPTER 15

"Such was the history of my beloved cottagers. It impressed me deeply. I learned, from the views of social life which it developed, to admire their virtues and to deprecate the vices of mankind.

"As yet I looked upon crime as a distant evil, benevolence and generosity were ever present before me, inciting within me a desire to become an actor in the busy scene where so many admirable qualities were called forth and displayed. But in giving an account of the progress of my intellect, I must not omit a circumstance which occurred in the beginning of the month of August of the same year.

"One night during my accustomed visit to the neighbouring wood where I collected my own food and brought home firing for my protectors, I found on the ground a leathern portmanteau containing several articles of dress and some books. I eagerly seized the prize and returned with it to my hovel. Fortunately the books were written in the language, the elements of which I had acquired at the cottage; they consisted of *Paradise Lost*, a volume of *Plutarch's Lives*, and the *Sorrows of Werter*. The possession of these treasures gave me extreme delight; I now continually studied and exercised my mind upon these histories, whilst my friends were employed in their ordinary occupations.

"I can hardly describe to you the effect of these books. They produced in me an infinity of new images and feelings, that sometimes raised me to ecstasy, but more frequently sunk me into the lowest dejection. In the *Sorrows of Werter*, besides the interest of its simple and affecting story, so many opinions are canvassed and so many lights thrown upon what had hitherto been to me obscure subjects that I found in it a never-ending source of speculation and astonishment. The gentle and domestic manners it described, combined with lofty sentiments and feelings, which had for their object something out of self, accorded well with my experience among my protectors and with the wants which were forever alive in my own bosom.

"But I thought Werter himself a more divine being than I had ever beheld or imagined; his character contained no pretension, but it sank deep. The disquisitions upon death and suicide were calculated to fill me with wonder. I did not pretend to enter into the merits of the case, yet I inclined towards the opinions of the hero, whose extinction I wept, without precisely understanding it.

"As I read, however, I applied much personally to my own feelings and condition. I found myself similar yet at the same time strangely unlike to the beings concerning whom I read and to whose conversation I was a listener. I sympathized with and partly understood them, but I was unformed in mind; I was dependent on none and related to none. "The path of my departure was free," and there was none to lament my annihilation. My person was hideous and my stature gigantic. What did this mean? Who was I? What was I? Whence did I come? What was my destination? These questions continually recurred, but I was unable to solve them.

"The volume of *Plutarch's Lives* which I possessed contained the histories of the first founders of the ancient republics. This book had a far different effect upon me from the Sorrows of Werter. I learned from Werter's imaginations despondency and gloom, but Plutarch taught me high thoughts; he elevated me above the wretched sphere of my own reflections, to admire and love the heroes of past ages. Many things I read surpassed my understanding and experience. I had a very confused knowledge of kingdoms, wide extents of country, mighty rivers, and boundless seas. But I was perfectly unacquainted with towns and large assemblages of men.

"The cottage of my protectors had been the only school in which I had studied human nature, but this book developed new and mightier scenes of action. I read of men concerned in public affairs, governing or massacring their species. I felt the greatest ardour for virtue rise within me, and abhorrence for vice, as far as I understood the signification of those terms, relative as they were, as I applied them, to pleasure and pain alone. Induced by these feelings, I was of course led to admire peaceable lawgivers, Numa, Solon, and Lycurgus, in preference to Romulus and Theseus. The patriarchal lives of my protectors caused these impressions to take a firm hold on my mind; perhaps, if my first introduction to humanity had been made by a young soldier, burning for glory and slaughter, I should have been imbued with different sensations.

"But Paradise Lost excited different and far deeper emotions. I read it, as I had read the other volumes which had fallen into my hands, as a true history. It moved every feeling of wonder and awe that the picture of an omnipotent God warring with his creatures was capable of exciting. I often referred the several situations, as their similarity struck me, to my own. Like Adam, I was apparently united by no link to any other being in existence; but his state was far different from mine in every other respect. He had come forth from the hands of God a perfect creature, happy and prosperous, guarded by the especial care of his Creator; he was allowed to converse with and acquire knowledge from beings of a superior nature, but I was wretched, helpless, and alone. Many times I considered Satan as the fitter emblem of my condition, for often, like him, when I viewed the bliss of my protectors, the bitter gall of envy rose within me.

"Another circumstance strengthened and confirmed these feelings. Soon after my arrival in the hovel I discovered some papers in the pocket of the dress which I had taken from your laboratory. At first I had neglected them, but now that I was able to decipher the characters in which they were written, I began to study them with diligence. It was your journal of the four months that preceded my creation. You minutely described in these papers every step you took in the progress of your work; this history was mingled with accounts of domestic occurrences.

"You doubtless recollect these papers. Here they are. Everything is related in them which bears reference to my accursed origin; the whole detail of that series of disgusting circumstances which produced it is set in view; the minutest description of my odious and loathsome person is given, in language which painted your own horrors and rendered mine indelible. I sickened as I read. 'Hateful day when I received life!' I exclaimed in agony. 'Accursed creator! Why did you form a monster so hideous that even YOU turned from me in disgust? God, in pity, made man beautiful and alluring, after his own image; but my form is a filthy type of yours, more horrid even from the very resemblance. Satan had his companions, fellow devils, to admire and encourage him, but I am solitary and abhorred.'

"These were the reflections of my hours of despondency and solitude; but when I contemplated the virtues of the cottagers, their amiable and benevolent dispositions, I persuaded myself that when they should become acquainted with my admiration of their virtues they would compassionate me and overlook my personal deformity. Could they turn from their door one, however monstrous, who solicited their compassion and friendship? I resolved, at least, not to despair, but in every way to fit myself for an interview with them which would decide my fate.

"I postponed this attempt for some months longer, for the importance attached to its success inspired me with a dread lest I should fail. Besides, I found that my understanding improved so much with every day's experience that I was unwilling to commence this undertaking until a few more months should have added to my sagacity.

"Several changes, in the meantime, took place in the cottage. The presence of Safie diffused happiness among its inhabitants, and I also found that a greater degree of plenty reigned there. Felix and Agatha spent more time in amusement and conversation, and were assisted in their labours by servants. They did not appear rich, but they were contented and happy; their feelings were serene and peaceful, while mine became every day more tumultuous. Increase of knowledge only discovered to me more clearly what a wretched outcast I was. I cherished hope, it is true, but it vanished when I beheld my person reflected in water or my shadow in the moonshine, even as that frail image and that inconstant shade.

"I endeavoured to crush these fears and to fortify myself for the trial which in a few months I resolved to undergo; and sometimes I allowed my thoughts, unchecked by reason, to ramble in the fields of Paradise, and dared to fancy amiable and lovely creatures sympathizing with my feelings and cheering my gloom; their angelic countenances breathed smiles of consolation. But it was all a dream; no Eve soothed my sorrows nor shared my thoughts; I was alone. I remembered Adam's supplication to his Creator. But where was mine? He had abandoned me, and in the bitterness of my heart I cursed him.

"Autumn passed thus. I saw, with surprise and grief, the leaves decay and fall, and nature again assume the barren and bleak appearance it had worn when I first beheld the woods and the lovely moon. Yet I did not heed the bleakness of the weather; I was better fitted by my conformation for the endurance of cold than heat. But my chief delights were the sight of the flowers, the birds, and all the gay apparel of summer; when those deserted me, I turned with more attention towards the cottagers. Their happiness was not decreased by the absence of summer. They loved and sympathized with one another; and their joys, depending on each other, were not interrupted by the casualties that took place around them.

"The more I saw of them, the greater became my desire to claim their protection and kindness; my heart yearned to be known and loved by these amiable creatures; to see their sweet looks directed towards me with affection was the utmost limit of my ambition. I dared not think that they would turn them from me with disdain and horror. The poor that stopped at their door were never driven away. I asked, it is true, for greater treasures than a little food or rest: I required kindness and sympathy; but I did not believe myself utterly unworthy of it.

"The winter advanced, and an entire revolution of the seasons had taken place since I awoke into life. My attention at this time was solely directed towards my plan of introducing myself into the cottage of my protectors. I revolved many projects, but that on which I finally fixed was to enter the dwelling when the blind old man should be alone. I had sagacity enough to discover that the unnatural hideousness of my person was the chief object of horror with those who had formerly beheld me. My voice, although harsh, had nothing terrible in it; I thought, therefore, that if in the absence of his children I could gain the good will and mediation of the old De Lacey, I might by his means be tolerated by my younger protectors.

"One day, when the sun shone on the red leaves that strewed the ground and diffused cheerfulness, although it denied warmth, Safie, Agatha, and Felix departed on a long country walk, and the old man, at his own desire, was left alone in the cottage. When his children had departed, he took up his guitar and played several mournful but sweet airs, more sweet and mournful than I had ever heard him play before. At first his countenance was illuminated with pleasure, but as he continued, thoughtfulness and sadness succeeded; at length, laying aside the instrument, he sat absorbed in reflection.

"My heart beat quick; this was the hour and moment of trial, which would decide my hopes or realize my fears. The servants were gone to a neighbouring fair. All was silent in and around the cottage; it was an excellent opportunity; yet, when I proceeded to execute my plan, my limbs failed me and I sank to the ground. Again I rose, and exerting all the firmness of which I was master, removed the planks which I had placed before my hovel to conceal my retreat. The fresh air revived me, and with renewed determination I approached the door of their cottage.

"I knocked. 'Who is there?' said the old man. 'Come in.'

"I entered. 'Pardon this intrusion,' said I; 'I am a traveller in want of a little rest; you would greatly oblige me if you would allow me to remain a few minutes before the fire.'

"'Enter,' said De Lacey, 'and I will try in what manner I can to relieve your wants; but, unfortunately, my children are from home, and as I am blind, I am afraid I shall find it difficult to procure food for you.'

"'Do not trouble yourself, my kind host; I have food; it is warmth and rest only that I need.'

"I sat down, and a silence ensued. I knew that every minute was precious to me, yet I remained irresolute in what manner to commence the interview, when the old man addressed me. 'By your language, stranger, I suppose you are my countryman; are you French?'

"'No; but I was educated by a French family and understand that language only. I am now going to claim the protection of some friends, whom I sincerely love, and of whose favour I have some hopes.'

"'Are they Germans?'

"'No, they are French. But let us change the subject. I am an unfortunate and deserted creature, I look around and I have no relation or friend upon earth. These amiable people to whom I go have never seen me and know little of me. I am full of fears, for if I fail there, I am an outcast in the world forever.'

"'Do not despair. To be friendless is indeed to be unfortunate, but the hearts of men, when unprejudiced by any obvious self-interest, are full of brotherly love and charity. Rely, therefore, on your hopes; and if these friends are good and amiable, do not despair.'

"'They are kind—they are the most excellent creatures in the world; but, unfortunately, they are prejudiced against me. I have good dispositions; my life has been hitherto harmless and in some degree beneficial; but a fatal prejudice clouds their eyes, and where they ought to see a feeling and kind friend, they behold only a detestable monster.'

"'That is indeed unfortunate; but if you are really blameless, cannot you undeceive them?'

"'I am about to undertake that task; and it is on that account that I feel so many overwhelming terrors. I tenderly love these friends; I have, unknown to them, been for many months in the habits of daily kindness towards them; but they believe that I wish to injure them, and it is that prejudice which I wish to overcome.'

"'Where do these friends reside?'

"'Near this spot.'

"The old man paused and then continued, 'If you will unreservedly confide to me the particulars of your tale, I perhaps may be of use in undeceiving them. I am blind and cannot judge of your countenance, but there is something in your words which persuades me that you are sincere. I am poor and an exile, but it will afford me true pleasure to be in any way serviceable to a human creature.'

"'Excellent man! I thank you and accept your generous offer. You raise me from the dust by this kindness; and I trust that, by your aid, I shall not be driven from the society and sympathy of your fellow creatures.'

"'Heaven forbid! Even if you were really criminal, for that can only drive you to desperation, and not instigate you to virtue. I also am unfortunate; I and my family have been condemned, although innocent; judge, therefore, if I do not feel for your misfortunes.'

"'How can I thank you, my best and only benefactor? From

your lips first have I heard the voice of kindness directed towards me; I shall be forever grateful; and your present humanity assures me of success with those friends whom I am on the point of meeting.'

"'May I know the names and residence of those friends?' "I paused. This, I thought, was the moment of decision, which was to rob me of or bestow happiness on me forever. I struggled vainly for firmness sufficient to answer him, but the effort destroyed all my remaining strength; I sank on the chair and sobbed aloud. At that moment I heard the steps of my younger protectors. I had not a moment to lose, but seizing the hand of the old man, I cried, 'Now is the time! Save and protect me! You and your family are the friends whom I seek. Do not you desert me in the hour of trial!'

"'Great God!' exclaimed the old man. 'Who are you?'

"At that instant the cottage door was opened, and Felix, Safie, and Agatha entered. Who can describe their horror and consternation on beholding me? Agatha fainted, and Safie, unable to attend to her friend, rushed out of the cottage. Felix darted forward, and with supernatural force tore me from his father, to whose knees I clung, in a transport of fury, he dashed me to the ground and struck me violently with a stick. I could have torn him limb from limb, as the lion rends the antelope. But my heart sank within me as with bitter sickness, and I refrained. I saw him on the point of repeating his blow, when, overcome by pain and anguish, I quitted the cottage, and in the general tumult escaped unperceived to my hovel."

CHAPTER 16

"Cursed, cursed creator! Why did I live? Why, in that instant, did I not extinguish the spark of existence which you had so wantonly bestowed? I know not; despair had not yet taken possession of me; my feelings were those of rage and revenge. I could with pleasure have destroyed the cottage and its inhabitants and have glutted myself with their shrieks and misery.

"When night came I quitted my retreat and wandered in

the wood; and now, no longer restrained by the fear of discovery, I gave vent to my anguish in fearful howlings. I was like a wild beast that had broken the toils, destroying the objects that obstructed me and ranging through the wood with a staglike swiftness. Oh! What a miserable night I passed! The cold stars shone in mockery, and the bare trees waved their branches above me; now and then the sweet voice of a bird burst forth amidst the universal stillness. All, save I, were at rest or in enjoyment; I, like the arch-fiend, bore a hell within me, and finding myself unsympathized with, wished to tear up the trees, spread havoc and destruction around me, and then to have sat down and enjoyed the ruin.

"But this was a luxury of sensation that could not endure; I became fatigued with excess of bodily exertion and sank on the damp grass in the sick impotence of despair. There was none among the myriads of men that existed who would pity or assist me; and should I feel kindness towards my enemies? No; from that moment I declared everlasting war against the species, and more than all, against him who had formed me and sent me forth to this insupportable misery.

"The sun rose; I heard the voices of men and knew that it was impossible to return to my retreat during that day. Accordingly I hid myself in some thick underwood, determining to devote the ensuing hours to reflection on my situation.

"The pleasant sunshine and the pure air of day restored me to some degree of tranquillity; and when I considered what had passed at the cottage, I could not help believing that I had been too hasty in my conclusions. I had certainly acted imprudently. It was apparent that my conversation had interested the father in my behalf, and I was a fool in having exposed my person to the horror of his children. I ought to have familiarized the old De Lacey to me, and by degrees to have discovered myself to the rest of his family, when they should have been prepared for my approach. But I did not believe my errors to be irretrievable, and after much consideration I resolved to return to the cottage, seek the old man, and by my representations win him to my party.

"These thoughts calmed me, and in the afternoon I sank into a profound sleep; but the fever of my blood did not allow me to be visited by peaceful dreams. The horrible scene of the preceding day was forever acting before my eyes; the females were flying and the enraged Felix tearing me from his father's feet. I awoke exhausted, and finding that it was already night, I crept forth from my hiding-place, and went in search of food.

"When my hunger was appeased, I directed my steps towards the wellknown path that conducted to the cottage. All there was at peace. I crept into my hovel and remained in silent expectation of the accustomed hour when the family arose. That hour passed, the sun mounted high in the heavens, but the cottagers did not appear. I trembled violently, apprehending some dreadful misfortune. The inside of the cottage was dark, and I heard no motion; I cannot describe the agony of this suspense.

"Presently two countrymen passed by, but pausing near the cottage, they entered into conversation, using violent gesticulations; but I did not understand what they said, as they spoke the language of the country, which differed from that of my protectors. Soon after, however, Felix approached with another man; I was surprised, as I knew that he had not quitted the cottage that morning, and waited anxiously to discover from his discourse the meaning of these unusual appearances.

"'Do you consider,' said his companion to him, 'that you will be obliged to pay three months' rent and to lose the produce of your garden? I do not wish to take any unfair advantage, and I beg therefore that you will take some days to consider of your determination.'

"'It is utterly useless,' replied Felix; 'we can never again inhabit your cottage. The life of my father is in the greatest danger, owing to the dreadful circumstance that I have related. My wife and my sister will never recover from their horror. I entreat you not to reason with me anymore. Take possession of your tenement and let me fly from this place.'

"Felix trembled violently as he said this. He and his companion entered the cottage, in which they remained for a few minutes, and then departed. I never saw any of the family of De Lacey more.

"I continued for the remainder of the day in my hovel in a state of utter and stupid despair. My protectors had departed and had broken the only link that held me to the world. For the first time the feelings of revenge and hatred filled my bosom, and I did not strive to control them, but allowing myself to be borne away by the stream, I bent my mind towards injury and death. When I thought of my friends, of the mild voice of De Lacey, the gentle eyes of Agatha, and the exquisite beauty of the Arabian, these thoughts vanished and a gush of tears somewhat soothed me.

"But again when I reflected that they had spurned and deserted me, anger returned, a rage of anger, and unable to injure anything human, I turned my fury towards inanimate objects. As night advanced I placed a variety of combustibles around the cottage, and after having destroyed every vestige of cultivation in the garden, I waited with forced impatience until the moon had sunk to commence my operations.

"As the night advanced, a fierce wind arose from the woods and quickly dispersed the clouds that had loitered in the heavens; the blast tore along like a mighty avalanche and produced a kind of insanity in my spirits that burst all bounds of reason and reflection. I lighted the dry branch of a tree and danced with fury around the devoted cottage, my eyes still fixed on the western horizon, the edge of which the moon nearly touched. A part of its orb was at length hid, and I waved my brand; it sank, and with a loud scream I fired the straw, and heath, and bushes, which I had collected. The wind fanned the fire, and the cottage was quickly enveloped by the flames, which clung to it and licked it with their forked and destroying tongues.

"As soon as I was convinced that no assistance could save any part of the habitation, I quitted the scene and sought for refuge in the woods.

"And now, with the world before me, whither should I bend

my steps? I resolved to fly far from the scene of my misfortunes; but to me, hated and despised, every country must be equally horrible. At length the thought of you crossed my mind. I learned from your papers that you were my father, my creator; and to whom could I apply with more fitness than to him who had given me life? Among the lessons that Felix had bestowed upon Safie, geography had not been omitted; I had learned from these the relative situations of the different countries of the earth. You had mentioned Geneva as the name of your native town, and towards this place I resolved to proceed.

"But how was I to direct myself? I knew that I must travel in a southwesterly direction to reach my destination, but the sun was my only guide. I did not know the names of the towns that I was to pass through, nor could I ask information from a single human being; but I did not despair. From you only could I hope for succour, although towards you I felt no sentiment but that of hatred. Unfeeling, heartless creator! You had endowed me with perceptions and passions and then cast me abroad an object for the scorn and horror of mankind. But on you only had I any claim for pity and redress, and from you I determined to seek that justice which I vainly attempted to gain from any other be-ing that wore the human form.

"My travels were long and the sufferings I endured intense. It was late in autumn when I quitted the district where I had so long resided. I travelled only at night, fearful of encounter-ing the visage of a human being. Nature decayed around me, and the sun became heatless; rain and snow poured around me; mighty rivers were frozen; the surface of the earth was hard and chill, and bare, and I found no shelter. Oh, earth! How often did I imprecate curses on the cause of my being! The mildness of my nature had fled, and all within me was turned to gall and bitterness.

"The nearer I approached to your habitation, the more deep-ly did I feel the spirit of revenge enkindled in my heart. Snow fell, and the waters were hardened, but I rested not. A few inci-dents now and then directed me, and I possessed a map of the country; but I often wandered wide from my path. The agony of my feelings allowed me no respite; no incident occurred from which my rage and misery could not extract its food; but a circumstance that happened when I arrived on the confines of Switzerland, when the sun had recovered its warmth and the earth again began to look green, confirmed in an especial manner the bitterness and horror of my feelings.

"I generally rested during the day and travelled only when I was secured by night from the view of man. One morning, however, finding that my path lay through a deep wood, I ventured to continue my journey after the sun had risen; the day, which was one of the first of spring, cheered even me by the loveliness of its sunshine and the balminess of the air. I felt emotions of gentleness and pleasure, that had long appeared dead, revive within me. Half surprised by the novelty of these sensations, I allowed myself to be borne away by them, and forgetting my solitude and deformity, dared to be happy. Soft tears again bedewed my cheeks, and I even raised my humid eyes with thankfulness towards the blessed sun, which bestowed such joy upon me.

"I continued to wind among the paths of the wood, until I came to its boundary, which was skirted by a deep and rapid river, into which many of the trees bent their branches, now budding with the fresh spring. Here I paused, not exactly knowing what path to pursue, when I heard the sound of voices, that induced me to conceal myself under the shade of a cypress. I was scarcely hid when a young girl came running towards the spot where I was concealed, laughing, as if she ran from someone in sport. She continued her course along the precipitous sides of the river, when suddenly her foot slipped, and she fell into the rapid stream.

"I rushed from my hiding-place and with extreme labour, from the force of the current, saved her and dragged her to shore. She was senseless, and I endeavoured by every means in my power to restore animation, when I was suddenly interrupted by the approach of a rustic, who was probably the person from whom she had playfully fled. On seeing me, he darted towards me, and tearing the girl from my arms, hastened towards the deeper parts of the wood. I followed speedily, I hardly knew why; but when the man saw me draw near, he aimed a gun, which he carried, at my body and fired. I sank to the ground, and my injurer, with increased swiftness, escaped into the wood.

"This was then the reward of my benevolence! I had saved a human being from destruction, and as a recompense I now writhed under the miserable pain of a wound which shattered the flesh and bone. The feelings of kindness and gentleness which I had entertained but a few moments before gave place to hellish rage and gnashing of teeth. Inflamed by pain, I vowed eternal hatred and vengeance to all mankind. But the agony of my wound overcame me; my pulses paused, and I fainted.

"For some weeks I led a miserable life in the woods, endeavouring to cure the wound which I had received. The ball had entered my shoulder, and I knew not whether it had remained there or passed through; at any rate I had no means of extracting it. My sufferings were augmented also by the oppressive sense of the injustice and ingratitude of their infliction. My daily vows rose for revenge—a deep and deadly revenge, such as would alone compensate for the outrages and anguish I had endured.

"After some weeks my wound healed, and I continued my journey. The labours I endured were no longer to be alleviated by the bright sun or gentle breezes of spring; all joy was but a mockery which insulted my desolate state and made me feel more painfully that I was not made for the enjoyment of pleasure.

"But my toils now drew near a close, and in two months from this time I reached the environs of Geneva.

"It was evening when I arrived, and I retired to a hiding-place among the fields that surround it to meditate in what manner I should apply to you. I was oppressed by fatigue and hunger and far too unhappy to enjoy the gentle breezes of evening or the prospect of the sun setting behind the stupendous mountains of Jura.

"At this time a slight sleep relieved me from the pain of reflection, which was disturbed by the approach of a beautiful child, who came running into the recess I had chosen, with all the sportiveness of infancy. Suddenly, as I gazed on him, an idea seized me that this little creature was unprejudiced and had lived too short a time to have imbibed a horror of deformity. If, therefore, I could seize him and educate him as my companion and friend, I should not be so desolate in this peopled earth.

"Urged by this impulse, I seized on the boy as he passed and drew him towards me. As soon as he beheld my form, he placed his hands before his eyes and uttered a shrill scream; I drew his hand forcibly from his face and said, 'Child, what is the meaning of this? I do not intend to hurt you; listen to me.'

"He struggled violently. 'Let me go,' he cried; 'monster! Ugly wretch! You wish to eat me and tear me to pieces. You are an ogre. Let me go, or I will tell my papa.'

"'Boy, you will never see your father again; you must come with me.'

"'Hideous monster! Let me go. My papa is a syndic—he is M. Frankenstein—he will punish you. You dare not keep me.'

"'Frankenstein! you belong then to my enemy—to him towards whom I have sworn eternal revenge; you shall be my first victim.'

"The child still struggled and loaded me with epithets which carried despair to my heart; I grasped his throat to silence him, and in a moment he lay dead at my feet.

"I gazed on my victim, and my heart swelled with exultation and hellish triumph; clapping my hands, I exclaimed, 'I too can create desolation; my enemy is not invulnerable; this death will carry despair to him, and a thousand other miseries shall torment and destroy him.'

"As I fixed my eyes on the child, I saw something glittering on his breast. I took it; it was a portrait of a most lovely woman. In spite of my malignity, it softened and attracted me. For a few moments I gazed with delight on her dark eyes, fringed by deep lashes, and her lovely lips; but presently my rage returned; I remembered that I was forever deprived of the delights that such beautiful creatures could bestow and that she whose resemblance I contemplated would, in regarding me, have changed that air of divine benignity to one expressive of disgust and affright.

"Can you wonder that such thoughts transported me with rage? I only wonder that at that moment, instead of venting my sensations in exclamations and agony, I did not rush among mankind and perish in the attempt to destroy them.

"While I was overcome by these feelings, I left the spot where I had committed the murder, and seeking a more secluded hiding-place, I entered a barn which had appeared to me to be empty. A woman was sleeping on some straw; she was young, not indeed so beautiful as her whose portrait I held, but of an agreeable aspect and blooming in the loveliness of youth and health. Here, I thought, is one of those whose joy-imparting smiles are bestowed on all but me. And then I bent over her and whispered, 'Awake, fairest, thy lover is near—he who would give his life but to obtain one look of affection from thine eyes; my beloved, awake!'

"The sleeper stirred; a thrill of terror ran through me. Should she indeed awake, and see me, and curse me, and denounce the murderer? Thus would she assuredly act if her darkened eyes opened and she beheld me. The thought was madness; it stirred the fiend within me—not I, but she, shall suffer; the murder I have committed because I am forever robbed of all that she could give me, she shall atone. The crime had its source in her; be hers the punishment! Thanks to the lessons of Felix and the sanguinary laws of man, I had learned now to work mischief. I bent over her and placed the portrait securely in one of the folds of her dress. She moved again, and I fled.

"For some days I haunted the spot where these scenes had taken place, sometimes wishing to see you, sometimes resolved to quit the world and its miseries forever. At length I wandered towards these mountains, and have ranged through their immense recesses, consumed by a burning passion which you alone can gratify. We may not part until you have promised to comply with my requisition. I am alone and miserable; man will not associate with me; but one as deformed and horrible as myself would not deny herself to me. My companion must be of the same species and have the same defects. This being you must create."

CHAPTER 17

The being finished speaking and fixed his looks upon me in the expectation of a reply. But I was bewildered, perplexed, and unable to arrange my ideas sufficiently to understand the full extent of his proposition. He continued,

"You must create a female for me with whom I can live in the interchange of those sympathies necessary for my being. This you alone can do, and I demand it of you as a right which you must not refuse to concede."

The latter part of his tale had kindled anew in me the anger that had died away while he narrated his peaceful life among the cottagers, and as he said this I could no longer suppress the rage that burned within me.

"I do refuse it," I replied; "and no torture shall ever extort a consent from me. You may render me the most miserable of men, but you shall never make me base in my own eyes. Shall I create another like yourself, whose joint wickedness might desolate the world. Begone! I have answered you; you may torture me, but I will never consent."

"You are in the wrong," replied the fiend; "and instead of threatening, I am content to reason with you. I am malicious because I am miserable. Am I not shunned and hated by all mankind? You, my creator, would tear me to pieces and triumph; remember that, and tell me why I should pity man more than he pities me? You would not call it murder if you could precipitate me into one of those ice-rifts and destroy my frame, the work of your own hands. Shall I respect man when he condemns me? Let him live with me in the interchange of kindness, and instead of injury I would bestow every benefit upon him with tears of gratitude at his acceptance. But that cannot be; the human senses are insurmountable barriers to our union. Yet mine shall not be the submission of abject slavery. I will revenge my injuries; if I cannot inspire love, I will cause fear, and chiefly towards you my archenemy, because my creator, do I swear inextinguishable hatred. Have a care; I will work at your destruction, nor finish until I desolate your heart, so that you shall curse the hour of your birth."

A fiendish rage animated him as he said this; his face was wrinkled into contortions too horrible for human eyes to behold; but presently he calmed himself and proceeded—

"I intended to reason. This passion is detrimental to me, for you do not reflect that YOU are the cause of its excess. If any being felt emotions of benevolence towards me, I should return them a hundred and a hundredfold; for that one creature's sake I would make peace with the whole kind! But I now indulge in dreams of bliss that cannot be realized. What I ask of you is reasonable and moderate; I demand a creature of another sex, but as hideous as myself; the gratification is small, but it is all that I can receive, and it shall content me.

"It is true, we shall be monsters, cut off from all the world; but on that account we shall be more attached to one another. Our lives will not be happy, but they will be harmless and free from the misery I now feel. Oh! My creator, make me happy; let me feel gratitude towards you for one benefit! Let me see that I excite the sympathy of some existing thing; do not deny me my request!"

I was moved. I shuddered when I thought of the possible consequences of my consent, but I felt that there was some justice in his argument. His tale and the feelings he now expressed proved him to be a creature of fine sensations, and did I not as his maker owe him all the portion of happiness that it was in my power to bestow? He saw my change of feeling and continued,

"If you consent, neither you nor any other human being shall ever see us again; I will go to the vast wilds of South America. My food is not that of man; I do not destroy the lamb and the kid to glut my appetite; acorns and berries afford me sufficient nourishment. My companion will be of the same nature as myself and will be content with the same fare. We shall make our bed of dried leaves; the sun will shine on us as on man and will ripen our food. The picture I present to you is peaceful and human, and you must feel that you could deny it only in the wantonness of power and cruelty. Pitiless as you have been towards me, I now see compassion in your eyes; let me seize the favourable moment and persuade you to promise what I so ardently desire."

"You propose," replied I, "to fly from the habitations of man, to dwell in those wilds where the beasts of the field will be your only companions. How can you, who long for the love and sympathy of man, persevere in this exile? You will return and again seek their kindness, and you will meet with their detestation; your evil passions will be renewed, and you will then have a companion to aid you in the task of destruction. This may not be; cease to argue the point, for I cannot consent."

"How inconstant are your feelings! But a moment ago you were moved by my representations, and why do you again harden yourself to my complaints? I swear to you, by the earth which I inhabit, and by you that made me, that with the companion you bestow I will quit the neighbourhood of man and dwell, as it may chance, in the most savage of places. My evil passions will have fled, for I shall meet with sympathy! My life will flow quietly away, and in my dying moments I shall not curse my maker."

His words had a strange effect upon me. I compassionated him and sometimes felt a wish to console him, but when I looked upon him, when I saw the filthy mass that moved and talked, my heart sickened and my feelings were altered to those of horror and hatred. I tried to stifle these sensations; I thought that as I could not sympathize with him, I had no right to withhold from him the small portion of happiness which was yet in my power to bestow.

"You swear," I said, "to be harmless; but have you not already shown a degree of malice that should reasonably make me distrust you? May not even this be a feint that will increase your triumph by affording a wider scope for your revenge?"

"How is this? I must not be trifled with, and I demand an answer. If I have no ties and no affections, hatred and vice must be my portion; the love of another will destroy the cause of my crimes, and I shall become a thing of whose existence everyone will be ignorant. My vices are the children of a forced solitude that I abhor, and my virtues will necessarily arise when I live in communion with an equal. I shall feel the affections of a sensitive being and became linked to the chain of existence and events from which I am now excluded."

I paused some time to reflect on all he had related and the various arguments which he had employed. I thought of the promise of virtues which he had displayed on the opening of his existence and the subsequent blight of all kindly feeling by the loathing and scorn which his protectors had manifested towards him. His power and threats were not omitted in my calculations; a creature who could exist in the ice caves of the glaciers and hide himself from pursuit among the ridges of inaccessible precipices was a being possessing faculties it would be vain to cope with. After a long pause of reflection I concluded that the justice due both to him and my fellow creatures demanded of me that I should comply with his request. Turning to him, therefore, I said,

"I consent to your demand, on your solemn oath to quit Europe forever, and every other place in the neighbourhood of man, as soon as I shall deliver into your hands a female who will accompany you in your exile."

"I swear," he cried, "by the sun, and by the blue sky of heaven, and by the fire of love that burns my heart, that if you grant my prayer, while they exist you shall never behold me again. Depart to your home and commence your labours; I shall watch their progress with unutterable anxiety; and fear not but that when you are ready I shall appear."

Saying this, he suddenly quitted me, fearful, perhaps, of any change in my sentiments. I saw him descend the mountain with greater speed than the flight of an eagle, and quickly lost among the undulations of the sea of ice.

His tale had occupied the whole day, and the sun was upon the verge of the horizon when he departed. I knew that I ought to hasten my descent towards the valley, as I should soon be encompassed in darkness; but my heart was heavy, and my steps slow. The labour of winding among the little paths of the mountain and fixing my feet firmly as I advanced perplexed me, occupied as I was by the emotions which the occurrences of the day had produced.

Night was far advanced when I came to the halfway resting-place and seated myself beside the fountain. The stars shone at intervals as the clouds passed from over them; the dark pines rose before me, and every here and there a broken tree lay on the ground; it was a scene of wonderful solemnity and stirred strange thoughts within me. I wept bitterly, and clasping my hands in agony, I exclaimed, "Oh! Stars and clouds and winds, ye are all about to mock me; if ye really pity me, crush sensation and memory; let me become as nought; but if not, depart, depart, and leave me in darkness."

These were wild and miserable thoughts, but I cannot describe to you how the eternal twinkling of the stars weighed upon me and how I listened to every blast of wind as if it were a dull ugly *siroc* on its way to consume me.

Morning dawned before I arrived at the village of Chamounix; I took no rest, but returned immediately to Geneva. Even in my own heart I could give no expression to my sensations-they weighed on me with a mountain's weight and their excess destroyed my agony beneath them. Thus I returned home, and entering the house, presented myself to the family. My haggard and wild appearance awoke intense alarm, but I answered no question, scarcely did I speak.

I felt as if I were placed under a ban—as if I had no right to claim their sympathies—as if never more might I enjoy companionship with them. Yet even thus I loved them to adoration; and to save them, I resolved to dedicate myself to my most abhorred task. The prospect of such an occupation made every other circumstance of existence pass before me like a dream, and that thought only had to me the reality of life.

CHAPTER 18

Day after day, week after week, passed away on my return to Geneva; and I could not collect the courage to recommence my work. I feared the vengeance of the disappointed fiend, yet I was unable to overcome my repugnance to the task which was enjoined me. I found that I could not compose a female without again devoting several months to profound study and laborious disquisition. I had heard of some discoveries having been made by an English philosopher, the knowledge of which was material to my success, and I sometimes thought of obtaining my father's consent to visit England for this purpose; but I clung to every pretence of delay and shrank from taking the first step in an undertaking whose immediate necessity began to appear less absolute to me.

A change indeed had taken place in me; my health, which had hitherto declined, was now much restored; and my spirits, when unchecked by the memory of my unhappy promise, rose proportionably. My father saw this change with pleasure, and he turned his thoughts towards the best method of eradicating the remains of my melancholy, which every now and then would return by fits, and with a devouring blackness overcast the approaching sunshine. At these moments I took refuge in the most perfect solitude. I passed whole days on the lake alone in a little boat, watching the clouds and listening to the rippling of the waves, silent and listless. But the fresh air and bright sun seldom failed to restore me to some degree of composure, and on my return I met the salutations of my friends with a readier smile and a more cheerful heart.

It was after my return from one of these rambles that my father, calling me aside, thus addressed me,

"I am happy to remark, my dear son, that you have resumed your former pleasures and seem to be returning to yourself. And yet you are still unhappy and still avoid our society. For some time I was lost in conjecture as to the cause of this, but yesterday an idea struck me, and if it is well founded, I conjure you to avow it. Reserve on such a point would be not only useless, but draw down treble misery on us all."

I trembled violently at his exordium, and my father continued—"I confess, my son, that I have always looked forward to your marriage with our dear Elizabeth as the tie of our domestic comfort and the stay of my declining years. You were attached to each other from your earliest infancy; you studied together, and appeared, in dispositions and tastes, entirely suited to one another. But so blind is the experience of man that what I conceived to be the best assistants to my plan may have entirely destroyed it. You, perhaps, regard her as your sister, without any wish that she might become your wife. Nay, you may have met with another whom you may love; and considering yourself as bound in honour to Elizabeth, this struggle may occasion the poignant misery which you appear to feel."

"My dear father, reassure yourself. I love my cousin tenderly and sincerely. I never saw any woman who excited, as Elizabeth does, my warmest admiration and affection. My future hopes and prospects are entirely bound up in the expectation of our union."

"The expression of your sentiments of this subject, my dear Victor, gives me more pleasure than I have for some time experienced. If you feel thus, we shall assuredly be happy, however present events may cast a gloom over us. But it is this gloom which appears to have taken so strong a hold of your mind that I wish to dissipate. Tell me, therefore, whether you object to an immediate solemnization of the marriage. We have been unfortunate, and recent events have drawn us from that everyday tranquillity befitting my years and infirmities. You are younger; yet l do not suppose, possessed as you are of a competent fortune, that an early marriage would at all interfere with any future plans of honour and utility that you may have formed.

"Do not suppose, however, that I wish to dictate happiness to you or that a delay on your part would cause me any serious uneasiness. Interpret my words with candour and answer me, I conjure you, with confidence and sincerity."

I listened to my father in silence and remained for some time incapable of offering any reply. I revolved rapidly in my mind a multitude of thoughts and endeavoured to arrive at some conclusion. Alas! To me the idea of an immediate union with my Elizabeth was one of horror and dismay. I was bound by a solemn promise which I had not yet fulfilled and dared not break, or if I did, what manifold miseries might not impend over me and my devoted family! Could I enter into a festival with this deadly weight yet hanging round my neck and bowing me to the ground? I must perform my engagement and let the monster depart with his mate before I allowed myself to enjoy the delight of a union from which I expected peace.

I remembered also the necessity imposed upon me of either journeying to England or entering into a long correspondence with those philosophers of that country whose knowledge and discoveries were of indispensable use to me in my present undertaking. The latter method of obtaining the desired intelligence was dilatory and unsatisfactory; besides, I had an insurmountable aversion to the idea of engaging myself in my loathsome task in my father's house while in habits of familiar intercourse with those I loved. I knew that a thousand fearful accidents might occur, the slightest of which would disclose a tale to thrill all connected with me with horror.

I was aware also that I should often lose all self-command, all capacity of hiding the harrowing sensations that would possess me during the progress of my unearthly occupation. I must absent myself from all I loved while thus employed. Once commenced, it would quickly be achieved, and I might be restored to my family in peace and happiness. My promise fulfilled, the monster would depart forever. Or (so my fond fancy imaged) some accident might meanwhile occur to destroy him and put an end to my slavery forever.

These feelings dictated my answer to my father. I expressed a wish to visit England, but concealing the true reasons of this request, I clothed my desires under a guise which excited no suspicion, while I urged my desire with an earnestness that easily induced my father to comply. After so long a period of an absorbing melancholy that resembled madness in its intensity and effects, he was glad to find that I was capable of taking pleasure in the idea of such a journey, and he hoped that change of scene and varied amusement would, before my return, have restored me entirely to myself.

The duration of my absence was left to my own choice; a few months, or at most a year, was the period contemplated. One paternal kind precaution he had taken to ensure my having a companion. Without previously communicating with me, he had, in concert with Elizabeth, arranged that Clerval should join me at Strasbourg. This interfered with the solitude I coveted for the prosecution of my task; yet at the commencement of my journey the presence of my friend could in no way be an impediment, and truly I rejoiced that thus I should be saved many hours of lonely, maddening reflection. Nay, Henry might stand between me and the intrusion of my foe. If I were alone, would he not at times force his abhorred presence on me to remind me of my task or to contemplate its progress?

To England, therefore, I was bound, and it was understood that my union with Elizabeth should take place immediately on my return. My father's age rendered him extremely averse to delay. For myself, there was one reward I promised myself from my detested toils—one consolation for my unparalleled sufferings; it was the prospect of that day when, enfranchised from my miserable slavery, I might claim Elizabeth and forget the past in my union with her.

I now made arrangements for my journey, but one feeling haunted me which filled me with fear and agitation. During my absence I should leave my friends unconscious of the existence of their enemy and unprotected from his attacks, exasperated as he might be by my departure. But he had promised to follow me wherever I might go, and would he not accompany me to England? This imagination was dreadful in itself, but soothing inasmuch as it supposed the safety of my friends. I was agonized with the idea of the possibility that the reverse of this might happen. But through the whole period during which I was the slave of my creature I allowed myself to be governed by the impulses of the moment; and my present sensations strongly intimated that the fiend would follow me and exempt my family from the danger of his machinations.

It was in the latter end of September that I again quitted my native country. My journey had been my own suggestion, and Elizabeth therefore acquiesced, but she was filled with disquiet at the idea of my suffering, away from her, the inroads of misery and grief. It had been her care which provided me a companion in Clerval—and yet a man is blind to a thousand minute circumstances which call forth a woman's sedulous attention. She longed to bid me hasten my return; a thousand conflicting emotions rendered her mute as she bade me a tearful, silent farewell.

I threw myself into the carriage that was to convey me away, hardly knowing whither I was going, and careless of what was passing around. I remembered only, and it was with a bitter anguish that I reflected on it, to order that my chemical instruments should be packed to go with me. Filled with dreary imaginations, I passed through many beautiful and majestic scenes, but my eyes were fixed and unobserving. I could only think of the bourne of my travels and the work which was to occupy me whilst they endured.

After some days spent in listless indolence, during which I traversed many leagues, I arrived at Strasbourg, where I waited two days for Clerval. He came. Alas, how great was the contrast between us! He was alive to every new scene, joyful when he saw the beauties of the setting sun, and more happy when he beheld it rise and recommence a new day. He pointed out to me the shifting colours of the landscape and the appearances of the sky.

"This is what it is to live," he cried; "how I enjoy existence! But you, my dear Frankenstein, wherefore are you desponding and sorrowful!" In truth, I was occupied by gloomy thoughts and neither saw the descent of the evening star nor the golden sunrise reflected in the Rhine. And you, my friend, would be far more amused with the journal of Clerval, who observed the scenery with an eye of feeling and delight, than in listening to my reflections. I, a miserable wretch, haunted by a curse that shut up every avenue to enjoyment.

We had agreed to descend the Rhine in a boat from Strasbourg to Rotterdam, whence we might take shipping for London. During this voyage we passed many willowy islands and saw several beautiful towns. We stayed a day at Mannheim, and on the fifth from our departure from Strasbourg, arrived at Mainz. The course of the Rhine below Mainz becomes much more picturesque. The river descends rapidly and winds between hills, not high, but steep, and of beautiful forms. We saw many ruined castles standing on the edges of precipices, surrounded by black woods, high and inaccessible. This part of the Rhine, indeed, presents a singularly variegated landscape. In one spot you view rugged hills, ruined castles overlooking tremendous precipices, with the dark Rhine rushing beneath; and on the sudden turn of a promontory, flourishing vineyards with green sloping banks and a meandering river and populous towns occupy the scene.

We travelled at the time of the vintage and heard the song of the labourers as we glided down the stream. Even I, depressed in mind, and my spirits continually agitated by gloomy feelings, even I was pleased. I lay at the bottom of the boat, and as I gazed on the cloudless blue sky, I seemed to drink in a tranquillity to which I had long been a stranger. And if these were my sensations, who can describe those of Henry? He felt as if he had been transported to fairyland and enjoyed a happiness seldom tasted by man.

"I have seen," he said, "the most beautiful scenes of my own country; I have visited the lakes of Lucerne and Uri, where the snowy mountains descend almost perpendicularly to the water, casting black and impenetrable shades, which would cause a gloomy and mournful appearance were it not for the most verdant islands that believe the eye by their gay appearance; I have seen this lake agitated by a tempest, when the wind tore up whirlwinds of water and gave you an idea of what the water-spout must be on the great ocean; and the waves dash with fury the base of the mountain, where the priest and his mistress were overwhelmed by an avalanche and where their dying voices are still said to be heard amid the pauses of the nightly wind; I have seen the mountains of La Valais, and the Pays de Vaud; but this country, Victor, pleases me more than all those wonders.

"The mountains of Switzerland are more majestic and strange, but there is a charm in the banks of this divine river that I never before saw equalled. Look at that castle which overhangs yon precipice; and that also on the island, almost concealed amongst the foliage of those lovely trees; and now that group of labourers coming from among their vines; and that village half hid in the recess of the mountain. Oh, surely the spirit that inhabits and guards this place has a soul more in harmony with man than those who pile the glacier or retire to the inaccessible peaks of the mountains of our own country."

Clerval! Beloved friend! Even now it delights me to record your words and to dwell on the praise of which you are so eminently deserving. He was a being formed in the "very poetry of nature." His wild and enthusiastic imagination was chastened by the sensibility of his heart. His soul overflowed with ardent affections, and his friendship was of that devoted and wondrous nature that the world-minded teach us to look for only in the imagination. But even human sympathies were not sufficient to satisfy his eager mind. The scenery of external nature, which others regard only with admiration, he loved with ardour:—

——The sounding cataract
Haunted him like a passion: the tall rock,
The mountain, and the deep and gloomy wood,
Their colours and their forms, were then to him
An appetite; a feeling, and a love,
That had no need of a remoter charm,
By thought supplied, or any interest

Unborrow'd from the eye.
[Wordsworth's *Tintern Abbey*.]

And where does he now exist? Is this gentle and lovely being lost forever? Has this mind, so replete with ideas, imaginations fanciful and magnificent, which formed a world, whose existence depended on the life of its creator;—has this mind perished? Does it now only exist in my memory? No, it is not thus; your form so divinely wrought, and beaming with beauty, has decayed, but your spirit still visits and consoles your unhappy friend.

Pardon this gush of sorrow; these ineffectual words are but a slight tribute to the unexampled worth of Henry, but they soothe my heart, overflowing with the anguish which his remembrance creates. I will proceed with my tale.

Beyond Cologne we descended to the plains of Holland; and we resolved to post the remainder of our way, for the wind was contrary and the stream of the river was too gentle to aid us. Our journey here lost the interest arising from beautiful scenery, but we arrived in a few days at Rotterdam, whence we proceeded by sea to England. It was on a clear morning, in the latter days of December, that I first saw the white cliffs of Britain. The banks of the Thames presented a new scene; they were flat but fertile, and almost every town was marked by the remembrance of some story. We saw Tilbury Fort and remembered the Spanish Armada, Gravesend, Woolwich, and Greenwich—places which I had heard of even in my country.

At length we saw the numerous steeples of London, St. Paul's towering above all, and the Tower famed in English history.

CHAPTER 19

London was our present point of rest; we determined to remain several months in this wonderful and celebrated city. Clerval desired the intercourse of the men of genius and talent who flourished at this time, but this was with me a secondary object; I was principally occupied with the means of obtaining the information necessary for the completion of my promise and quickly availed myself of the letters of introduction that I had brought with me, addressed to the most distinguished natural philosophers.

If this journey had taken place during my days of study and happiness, it would have afforded me inexpressible pleasure. But a blight had come over my existence, and I only visited these people for the sake of the information they might give me on the subject in which my interest was so terribly profound. Company was irksome to me; when alone, I could fill my mind with the sights of heaven and earth; the voice of Henry soothed me, and I could thus cheat myself into a transitory peace. But busy, uninteresting, joyous faces brought back despair to my heart. I saw an insurmountable barrier placed between me and my fellow men; this barrier was sealed with the blood of William and Justine, and to reflect on the events connected with those names filled my soul with anguish.

But in Clerval I saw the image of my former self; he was inquisitive and anxious to gain experience and instruction. The difference of manners which he observed was to him an inexhaustible source of instruction and amusement. He was also pursuing an object he had long had in view. His design was to visit India, in the belief that he had in his knowledge of its various languages, and in the views he had taken of its society, the means of materially assisting the progress of European colonization and trade. In Britain only could he further the execution of his plan. He was forever busy, and the only check to his enjoyments was my sorrowful and dejected mind.

I tried to conceal this as much as possible, that I might not debar him from the pleasures natural to one who was entering on a new scene of life, undisturbed by any care or bitter recollection. I often refused to accompany him, alleging another engagement, that I might remain alone. I now also began to collect the materials necessary for my new creation, and this was to me like the torture of single drops of water continually falling on the head. Every thought that was devoted to it was an extreme anguish, and every word that I spoke in allusion to it caused my lips to quiver, and my heart to palpitate.

After passing some months in London, we received a letter from a person in Scotland who had formerly been our visitor at Geneva. He mentioned the beauties of his native country and asked us if those were not sufficient allurements to induce us to prolong our journey as far north as Perth, where he resided. Clerval eagerly desired to accept this invitation, and I, although I abhorred society, wished to view again mountains and streams and all the wondrous works with which Nature adorns her chosen dwelling-places.

We had arrived in England at the beginning of October, and it was now February. We accordingly determined to commence our journey towards the north at the expiration of another month. In this expedition we did not intend to follow the great road to Edinburgh, but to visit Windsor, Oxford, Matlock, and the Cumberland lakes, resolving to arrive at the completion of this tour about the end of July. I packed up my chemical instruments and the materials I had collected, resolving to finish my labours in some obscure nook in the northern highlands of Scotland.

We quitted London on the 27th of March and remained a few days at Windsor, rambling in its beautiful forest. This was a new scene to us mountaineers; the majestic oaks, the quantity of game, and the herds of stately deer were all novelties to us.

From thence we proceeded to Oxford. As we entered this city our minds were filled with the remembrance of the events that had been transacted there more than a century and a half before. It was here that Charles I had collected his forces. This city had remained faithful to him, after the whole nation had forsaken his cause to join the standard of Parliament and liberty. The memory of that unfortunate king and his companions, the amiable Falkland, the insolent Goring, his queen, and son, gave a peculiar interest to every part of the city which they might be supposed to have inhabited.

The spirit of elder days found a dwelling here, and we delighted to trace its footsteps. If these feelings had not found an imaginary gratification, the appearance of the city had yet in itself sufficient beauty to obtain our admiration. The colleges are ancient and picturesque; the streets are almost magnificent; and the lovely Isis, which flows beside it through meadows of exquisite verdure, is spread forth into a placid expanse of waters, which reflects its majestic assemblage of towers, and spires, and domes, embosomed among aged trees.

I enjoyed this scene, and yet my enjoyment was embittered both by the memory of the past and the anticipation of the future. I was formed for peaceful happiness. During my youthful days discontent never visited my mind, and if I was ever overcome by ennui, the sight of what is beautiful in nature or the study of what is excellent and sublime in the productions of man could always interest my heart and communicate elasticity to my spirits. But I am a blasted tree; the bolt has entered my soul; and I felt then that I should survive to exhibit what I shall soon cease to be—a miserable spectacle of wrecked humanity, pitiable to others and intolerable to myself.

We passed a considerable period at Oxford, rambling among its environs and endeavouring to identify every spot which might relate to the most animating epoch of English history. Our little voyages of discovery were often prolonged by the successive objects that presented themselves. We visited the tomb of the illustrious Hampden and the field on which that patriot fell. For a moment my soul was elevated from its debasing and miserable fears to contemplate the divine ideas of liberty and self sacrifice of which these sights were the monuments and the remembrancers. For an instant I dared to shake off my chains and look around me with a free and lofty spirit, but the iron had eaten into my flesh, and I sank again, trembling and hopeless, into my miserable self.

We left Oxford with regret and proceeded to Matlock, which was our next place of rest. The country in the neighbourhood of this village resembled, to a greater degree, the scenery of Switzerland; but everything is on a lower scale, and the green hills want the crown of distant white Alps which always attend on the piny mountains of my native country. We visited the wondrous cave and the little cabinets of natural history, where the curiosities are disposed in the same manner as in the collections at Servox and Chamounix. The latter name made me tremble when pronounced by Henry, and I hastened to quit Matlock, with which that terrible scene was thus associated.

From Derby, still journeying northwards, we passed two months in Cumberland and Westmorland. I could now almost fancy myself among the Swiss mountains. The little patches of snow which yet lingered on the northern sides of the mountains, the lakes, and the dashing of the rocky streams were all familiar and dear sights to me. Here also we made some acquaintances, who almost contrived to cheat me into happiness. The delight of Clerval was proportionably greater than mine; his mind expanded in the company of men of talent, and he found in his own nature greater capacities and resources than he could have imagined himself to have possessed while he associated with his inferiors. "I could pass my life here," said he to me; "and among these mountains I should scarcely regret Switzerland and the Rhine."

But he found that a traveller's life is one that includes much pain amidst its enjoyments. His feelings are forever on the stretch; and when he begins to sink into repose, he finds himself obliged to quit that on which he rests in pleasure for something new, which again engages his attention, and which also he forsakes for other novelties.

We had scarcely visited the various lakes of Cumberland and Westmorland and conceived an affection for some of the inhabitants when the period of our appointment with our Scotch friend approached, and we left them to travel on. For my own part I was not sorry. I had now neglected my promise for some time, and I feared the effects of the daemon's disappointment. He might remain in Switzerland and wreak his vengeance on my relatives. This idea pursued me and tormented me at every moment from which I might otherwise have snatched repose and peace.

I waited for my letters with feverish impatience; if they were delayed I was miserable and overcome by a thousand fears; and when they arrived and I saw the superscription of Elizabeth or my father, I hardly dared to read and ascertain my fate. Sometimes I thought that the fiend followed me and might expedite my remissness by murdering my companion. When these thoughts possessed me, I would not quit Henry for a moment, but followed him as his shadow, to protect him from the fancied rage of his destroyer. I felt as if I had committed some great crime, the consciousness of which haunted me. I was guiltless, but I had indeed drawn down a horrible curse upon my head, as mortal as that of crime.

I visited Edinburgh with languid eyes and mind; and yet that city might have interested the most unfortunate being. Clerval did not like it so well as Oxford, for the antiquity of the latter city was more pleasing to him. But the beauty and regularity of the new town of Edinburgh, its romantic castle and its environs, the most delightful in the world, Arthur's Seat, St. Bernard's Well, and the Pentland Hills compensated him for the change and filled him with cheerfulness and admiration. But I was impatient to arrive at the termination of my journey.

We left Edinburgh in a week, passing through Coupar, St. Andrew's, and along the banks of the Tay, to Perth, where our friend expected us. But I was in no mood to laugh and talk with strangers or enter into their feelings or plans with the good humour expected from a guest; and accordingly I told Clerval that I wished to make the tour of Scotland alone. "Do you," said I, "enjoy yourself, and let this be our rendezvous. I may be absent a month or two; but do not interfere with my motions, I entreat you; leave me to peace and solitude for a short time; and when I return, I hope it will be with a lighter heart, more congenial to your own temper."

Henry wished to dissuade me, but seeing me bent on this plan, ceased to remonstrate. He entreated me to write often. "I had rather be with you," he said, "in your solitary rambles, than with these Scotch people, whom I do not know; hasten, then, my dear friend, to return, that I may again feel myself somewhat at home, which I cannot do in your absence."

Having parted from my friend, I determined to visit some remote spot of Scotland and finish my work in solitude. I did not doubt but that the monster followed me and would discover himself to me when I should have finished, that he might receive his companion. With this resolution I traversed the northern highlands and fixed on one of the remotest of the Orkneys as the scene of my labours. It was a place fitted for such a work, being hardly more than a rock whose high sides were continually beaten upon by the waves. The soil was barren, scarcely affording pasture for a few miserable cows, and oatmeal for its inhabitants, which consisted of five persons, whose gaunt and scraggy limbs gave tokens of their miserable fare. Vegetables and bread, when they indulged in such luxuries, and even fresh water, was to be procured from the mainland, which was about five miles distant.

On the whole island there were but three miserable huts, and one of these was vacant when I arrived. This I hired. It contained but two rooms, and these exhibited all the squalidness of the most miserable penury. The thatch had fallen in, the walls were unplastered, and the door was off its hinges. I ordered it to be repaired, bought some furniture, and took possession, an incident which would doubtless have occasioned some surprise had not all the senses of the cottagers been benumbed by want and squalid poverty. As it was, I lived ungazed at and unmolested, hardly thanked for the pittance of food and clothes which I gave, so much does suffering blunt even the coarsest sensations of men.

In this retreat I devoted the morning to labour; but in the evening, when the weather permitted, I walked on the stony beach of the sea to listen to the waves as they roared and dashed at my feet. It was a monotonous yet ever-changing scene. I thought of Switzerland; it was far different from this desolate and appalling landscape. Its hills are covered with vines, and its cottages are scattered thickly in the plains. Its fair lakes reflect a blue and gentle sky, and when troubled by the winds, their tumult is but as the play of a lively infant when compared to the roarings of the giant ocean.

In this manner I distributed my occupations when I first arrived, but as I proceeded in my labour, it became every day more horrible and irksome to me. Sometimes I could not prevail on myself to enter my laboratory for several days, and at other times I toiled day and night in order to complete my work. It was, indeed, a filthy process in which I was engaged. During my first experiment, a kind of enthusiastic frenzy had blinded me to the horror of my employment; my mind was intently fixed on the consummation of my labour, and my eyes were shut to the horror of my proceedings. But now I went to it in cold blood, and my heart often sickened at the work of my hands.

Thus situated, employed in the most detestable occupation, immersed in a solitude where nothing could for an instant call my attention from the actual scene in which I was engaged, my spirits became unequal; I grew restless and nervous. Every moment I feared to meet my persecutor. Sometimes I sat with my eyes fixed on the ground, fearing to raise them lest they should encounter the object which I so much dreaded to behold. I feared to wander from the sight of my fellow creatures lest when alone he should come to claim his companion.

In the meantime I worked on, and my labour was already considerably advanced. I looked towards its completion with a tremulous and eager hope, which I dared not trust myself to question but which was intermixed with obscure forebodings of evil that made my heart sicken in my bosom.

CHAPTER 20

I sat one evening in my laboratory; the sun had set, and the moon was just rising from the sea; I had not sufficient light for my employment, and I remained idle, in a pause of consideration of whether I should leave my labour for the night or hasten its conclusion by an unremitting attention to it. As I sat, a train of reflection occurred to me which led me to consider the effects of what I was now doing. Three years before, I was engaged in the same manner and had created a fiend whose unparalleled barbarity had desolated my heart and filled it forever with the bitterest remorse. I was now about to form another being of whose dispositions I was alike ignorant; she might become ten thousand times more malignant than her mate and delight, for its own sake, in murder and wretchedness.

He had sworn to quit the neighbourhood of man and hide himself in deserts, but she had not; and she, who in all probability was to become a thinking and reasoning animal, might refuse to comply with a compact made before her creation. They might even hate each other; the creature who already lived loathed his own deformity, and might he not conceive a greater abhorrence for it when it came before his eyes in the female form? She also might turn with disgust from him to the superior beauty of man; she might quit him, and he be again alone, exasperated by the fresh provocation of being deserted by one of his own species.

Even if they were to leave Europe and inhabit the deserts of the new world, yet one of the first results of those sympathies for which the daemon thirsted would be children, and a race of devils would be propagated upon the earth who might make the very existence of the species of man a condition precarious and full of terror. Had I right, for my own benefit, to inflict this curse upon everlasting generations? I had before been moved by the sophisms of the being I had created; I had been struck senseless by his fiendish threats; but now, for the first time, the wickedness of my promise burst upon me; I shuddered to think that future ages might curse me as their pest, whose selfishness had not hesitated to buy its own peace at the price, perhaps, of the existence of the whole human race.

I trembled and my heart failed within me, when, on looking up, I saw by the light of the moon the daemon at the casement. A ghastly grin wrinkled his lips as he gazed on me, where I sat fulfilling the task which he had allotted to me. Yes, he had followed me in my travels; he had loitered in forests, hid himself in caves, or taken refuge in wide and desert heaths; and he now came to mark my progress and claim the fulfilment of my promise.

As I looked on him, his countenance expressed the utmost extent of malice and treachery. I thought with a sensation of madness on my promise of creating another like to him, and trembling with passion, tore to pieces the thing on which I was engaged. The wretch saw me destroy the creature on whose future existence he depended for happiness, and with a howl of devilish despair and revenge, withdrew.

I left the room, and locking the door, made a solemn vow in my own heart never to resume my labours; and then, with trembling steps, I sought my own apartment. I was alone; none were near me to dissipate the gloom and relieve me from the sickening oppression of the most terrible reveries.

Several hours passed, and I remained near my window gazing on the sea; it was almost motionless, for the winds were hushed, and all nature reposed under the eye of the quiet moon. A few fishing vessels alone specked the water, and now and then the gentle breeze wafted the sound of voices as the fishermen called to one another. I felt the silence, although I was hardly conscious of its extreme profundity, until my ear was suddenly arrested by the paddling of oars near the shore, and a person landed close to my house.

In a few minutes after, I heard the creaking of my door, as if someone endeavoured to open it softly. I trembled from head to foot; I felt a presentiment of who it was and wished to rouse one of the peasants who dwelt in a cottage not far from mine; but I was overcome by the sensation of helplessness, so often felt in frightful dreams, when you in vain endeavour to fly from an impending danger, and was rooted to the spot. Presently I heard the sound of footsteps along the passage; the door opened, and the wretch whom I dreaded appeared.

Shutting the door, he approached me and said in a smothered voice, "You have destroyed the work which you began; what is it that you intend? Do you dare to break your promise? I have endured toil and misery; I left Switzerland with you; I crept along the shores of the Rhine, among its willow islands and over the summits of its hills. I have dwelt many months in the heaths of England and among the deserts of Scotland. I have endured incalculable fatigue, and cold, and hunger; do you dare destroy my hopes?"

"Begone! I do break my promise; never will I create another like yourself, equal in deformity and wickedness."

"Slave, I before reasoned with you, but you have proved yourself unworthy of my condescension. Remember that I have power; you believe yourself miserable, but I can make you so wretched that the light of day will be hateful to you. You are my creator, but I am your master; obey!"

"The hour of my irresolution is past, and the period of your power is arrived. Your threats cannot move me to do an act of wickedness; but they confirm me in a determination of not creating you a companion in vice. Shall I, in cool blood, set loose upon the earth a daemon whose delight is in death and wretchedness? Begone! I am firm, and your words will only exasperate my rage."

The monster saw my determination in my face and gnashed his teeth in the impotence of anger. "Shall each man," cried he, "find a wife for his bosom, and each beast have his mate, and I be alone? I had feelings of affection, and they were requited by detestation and scorn. Man! You may hate, but beware! Your hours will pass in dread and misery, and soon the bolt will fall which must ravish from you your happiness forever. Are you to be happy while I grovel in the intensity of my wretchedness? You can blast my other passions, but revenge remains—revenge, henceforth dearer than light or food! I may die, but first you, my tyrant and tormentor, shall curse the sun that gazes on your misery. Beware, for I am fearless and therefore powerful. I will watch with the wiliness of a snake, that I may sting with its venom. Man, you shall repent of the injuries you inflict."

"Devil, cease; and do not poison the air with these sounds of malice. I have declared my resolution to you, and I am no coward to bend beneath words. Leave me; I am inexorable."

"It is well. I go; but remember, I shall be with you on your wedding-night."

I started forward and exclaimed, "Villain! Before you sign my death-warrant, be sure that you are yourself safe."

I would have seized him, but he eluded me and quitted the house with precipitation. In a few moments I saw him in his boat, which shot across the waters with an arrowy swiftness and was soon lost amidst the waves.

All was again silent, but his words rang in my ears. I burned with rage to pursue the murderer of my peace and precipitate him into the ocean. I walked up and down my room hastily and perturbed, while my imagination conjured up a thousand images to torment and sting me. Why had I not followed him and closed with him in mortal strife? But I had suffered him to depart, and he had directed his course towards the mainland. I shuddered to think who might be the next victim sacrificed to his insatiate revenge.

And then I thought again of his words—"I WILL BE WITH YOU ON YOUR WEDDING-NIGHT." That, then, was the period fixed for the fulfilment of my destiny. In that hour I should die and at once satisfy and extinguish his malice. The prospect did not move me to fear; yet when I thought of my beloved Elizabeth, of her tears and endless sorrow, when she should find her lover so barbarously snatched from her, tears, the first I had shed for many months, streamed from my eyes, and I resolved not to fall before my enemy without a bitter struggle.

The night passed away, and the sun rose from the ocean; my feelings became calmer, if it may be called calmness when the violence of rage sinks into the depths of despair. I left the house, the horrid scene of the last night's contention, and walked on the beach of the sea, which I almost regarded as an insuperable barrier between me and my fellow creatures; nay, a wish that such should prove the fact stole across me.

I desired that I might pass my life on that barren rock, wearily, it is true, but uninterrupted by any sudden shock of misery. If

I returned, it was to be sacrificed or to see those whom I most loved die under the grasp of a daemon whom I had myself created.

I walked about the isle like a restless spectre, separated from all it loved and miserable in the separation. When it became noon, and the sun rose higher, I lay down on the grass and was overpowered by a deep sleep. I had been awake the whole of the preceding night, my nerves were agitated, and my eyes inflamed by watching and misery. The sleep into which I now sank refreshed me; and when I awoke, I again felt as if I belonged to a race of human beings like myself, and I began to reflect upon what had passed with greater composure; yet still the words of the fiend rang in my ears like a death-knell; they appeared like a dream, yet distinct and oppressive as a reality.

The sun had far descended, and I still sat on the shore, satisfying my appetite, which had become ravenous, with an oaten cake, when I saw a fishing-boat land close to me, and one of the men brought me a packet; it contained letters from Geneva, and one from Clerval entreating me to join him. He said that he was wearing away his time fruitlessly where he was, that letters from the friends he had formed in London desired his return to complete the negotiation they had entered into for his Indian enterprise. He could not any longer delay his departure; but as his journey to London might be followed, even sooner than he now conjectured, by his longer voyage, he entreated me to bestow as much of my society on him as I could spare.

He besought me, therefore, to leave my solitary isle and to meet him at Perth, that we might proceed southwards together. This letter in a degree recalled me to life, and I determined to quit my island at the expiration of two days. Yet, before I departed, there was a task to perform, on which I shuddered to reflect; I must pack up my chemical instruments, and for that purpose I must enter the room which had been the scene of my odious work, and I must handle those utensils the sight of which was sickening to me. The next morning, at daybreak, I summoned sufficient courage and unlocked the door of my laboratory. The remains of the half-finished creature, whom I had destroyed, lay scattered on the floor, and I almost felt as if I had mangled the living flesh of a human being. I paused to collect myself and then entered the chamber.

With trembling hand I conveyed the instruments out of the room, but I reflected that I ought not to leave the relics of my work to excite the horror and suspicion of the peasants; and I accordingly put them into a basket, with a great quantity of stones, and laying them up, determined to throw them into the sea that very night; and in the meantime I sat upon the beach, employed in cleaning and arranging my chemical apparatus.

Nothing could be more complete than the alteration that had taken place in my feelings since the night of the appearance of the daemon. I had before regarded my promise with a gloomy despair as a thing that, with whatever consequences, must be fulfilled; but I now felt as if a film had been taken from before my eyes and that I for the first time saw clearly. The idea of renewing my labours did not for one instant occur to me; the threat I had heard weighed on my thoughts, but I did not reflect that a voluntary act of mine could avert it. I had resolved in my own mind that to create another like the fiend I had first made would be an act of the basest and most atrocious selfishness, and I banished from my mind every thought that could lead to a different conclusion.

Between two and three in the morning the moon rose; and I then, putting my basket aboard a little skiff, sailed out about four miles from the shore. The scene was perfectly solitary; a few boats were returning towards land, but I sailed away from them. I felt as if I was about the commission of a dreadful crime and avoided with shuddering anxiety any encounter with my fellow creatures. At one time the moon, which had before been clear, was suddenly overspread by a thick cloud, and I took advantage of the moment of darkness and cast my basket into the sea; I listened to the gurgling sound as it sank and then sailed away from the spot.

The sky became clouded, but the air was pure, although

chilled by the northeast breeze that was then rising. But it re-freshed me and filled me with such agreeable sensations that I resolved to prolong my stay on the water, and fixing the rud-der in a direct position, stretched myself at the bottom of the boat. Clouds hid the moon, everything was obscure, and I heard only the sound of the boat as its keel cut through the waves; the murmur lulled me, and in a short time I slept soundly. I do not know how long I remained in this situation, but when I awoke I found that the sun had already mounted considerably. The wind was high, and the waves continually threatened the safety of my little skiff.

I found that the wind was northeast and must have driven me far from the coast from which I had embarked. I endeavoured to change my course but quickly found that if I again made the attempt the boat would be instantly filled with water. Thus situ-ated, my only resource was to drive before the wind. I confess that I felt a few sensations of terror. I had no compass with me and was so slenderly acquainted with the geography of this part of the world that the sun was of little benefit to me. I might be driven into the wide Atlantic and feel all the tortures of starva-tion or be swallowed up in the immeasurable waters that roared and buffeted around me.

I had already been out many hours and felt the torment of a burning thirst, a prelude to my other sufferings. I looked on the heavens, which were covered by clouds that flew before the wind, only to be replaced by others; I looked upon the sea; it was to be my grave. "Fiend," I exclaimed, "your task is already ful-filled!" I thought of Elizabeth, of my father, and of Clerval—all left behind, on whom the monster might satisfy his sanguinary and merciless passions. This idea plunged me into a reverie so despairing and frightful that even now, when the scene is on the point of closing before me forever, I shudder to reflect on it.

Some hours passed thus; but by degrees, as the sun declined towards the horizon, the wind died away into a gentle breeze and the sea became free from breakers. But these gave place to a heavy swell; I felt sick and hardly able to hold the rudder, when suddenly I saw a line of high land towards the south.

Almost spent, as I was, by fatigue and the dreadful suspense I endured for several hours, this sudden certainty of life rushed like a flood of warm joy to my heart, and tears gushed from my eyes.

How mutable are our feelings, and how strange is that clinging love we have of life even in the excess of misery! I constructed another sail with a part of my dress and eagerly steered my course towards the land. It had a wild and rocky appearance, but as I approached nearer I easily perceived the traces of cultivation. I saw vessels near the shore and found myself suddenly transported back to the neighbourhood of civilized man. I carefully traced the windings of the land and hailed a steeple which I at length saw issuing from behind a small promontory. As I was in a state of extreme debility, I resolved to sail directly towards the town, as a place where I could most easily procure nourishment. Fortunately I had money with me.

As I turned the promontory I perceived a small neat town and a good harbour, which I entered, my heart bounding with joy at my unexpected escape.

As I was occupied in fixing the boat and arranging the sails, several people crowded towards the spot. They seemed much surprised at my appearance, but instead of offering me any assistance, whispered together with gestures that at any other time might have produced in me a slight sensation of alarm. As it was, I merely remarked that they spoke English, and I therefore addressed them in that language. "My good friends," said I, "will you be so kind as to tell me the name of this town and inform me where I am?"

"You will know that soon enough," replied a man with a hoarse voice. "Maybe you are come to a place that will not prove much to your taste, but you will not be consulted as to your quarters, I promise you."

I was exceedingly surprised on receiving so rude an answer from a stranger, and I was also disconcerted on perceiving the frowning and angry countenances of his companions. "Why do you answer me so roughly?" I replied. "Surely it is not the custom of Englishmen to receive strangers so inhospitably."

"I do not know," said the man, "what the custom of the English may be, but it is the custom of the Irish to hate villains." While this strange dialogue continued, I perceived the crowd rapidly increase. Their faces expressed a mixture of curiosity and anger, which annoyed and in some degree alarmed me.

I inquired the way to the inn, but no one replied. I then moved forward, and a murmuring sound arose from the crowd as they followed and surrounded me, when an ill-looking man approaching tapped me on the shoulder and said, "Come, sir, you must follow me to Mr. Kirwin's to give an account of yourself."

"Who is Mr. Kirwin? Why am I to give an account of myself? Is not this a free country?"

"Ay, sir, free enough for honest folks. Mr. Kirwin is a magistrate, and you are to give an account of the death of a gentleman who was found murdered here last night."

This answer startled me, but I presently recovered myself. I was innocent; that could easily be proved; accordingly I followed my conductor in silence and was led to one of the best houses in the town. I was ready to sink from fatigue and hunger, but being surrounded by a crowd, I thought it politic to rouse all my strength, that no physical debility might be construed into apprehension or conscious guilt. Little did I then expect the calamity that was in a few moments to overwhelm me and extinguish in horror and despair all fear of ignominy or death. I must pause here, for it requires all my fortitude to recall the memory of the frightful events which I am about to relate, in proper detail, to my recollection. dared not trust myself to question but which was intermixed with obscure forebodings of evil that made my heart sicken in my bosom.

CHAPTER 21

I was soon introduced into the presence of the magistrate, an old benevolent man with calm and mild manners. He looked upon me, however, with some degree of severity, and then, turning towards my conductors, he asked who appeared as witnesses on this occasion.

About half a dozen men came forward; and, one being selected by the magistrate, he deposed that he had been out fishing the night before with his son and brother-in-law, Daniel Nugent, when, about ten o'clock, they observed a strong northerly blast rising, and they accordingly put in for port. It was a very dark night, as the moon had not yet risen; they did not land at the harbour, but, as they had been accustomed, at a creek about two miles below. He walked on first, carrying a part of the fishing tackle, and his companions followed him at some distance.

As he was proceeding along the sands, he struck his foot against something and fell at his length on the ground. His companions came up to assist him, and by the light of their lantern they found that he had fallen on the body of a man, who was to all appearance dead. Their first supposition was that it was the corpse of some person who had been drowned and was thrown on shore by the waves, but on examination they found that the clothes were not wet and even that the body was not then cold. They instantly carried it to the cottage of an old woman near the spot and endeavoured, but in vain, to restore it to life. It appeared to be a handsome young man, about five and twenty years of age. He had apparently been strangled, for there was no sign of any violence except the black mark of fingers on his neck.

The first part of this deposition did not in the least interest me, but when the mark of the fingers was mentioned I remembered the murder of my brother and felt myself extremely agitated; my limbs trembled, and a mist came over my eyes, which obliged me to lean on a chair for support. The magistrate observed me with a keen eye and of course drew an unfavourable augury from my manner.

The son confirmed his father's account, but when Daniel Nugent was called he swore positively that just before the fall of his companion, he saw a boat, with a single man in it, at a short distance from the shore; and as far as he could judge by the light of a few stars, it was the same boat in which I had just landed. A woman deposed that she lived near the beach and was standing at the door of her cottage, waiting for the return of the fishermen, about an hour before she heard of the discovery of the body, when she saw a boat with only one man in it push off from that part of the shore where the corpse was afterwards found.

Another woman confirmed the account of the fishermen having brought the body into her house; it was not cold. They put it into a bed and rubbed it, and Daniel went to the town for an apothecary, but life was quite gone.

Several other men were examined concerning my landing, and they agreed that, with the strong north wind that had arisen during the night, it was very probable that I had beaten about for many hours and had been obliged to return nearly to the same spot from which I had departed. Besides, they observed that it appeared that I had brought the body from another place, and it was likely that as I did not appear to know the shore, I might have put into the harbour ignorant of the distance of the town of —— from the place where I had deposited the corpse.

Mr. Kirwin, on hearing this evidence, desired that I should be taken into the room where the body lay for interment, that it might be observed what effect the sight of it would produce upon me. This idea was probably suggested by the extreme agitation I had exhibited when the mode of the murder had been described. I was accordingly conducted, by the magistrate and several other persons, to the inn. I could not help being struck by the strange coincidences that had taken place during this eventful night; but, knowing that I had been conversing with several persons in the island I had inhabited about the time that the body had been found, I was perfectly tranquil as to the consequences of the affair. I entered the room where the corpse lay and was led up to the coffin. How can I describe my sensations on beholding it? I feel yet parched with horror, nor can I reflect on that terrible moment without shuddering and agony. The examination, the presence of the magistrate and witnesses, passed like a dream from my memory when I saw the lifeless form of Henry Clerval stretched before me. I gasped for breath, and throwing myself on the body, I exclaimed, "Have my murderous machinations deprived you also, my dearest Henry, of life? Two I have already destroyed; other victims await their destiny; but you, Clerval, my friend, my benefactor—"

The human frame could no longer support the agonies that I endured, and I was carried out of the room in strong convulsions. A fever succeeded to this. I lay for two months on the point of death; my ravings, as I afterwards heard, were frightful; I called myself the murderer of William, of Justine, and of Clerval. Sometimes I entreated my attendants to assist me in the destruction of the fiend by whom I was tormented; and at others I felt the fingers of the monster already grasping my neck, and screamed aloud with agony and terror.

Fortunately, as I spoke my native language, Mr. Kirwin alone understood me; but my gestures and bitter cries were sufficient to affright the other witnesses. Why did I not die? More miserable than man ever was before, why did I not sink into forgetfulness and rest? Death snatches away many blooming children, the only hopes of their doting parents; how many brides and youthful lovers have been one day in the bloom of health and hope, and the next a prey for worms and the decay of the tomb! Of what materials was I made that I could thus resist so many shocks, which, like the turning of the wheel, continually renewed the torture?

But I was doomed to live and in two months found myself as awaking from a dream, in a prison, stretched on a wretched bed, surrounded by jailers, turnkeys, bolts, and all the miserable apparatus of a dungeon. It was morning, I remember, when I thus awoke to understanding; I had forgotten the particulars of what had happened and only felt as if some great misfortune had suddenly overwhelmed me; but when I looked around and saw the barred windows and the squalidness of the room in which I was, all flashed across my memory and I groaned bitterly.

This sound disturbed an old woman who was sleeping in a chair beside me. She was a hired nurse, the wife of one of the turnkeys, and her countenance expressed all those bad qualities which often characterize that class. The lines of her face were hard and rude, like that of persons accustomed to see without sympathizing in sights of misery. Her tone expressed her entire indifference; she addressed me in English, and the voice struck me as one that I had heard during my sufferings. "Are you better now, sir?" said she.

I replied in the same language, with a feeble voice, "I believe I am; but if it be all true, if indeed I did not dream, I am sorry that I am still alive to feel this misery and horror."

"For that matter," replied the old woman, "if you mean about the gentleman you murdered, I believe that it were better for you if you were dead, for I fancy it will go hard with you! However, that's none of my business; I am sent to nurse you and get you well; I do my duty with a safe conscience; it were well if everybody did the same."

I turned with loathing from the woman who could utter so unfeeling a speech to a person just saved, on the very edge of death; but I felt languid and unable to reflect on all that had passed. The whole series of my life appeared to me as a dream; I sometimes doubted if indeed it were all true, for it never presented itself to my mind with the force of reality.

As the images that floated before me became more distinct, I grew feverish; a darkness pressed around me; no one was near me who soothed me with the gentle voice of love; no dear hand supported me. The physician came and prescribed medicines, and the old woman prepared them for me; but utter carelessness was visible in the first, and the expression of brutality was strongly marked in the visage of the second. Who could be interested in the fate of a murderer but the hangman who would gain his fee?

These were my first reflections, but I soon learned that Mr. Kirwin had shown me extreme kindness. He had caused the best room in the prison to be prepared for me (wretched indeed was the best); and it was he who had provided a physician and a nurse. It is true, he seldom came to see me, for although he ardently desired to relieve the sufferings of every human creature, he did not wish to be present at the agonies and miserable ravings of a murderer. He came, therefore, sometimes to see that I was not neglected, but his visits were short and with long intervals.

One day, while I was gradually recovering, I was seated in a chair, my eyes half open and my cheeks livid like those in death. I was overcome by gloom and misery and often reflected I had better seek death than desire to remain in a world which to me was replete with wretchedness. At one time I considered whether I should not declare myself guilty and suffer the penalty of the law, less innocent than poor Justine had been. Such were my thoughts when the door of my apartment was opened and Mr. Kirwin entered. His countenance expressed sympathy and compassion; he drew a chair close to mine and addressed me in French, "I fear that this place is very shocking to you; can I do anything to make you more comfortable?"

"I thank you, but all that you mention is nothing to me; on the whole earth there is no comfort which I am capable of receiving."

"I know that the sympathy of a stranger can be but of little relief to one borne down as you are by so strange a misfortune. But you will, I hope, soon quit this melancholy abode, for doubtless evidence can easily be brought to free you from the criminal charge."

"That is my least concern; I am, by a course of strange events, become the most miserable of mortals. Persecuted and tortured as I am and have been, can death be any evil to me?"

"Nothing indeed could be more unfortunate and agonizing than the strange chances that have lately occurred. You were thrown, by some surprising accident, on this shore, renowned for its hospitality, seized immediately, and charged with murder. The first sight that was presented to your eyes was the body of your friend, murdered in so unaccountable a manner and placed, as it were, by some fiend across your path."

As Mr. Kirwin said this, notwithstanding the agitation I endured on this retrospect of my sufferings, I also felt considerable surprise at the knowledge he seemed to possess concerning me. I suppose some astonishment was exhibited in my countenance, for Mr. Kirwin hastened to say, "Immediately upon your being taken ill, all the papers that were on your person were brought me, and I examined them that I might discover some trace by which I could send to your relations an account of your misfortune and illness. I found several letters, and, among others, one which I discovered from its commencement to be from your father. I instantly wrote to Geneva; nearly two months have elapsed since the departure of my letter. But you are ill; even now you tremble; you are unfit for agitation of any kind."

"This suspense is a thousand times worse than the most horrible event; tell me what new scene of death has been acted, and whose murder I am now to lament?"

"Your family is perfectly well," said Mr. Kirwin with gentleness; "and someone, a friend, is come to visit you."

I know not by what chain of thought the idea presented itself, but it instantly darted into my mind that the murderer had come to mock at my misery and taunt me with the death of Clerval, as a new incitement for me to comply with his hellish desires. I put my hand before my eyes, and cried out in agony, "Oh! Take him away! I cannot see him; for God's sake, do not let him enter!"

Mr. Kirwin regarded me with a troubled countenance. He could not help regarding my exclamation as a presumption of my guilt and said in rather a severe tone, "I should have thought, young man, that the presence of your father would have been welcome instead of inspiring such violent repugnance."

"My father!" cried I, while every feature and every muscle was relaxed from anguish to pleasure. "Is my father indeed come? How kind, how very kind! But where is he, why does he not hasten to me?"

My change of manner surprised and pleased the magistrate;

perhaps he thought that my former exclamation was a momentary return of delirium, and now he instantly resumed his former benevolence. He rose and quitted the room with my nurse, and in a moment my father entered it.

Nothing, at this moment, could have given me greater pleasure than the arrival of my father. I stretched out my hand to him and cried, "Are you, then, safe—and Elizabeth—and Ernest?" My father calmed me with assurances of their welfare and endeavoured, by dwelling on these subjects so interesting to my heart, to raise my desponding spirits; but he soon felt that a prison cannot be the abode of cheerfulness.

"What a place is this that you inhabit, my son!" said he, looking mournfully at the barred windows and wretched appearance of the room. "You travelled to seek happiness, but a fatality seems to pursue you. And poor Clerval—"

The name of my unfortunate and murdered friend was an agitation too great to be endured in my weak state; I shed tears. "Alas! Yes, my father," replied I; "some destiny of the most horrible kind hangs over me, and I must live to fulfil it, or surely I should have died on the coffin of Henry."

We were not allowed to converse for any length of time, for the precarious state of my health rendered every precaution necessary that could ensure tranquillity. Mr. Kirwin came in and insisted that my strength should not be exhausted by too much exertion. But the appearance of my father was to me like that of my good angel, and I gradually recovered my health.

As my sickness quitted me, I was absorbed by a gloomy and black melancholy that nothing could dissipate. The image of Clerval was forever before me, ghastly and murdered. More than once the agitation into which these reflections threw me made my friends dread a dangerous relapse. Alas! Why did they preserve so miserable and detested a life? It was surely that I might fulfil my destiny, which is now drawing to a close. Soon, oh, very soon, will death extinguish these throbbings and relieve me from the mighty weight of anguish that bears me to the dust; and, in executing the award of justice, I shall also sink to rest. Then the appearance of death was distant, although the wish was ever present to my thoughts; and I often sat for hours motionless and speechless, wishing for some mighty revolution that might bury me and my destroyer in its ruins.

The season of the assizes approached. I had already been three months in prison, and although I was still weak and in continual danger of a relapse, I was obliged to travel nearly a hundred miles to the country town where the court was held. Mr. Kirwin charged himself with every care of collecting witnesses and arranging my defence. I was spared the disgrace of appearing publicly as a criminal, as the case was not brought before the court that decides on life and death. The grand jury rejected the bill, on its being proved that I was on the Orkney Islands at the hour the body of my friend was found; and a fortnight after my removal I was liberated from prison.

My father was enraptured on finding me freed from the vexations of a criminal charge, that I was again allowed to breathe the fresh atmosphere and permitted to return to my native country. I did not participate in these feelings, for to me the walls of a dungeon or a palace were alike hateful. The cup of life was poisoned forever, and although the sun shone upon me, as upon the happy and gay of heart, I saw around me nothing but a dense and frightful darkness, penetrated by no light but the glimmer of two eyes that glared upon me. Sometimes they were the expressive eyes of Henry, languishing in death, the dark orbs nearly covered by the lids and the long black lashes that fringed them; sometimes it was the watery, clouded eyes of the monster, as I first saw them in my chamber at Ingolstadt.

My father tried to awaken in me the feelings of affection. He talked of Geneva, which I should soon visit, of Elizabeth and Ernest; but these words only drew deep groans from me. Sometimes, indeed, I felt a wish for happiness and thought with melancholy delight of my beloved cousin or longed, with a devouring *maladie du pays*, to see once more the blue lake and rapid Rhone, that had been so dear to me in early childhood; but my general state of feeling was a torpor in which a prison was as welcome a residence as the divinest scene in nature; and these fits were seldom interrupted but by paroxysms of anguish and despair. At these moments I often endeavoured to put an end to the existence I loathed, and it required unceasing attendance and vigilance to restrain me from committing some dreadful act of violence.

Yet one duty remained to me, the recollection of which finally triumphed over my selfish despair. It was necessary that I should return without delay to Geneva, there to watch over the lives of those I so fondly loved and to lie in wait for the murderer, that if any chance led me to the place of his concealment, or if he dared again to blast me by his presence, I might, with unfailing aim, put an end to the existence of the monstrous image which I had endued with the mockery of a soul still more monstrous. My father still desired to delay our departure, fearful that I could not sustain the fatigues of a journey, for I was a shattered wreck—the shadow of a human being.

My strength was gone. I was a mere skeleton, and fever night and day preyed upon my wasted frame. Still, as I urged our leaving Ireland with such inquietude and impatience, my father thought it best to yield. We took our passage on board a vessel bound for Havre-de-Grace and sailed with a fair wind from the Irish shores. It was midnight. I lay on the deck looking at the stars and listening to the dashing of the waves. I hailed the darkness that shut Ireland from my sight, and my pulse beat with a feverish joy when I reflected that I should soon see Geneva.

The past appeared to me in the light of a frightful dream; yet the vessel in which I was, the wind that blew me from the detested shore of Ireland, and the sea which surrounded me told me too forcibly that I was deceived by no vision and that Clerval, my friend and dearest companion, had fallen a victim to me and the monster of my creation. I repassed, in my memory, my whole life—my quiet happiness while residing with my family in Geneva, the death of my mother, and my departure for Ingolstadt.

I remembered, shuddering, the mad enthusiasm that hurried

me on to the creation of my hideous enemy, and I called to mind the night in which he first lived. I was unable to pursue the train of thought; a thousand feelings pressed upon me, and I wept bitterly. Ever since my recovery from the fever I had been in the custom of taking every night a small quantity of laudanum, for it was by means of this drug only that I was enabled to gain the rest necessary for the preservation of life. Oppressed by the recollection of my various misfortunes, I now swallowed double my usual quantity and soon slept profoundly. But sleep did not afford me respite from thought and misery; my dreams presented a thousand objects that scared me.

Towards morning I was possessed by a kind of nightmare; I felt the fiend's grasp in my neck and could not free myself from it; groans and cries rang in my ears. My father, who was watching over me, perceiving my restlessness, awoke me; the dashing waves were around, the cloudy sky above, the fiend was not here: a sense of security, a feeling that a truce was established between the present hour and the irresistible, disastrous future imparted to me a kind of calm forgetfulness, of which the human mind is by its structure peculiarly susceptible.

CHAPTER 22

The voyage came to an end. We landed, and proceeded to Paris. I soon found that I had overtaxed my strength and that I must repose before I could continue my journey. My father's care and attentions were indefatigable, but he did not know the origin of my sufferings and sought erroneous methods to remedy the incurable ill. He wished me to seek amusement in society. I abhorred the face of man. Oh, not abhorred! They were my brethren, my fellow beings, and I felt attracted even to the most repulsive among them, as to creatures of an angelic nature and celestial mechanism. But I felt that I had no right to share their intercourse. I had unchained an enemy among them whose joy it was to shed their blood and to revel in their groans. How they would, each and all, abhor me and hunt me from the world did they know my unhallowed acts and the crimes which had their source in me!

My father yielded at length to my desire to avoid society and strove by various arguments to banish my despair. Sometimes he thought that I felt deeply the degradation of being obliged to answer a charge of murder, and he endeavoured to prove to me the futility of pride.

"Alas! My father," said I, "how little do you know me. Human beings, their feelings and passions, would indeed be degraded if such a wretch as I felt pride. Justine, poor unhappy Justine, was as innocent as I, and she suffered the same charge; she died for it; and I am the cause of this—I murdered her. William, Justine, and Henry—they all died by my hands."

My father had often, during my imprisonment, heard me make the same assertion; when I thus accused myself, he sometimes seemed to desire an explanation, and at others he appeared to consider it as the offspring of delirium, and that, during my illness, some idea of this kind had presented itself to my imagination, the remembrance of which I preserved in my convalescence.

I avoided explanation and maintained a continual silence concerning the wretch I had created. I had a persuasion that I should be supposed mad, and this in itself would forever have chained my tongue. But, besides, I could not bring myself to disclose a secret which would fill my hearer with consternation and make fear and unnatural horror the inmates of his breast. I checked, therefore, my impatient thirst for sympathy and was silent when I would have given the world to have confided the fatal secret. Yet, still, words like those I have recorded would burst uncontrollably from me. I could offer no explanation of them, but their truth in part relieved the burden of my mysterious woe.

Upon this occasion my father said, with an expression of unbounded wonder, "My dearest Victor, what infatuation is this? My dear son, I entreat you never to make such an assertion again."

"I am not mad," I cried energetically; "the sun and the heavens, who have viewed my operations, can bear witness of my truth. I am the assassin of those most innocent victims; they died by my machinations. A thousand times would I have shed my own blood, drop by drop, to have saved their lives; but I could not, my father, indeed I could not sacrifice the whole human race."

The conclusion of this speech convinced my father that my ideas were deranged, and he instantly changed the subject of our conversation and endeavoured to alter the course of my thoughts. He wished as much as possible to obliterate the memory of the scenes that had taken place in Ireland and never alluded to them or suffered me to speak of my misfortunes.

As time passed away I became more calm; misery had her dwelling in my heart, but I no longer talked in the same incoherent manner of my own crimes; sufficient for me was the consciousness of them. By the utmost self-violence I curbed the imperious voice of wretchedness, which sometimes desired to declare itself to the whole world, and my manners were calmer and more composed than they had ever been since my journey to the sea of ice. A few days before we left Paris on our way to Switzerland, I received the following letter from Elizabeth:

My dear Friend,

It gave me the greatest pleasure to receive a letter from my uncle dated at Paris; you are no longer at a formidable distance, and I may hope to see you in less than a fortnight. My poor cousin, how much you must have suffered! I expect to see you looking even more ill than when you quitted Geneva. This winter has been passed most miserably, tortured as I have been by anxious suspense; yet I hope to see peace in your countenance and to find that your heart is not totally void of comfort and tranquillity.

Yet I fear that the same feelings now exist that made you so miserable a year ago, even perhaps augmented by time. I would not disturb you at this period, when so many misfortunes weigh upon you, but a conversation that I had with my uncle previous to his departure renders some explanation necessary before we meet. Explanation! You may possibly say, What can Elizabeth have to explain? If you really say this, my questions are answered and all my doubts satisfied. But you are distant from me, and it is possible that you may dread and yet be pleased with this explanation; and in a probability of this being the case, I dare not any longer postpone writing what, during your absence, I have often wished to express to you but have never had the courage to begin.

You well know, Victor, that our union had been the favourite plan of your parents ever since our infancy. We were told this when young, and taught to look forward to it as an event that would certainly take place. We were affectionate playfellows during childhood, and, I believe, dear and valued friends to one another as we grew older. But as brother and sister often entertain a lively affection towards each other without desiring a more intimate union, may not such also be our case? Tell me, dearest Victor. Answer me, I conjure you by our mutual happiness, with simple truth—Do you not love another?

You have travelled; you have spent several years of your life at Ingolstadt; and I confess to you, my friend, that when I saw you last autumn so unhappy, flying to solitude from the society of every creature, I could not help supposing that you might regret our connection and believe yourself bound in honour to fulfil the wishes of your parents, although they opposed themselves to your inclinations. But this is false reasoning. I confess to you, my friend, that I love you and that in my airy dreams of futurity you have been my constant friend and companion.

But it is your happiness I desire as well as my own when I declare to you that our marriage would render me eternally miserable unless it were the dictate of your own free choice. Even now I weep to think that, borne down as you are by the cruellest misfortunes, you may stifle, by the word "honour," all hope of that love and happiness which would alone restore you to yourself. I, who have so disinterested an affection for you, may increase your miseries tenfold by being an obstacle to your wishes. Ah! Victor, be assured that your cousin and playmate has too sincere a love for you not to be made miserable by this supposition. Be happy, my friend; and if you obey me in this one request, remain satisfied that nothing on earth will have the power to interrupt my tranquillity.

Do not let this letter disturb you; do not answer tomorrow, or the next day, or even until you come, if it will give you pain. My uncle will send me news of your health, and if I see but one smile on your lips when we meet, occasioned by this or any other exertion of mine, I shall need no other happiness.

Elizabeth Lavenza

Geneva, May 18th, 17—

This letter revived in my memory what I had before forgotten, the threat of the fiend—"I WILL BE WITH YOU ON YOUR WEDDING-NIGHT!" Such was my sentence, and on that night would the daemon employ every art to destroy me and tear me from the glimpse of happiness which promised partly to console my sufferings. On that night he had determined to consummate his crimes by my death. Well, be it so; a deadly struggle would then assuredly take place, in which if he were victorious I should be at peace and his power over me be at an end.

If he were vanquished, I should be a free man. Alas! What freedom? Such as the peasant enjoys when his family have been massacred before his eyes, his cottage burnt, his lands laid waste, and he is turned adrift, homeless, penniless, and alone, but free. Such would be my liberty except that in my Elizabeth I possessed a treasure, alas, balanced by those horrors of remorse and guilt which would pursue me until death.

Sweet and beloved Elizabeth! I read and reread her letter, and some softened feelings stole into my heart and dared to whisper paradisiacal dreams of love and joy; but the apple was already eaten, and the angel's arm bared to drive me from all hope. Yet I would die to make her happy. If the monster executed his threat, death was inevitable; yet, again, I considered whether my marriage would hasten my fate. My destruction might indeed arrive a few months sooner, but if my torturer should suspect that I postponed it, influenced by his menaces, he would surely find other and perhaps more dreadful means of revenge.

He had vowed TO BE WITH ME ON MY WEDDING-NIGHT, yet he did not consider that threat as binding him to peace in the meantime, for as if to show me that he was not yet satiated with blood, he had murdered Clerval immediately after the enunciation of his threats. I resolved, therefore, that if my immediate union with my cousin would conduce either to hers or my father's happiness, my adversary's designs against my life should not retard it a single hour.

In this state of mind I wrote to Elizabeth. My letter was calm and affectionate.

"I fear, my beloved girl," I said, "little happiness remains for us on earth; yet all that I may one day enjoy is centred in you. Chase away your idle fears; to you alone do I consecrate my life and my endeavours for contentment. I have one secret, Elizabeth, a dreadful one; when revealed to you, it will chill your frame with horror, and then, far from being surprised at my misery, you will only wonder that I survive what I have endured. I will confide this tale of misery and terror to you the day after our marriage shall take place, for, my sweet cousin, there must be perfect confidence between us. But until then, I conjure you, do not mention or allude to it. This I most earnestly entreat, and I know you will comply."

In about a week after the arrival of Elizabeth's letter we returned to Geneva. The sweet girl welcomed me with warm affection, yet tears were in her eyes as she beheld my emaciated frame and feverish cheeks. I saw a change in her also. She was thinner and had lost much of that heavenly vivacity that had before charmed me; but her gentleness and soft looks of compassion made her a more fit companion for one blasted and miserable as I was. The tranquillity which I now enjoyed did not endure. Memory brought madness with it, and when I thought of what had passed, a real insanity possessed me; sometimes I was furious and burnt with rage, sometimes low and despondent. I neither spoke nor looked at anyone, but sat motionless, bewildered by the multitude of miseries that overcame me.

Elizabeth alone had the power to draw me from these fits; her gentle voice would soothe me when transported by passion and inspire me with human feelings when sunk in torpor. She wept with me and for me. When reason returned, she would remonstrate and endeavour to inspire me with resignation. Ah! It is well for the unfortunate to be resigned, but for the guilty there is no peace. The agonies of remorse poison the luxury there is otherwise sometimes found in indulging the excess of grief. Soon after my arrival my father spoke of my immediate marriage with Elizabeth. I remained silent.

"Have you, then, some other attachment?"

"None on earth. I love Elizabeth and look forward to our union with delight. Let the day therefore be fixed; and on it I will consecrate myself, in life or death, to the happiness of my cousin."

"My dear Victor, do not speak thus. Heavy misfortunes have befallen us, but let us only cling closer to what remains and transfer our love for those whom we have lost to those who yet live. Our circle will be small but bound close by the ties of affection and mutual misfortune. And when time shall have softened your despair, new and dear objects of care will be born to replace those of whom we have been so cruelly deprived."

Such were the lessons of my father. But to me the remembrance of the threat returned; nor can you wonder that, omnipotent as the fiend had yet been in his deeds of blood, I should almost regard him as invincible, and that when he had pronounced the words "I SHALL BE WITH YOU ON YOUR WEDDING-NIGHT," I should regard the threatened fate as unavoidable. But death was no evil to me if the loss of Elizabeth were balanced with it, and I therefore, with a contented and even cheerful countenance, agreed with my father that if my cousin would consent, the ceremony should take place in ten days, and thus put, as I imagined, the seal to my fate.

Great God! If for one instant I had thought what might be the hellish intention of my fiendish adversary, I would rather have banished myself forever from my native country and wandered a friendless outcast over the earth than have consented to this miserable marriage. But, as if possessed of magic powers, the monster had blinded me to his real intentions; and when I thought that I had prepared only my own death, I hastened that of a far dearer victim.

As the period fixed for our marriage drew nearer, whether from cowardice or a prophetic feeling, I felt my heart sink within me. But I concealed my feelings by an appearance of hilarity that brought smiles and joy to the countenance of my father, but hardly deceived the everwatchful and nicer eye of Elizabeth. She looked forward to our union with placid contentment, not unmingled with a little fear, which past misfortunes had impressed, that what now appeared certain and tangible happiness might soon dissipate into an airy dream and leave no trace but deep and everlasting regret.

Preparations were made for the event, congratulatory visits were received, and all wore a smiling appearance. I shut up, as well as I could, in my own heart the anxiety that preyed there and entered with seeming earnestness into the plans of my father, although they might only serve as the decorations of my tragedy. Through my father's exertions a part of the inheritance of Elizabeth had been restored to her by the Austrian government. A small possession on the shores of Como belonged to her. It was agreed that, immediately after our union, we should proceed to Villa Lavenza and spend our first days of happiness beside the beautiful lake near which it stood.

In the meantime I took every precaution to defend my person in case the fiend should openly attack me. I carried pistols and a dagger constantly about me and was ever on the watch to prevent artifice, and by these means gained a greater degree of tranquillity. Indeed, as the period approached, the threat appeared more as a delusion, not to be regarded as worthy to disturb my peace, while the happiness I hoped for in my marriage wore a greater appearance of certainty as the day fixed for its solemnization drew nearer and I heard it continually spoken of as an occurrence which no accident could possibly prevent.

Elizabeth seemed happy; my tranquil demeanour contributed greatly to calm her mind. But on the day that was to fulfil my wishes and my destiny, she was melancholy, and a presentiment of evil pervaded her; and perhaps also she thought of the dreadful secret which I had promised to reveal to her on the following day. My father was in the meantime overjoyed and in the bustle of preparation only recognized in the melancholy of his niece the diffidence of a bride.

After the ceremony was performed a large party assembled at my father's, but it was agreed that Elizabeth and I should commence our journey by water, sleeping that night at Evian and continuing our voyage on the following day. The day was fair, the wind favourable; all smiled on our nuptial embarkation.

Those were the last moments of my life during which I enjoyed the feeling of happiness. We passed rapidly along; the sun was hot, but we were sheltered from its rays by a kind of canopy while we enjoyed the beauty of the scene, sometimes on one side of the lake, where we saw Mont Saleve, the pleasant banks of Montalegre, and at a distance, surmounting all, the beautiful Mont Blanc and the assemblage of snowy mountains that in vain endeavour to emulate her; sometimes coasting the opposite banks, we saw the mighty Jura opposing its dark side to the ambition that would quit its native country, and an almost insurmountable barrier to the invader who should wish to enslave it.

I took the hand of Elizabeth. "You are sorrowful, my love. Ah! If you knew what I have suffered and what I may yet endure, you would endeavour to let me taste the quiet and freedom from despair that this one day at least permits me to enjoy."

"Be happy, my dear Victor," replied Elizabeth; "there is, I hope, nothing to distress you; and be assured that if a lively joy is not painted in my face, my heart is contented. Something whispers to me not to depend too much on the prospect that is opened before us, but I will not listen to such a sinister voice. Observe how fast we move along and how the clouds, which sometimes obscure and sometimes rise above the dome of Mont Blanc, render this scene of beauty still more interesting. Look also at the innumerable fish that are swimming in the clear waters, where we can distinguish every pebble that lies at the bottom. What a divine day! How happy and serene all nature appears!"

Thus Elizabeth endeavoured to divert her thoughts and mine from all reflection upon melancholy subjects. But her temper was fluctuating; joy for a few instants shone in her eyes, but it continually gave place to distraction and reverie.

The sun sank lower in the heavens; we passed the river Drance and observed its path through the chasms of the higher and the glens of the lower hills. The Alps here come closer to the lake, and we approached the amphitheatre of mountains which forms its eastern boundary. The spire of Evian shone under the woods that surrounded it and the range of mountain above mountain by which it was overhung.

The wind, which had hitherto carried us along with amazing rapidity, sank at sunset to a light breeze; the soft air just ruffled the water and caused a pleasant motion among the trees as we approached the shore, from which it wafted the most delightful scent of flowers and hay. The sun sank beneath the horizon as we landed, and as I touched the shore I felt those cares and fears revive which soon were to clasp me and cling to me forever.

Chapter 23

It was eight o'clock when we landed; we walked for a short time on the shore, enjoying the transitory light, and then retired to the inn and contemplated the lovely scene of waters, woods, and mountains, obscured in darkness, yet still displaying their black outlines.

The wind, which had fallen in the south, now rose with great violence in the west. The moon had reached her summit in the heavens and was beginning to descend; the clouds swept across it swifter than the flight of the vulture and dimmed her rays, while the lake reflected the scene of the busy heavens, rendered still busier by the restless waves that were beginning to rise. Suddenly a heavy storm of rain descended.

I had been calm during the day, but so soon as night obscured the shapes of objects, a thousand fears arose in my mind. I was anxious and watchful, while my right hand grasped a pistol which was hidden in my bosom; every sound terrified me, but I resolved that I would sell my life dearly and not shrink from the conflict until my own life or that of my adversary was extinguished. Elizabeth observed my agitation for some time in timid and fearful silence, but there was something in my glance which communicated terror to her, and trembling, she asked, "What is it that agitates you, my dear Victor? What is it you fear?"

"Oh! Peace, peace, my love," replied I; "this night, and all will be safe; but this night is dreadful, very dreadful."

I passed an hour in this state of mind, when suddenly I reflected how fearful the combat which I momentarily expected would be to my wife, and I earnestly entreated her to retire, resolving not to join her until I had obtained some knowledge as to the situation of my enemy.

She left me, and I continued some time walking up and down the passages of the house and inspecting every corner that might afford a retreat to my adversary. But I discovered no trace of him and was beginning to conjecture that some fortunate chance had intervened to prevent the execution of his menaces when suddenly I heard a shrill and dreadful scream. It came from the room into which Elizabeth had retired. As I heard it, the whole truth rushed into my mind, my arms dropped, the motion of every muscle and fibre was suspended; I could feel the blood trickling in my veins and tingling in the extremities of my limbs.

This state lasted but for an instant; the scream was repeated, and I rushed into the room. Great God! Why did I not then expire! Why am I here to relate the destruction of the best hope and the purest creature on earth? She was there, lifeless and inanimate, thrown across the bed, her head hanging down and her pale and distorted features half covered by her hair. Everywhere I turn I see the same figure—her bloodless arms and relaxed form flung by the murderer on its bridal bier. Could I behold this and live? Alas! Life is obstinate and clings closest where it is most hated. For a moment only did I lose recollection; I fell senseless on the ground.

When I recovered I found myself surrounded by the people of the inn; their countenances expressed a breathless terror, but the horror of others appeared only as a mockery, a shadow of the feelings that oppressed me. I escaped from them to the room where lay the body of Elizabeth, my love, my wife, so lately living, so dear, so worthy. She had been moved from the posture in which I had first beheld her, and now, as she lay, her head upon her arm and a handkerchief thrown across her face and neck, I might have supposed her asleep. I rushed towards her and embraced her with ardour, but the deadly languor and coldness of the limbs told me that what I now held in my arms had ceased to be the Elizabeth whom I had loved and cherished.

The murderous mark of the fiend's grasp was on her neck, and the breath had ceased to issue from her lips. While I still hung over her in the agony of despair, I happened to look up. The windows of the room had before been darkened, and I felt a kind of panic on seeing the pale yellow light of the moon illuminate the chamber. The shutters had been thrown back, and with a sensation of horror not to be described, I saw at the open window a figure the most hideous and abhorred. A grin was on the face of the monster; he seemed to jeer, as with his fiendish finger he pointed towards the corpse of my wife. I rushed towards the window, and drawing a pistol from my bosom, fired; but he eluded me, leaped from his station, and running with the swiftness of lightning, plunged into the lake.

The report of the pistol brought a crowd into the room. I pointed to the spot where he had disappeared, and we followed the track with boats; nets were cast, but in vain. After passing several hours, we returned hopeless, most of my companions believing it to have been a form conjured up by my fancy. After having landed, they proceeded to search the country, parties going in different directions among the woods and vines.

I attempted to accompany them and proceeded a short distance from the house, but my head whirled round, my steps were like those of a drunken man, I fell at last in a state of utter exhaustion; a film covered my eyes, and my skin was parched with the heat of fever. In this state I was carried back and placed on a bed, hardly conscious of what had happened; my eyes wandered round the room as if to seek something that I had lost.

After an interval I arose, and as if by instinct, crawled into the room where the corpse of my beloved lay. There were women weeping around; I hung over it and joined my sad tears to theirs; all this time no distinct idea presented itself to my mind, but my thoughts rambled to various subjects, reflecting confusedly on my misfortunes and their cause. I was bewildered, in a cloud of wonder and horror. The death of William, the execution of Justine, the murder of Clerval, and lastly of my wife; even at that moment I knew not that my only remaining friends were safe from the malignity of the fiend; my father even now might be writhing under his grasp, and Ernest might be dead at his feet. This idea made me shudder and recalled me to action. I started up and resolved to return to Geneva with all possible speed.

There were no horses to be procured, and I must return by the lake; but the wind was unfavourable, and the rain fell in torrents. However, it was hardly morning, and I might reasonably hope to arrive by night. I hired men to row and took an oar myself, for I had always experienced relief from mental torment in bodily exercise. But the overflowing misery I now felt, and the excess of agitation that I endured rendered me incapable of any exertion. I threw down the oar, and leaning my head upon my hands, gave way to every gloomy idea that arose.

If I looked up, I saw scenes which were familiar to me in my happier time and which I had contemplated but the day before in the company of her who was now but a shadow and a recollection. Tears streamed from my eyes. The rain had ceased for a moment, and I saw the fish play in the waters as they had done a few hours before; they had then been observed by Elizabeth. Nothing is so painful to the human mind as a great and sudden change. The sun might shine or the clouds might lower, but nothing could appear to me as it had done the day before. A fiend had snatched from me every hope of future happiness; no creature had ever been so miserable as I was; so frightful an event is single in the history of man.

But why should I dwell upon the incidents that followed this last overwhelming event? Mine has been a tale of horrors; I have reached their acme, and what I must now relate can but be tedious to you. Know that, one by one, my friends were snatched away; I was left desolate. My own strength is exhausted, and I must tell, in a few words, what remains of my hideous narration. I arrived at Geneva. My father and Ernest yet lived, but the former sunk under the tidings that I bore.

I see him now, excellent and venerable old man! His eyes wandered in vacancy, for they had lost their charm and their delight—his Elizabeth, his more than daughter, whom he doted on with all that affection which a man feels, who in the decline of life, having few affections, clings more earnestly to those that remain. Cursed, cursed be the fiend that brought misery on his grey hairs and doomed him to waste in wretchedness! He could not live under the horrors that were accumulated around him; the springs of existence suddenly gave way; he was unable to rise from his bed, and in a few days he died in my arms.

What then became of me? I know not; I lost sensation, and chains and darkness were the only objects that pressed upon me. Sometimes, indeed, I dreamt that I wandered in flowery meadows and pleasant vales with the friends of my youth, but I awoke and found myself in a dungeon. Melancholy followed, but by degrees I gained a clear conception of my miseries and situation and was then released from my prison. For they had called me mad, and during many months, as I understood, a solitary cell had been my habitation.

Liberty, however, had been a useless gift to me, had I not, as I awakened to reason, at the same time awakened to revenge. As the memory of past misfortunes pressed upon me, I began to reflect on their cause—the monster whom I had created, the miserable daemon whom I had sent abroad into the world for my destruction. I was possessed by a maddening rage when I thought of him, and desired and ardently prayed that I might have him within my grasp to wreak a great and signal revenge on his cursed head.

Nor did my hate long confine itself to useless wishes; I began to reflect on the best means of securing him; and for this purpose, about a month after my release, I repaired to a criminal judge in the town and told him that I had an accusation to make, that I knew the destroyer of my family, and that I required him to exert his whole authority for the apprehension of the murderer. The magistrate listened to me with attention and kindness.

"Be assured, sir," said he, "no pains or exertions on my part shall be spared to discover the villain."

"I thank you," replied I; "listen, therefore, to the deposition that I have to make. It is indeed a tale so strange that I should fear you would not credit it were there not something in truth which, however wonderful, forces conviction. The story is too connected to be mistaken for a dream, and I have no motive for falsehood." My manner as I thus addressed him was impressive but calm; I had formed in my own heart a resolution to pursue my destroyer to death, and this purpose quieted my agony and for an interval reconciled me to life. I now related my history briefly but with firmness and precision, marking the dates with accuracy and never deviating into invective or exclamation.

The magistrate appeared at first perfectly incredulous, but as I continued he became more attentive and interested; I saw him sometimes shudder with horror; at others a lively surprise, un-mingled with disbelief, was painted on his countenance. When

I had concluded my narration I said, "This is the being whom I accuse and for whose seizure and punishment I call upon you to exert your whole power. It is your duty as a magistrate, and I believe and hope that your feelings as a man will not revolt from the execution of those functions on this occasion."

This address caused a considerable change in the physiognomy of my own auditor. He had heard my story with that half kind of belief that is given to a tale of spirits and supernatural events; but when he was called upon to act officially in consequence, the whole tide of his incredulity returned. He, however, answered mildly, "I would willingly afford you every aid in your pursuit, but the creature of whom you speak appears to have powers which would put all my exertions to defiance. Who can follow an animal which can traverse the sea of ice and inhabit caves and dens where no man would venture to intrude? Besides, some months have elapsed since the commission of his crimes, and no one can conjecture to what place he has wandered or what region he may now inhabit."

"I do not doubt that he hovers near the spot which I inhabit, and if he has indeed taken refuge in the Alps, he may be hunted like the chamois and destroyed as a beast of prey. But I perceive your thoughts; you do not credit my narrative and do not intend to pursue my enemy with the punishment which is his desert." As I spoke, rage sparkled in my eyes; the magistrate was intimidated. "You are mistaken," said he. "I will exert myself, and if it is in my power to seize the monster, be assured that he shall suffer punishment proportionate to his crimes. But I fear, from what you have yourself described to be his properties, that this will prove impracticable; and thus, while every proper measure is pursued, you should make up your mind to disappointment."

"That cannot be; but all that I can say will be of little avail. My revenge is of no moment to you; yet, while I allow it to be a vice, I confess that it is the devouring and only passion of my soul. My rage is unspeakable when I reflect that the murderer, whom I have turned loose upon society, still exists. You refuse my just demand; I have but one resource, and I devote myself, either in my life or death, to his destruction."

I trembled with excess of agitation as I said this; there was a frenzy in my manner, and something, I doubt not, of that haughty fierceness which the martyrs of old are said to have possessed. But to a Genevan magistrate, whose mind was occupied by far other ideas than those of devotion and heroism, this elevation of mind had much the appearance of madness. He endeavoured to soothe me as a nurse does a child and reverted to my tale as the effects of delirium.

"Man," I cried, "how ignorant art thou in thy pride of wisdom! Cease; you know not what it is you say."

I broke from the house angry and disturbed and retired to meditate on some other mode of action.

CHAPTER 24

My present situation was one in which all voluntary thought was swallowed up and lost. I was hurried away by fury; revenge alone endowed me with strength and composure; it moulded my feelings and allowed me to be calculating and calm at periods when otherwise delirium or death would have been my portion.

My first resolution was to quit Geneva forever; my country, which, when I was happy and beloved, was dear to me, now, in my adversity, became hateful. I provided myself with a sum of money, together with a few jewels which had belonged to my mother, and departed. And now my wanderings began which are to cease but with life. I have traversed a vast portion of the earth and have endured all the hardships which travellers in deserts and barbarous countries are wont to meet. How I have lived I hardly know; many times have I stretched my failing limbs upon the sandy plain and prayed for death. But revenge kept me alive; I dared not die and leave my adversary in being.

When I quitted Geneva my first labour was to gain some clue by which I might trace the steps of my fiendish enemy. But my plan was unsettled, and I wandered many hours round the confines of the town, uncertain what path I should pursue. As night approached I found myself at the entrance of the cemetery where William, Elizabeth, and my father reposed. I entered it and approached the tomb which marked their graves. Everything was silent except the leaves of the trees, which were gently agitated by the wind; the night was nearly dark, and the scene would have been solemn and affecting even to an uninterested observer. The spirits of the departed seemed to flit around and to cast a shadow, which was felt but not seen, around the head of the mourner.

The deep grief which this scene had at first excited quickly gave way to rage and despair. They were dead, and I lived; their murderer also lived, and to destroy him I must drag out my weary existence. I knelt on the grass and kissed the earth and with quivering lips exclaimed, "By the sacred earth on which I kneel, by the shades that wander near me, by the deep and eternal grief that I feel, I swear; and by thee, O Night, and the spirits that preside over thee, to pursue the daemon who caused this misery, until he or I shall perish in mortal conflict.

For this purpose I will preserve my life; to execute this dear revenge will I again behold the sun and tread the green herbage of earth, which otherwise should vanish from my eyes forever. And I call on you, spirits of the dead, and on you, wandering ministers of vengeance, to aid and conduct me in my work. Let the cursed and hellish monster drink deep of agony; let him feel the despair that now torments me." I had begun my adjuration with solemnity and an awe which almost assured me that the shades of my murdered friends heard and approved my devotion, but the furies possessed me as I concluded, and rage choked my utterance.

I was answered through the stillness of night by a loud and fiendish laugh. It rang on my ears long and heavily; the mountains re-echoed it, and I felt as if all hell surrounded me with mockery and laughter. Surely in that moment I should have been possessed by frenzy and have destroyed my miserable existence but that my vow was heard and that I was reserved for vengeance. The laughter died away, when a well-known and abhorred voice, apparently close to my ear, addressed me in an audible whisper, "I am satisfied, miserable wretch! You have determined to live, and I am satisfied."

I darted towards the spot from which the sound proceeded, but the devil eluded my grasp. Suddenly the broad disk of the moon arose and shone full upon his ghastly and distorted shape as he fled with more than mortal speed.

I pursued him, and for many months this has been my task. Guided by a slight clue, I followed the windings of the Rhone, but vainly. The blue Mediterranean appeared, and by a strange chance, I saw the fiend enter by night and hide himself in a vessel bound for the Black Sea. I took my passage in the same ship, but he escaped, I know not how.

Amidst the wilds of Tartary and Russia, although he still evaded me, I have ever followed in his track. Sometimes the peasants, scared by this horrid apparition, informed me of his path; sometimes he himself, who feared that if I lost all trace of him I should despair and die, left some mark to guide me. The snows descended on my head, and I saw the print of his huge step on the white plain. To you first entering on life, to whom care is new and agony unknown, how can you understand what I have felt and still feel? Cold, want, and fatigue were the least pains which I was destined to endure; I was cursed by some devil and carried about with me my eternal hell; yet still a spirit of good followed and directed my steps and when I most murmured would suddenly extricate me from seemingly insurmountable difficulties.

Sometimes, when nature, overcome by hunger, sank under the exhaustion, a repast was prepared for me in the desert that restored and inspirited me. The fare was, indeed, coarse, such as the peasants of the country ate, but I will not doubt that it was set there by the spirits that I had invoked to aid me. Often, when all was dry, the heavens cloudless, and I was parched by thirst, a slight cloud would bedim the sky, shed the few drops that revived me, and vanish.

I followed, when I could, the courses of the rivers; but the daemon generally avoided these, as it was here that the population of the country chiefly collected. In other places human beings were seldom seen, and I generally subsisted on the wild animals that crossed my path. I had money with me and gained the friendship of the villagers by distributing it; or I brought with me some food that I had killed, which, after taking a small part, I always presented to those who had provided me with fire and utensils for cooking.

My life, as it passed thus, was indeed hateful to me, and it was during sleep alone that I could taste joy. O blessed sleep! Often, when most miserable, I sank to repose, and my dreams lulled me even to rapture. The spirits that guarded me had provided these moments, or rather hours, of happiness that I might retain strength to fulfil my pilgrimage. Deprived of this respite, I should have sunk under my hardships. During the day I was sustained and inspirited by the hope of night, for in sleep I saw my friends, my wife, and my beloved country; again I saw the benevolent countenance of my father, heard the silver tones of my Elizabeth's voice, and beheld Clerval enjoying health and youth.

Often, when wearied by a toilsome march, I persuaded myself that I was dreaming until night should come and that I should then enjoy reality in the arms of my dearest friends. What agonizing fondness did I feel for them! How did I cling to their dear forms, as sometimes they haunted even my waking hours, and persuade myself that they still lived! At such moments vengeance, that burned within me, died in my heart, and I pursued my path towards the destruction of the daemon more as a task enjoined by heaven, as the mechanical impulse of some power of which I was unconscious, than as the ardent desire of my soul.

What his feelings were whom I pursued I cannot know. Sometimes, indeed, he left marks in writing on the barks of the trees or cut in stone that guided me and instigated my fury. "My reign is not yet over"—these words were legible in one of these inscriptions—"you live, and my power is complete. Follow me; I seek the everlasting ices of the north, where you will feel the misery of cold and frost, to which I am impassive. You will find near this place, if you follow not too tardily, a dead hare; eat and be refreshed. Come on, my enemy; we have yet to wrestle for our lives, but many hard and miserable hours must you endure until that period shall arrive."

Scoffing devil! Again do I vow vengeance; again do I devote thee, miserable fiend, to torture and death. Never will I give up my search until he or I perish; and then with what ecstasy shall I join my Elizabeth and my departed friends, who even now prepare for me the reward of my tedious toil and horrible pilgrimage!

As I still pursued my journey to the northward, the snows thickened and the cold increased in a degree almost too severe to support. The peasants were shut up in their hovels, and only a few of the most hardy ventured forth to seize the animals whom starvation had forced from their hiding-places to seek for prey. The rivers were covered with ice, and no fish could be procured; and thus I was cut off from my chief article of maintenance. The triumph of my enemy increased with the difficulty of my labours. One inscription that he left was in these words: "Prepare! Your toils only begin; wrap yourself in furs and provide food, for we shall soon enter upon a journey where your sufferings will satisfy my everlasting hatred."

My courage and perseverance were invigorated by these scoffing words; I resolved not to fail in my purpose, and calling on heaven to support me, I continued with unabated fervour to traverse immense deserts, until the ocean appeared at a distance and formed the utmost boundary of the horizon. Oh! How unlike it was to the blue seasons of the south! Covered with ice, it was only to be distinguished from land by its superior wildness and ruggedness. The Greeks wept for joy when they beheld the Mediterranean from the hills of Asia, and hailed with rapture the boundary of their toils. I did not weep, but I knelt down and with a full heart thanked my guiding spirit for conducting me in safety to the place where I hoped, notwithstanding my adversary's gibe, to meet and grapple with him.

Some weeks before this period I had procured a sledge and dogs and thus traversed the snows with inconceivable speed. I know not whether the fiend possessed the same advantages, but I found that, as before I had daily lost ground in the pursuit, I now gained on him, so much so that when I first saw the ocean he was but one day's journey in advance, and I hoped to intercept him before he should reach the beach. With new courage, therefore, I pressed on, and in two days arrived at a wretched hamlet on the seashore. I inquired of the inhabitants concerning the fiend and gained accurate information.

A gigantic monster, they said, had arrived the night before, armed with a gun and many pistols, putting to flight the inhabitants of a solitary cottage through fear of his terrific appearance. He had carried off their store of winter food, and placing it in a sledge, to draw which he had seized on a numerous drove of trained dogs, he had harnessed them, and the same night, to the joy of the horror-struck villagers, had pursued his journey across the sea in a direction that led to no land; and they conjectured that he must speedily be destroyed by the breaking of the ice or frozen by the eternal frosts.

On hearing this information I suffered a temporary access of despair. He had escaped me, and I must commence a destructive and almost endless journey across the mountainous ices of the ocean, amidst cold that few of the inhabitants could long endure and which I, the native of a genial and sunny climate, could not hope to survive. Yet at the idea that the fiend should live and be triumphant, my rage and vengeance returned, and like a mighty tide, overwhelmed every other feeling. After a slight repose, during which the spirits of the dead hovered round and instigated me to toil and revenge, I prepared for my journey. I exchanged my land-sledge for one fashioned for the inequalities of the frozen ocean, and purchasing a plentiful stock of provisions, I departed from land.

I cannot guess how many days have passed since then, but I have endured misery which nothing but the eternal sentiment of a just retribution burning within my heart could have enabled me to support. Immense and rugged mountains of ice often barred up my passage, and I often heard the thunder of the ground sea, which threatened my destruction. But again the frost came and made the paths of the sea secure.

By the quantity of provision which I had consumed, I should guess that I had passed three weeks in this journey; and the continual protraction of hope, returning back upon the heart, often wrung bitter drops of despondency and grief from my eyes. Despair had indeed almost secured her prey, and I should soon have sunk beneath this misery. Once, after the poor animals that conveyed me had with incredible toil gained the summit of a sloping ice mountain, and one, sinking under his fatigue, died, I viewed the expanse before me with anguish, when suddenly my eye caught a dark speck upon the dusky plain.

I strained my sight to discover what it could be and uttered a wild cry of ecstasy when I distinguished a sledge and the distorted proportions of a well-known form within. Oh! With what a burning gush did hope revisit my heart! Warm tears filled my eyes, which I hastily wiped away, that they might not intercept the view I had of the daemon; but still my sight was dimmed by the burning drops, until, giving way to the emotions that oppressed me, I wept aloud.

But this was not the time for delay; I disencumbered the dogs of their dead companion, gave them a plentiful portion of food, and after an hour's rest, which was absolutely necessary, and yet which was bitterly irksome to me, I continued my route. The sledge was still visible, nor did I again lose sight of it except at the moments when for a short time some ice-rock concealed it with its intervening crags. I indeed perceptibly gained on it, and when, after nearly two days' journey, I beheld my enemy at no more than a mile distant, my heart bounded within me.

But now, when I appeared almost within grasp of my foe, my hopes were suddenly extinguished, and I lost all trace of him more utterly than I had ever done before. A ground sea was heard; the thunder of its progress, as the waters rolled and swelled beneath me, became every moment more ominous and terrific. I pressed on, but in vain. The wind arose; the sea roared; and, as with the mighty shock of an earthquake, it split and cracked with a tremendous and overwhelming sound. The work was soon finished; in a few minutes a tumultuous sea rolled between me and my enemy, and I was left drifting on a scattered piece of ice that was continually lessening and thus preparing for me a hideous death. In this manner many appalling hours passed; several of my dogs died, and I myself was about to sink under the accumulation of distress when I saw your vessel riding at anchor and holding forth to me hopes of succour and life.

I had no conception that vessels ever came so far north and was astounded at the sight. I quickly destroyed part of my sledge to construct oars, and by these means was enabled, with infinite fatigue, to move my ice raft in the direction of your ship. I had determined, if you were going southwards, still to trust myself to the mercy of the seas rather than abandon my purpose. I hoped to induce you to grant me a boat with which I could pursue my enemy. But your direction was northwards. You took me on board when my vigour was exhausted, and I should soon have sunk under my multiplied hardships into a death which I still dread, for my task is unfulfilled.

Oh! When will my guiding spirit, in conducting me to the daemon, allow me the rest I so much desire; or must I die, and he yet live? If I do, swear to me, Walton, that he shall not escape, that you will seek him and satisfy my vengeance in his death. And do I dare to ask of you to undertake my pilgrimage, to endure the hardships that I have undergone? No; I am not so selfish. Yet, when I am dead, if he should appear, if the ministers of vengeance should conduct him to you, swear that he shall not live—swear that he shall not triumph over my accumulated woes and survive to add to the list of his dark crimes. He is eloquent and persuasive, and once his words had even power over my heart; but trust him not. His soul is as hellish as his form, full of treachery and fiendlike malice. Hear him not; call on the names of William, Justine, Clerval, Elizabeth, my father, and of the wretched Victor, and thrust your sword into his heart. I will hover near and direct the steel aright.

Walton, in continuation.

August 26th, 17—

You have read this strange and terrific story, Margaret; and do you not feel your blood congeal with horror, like that which even now curdles mine? Sometimes, seized with sudden agony, he could not continue his tale; at others, his voice broken, yet piercing, uttered with difficulty the words so replete with anguish. His fine and lovely eyes were now lighted up with indignation, now subdued to downcast sorrow and quenched in infinite wretchedness. Sometimes he commanded his countenance and tones and related the most horrible incidents with a tranquil voice, suppressing every mark of agitation; then, like a volcano bursting forth, his face would suddenly change to an expression of the wildest rage as he shrieked out imprecations on his persecutor.

His tale is connected and told with an appearance of the simplest truth, yet I own to you that the letters of Felix and Safie, which he showed me, and the apparition of the monster seen from our ship, brought to me a greater conviction of the truth of his narrative than his asseverations, however earnest and connected. Such a monster has, then, really existence! I cannot doubt it, yet I am lost in surprise and admiration. Sometimes I endeavoured to gain from Frankenstein the particulars of his creature's formation, but on this point he was impenetrable. "Are you mad, my friend?" said he. "Or whither does your senseless curiosity lead you? Would you also create for yourself and the world a demoniacal enemy? Peace, peace! Learn my miseries and do not seek to increase your own."

Frankenstein discovered that I made notes concerning his history; he asked to see them and then himself corrected and augmented them in many places, but principally in giving the life and spirit to the conversations he held with his enemy. "Since you have preserved my narration," said he, "I would not that a mutilated one should go down to posterity."

Thus has a week passed away, while I have listened to the strangest tale that ever imagination formed. My thoughts and every feeling of my soul have been drunk up by the interest for my guest which this tale and his own elevated and gentle manners have created. I wish to soothe him, yet can I counsel one so infinitely miserable, so destitute of every hope of consolation, to live? Oh, no! The only joy that he can now know will be when he composes his shattered spirit to peace and death.

Yet he enjoys one comfort, the offspring of solitude and delirium; he believes that when in dreams he holds converse with his friends and derives from that communion consolation for his miseries or excitements to his vengeance, that they are not the creations of his fancy, but the beings themselves who visit him from the regions of a remote world. This faith gives a solemnity to his reveries that render them to me almost as imposing and interesting as truth.

Our conversations are not always confined to his own history and misfortunes. On every point of general literature he displays unbounded knowledge and a quick and piercing apprehension. His eloquence is forcible and touching; nor can I hear him, when he relates a pathetic incident or endeavours to move the passions of pity or love, without tears. What a glorious creature must he have been in the days of his prosperity, when he is thus noble and godlike in ruin! He seems to feel his own worth and the greatness of his fall.

"When younger," said he, "I believed myself destined for some great enterprise. My feelings are profound, but I possessed a coolness of judgment that fitted me for illustrious achievements. This sentiment of the worth of my nature supported me when others would have been oppressed, for I deemed it criminal to throw away in useless grief those talents that might be useful to my fellow creatures. When I reflected on the work I had completed, no less a one than the creation of a sensitive and rational animal, I could not rank myself with the herd of common projectors. But this thought, which supported me in the commencement of my career, now serves only to plunge me lower in the dust.

All my speculations and hopes are as nothing, and like the archangel who aspired to omnipotence, I am chained in an eternal hell. My imagination was vivid, yet my powers of analysis and application were intense; by the union of these qualities I conceived the idea and executed the creation of a man. Even now I cannot recollect without passion my reveries while the work was incomplete. I trod heaven in my thoughts, now exulting in my powers, now burning with the idea of their effects. From my infancy I was imbued with high hopes and a lofty ambition; but how am I sunk! Oh! My friend, if you had known me as I once was, you would not recognize me in this state of degradation.

Despondency rarely visited my heart; a high destiny seemed to bear me on, until I fell, never, never again to rise." Must I then lose this admirable being? I have longed for a friend; I have sought one who would sympathize with and love me. Behold, on these desert seas I have found such a one, but I fear I have gained him only to know his value and lose him. I would reconcile him to life, but he repulses the idea.

"I thank you, Walton," he said, "for your kind intentions towards so miserable a wretch; but when you speak of new ties and fresh affections, think you that any can replace those who are gone? Can any man be to me as Clerval was, or any woman another Elizabeth? Even where the affections are not strongly moved by any superior excellence, the companions of our childhood always possess a certain power over our minds which hardly any later friend can obtain. They know our infantine dispositions, which, however they may be afterwards modified, are never eradicated; and they can judge of our actions with more certain conclusions as to the integrity of our motives.

"A sister or a brother can never, unless indeed such symptoms have been shown early, suspect the other of fraud or false dealing, when another friend, however strongly he may be attached, may, in spite of himself, be contemplated with suspicion. But I enjoyed friends, dear not only through habit and association, but from their own merits; and wherever I am, the soothing voice of my Elizabeth and the conversation of Clerval will be ever whispered in my ear. They are dead, and but one feeling in such a solitude can persuade me to preserve my life. If I were engaged in any high undertaking or design, fraught with extensive utility to my fellow creatures, then could I live to fulfil it. But such is not my destiny; I must pursue and destroy the being to whom I gave existence; then my lot on earth will be fulfilled and I may die."

My beloved Sister,   September 2nd
I write to you, encompassed by peril and ignorant whether I am ever doomed to see again dear England and the dearer friends that inhabit it. I am surrounded by mountains of ice which admit of no escape and threaten every moment to crush my vessel. The brave fellows whom I have persuaded to be my companions look towards me for aid, but I have none to bestow. There is something terribly appalling in our situation, yet my courage and hopes do not desert me. Yet it is terrible to reflect that the lives of all these men are endangered through me. If we are lost, my mad schemes are the cause.

And what, Margaret, will be the state of your mind? You will not hear of my destruction, and you will anxiously await my return. Years will pass, and you will have visitings of despair and yet be tortured by hope. Oh! My beloved sister, the sickening failing of your heart-felt expectations is, in prospect, more terrible to me than my own death. But you have a husband and lovely children; you may be happy. Heaven bless you and make you so!

My unfortunate guest regards me with the tenderest compassion. He endeavours to fill me with hope and talks as if life were a possession which he valued. He reminds me how often the same accidents have happened to other navigators who have attempted this sea, and in spite of myself, he fills me with cheerful auguries. Even the sailors feel the power of his eloquence; when he speaks, they no longer despair; he rouses their energies, and while they hear his voice they believe these vast mountains of ice are molehills which will vanish before the resolutions of man. These feelings are transitory; each day of expectation delayed fills them with fear, and I almost dread a mutiny caused by this despair.

September 5th

A scene has just passed of such uncommon interest that, although it is highly probable that these papers may never reach you, yet I cannot forbear recording it.

We are still surrounded by mountains of ice, still in imminent danger of being crushed in their conflict. The cold is excessive, and many of my unfortunate comrades have already found a grave amidst this scene of desolation. Frankenstein has daily declined in health; a feverish fire still glimmers in his eyes, but he is exhausted, and when suddenly roused to any exertion, he speedily sinks again into apparent lifelessness.

I mentioned in my last letter the fears I entertained of a mutiny. This morning, as I sat watching the wan countenance of my friend—his eyes half closed and his limbs hanging listlessly—I was roused by half a dozen of the sailors, who demanded admission into the cabin. They entered, and their leader addressed me. He told me that he and his companions had been chosen by the other sailors to come in deputation to me to make me a requisition which, in justice, I could not refuse.

We were immured in ice and should probably never escape, but they feared that if, as was possible, the ice should dissipate and a free passage be opened, I should be rash enough to continue my voyage and lead them into fresh dangers, after they might happily have surmounted this. They insisted, therefore, that I should engage with a solemn promise that if the vessel should be freed I would instantly direct my course southwards.

This speech troubled me. I had not despaired, nor had I yet conceived the idea of returning if set free. Yet could I, in justice, or even in possibility, refuse this demand? I hesitated before I answered, when Frankenstein, who had at first been silent, and indeed appeared hardly to have force enough to attend, now roused himself; his eyes sparkled, and his cheeks flushed with momentary vigour. Turning towards the men, he said,:

"What do you mean? What do you demand of your captain? Are you, then, so easily turned from your design? Did you not call this a glorious expedition? And wherefore was it glorious? Not because the way was smooth and placid as a southern sea, but because it was full of dangers and terror, because at every new incident your fortitude was to be called forth and your courage exhibited, because danger and death surrounded it, and these you were to brave and overcome. For this was it a glorious, for this was it an honourable undertaking. You were hereafter to be hailed as the benefactors of your species, your names adored as belonging to brave men who encountered death for honour and the benefit of mankind.

"And now, behold, with the first imagination of danger, or, if you will, the first mighty and terrific trial of your courage, you shrink away and are content to be handed down as men who had not strength enough to endure cold and peril; and so, poor souls, they were chilly and returned to their warm firesides. Why, that requires not this preparation; ye need not have come thus far and dragged your captain to the shame of a defeat merely to prove yourselves cowards. Oh! Be men, or be more than men. Be steady to your purposes and firm as a rock. This ice is not made of such stuff as your hearts may be; it is mutable and cannot withstand you if you say that it shall not. Do not return to your families with the stigma of disgrace marked on your brows. Return as heroes who have fought and conquered and who know not what it is to turn their backs on the foe."

He spoke this with a voice so modulated to the different feelings expressed in his speech, with an eye so full of lofty design and heroism, that can you wonder that these men were moved? They looked at one another and were unable to reply. I spoke; I told them to retire and consider of what had been said, that I would not lead them farther north if they strenuously desired the contrary, but that I hoped that, with reflection, their courage would return. They retired and I turned towards my friend, but he was sunk in languor and almost deprived of life.

How all this will terminate, I know not, but I had rather die than return shamefully, my purpose unfulfilled. Yet I fear such will be my fate; the men, unsupported by ideas of glory and honour, can never willingly continue to endure their present hardships.

September 7th

The die is cast; I have consented to return if we are not destroyed. Thus are my hopes blasted by cowardice and indecision; I come back ignorant and disappointed. It requires more philosophy than I possess to bear this injustice with patience.

September 12th

It is past; I am returning to England. I have lost my hopes of utility and glory; I have lost my friend. But I will endeavour to detail these bitter circumstances to you, my dear sister; and while I am wafted towards England and towards you, I will not despond.

September 9th, the ice began to move, and roarings like thunder were heard at a distance as the islands split and cracked in every direction. We were in the most imminent peril, but as we could only remain passive, my chief attention was occupied by my unfortunate guest whose illness increased in such a degree that he was entirely confined to his bed. The ice cracked behind us and was driven with force towards the north; a breeze sprang from the west, and on the 11th the passage towards the south became perfectly free. When the sailors saw this and that their return to their native country was apparently assured, a shout of tumultuous joy broke from them, loud and long-continued. Frankenstein, who was dozing, awoke and asked the cause of the tumult. "They shout," I said, "because they will soon return to England."

"Do you, then, really return?"

"Alas! Yes; I cannot withstand their demands. I cannot lead them unwillingly to danger, and I must return."

"Do so, if you will; but I will not. You may give up your purpose, but mine is assigned to me by heaven, and I dare not. I am weak, but surely the spirits who assist my vengeance will endow me with sufficient strength." Saying this, he endeavoured to spring from the bed, but the exertion was too great for him; he fell back and fainted.

It was long before he was restored, and I often thought that life was entirely extinct. At length he opened his eyes; he breathed with difficulty and was unable to speak. The surgeon gave him a composing draught and ordered us to leave him undisturbed. In the meantime he told me that my friend had certainly not many hours to live.

His sentence was pronounced, and I could only grieve and be patient. I sat by his bed, watching him; his eyes were closed, and I thought he slept; but presently he called to me in a feeble voice, and bidding me come near, said,

"Alas! The strength I relied on is gone; I feel that I shall soon die, and he, my enemy and persecutor, may still be in being. Think not, Walton, that in the last moments of my existence I feel that burning hatred and ardent desire of revenge I once expressed; but I feel myself justified in desiring the death of my adversary. During these last days I have been occupied in examining my past conduct; nor do I find it blameable. In a fit of enthusiastic madness I created a rational creature and was bound towards him to assure, as far as was in my power, his happiness and well-being.

This was my duty, but there was another still paramount to that. My duties towards the beings of my own species had greater claims to my attention because they included a greater proportion of happiness or misery. Urged by this view, I refused, and I did right in refusing, to create a companion for the first creature. He showed unparalleled malignity and selfishness in evil; he destroyed my friends; he devoted to destruction beings who possessed exquisite sensations, happiness, and wisdom; nor do I know where this thirst for vengeance may end. Miserable himself that he may render no other wretched, he ought to die. The task of his destruction was mine, but I have failed. When actuated by selfish and vicious motives, I asked you to undertake my unfinished work, and I renew this request now, when I am only induced by reason and virtue.

"Yet I cannot ask you to renounce your country and friends to fulfil this task; and now that you are returning to England, you will have little chance of meeting with him. But the consideration of these points, and the well balancing of what you may esteem your duties, I leave to you; my judgment and ideas are already disturbed by the near approach of death. I dare not ask you to do what I think right, for I may still be misled by passion.

"That he should live to be an instrument of mischief disturbs me; in other respects, this hour, when I momentarily expect my release, is the only happy one which I have enjoyed for several years. The forms of the beloved dead flit before me, and I hasten to their arms. Farewell, Walton! Seek happiness in tranquillity and avoid ambition, even if it be only the apparently innocent one of distinguishing yourself in science and discoveries. Yet why do I say this? I have myself been blasted in these hopes, yet another may succeed."

His voice became fainter as he spoke, and at length, exhausted by his effort, he sank into silence. About half an hour afterwards he attempted again to speak but was unable; he pressed my hand feebly, and his eyes closed forever, while the irradiation of a gentle smile passed away from his lips.

Margaret, what comment can I make on the untimely extinction of this glorious spirit? What can I say that will enable you to understand the depth of my sorrow? All that I should express would be inadequate and feeble. My tears flow; my mind is overshadowed by a cloud of disappointment. But I journey towards England, and I may there find consolation.

I am interrupted. What do these sounds portend? It is midnight; the breeze blows fairly, and the watch on deck scarcely stir. Again there is a sound as of a human voice, but hoarser; it comes from the cabin where the remains of Frankenstein still lie. I must arise and examine. Goodnight, my sister.

Great God! what a scene has just taken place! I am yet dizzy with the remembrance of it. I hardly know whether I shall have the power to detail it; yet the tale which I have recorded would be incomplete without this final and wonderful catastrophe. I entered the cabin where lay the remains of my ill-fated and admirable friend. Over him hung a form which I cannot find words to describe—gigantic in stature, yet uncouth and distorted in its proportions. As he hung over the coffin, his face was concealed by long locks of ragged hair; but one vast hand was extended, in colour and apparent texture like that of a mummy. When he heard the sound of my approach, he ceased to utter exclamations of grief and horror and sprung towards the window. Never did I behold a vision so horrible as his face, of such loathsome yet appalling hideousness. I shut my eyes involuntarily and endeavoured to recollect what were my duties with regard to this destroyer. I called on him to stay.

He paused, looking on me with wonder, and again turning towards the lifeless form of his creator, he seemed to forget my presence, and every feature and gesture seemed instigated by the wildest rage of some uncontrollable passion.

"That is also my victim!" he exclaimed. "In his murder my crimes are consummated; the miserable series of my being is wound to its close! Oh, Frankenstein! Generous and self-devoted being! What does it avail that I now ask thee to pardon me? I, who irretrievably destroyed thee by destroying all thou lovedst. Alas! He is cold, he cannot answer me." His voice seemed suffocated, and my first impulses, which had suggested to me the duty of obeying the dying request of my friend in destroying his enemy, were now suspended by a mixture of curiosity and compassion. I approached this tremendous being; I dared not again raise my eyes to his face, there was something so scaring and unearthly in his ugliness. I attempted to speak, but the words died away on my lips. The monster continued to utter wild and incoherent self-reproaches. At length I gathered resolution to address him in a pause of the tempest of his passion.

"Your repentance," I said, "is now superfluous. If you had listened to the voice of conscience and heeded the stings of remorse before you had urged your diabolical vengeance to this extremity, Frankenstein would yet have lived."

"And do you dream?" said the daemon. "Do you think

that I was then dead to agony and remorse? He," he continued, pointing to the corpse, "he suffered not in the consummation of the deed. Oh! Not the ten-thousandth portion of the anguish that was mine during the lingering detail of its execution. A frightful selfishness hurried me on, while my heart was poisoned with remorse. Think you that the groans of Clerval were music to my ears? My heart was fashioned to be susceptible of love and sympathy, and when wrenched by misery to vice and hatred, it did not endure the violence of the change without torture such as you cannot even imagine.

"After the murder of Clerval I returned to Switzerland, heart-broken and overcome. I pitied Frankenstein; my pity amounted to horror; I abhorred myself. But when I discovered that he, the author at once of my existence and of its unspeakable torments, dared to hope for happiness, that while he accumulated wretchedness and despair upon me he sought his own enjoyment in feelings and passions from the indulgence of which I was forever barred, then impotent envy and bitter indignation filled me with an insatiable thirst for vengeance.

"I recollected my threat and resolved that it should be accomplished. I knew that I was preparing for myself a deadly torture, but I was the slave, not the master, of an impulse which I detested yet could not disobey. Yet when she died! Nay, then I was not miserable. I had cast off all feeling, subdued all anguish, to riot in the excess of my despair. Evil thenceforth became my good. Urged thus far, I had no choice but to adapt my nature to an element which I had willingly chosen. The completion of my demoniacal design became an insatiable passion. And now it is ended; there is my last victim!"

I was at first touched by the expressions of his misery; yet, when I called to mind what Frankenstein had said of his powers of eloquence and persuasion, and when I again cast my eyes on the lifeless form of my friend, indignation was rekindled within me. "Wretch!" I said. "It is well that you come here to whine over the desolation that you have made. You throw a torch into a pile of buildings, and when they are consumed, you sit among the ruins and lament the fall. Hypocritical fiend! If he whom you mourn still lived, still would he be the object, again would he become the prey, of your accursed vengeance. It is not pity that you feel; you lament only because the victim of your malignity is withdrawn from your power."

"Oh, it is not thus—not thus," interrupted the being. "Yet such must be the impression conveyed to you by what appears to be the purport of my actions. Yet I seek not a fellow feeling in my misery. No sympathy may I ever find. When I first sought it, it was the love of virtue, the feelings of happiness and affection with which my whole being overflowed, that I wished to be participated. But now that virtue has become to me a shadow, and that happiness and affection are turned into bitter and loathing despair, in what should I seek for sympathy? I am content to suffer alone while my sufferings shall endure; when I die, I am well satisfied that abhorrence and opprobrium should load my memory.

"Once my fancy was soothed with dreams of virtue, of fame, and of enjoyment. Once I falsely hoped to meet with beings who, pardoning my outward form, would love me for the excellent qualities which I was capable of unfolding. I was nourished with high thoughts of honour and devotion. But now crime has degraded me beneath the meanest animal. No guilt, no mischief, no malignity, no misery, can be found comparable to mine. When I run over the frightful catalogue of my sins, I cannot believe that I am the same creature whose thoughts were once filled with sublime and transcendent visions of the beauty and the majesty of goodness. But it is even so; the fallen angel becomes a malignant devil. Yet even that enemy of God and man had friends and associates in his desolation;

I am alone.

"You, who call Frankenstein your friend, seem to have a knowledge of my crimes and his misfortunes. But in the detail which he gave you of them he could not sum up the hours and months of misery which I endured wasting in impotent passions. For while I destroyed his hopes, I did not satisfy my own desires. They were forever ardent and craving; still I desired love and fellowship, and I was still spurned. Was there no injustice in this? Am I to be thought the only criminal, when all humankind sinned against me? Why do you not hate Felix, who drove his friend from his door with contumely? Why do you not execrate the rustic who sought to destroy the saviour of his child? Nay, these are virtuous and immaculate beings! I, the miserable and the abandoned, am an abortion, to be spurned at, and kicked, and trampled on. Even now my blood boils at the recollection of this injustice.

"But it is true that I am a wretch. I have murdered the lovely and the helpless; I have strangled the innocent as they slept and grasped to death his throat who never injured me or any other living thing. I have devoted my creator, the select specimen of all that is worthy of love and admiration among men, to misery; I have pursued him even to that irremediable ruin. There he lies, white and cold in death. You hate me, but your abhorrence cannot equal that with which I regard myself. I look on the hands which executed the deed; I think on the heart in which the imagination of it was conceived and long for the moment when these hands will meet my eyes, when that imagination will haunt my thoughts no more.

"Fear not that I shall be the instrument of future mischief. My work is nearly complete. Neither yours nor any man's death is needed to consummate the series of my being and accomplish that which must be done, but it requires my own. Do not think that I shall be slow to perform this sacrifice. I shall quit your vessel on the ice raft which brought me thither and shall seek the most northern extremity of the globe; I shall collect my funeral pile and consume to ashes this miserable frame, that its remains may afford no light to any curious and unhallowed wretch who would create such another as I have been. I shall die. I shall no longer feel the agonies which now consume me or be the prey of feelings unsatisfied, yet unquenched. He is dead who called me into being; and when I shall be no more, the very remembrance of us both will speedily vanish. I shall no longer see the sun or stars or feel the winds play on my cheeks.

"Light, feeling, and sense will pass away; and in this condition must I find my happiness. Some years ago, when the images which this world affords first opened upon me, when I felt the cheering warmth of summer and heard the rustling of the leaves and the warbling of the birds, and these were all to me, I should have wept to die; now it is my only consolation. Polluted by crimes and torn by the bitterest remorse, where can I find rest but in death?

"Farewell! I leave you, and in you the last of humankind whom these eyes will ever behold. Farewell, Frankenstein! If thou wert yet alive and yet cherished a desire of revenge against me, it would be better satiated in my life than in my destruction. But it was not so; thou didst seek my extinction, that I might not cause greater wretchedness; and if yet, in some mode unknown to me, thou hadst not ceased to think and feel, thou wouldst not desire against me a vengeance greater than that which I feel. Blasted as thou wert, my agony was still superior to thine, for the bitter sting of remorse will not cease to rankle in my wounds until death shall close them forever.

"But soon," he cried with sad and solemn enthusiasm, "I shall die, and what I now feel be no longer felt. Soon these burning miseries will be extinct. I shall ascend my funeral pile triumphantly and exult in the agony of the torturing flames. The light of that conflagration will fade away; my ashes will be swept into the sea by the winds. My spirit will sleep in peace, or if it thinks, it will not surely think thus. Farewell."

He sprang from the cabin window as he said this, upon the ice raft which lay close to the vessel. He was soon borne away by the waves and lost in darkness and distance.

The Dream

The time of the occurrence of the little legend about to be narrated, was that of the commencement of the reign of Henry IV of France, whose accession and conversion, while they brought peace to the kingdom whose throne he ascended, were inadequate to heal the deep wounds mutually inflicted by the inimical parties. Private feuds, and the memory of mortal injuries, existed between those now apparently united; and often did the hands that had clasped each other in seeming friendly greeting, involuntarily, as the grasp was released, clasp the dagger's hilt, as fitter spokesman to their passions than the words of courtesy that had just fallen from their lips. Many of the fiercer Catholics retreated to their distant provinces; and while they concealed in solitude their rankling discontent, not less keenly did they long for the day when they might show it openly.

In a large and fortified *chateau* built on a rugged steep overlooking the Loire, not far from the town of Nantes, dwelt the last of her race, and the heiress of their fortunes, the young and beautiful Countess de Villeneuve. She had spent the preceding year in complete solitude in her secluded abode; and the mourning she wore for a father and two brothers, the victims of the civil wars, was a graceful and good reason why she did not appear at court, and mingle with its festivities. But the orphan countess inherited a high name and broad lands; and it was soon signified to her that the king, her guardian, desired that she should bestow them, together with her hand, upon some noble whose birth and accomplishments should entitle him to the gift.

Constance, in reply, expressed her intention of taking vows, and retiring to a convent.

The king earnestly and resolutely forbade this act, believing such an idea to be the result of sensibility overwrought by sorrow, and relying on the hope that, after a time, the genial spirit of youth would break through this cloud.

A year passed, and still the countess persisted; and at last Henry, unwilling, to exercise compulsion,—desirous, too, of judging for himself of the motives that led one so beautiful, young, and gifted with fortune's favours, to desire to bury herself in a cloister,—announced his intention, now that the period of her mourning was expired, of visiting her *chateau*; and if he brought not with him, the monarch said, inducement sufficient to change her design, he would yield his consent to its fulfilment.

Many a sad hour had Constance passed—many a day of tears, and many a night of restless misery. She had closed her gates against every visitant; and, like the Lady Olivia in *Twelfth Night*, vowed herself to loneliness and weeping. Mistress of herself, she easily silenced the entreaties and remonstrances of underlings, and nursed her grief as it had been the thing she loved. Yet it was too keen, too bitter, too burning, to be a favoured guest. In fact, Constance, young, ardent, and vivacious, battled with it, struggled and longed to cast it off; but all that was joyful in itself, or fair in outward show, only served to renew it; and she could best support the burden of her sorrow with patience, when, yielding to it, it oppressed but did not torture her.

Constance had left the castle to wander in the neighbouring grounds. Lofty and extensive as were the apartments of her abode, she felt pent up within their walls, beneath their fretted roofs. The spreading uplands and the antique wood, associated to her with every dear recollection of her past life, enticed her to spend hours and days beneath their leafy coverts. The motion and change eternally working, as the wind stirred among the boughs, or the journeying sun rained its beams through them, soothed and called her out of that dull sorrow which clutched her heart with so unrelenting a pang beneath her castle roof.

There was one spot on the verge of the well-wooded park, one nook of ground, whence she could discern the country extended beyond, yet which was in itself thick set with tall umbrageous trees—a spot which she had forsworn, yet whither unconsciously her steps for ever tended, and where again for the twentieth time that day, she had unaware found herself. She sat upon a grassy mound, and looked wistfully on the flowers she had herself planted to adorn the verdurous recess—to her the temple of memory and love. She held the letter from the king which was the parent to her of so much despair. Dejection sat upon her features, and her gentle heart asked fate why, so young, unprotected, and forsaken, she should have to struggle with this new form of wretchedness.

'I but ask,' she thought, 'to live in my father's halls—in the spot familiar to my infancy—to water with my frequent tears the graves of those I loved; and here in these woods, where such a mad dream of happiness was mine, to celebrate forever the obsequies of Hope!'

A rustling among the boughs now met her ear—her heart beat quick—all again was still.

'Foolish girl!' she half muttered; 'dupe of thine own passionate fancy: because here we met; because seated here I have expected, and sounds like these have announced, his dear approach; so now every coney as it stirs, and every bird as it awakens silence, speaks of him. O Gaspar!—mine once—never again will this beloved spot be made glad by thee—never more!'

Again the bushes were stirred, and footsteps were heard in the brake. She rose; her heart beat high; it must be that silly Manon, with her impertinent entreaties for her to return. But the steps were firmer and slower than would be those of her waiting-woman; and now emerging from the shade, she too plainly discerned the intruder. He first impulse was to fly: but once again to see him—to hear his voice:—once again before she placed eternal vows between them, to stand together, and find the wide chasm filled which absence had made, could not injure the dead, and would soften the fatal sorrow that made her cheek so pale.

And now he was before, her, the same beloved one with whom she had exchanged vows of constancy. He, like her, seemed sad; nor could she resist the imploring glance that entreated her for one moment to remain.

'I come, lady,' said the young knight, 'without a hope to bend your inflexible will. I come but once again to see you, and to bid you farewell before I depart for the Holy Land. I come to beseech you not to immure yourself in the dark cloister to avoid one as hateful as myself,—one you will never see more. Whether I die or live, France and I are parted forever!'

'That were fearful, were it true,' said Constance; 'but King Henry will never so lose his favourite cavalier. The throne you helped to build, you still will guard. Nay, as I ever had power over thought of thine, go not to Palestine.'

'One word of yours could detain me—one smile—Constance'—and the youthful lover knelt before her; but her harsher purpose was recalled by the image once so dear and familiar, now so strange and so forbidden.

'Linger no longer here!' she cried. 'No smile, no word of mine will ever again be yours. Why are you here—here, where the spirits of the dead wander, and claiming these shades as their own, curse the false girl who permits their murderer to disturb their sacred repose?'

'When love was young and you were kind,' replied the knight, 'you taught me to thread the intricacies of these woods you welcomed me to this dear spot, where once you vowed to be my own—even beneath these ancient trees.'

'A wicked sin it was,' said Constance, 'to unbar my father's doors to the son of his enemy, and dearly is it punished!'

The young knight gained courage as she spoke; yet he dared not move, lest she, who, every instant, appeared ready to take flight, should be startled from her momentary tranquillity, but he slowly replied:—'Those were happy days, Constance, full of terror and deep joy, when evening brought me to your feet; and while hate and vengeance were as its atmosphere to yonder frowning castle, this leafy, starlit bower was the shrine of love.'

'*Happy?*—miserable days!' echoed Constance; 'when I imagined good could arise from failing in my duty, and that disobedience would be rewarded of God. Speak not of love, Gaspar!—a sea of blood divides us forever! Approach me not! The dead and the beloved stand even now between us: their pale shadows warn me of my fault, and menace me for listening to their murderer.'

'That am not I!' exclaimed the youth. 'Behold, Constance, we are each the last of our race. Death has dealt cruelly with us, and we are alone. It was not so when first we loved—when parent, kinsman, brother, nay, my own mother breathed curses on the house of Villeneuve; and in spite of all I blessed it. I saw thee, my lovely one, and blessed it. The God of peace planted love in our hearts, and with mystery and secrecy we met during many a summer night in the moonlit dells; and when daylight was abroad, in this sweet recess we fled to avoid its scrutiny, and here, even here, where now I kneel in supplication, we both knelt and made our vows. Shall they be broken?'

Constance wept as her lover recalled the images of happy hours. 'Never,' she exclaimed, 'O never! Thou knowest, or wilt soon know, Gaspar, the faith and resolves of one who dare not be yours. Was it for us to talk of love and happiness, when war, and hate, and blood were raging around! The fleeting flowers our young hands strewed were trampled by the deadly encounter of mortal foes. By your father's hand mine died; and little boots it to know whether, as my brother swore, and you deny, your hand did or did not deal the blow that destroyed him. You fought among those by whom he died. Say no more—no other word: it is impiety towards the unreposing dead to hear you. Go, Gaspar; forget me. Under the chivalrous and gallant Henry your career may be glorious; and some fair girl will listen, as once I did, to your vows, and be made happy by them. Farewell! May the Virgin bless you! In my cell and cloister-home I will not forget the best Christian lesson—to pray for our enemies. Gaspar, farewell!'

She glided hastily from the bower: with swift steps she threaded the glade and sought the castle. Once within the seclusion of her own apartment she gave way to the burst of grief that tore her gentle bosom like a tempest; for hers was that worst sorrow, which taints past joys, making wait upon the memory of bliss, and linking love and fancied guilt in such fearful society as that of the tyrant when he bound a living body to a corpse. Suddenly a thought darted into her mind. At first she rejected it as puerile and superstitious; but it would not be driven away. She called hastily for her attendant. 'Manon,' she said, 'didst thou ever sleep on St Catherine's couch?'

Manon crossed herself. 'Heaven forefend! None ever did, since I was born, but two: one fell into the Loire and was drowned; the other only looked upon the narrow bed, and turned to her own home without a word. It is an awful place; and if the votary have not led a pious and good life, woe betide the hour when she rests her head on the holy stone!'

Constance crossed herself also. 'As for our lives, it is only through our Lord and the blessed saints that we can any of us hope for righteousness. I will sleep on that couch tomorrow night!'

'Dear, my lady! and the king arrives tomorrow.'

'The more need that I resolve. It cannot be that misery so intense should dwell in any heart, and no cure be found. I had hoped to be the bringer of peace to our houses; and if the good work to be for me a crown of thorns Heaven shall direct me. I will rest tomorrow night on St Catherine's bed: and if, as I have heard, the saint deigns to direct her votaries in dreams, I will be guided by her; and, believing that I act according to the dictates of Heaven, I shall feel resigned even to the worst.'

The king was on his way to Nantes from Paris, and he slept on this night at a castle but a few miles distant Before dawn a young cavalier was introduced into his chamber. The knight had a serious, nay, a sad aspect; and all beautiful as he was in feature and limb, looked wayworn and haggard. He stood silent in Henry's presence, who, alert and gay, turned his lively blue eyes upon his guest, saying gently, 'So thou foundest her obdurate, Gaspar?'

'I found her resolved on our mutual misery. Alas! my liege, it is not, credit me, the least of my grief, that Constance sacrifices her own happiness when she destroys mine.'

'And thou believest that she will say nay to the gaillard chevalier whom we ourselves present to her?'

'Oh, my liege, think not that thought! it cannot be. My heart deeply, most deeply, thanks you for your generous condescension. But she whom her lover's voice in solitude—whose entreaties, when memory and seclusion aided the spell—could not persuade, will resist even your majesty's commands. She is bent upon entering a cloister; and I, so please you, will now take my leave:—I am henceforth a soldier of the cross.'

'Gaspar,' said the monarch, 'I know woman better than thou. It is not by submission nor tearful plaints she is to be won. The death of her relatives naturally sits heavy at the young countess' heart; and nourishing in solitude her regret and her repentance, she fancies that Heaven itself forbids your union. Let the voice of the world reach her—the voice of earthly power and earthly kindness—the one commanding, the other pleading, and both finding response in her own heart—and by my say and the Holy Cross she will be yours. Let our plan still hold. And now to horse: the morning wears, and the sun is risen.'

The king arrived at the bishop's palace, and proceeded forthwith to mass in the cathedral. A sumptuous dinner succeeded, and it was afternoon before the monarch proceeded through the town beside the Loire to where, a little above Nantes, the Chateau Villeneuve was situated. The, young countess received him at the gate. Henry looked in vain for the cheek blanched by misery, the aspect of downcast despair which he had been taught to expect. Her cheek was flushed, her manner animated, her voice scarce tremulous. 'She loves him not,' thought Henry, or already her heart has consented.'

A collation was prepared for the monarch; and after some little hesitation, arising from the cheerfulness of her mien, he mentioned the name of Gaspar. Constance blushed instead of turning pale, and replied very quickly, 'Tomorrow, good my liege; I ask for a respite but until tomorrow;—all will then be decided;—tomorrow I am vowed to God—or'—

She looked confused, and the king, at once surprised and pleased, said, 'Then you hate not young De Vaudemont;—you forgive him for the inimical blood that warms his veins.'

'We are taught that we should forgive, that we should love our enemies,' the countess replied, with some trepidation.

'Now, by Saint Denis, that is a right welcome answer for the novice,' said the king, laughing. 'What ho! my faithful serving-man, Don Apollo in disguise! come forward, and thank your lady for her love.'

In such disguise as had concealed him from all, the cavalier had hung behind, and viewed with infinite surprise the demean-our and calm countenance of the lady. He could not hear her words: but was this even she whom he had seen trembling and weeping the evening before? this she whose very heart was torn by conflicting passion?—who saw the pale ghosts of parent and kinsman stand between her and the lover whom more than her life she adored? It was a riddle hard to solve. The king's call was in unison with his impatience, and he sprang forward. He was at her feet; while she, still passion-driven overwrought by the very calmness she had assumed, uttered one cry as she recognized him. and sank senseless on the floor.

All this was very unintelligible. Even when her attendants had brought her to life, another fit succeeded, and then pas-sionate floods of tears; while the monarch, waiting in the hall, eyeing the half-eaten collation, and, humming some romance in commemoration of woman's waywardness, knew not how to reply to Vaudemont's look of bitter disappointment and anxiety. At length the countess' chief attendant came with an apology. 'Her lady was ill, very ill. The next day she would throw herself at the king's feet, at once to solicit his excuse, and to disclose her purpose.'

'Tomorrow—again tomorrow! Does tomorrow bear some charm, maiden?' said the king. 'Can you read us the riddle pretty one? What strange tale belongs to tomorrow, that all rests on its advent?

Manon coloured, looked down, and hesitated. But Henry was no tyro in the art of enticing ladies' attendants to disclose their ladies' council. Manon was besides, frightened by the countess' scheme, on which she was still obstinately bent, so she was the more readily induced to betray it. To sleep in St Catherine's bed, to rest on a narrow ledge overhanging the deep rapid Loire, and if, as was most probable, the luckless dreamer escaped from falling into it, to take the disturbed visions that, such uneasy slumber might produce for the dictate of Heaven, was a madness of which even Henry himself could scarcely deem any woman capable.

But could Constance, her whose beauty was so highly intellectual, and whom he had heard perpetually praised for her strength of mind and talents, could *she* be so strangely infatuated! And can passion play such freaks with us?—like death, levelling even the aristocracy of the soul, and bringing noble and peasant, the wise and foolish, under one thraldom? It was strange—yes she must have her way. That she hesitated in her decision was much; and it was to be hoped that St Catherine would play no ill-natured part. Should it be otherwise, a purpose to be swayed by a dream might be influenced by other waking thoughts. To the more material kind of danger some safeguard should be brought.

There is no feeling more awful than that which invades a weak human heart bent upon gratifying its ungovernable impulses in contradiction to the dictates of conscience. Forbidden pleasures are said to be the most agreeable;—it may be so to rude natures, to those who love to struggle, combat, and contest; who find happiness in a fray, and joy in the conflict of passion. But softer and sweeter was the gentle spirit of Constance; and love and duty contending crushed and tortured her poor heart. To commit her conduct to the inspirations of religion, or, if it was so to be named, of superstition, was a blessed relief.

The very perils that threatened her undertaking gave zest to it;—to dare for his sake was happiness;—the very difficulty of

the way that led to the completion of her wishes at once gratified her love and distracted her thoughts from her despair. Or if
it was decreed that she must sacrifice all, the risk of danger and
of death were of trifling import in comparison with the anguish
which would then be her portion forever.

The night threatened to be stormy, the raging wind shook
the casements, and the trees waved their huge shadowy arms, as
giants might in fantastic dance and mortal broil. Constance and
Manon, unattended, quitted the *chateau* by a postern, and began
to descend the hillside. The moon had not yet risen; and though
the way was familiar to both, Manon tottered and trembled;
while the countess, drawing her silken cloak around her, walked
with a firm step down the steep. They came to the river's side,
where a small boat was moored, and one man was in waiting.
Constance stepped lightly in, and then aided her fearful companion.

In a few moments they were in the middle of the stream. The
warm, tempestuous, animating, equinoctial wind swept over
them. For the first time since her mourning, a thrill of pleasure
swelled the bosom of Constance. She hailed the emotion with
double joy. It cannot be, she thought, that Heaven will forbid
me to love one so brave, so generous, and so good as the noble
Gaspar. Another I can never love; I shall die if divided from him;
and this heart, these limbs, so alive with glowing sensation, are
they already predestined to an early grave? Oh no! life speaks
aloud within them: I shall live to love. Do not all things love?—
the winds as they whisper to the rushing waters? the waters as
they kiss the flowery banks, and speed to mingle with the sea?
Heaven and earth are sustained by, and live through, love; and
shall Constance alone, whose heart has ever been a deep, gush-
ing, overflowing well of true affection, be compelled to set a
stone upon the fount to lock it up forever?

These thoughts bade fair for pleasant dreams; and perhaps
the countess, an adept in the blind god's lore, therefore indulged
them the more readily. But as thus she was engrossed by soft
emotions, Manon caught her arm:—'Lady, look,' she cried; 'it

comes yet the oars have no sound. Now the Virgin shield us! Would we were at home!'

A dark boat glided by them. Four rowers, habited in black cloaks, pulled at oars which, as Manon said, gave no sound; another sat at the helm: like the rest, his person was veiled in a dark mantle, but he wore no cap; and though his face was turned from them, Constance recognized her lover. 'Gaspar,' she cried aloud, 'dost thou live?'—but the figure in the boat neither turned its head nor replied, and quickly it was lost. in the shadowy waters.

How changed now was the fair countess' reverie! Already Heaven had begun its spell, and unearthly forms were around, as she strained her eyes through the gloom. Now she saw and now she lost view of the bark that occasioned her terror; and now it seemed that another was there, which held the spirits of the dead; and her father waved to her from shore, and her brothers frowned on her.

Meanwhile they neared the landing. Her bark was moored in a little cove, and Constance stood upon the bank. Now she trembled, and half yielded to Manon's entreaty to return; till the unwise *suivante* mentioned the king's and De Vaudemont's name, and spoke of the answer to be given tomorrow. What answer, if she turned back from her intent?

She now hurried forward up the broken ground of the bank, and then along its edge, till they came to a bill which abruptly hung over the tide. A small chapel stood near. With trembling fingers the countess drew forth the key and unlocked its. door. They entered. It was dark—save that a little lamp, flickering in the wind, showed an uncertain light from before the figure of Saint Catherine. The two women knelt; they prayed; and then rising, with a cheerful accent the countess bade her attendant good-night. She unlocked a little low iron door. It opened on a narrow cavern. The roar of waters was heard beyond. 'Thou mayest not follow, my poor Manon,' said Constance,—'nor dost thou much desire:—this adventure is for me alone.'

It was hardly fair to leave the trembling servant in the chapel alone, who had neither hope nor fear, nor love, nor grief to beguile her; but, in those days, esquires and waiting-women often played the part of subalterns in the army, gaming knocks and no fame. Besides, Manon was safe in holy ground. The countess meanwhile pursued her way groping in the dark through the narrow tortuous passage.

At length what seemed light to her long darkened sense gleamed on her. She reached an open cavern in the overhanging hill's side, looking over the rushing tide beneath. She looked out upon the night. The waters of the Loire were speeding, as since that day have they ever sped—changeful, yet the same; the heavens were thickly veiled with clouds, and the wind in the trees was as mournful and ill-omened as if it rushed round a murderer's tomb. Constance shuddered a little, and looked upon her, bed,—a narrow ledge of earth and a grown stone bordering on the very verge of the precipice. She doffed her mantle,—such was one of the conditions of the spell;—she bowed her head, and loosened the tresses of her dark hair; she bared her feet; and thus, fully prepared for suffering to the utmost the chill influence of the cold night, she stretched herself on the narrow couch that scarce afforded room for her repose, and whence, if she moved in sleep, she must be precipitated into the cold waters below.

At first it seemed to her as if she never should sleep again. No great wonder that exposure to the blast and her perilous position should forbid her eyelids to close. At length she fell into a reverie so soft and soothing that she wished even to watch; and then by degrees her senses became confused; and now she was on St Catherine's bed—the Loire rushing beneath, and the wild wind sweeping by—and now—oh whither?—and what dreams did the saint send, to drive her to despair, or to bid her be blest forever?

Beneath the rugged hill, upon the dark tide, another watched, who feared a thousand things, and scarce dared hope. He had meant to precede the lady on her way, but when he found that he had outstayed his time, with muffled oars and breathless haste he had shot by the bark that contained his Constance, nor even turned at her voice, fearful to incur her blame, and her commands to return. He had seen her emerge from the passage, and shuddered as she leant over the cliff. He saw her step forth, clad as she was in white, and could mark her as she lay on the edge beetling above.

What a vigil did the lovers keep!—she given up to visionary thoughts, he knowing—and the consciousness thrilled his bosom with strange emotion—that love, and love for him, had led her to that perilous couch; and that while angers surrounded her in every shape, she was alive only to a small still voice that whispered to her heart the dream which was to decide their destinies. She slept perhaps—but he waked and watched; and night wore away, as now praying, now entranced by alternating hope and fear, he sat in his boat, his eyes fixed on the white garb of the slumberer above.

Morning—was it morning that struggled in the clouds? Would morning ever come to waken her? And had she slept? and what dreams of weal or woe had peopled her sleep? Gaspar grew impatient. He commanded his boatmen still to wait, and he sprang forward, intent on clambering the precipice. In vain they urged the danger, nay, the impossibility of the attempt; he clung to the rugged face of the hill, and found footing where it would seem no footing was. The acclivity, indeed, was not high; the dangers of St Catherine's bed arising from the likelihood that anyone who slept on so narrow a couch would be precipitated into the waters beneath.

Up the steep ascent Gaspar continued to toil, and at last reached the roots of a tree that grew near the summit. Aided by its branches, he made good his stand at the very extremity of the ledge, near the pillow on which lay the uncovered head of his beloved. Her hands were folded on her bosom; her dark hair fell round her throat and pillowed her cheek; her face was serene: sleep was there in all its innocence and in all its helplessness; every wilder emotion was hushed, and her bosom heaved in regular breathing. He could see her heart beat as it lifted her fair hands crossed above. No statue hewn of marble in monumental effigy was ever half so fair; and within that surpassing form dwelt a soul true, tender, self-devoted, and affectionate as ever warmed a human breast.

With what deep passion did Gaspar gaze, gathering hope from the placidity of her angel countenance! A smile wreathed her lips, and he too involuntarily smiled, as he hailed the happy omen; when suddenly her cheek was flushed, her bosom heaved, a tear stole from her dark lashes, and then a whole shower fell, as starting up she cried, 'No!—he shall not die!—I will unloose his chains!—I will save him!' Gaspar's hand was there. He caught her light form ready to fall from the perilous couch. She opened her eyes and beheld her lover, who had watched over her dream of fate, and who had saved her.

Manon also had slept well, dreaming or not, and was startled in the morning to find that she waked surrounded by a crowd. The little desolate chapel was hung with tapestry, the altar adorned with golden chalices—the priest was chanting mass to a goodly array of kneeling knights. Manon saw that King Henry was there; and she looked for another whom she found not, when the iron door of the cavern passage opened, and Gaspar de Vaudemont entered from it, leading the fair form of Constance; who, in her white robes and dark dishevelled hair, with a face in which smiles and blushes contended with deeper emotion, approached the altar, and, kneeling with her lover, pronounced the vows that united them forever.

It was long before the happy Gaspar could win from his lady the secret of her dream. In spite of the happiness she now enjoyed, she had suffered too much not to look back even with terror to those days when she thought love a crime, and every event connected with them wore an awful aspect.

'Many a vision,' she said, 'she had that fearful night. She had seen the spirits of her father and brothers in Paradise; she had beheld Gaspar victoriously combating among the infidels; she had beheld him in King Henry's court, favoured and beloved; and she herself—now pining in a cloister, now a bride, now grateful to Heaven for the full measure of bliss presented to her, now weeping away her sad days—till suddenly she thought herself in Paynim land; and the saint herself, St Catherine, guiding her unseen through the city of the infidels. She entered a palace, and beheld the miscreants rejoicing in victory; and then, descending to the dungeons beneath, they groped their way through damp vaults, and low, mildewed passages, to one cell, darker more frightful than the rest. On the floor lay one with soiled tattered garments, with unkempt locks and wild, matted beard. His cheek was worn and thin; his eyes had lost their fire; his form was a mere skeleton; the chains hung loosely on the fleshless bones.'

'And was it my appearance in that attractive state and winning costume that softened the hard heart of Constance?' asked Gaspar, smiling at this painting of what would never be.

'Even so,' replied Constance; 'for my heart whispered me that this was my doing; and who could recall the life that waned in your pulses—who restore, save the destroyer? My heart never warmed to my living, happy knight as then it did to his wasted image as it lay, in the visions of night, at my feet. A veil fell from my eyes; a darkness was dispelled from before me. Methought I then knew for the first time what life and what death was. I was bid believe that to make the living happy was not to injure the dead; and I felt how wicked and how vain was that false philosophy which placed virtue and good in hatred, and unkindness. You should not die; I would loosen your chains and save you, and bid you live for love. I sprang forward, and the death I deprecated for you would, in my presumption, have been mine,—then, when first I felt the real value of life,—but that your arm was there to save me, your dear voice to bid me be blest for evermore.'

The Mortal Immortal

July 16, 1833.—This is a memorable anniversary for me; on it I complete my three hundred and twenty-third year!

The Wandering Jew?—certainly not. More than eighteen centuries have passed over his head. In comparison with him, I am a very young Immortal.

Am I, then, immortal? This is a question which I have asked myself, by day and night, for now three hundred and three years, and yet cannot answer it. I detected a gray hair amidst my brown locks this very day—that surely signifies decay. Yet it may have remained concealed there for three hundred years—for some persons have become entirely white headed before twenty years of age.

I will tell my story, and my reader shall judge for me. I will tell my story, and so contrive to pass some few hours of a long eternity, become so wearisome to me. Forever! Can it be? to live forever! I have heard of enchantments, in which the victims were plunged into a deep sleep, to wake, after a hundred years, as fresh as ever: I have heard of the Seven Sleepers—thus to be immortal would not be so burthensome: but, oh! the weight of never-ending time—the tedious passage of the still-succeeding hours! How happy was the fabled Nourjahad!——But to my task.

All the world has heard of Cornelius Agrippa. His memory is as immortal as his arts have made me. All the world has also heard of his scholar, who, unawares, raised the foul fiend during his master's absence, and was destroyed by him. The report, true or false, of this accident, was attended with many inconveniences to the renowned philosopher. All his scholars at once deserted him—his servants disappeared. He had no one near him to put coals on his ever-burning fires while he slept, or to attend to the changeful colours of his medicines while he studied. Experiment after experiment failed, because one pair of hands was insufficient to complete them: the dark spirits laughed at him for not being able to retain a single mortal in his service.

I was then very young—very poor—and very much. in love. I had been for about a year the pupil of Cornelius, though I was absent when this accident took place. On my return, my friends implored me not to return to the alchymist's abode. I trembled as I listened to the dire tale they told; I required no second warning; and when Cornelius came and offered me a purse of gold if I would remain under his roof, I felt as if Satan himself tempted me. My teeth chattered—my hair stood on end:—I ran off as fast as my trembling knees would permit.

My failing steps were directed whither for two years they had every evening been attracted,—a gently bubbling spring of pure living waters, beside which lingered a dark-haired girl, whose beaming eyes were fixed on the path I was accustomed each night to tread. I cannot remember the hour when I did not love Bertha; we had been neighbours and playmates from infancy-her parents, like mine, were of humble life, yet respectable—our attachment had been a source of pleasure to them.

In an evil hour, a malignant fever carried off both her father and mother, and Bertha became an orphan. She would have found a home beneath my paternal roof, but, unfortunately, the old lady of the near castle, rich, childless, and solitary, declared her intention to adopt her. Henceforth Bertha was clad in silk—inhabited a marble palace—and was looked on as being highly favoured by fortune. But in her new situation among her new associates, Bertha remained true to the friend of her humbler days; she often visited the cottage of my father, and when forbidden to go thither, she would stray towards the neighbouring wood, and meet me beside its shady fountain.

She often declared that she owed no duty to her new pro-tectress equal in sanctity to that which bound us. Yet still I was too poor to marry, and she grew weary of being tormented on my account. She had a haughty but an impatient spirit, and grew angry at the obstacles that prevented our union. We met now after an absence, and she had been sorely beset while I was away; she complained bitterly, and almost reproached me for being poor. I replied hastily,—

"I am honest, if I am poor!—were I not, I might soon be-come rich!"

This exclamation produced a thousand questions. I feared to shock her by owning the truth, but she drew it from me; and then, casting a look of disdain on me, she said—"You pretend to love, and you fear to face the Devil for my sake!" I protested that I had only dreaded to offend her;—while she dwelt on the mag-nitude of the reward that I should receive. Thus encouraged—shamed by her—led on by love and hope, laughing at my late fears, with quick steps and a light heart, I returned to accept the offers of the alchymist, and was instantly installed in my office. A year passed away. I became possessed of no insignificant sum of money. Custom had banished my fears.

In spite of the most painful vigilance, I had never detected the trace of a cloven foot; nor was the studious silence of our abode ever disturbed by demoniac howls. I still continued my stolen interviews with Bertha, and Hope dawned on me— Hope—but not perfect joy; for Bertha fancied that love and security were enemies, and her pleasure was to divide them in my bosom. Though true of heart, she was somewhat of a *coquette* in manner; and I was jealous as a Turk. She slighted me in a thousand ways, yet would never acknowledge herself to be in the wrong. She would drive me mad with anger, and then force me to beg her pardon. Sometimes she fancied that I was not sufficiently sub-missive, and then she had some story of a rival, favoured by her protectress. She was surrounded by silk-clad youths—the rich and gay—What chance had the sad-robed scholar of Cornelius compared with these?

On one occasion, the philosopher made such large demands upon my time, that I was unable to meet her as I was wont. He was engaged in some mighty work, and I was forced to remain, day and night, feeding his furnaces and watching his chemical preparations. Bertha waited for me in vain at the fountain. Her haughty spirit fired at this neglect; and when at last I stole out during the few short minutes allotted to me for slumber, and hoped to be consoled by her, she received me with disdain, dismissed me in scorn, and vowed that any man should possess her hand rather than he who could not be in two places at once for her sake. She would be revenged!—And truly she was. In my dingy retreat I heard that she had been hunting, attended by Albert Hoffer. Albert Hoffer was favoured by her protectress, and the three passed in cavalcade before my smoky window. Methought that they mentioned my name—it was followed by a laugh of derision, as her dark eyes glanced contemptuously towards my abode.

Jealousy, with all its venom, and all its misery, entered my breast. Now I shed a torrent of tears, to think that I should never call her mine; and, anon, I imprecated a thousand curses on her inconstancy. Yet, still I must stir the fires of the alchymist, still attend on the changes of his unintelligible medicines.

Cornelius had watched for three days and nights, nor closed his eyes. The progress of his alembics was slower than he expected: in spite of his anxiety, sleep weighed upon his eyelids. Again and again he threw off drowsiness with more than human energy; again and again it stole away his senses. He eyed his crucibles wistfully. "Not ready yet," he murmured; "will another night pass before the work is accomplished? Winzy, you are vigilant—you are faithful—you have slept, my boy—you slept last night. Look at that glass vessel. The liquid it contains is of a soft rose-colour: the moment it begins to change its hue, awaken me—till then I may close my eyes. First, it will turn white, and then emit golden flashes; but wait not till then; when the rose-colour fades, rouse me."

I scarcely heard the last words, muttered, as they were, in

sleep. Even then he did not quite yield to nature. "Winzy, my boy," he again said, "do not touch the vessel—do not put it to your lips; it is a philter—a philter to cure love; you would not cease to love your Bertha—beware to drink!"

And he slept. His venerable head sunk on his breast, and I scarce heard his regular breathing. For a few minutes I watched the vessel—the rosy hue of the liquid remained unchanged. Then my thoughts wandered—they visited the fountain, and dwelt on a thousand charming scenes never to be renewed—never! Serpents and adders were in my heart as the word "Never!" half formed itself on my lips. False girl!—false and cruel! Never more would she smile on me as that evening she smiled on Albert. Worthless, detested woman! I would not remain unrevenged- she should see Albert expire at her feet—she should die beneath my vengeance. She had smiled in disdain and triumph- she knew my wretchedness and her power. Yet what power had she?—the power of exciting my hate—my utter scorn—my— oh, all but indifference! Could I attain that—could I regard her with careless eyes, transferring my rejected love to one fairer and more true, that were indeed a victory!

A bright flash darted before my eyes. I had forgotten the medicine of the adept; I gazed on it with wonder: flashes of admirable beauty, more bright than those which the diamond emits when the sun's rays are on it, glanced from the surface of the liquid; an odour the most fragrant and grateful stole over my sense; the vessel seemed one globe of living radiance, lovely to the eye, and most inviting to the taste. The first thought, instinc- tively inspired by the grosser sense, was, I will—I must drink. I raised the vessel to my lips. "It will cure me of love—of torture!" Already I had quaffed half of the most delicious liquor ever tasted by the palate of man, when the philosopher stirred. I started—I dropped the glass—the fluid flamed and glanced along the floor, while I felt Cornelius's gripe at my throat, as he shrieked aloud, "Wretch! you have destroyed the labour of my life!"

The philosopher was totally unaware that I had drunk any portion of his drug. His idea was, and I gave a tacit assent to it, that I had raised the vessel from curiosity, and that, frighted at its brightness, and the flashes of intense light it gave forth, I had let it fall. I never undeceived him. The fire of the medicine was quenched—the fragrance died away—he grew calm, as a philosopher should under the heaviest trials, and dismissed me to rest.

I will not attempt to describe the sleep of glory and bliss which bathed my soul in paradise during the remaining hours of that memorable night. Words would be faint and shallow types of my enjoyment, or of the gladness that possessed my bosom when I woke. I trod air—my thoughts were in heaven. Earth appeared heaven, and my inheritance upon it was to be one trance of delight. "This it is to be cured of love," I thought; "I will see Bertha this day, and she will find her lover cold and regardless: too happy to be disdainful, yet how utterly indifferent to her!"

The hours danced away. The philosopher, secure that he had once succeeded, and believing that he might again, began to concoct the same medicine once more. He was shut up with his books and drugs, and I had a holiday. I dressed myself with care; I looked in an old but polished shield, which served me for a mirror; methought my good looks had wonderfully improved. I hurried beyond the precincts of the town, joy in my soul, the beauty of heaven and earth around me.

I turned my steps towards the castle—I could look on its lofty turrets with lightness of heart, for I was cured of love. My Bertha saw me afar off, as I came up the avenue. I know not what sudden impulse animated her bosom, but at the sight, she sprung with a light fawn-like bound down the marble steps, and was hastening towards me. But I had been perceived by another person. The old high-born hag, who called herself her protectress, and was her tyrant, had seen me, also; she hobbled, panting, up the terrace; a page, as ugly as herself, held up her train, and fanned her as she hurried along, and stopped my fair girl with a "How, now, my bold mistress? whither so fast? Back to your cage—hawks are abroad!"

Bertha clasped her hands—her eyes were still bent on my

approaching figure. I saw the contest. How I abhorred the old crone who checked the kind impulses of my Bertha's softening heart. Hitherto, respect for her rank had caused me to avoid the lady of the castle; now I disdained such trivial considerations. I was cured of love, and lifted above all human fears; I hastened forwards, and soon reached the terrace. How lovely Bertha looked! her eyes flashing fire, her cheeks glowing with impatience and anger, she was a thousand times more graceful and charming than ever—I no longer loved—Oh! no, I adored—worshipped—idolized her!

She had that morning been persecuted, with more than usual vehemence, to consent to an immediate marriage with my rival. She was reproached with the encouragement that she had shown him—she was threatened with being turned out of doors with disgrace and shame. Her proud spirit rose in arms at the threat; but when she remembered the scorn that she had heaped upon me, and how, perhaps, she had thus lost one whom she now regarded as her only friend, she wept with remorse and rage. At that moment I appeared. "O, Winzy!" she exclaimed, "take me to your mother's cot; swiftly let me leave the detested luxuries and wretchedness of this noble dwelling—take me to poverty and happiness."

I clasped her in my arms with transport. The old lady was speechless with fury, and broke forth into invective only when we were far on our road to my natal cottage. My mother received the fair fugitive, escaped from a gilt cage to nature and liberty, with tenderness and joy; my father, who loved her, welcomed her heartily; it was a day of rejoicing, which did not need the addition of the celestial potion of the alchymist to steep me in delight.

Soon after this eventful day, I became the husband of Bertha. I ceased to be the scholar of Cornelius, but I continued his friend. I always felt grateful to him for having, unawares, procured me that delicious draught of a divine elixir, which, instead of curing me of love (sad cure! solitary and joyless remedy for evils which seem blessings to the memory), had inspired me with courage and resolution, thus winning for me an inestimable treasure in my Bertha.

I often called to mind that period of trance-like inebriation with wonder. The drink of Cornelius had not fulfilled the task for which he affirmed that it had been prepared, but its effects were more potent and blissful than words can express.

They had faded by degrees, yet they lingered long—and painted life in hues of splendour. Bertha often wondered at my lightness of heart and unaccustomed gaiety; for, before, I had been rather serious, or even sad, in my disposition. She loved me the better for my cheerful temper, and our days were winged by joy.

Five years afterwards I was suddenly summoned to the bed-side of the dying Cornelius. He had sent for me in haste, con-juring my instant presence. I found him stretched on his pallet, enfeebled even to death; all of life that yet remained animated his piercing eyes, and they were fixed on a glass vessel, full of a roseate liquid.

"Behold," he said, in a broken and inward voice, "the van-ity of human wishes! a second time my hopes are about to be crowned, a second time they are destroyed. Look at that liquor-you remember five years ago I had prepared the same, with the same success;—then, as now, my thirsting lips expected to taste the immortal elixir—you dashed it from me! and at present it is too late."

He spoke with difficulty, and fell back on his pillow. I could not help saying,—"How, revered master, can a cure for love re-store you to life?"

A faint smile gleamed across his face as I listened earnestly to his scarcely intelligible answer. "A cure for love and for all things—the Elixir of Immortality. Ah! if now I might drink, I should live forever!"

As he spoke, a golden flash gleamed from the fluid; a well-remembered fragrance stole over the air; he raised himself, all weak as he was—strength seemed miraculously to re-enter his frame—he stretched forth his hand—a loud explosion startled me—a ray of fire shot up from the elixir, and the glass vessel which contained it was shivered to atoms! I turned my eyes towards the philosopher; he had fallen back—his eyes were glassy—his features rigid—he was dead!

But I lived, and was to live forever! So said the unfortunate alchymist, and for a few days I believed his words. I remembered the glorious drunkenness that had followed my stolen draught. I reflected on the change I had felt in my frame—in my soul. The bounding elasticity of the one—the buoyant lightness of the other. I surveyed myself in a mirror, and could perceive no change in my features during the space of the five years which had elapsed. I remembered the radiant hues and grateful scent of that delicious beverage—worthy the gift it was capable of bestowing——I was, then, IMMORTAL!

A few days after I laughed at my credulity. The old proverb, that *a prophet is least regarded in his own country*, was true with respect to me and my defunct master. I loved him as a man—I respected him as a sage—but I derided the notion that he could command the powers of darkness, and laughed at the superstitious fears with which he was regarded by the vulgar. He was a wise philosopher, but had no acquaintance with any spirits but those clad in flesh and blood. His science was simply human; and human science, I soon persuaded myself, could never conquer nature's laws so far as to imprison the soul for ever within its carnal habitation.

Cornelius had brewed a soul-refreshing drink—more inebriating than wine—sweeter and more fragrant than any fruit: it possessed probably strong medicinal powers, imparting gladness to the heart and vigor to the limbs; but its effects would wear out; already were they diminished in my frame. I was a lucky fellow to have quaffed health and joyous spirits, and perhaps long life, at my master's hands; but my good fortune ended there: longevity was far different from immortality.

I continued to entertain this belief for many years. Sometimes a thought stole across me—Was the alchymist indeed deceived? But my habitual credence was, that I should meet the fate of all the children of Adam at my appointed time—a little late, but still at a natural age. Yet it was certain that I retained a wonderfully youthful look. I was laughed at for my vanity in consulting the mirror so often, but I consulted it in vain—my brow was untrenched—my cheeks—my eyes—my whole person continued as untarnished as in my twentieth year.

I was troubled. I looked at the faded beauty of Bertha—I seemed more like her son. By degrees our neighbours began to make similar observations, and I found at last that I went by the name of the Scholar bewitched. Bertha herself grew uneasy. She became jealous and peevish, and at length she began to question me. We had no children; we were all in all to each other; and though, as she grew older, her vivacious spirit became a little allied to ill-temper, and her beauty sadly diminished, I cherished her in my heart as the mistress I had idolized, the wife I had sought and won with such perfect love.

At last our situation became intolerable: Bertha was fifty—I twenty years of age. I had, in very shame, in some measure adopted the habits of a more advanced age; I no longer mingled in the dance among the young and gay, but my heart bounded along with them while I restrained my feet; and a sorry figure I cut among the Nestors of our village. But before the time I mention, things were altered—we were universally shunned; we were—at least, I was—reported to have kept up an iniquitous acquaintance with some of my former master's supposed friends. Poor Bertha was pitied, but deserted. I was regarded with horror and detestation.

What was to be done? we sat by our winter fire—poverty had made itself felt, for none would buy the produce of my farm; and often I had been forced to journey twenty miles, to some place where I was not known, to dispose of our property. It is true we had saved something for an evil day—that day was come.

We sat by our lone fireside—the old-hearted youth and his antiquated wife. Again Bertha insisted on knowing the truth; she recapitulated all she had ever heard said about me, and added her own observations. She conjured me to cast off the spell; she described how much more comely grey hairs were than my chestnut locks; she descanted on the reverence and respect due to age—how preferable to the slight regard paid to mere children: could I imagine that the despicable gifts of youth and good looks outweighed disgrace, hatred, and scorn?

Nay, in the end I should be burnt as a dealer in the black art, while she, to whom I had not deigned to communicate any portion of my good fortune, might be stoned as my accomplice. At length she insinuated that I must share my secret with her, and bestow on her like benefits to those I myself enjoyed, or she would denounce me—and then she burst into tears.

Thus beset, methought it was the best way to tell the truth. I revealed it as tenderly as I could, and spoke only of a *very long life*, not of immortality—which representation, indeed, coincided best with my own ideas. When I ended, I rose and said,

"And now, my Bertha, will you denounce the lover of your youth?—You will not, I know. But it is too hard, my poor wife, that you should suffer from my ill-luck and the accursed arts of Cornelius. I will leave you—you have wealth enough, and friends will return in my absence. I will go; young as I seem, and strong as I am, I can work and gain my bread among strangers, unsuspected and unknown. I loved you in youth; God is my witness that I would not desert you in age, but that your safety and happiness require it."

I took my cap and moved towards the door; in a moment Bertha's arms were round my neck, and her lips were pressed to mine. "No, my husband, my Winzy," she said, "you shall not go alone—take me with you; we will remove from this place, and, as you say, among strangers we shall be unsuspected and safe. I am not so very old as quite to shame you, my Winzy; and I dare say the charm will soon wear off, and, with the blessing of God, you will become more elderly-looking, as is fitting; you shall not leave me."

I returned the good soul's embrace heartily. "I will not, my Bertha; but for your sake I had not thought of such a thing. I will be your true, faithful husband while you are spared to me, and do my duty by you to the last."

The next day we prepared secretly for our emigration. We were obliged to make great pecuniary sacrifices—it could not be helped. We realised a sum sufficient, at least, to maintain us while Bertha lived; and, without saying *adieu* to any one, quitted our native country to take refuge in a remote part of western France.

It was a cruel thing to transport poor Bertha from her native village, and the friends of her youth, to a new country, new language, new customs. The strange secret of my destiny rendered this removal immaterial to me; but I compassionated her deeply, and was glad to perceive that she found compensation for her misfortunes in a variety of little ridiculous circumstances. Away from all tell-tale chroniclers, she sought to decrease the apparent disparity of our ages by a thousand feminine arts—rouge, youthful dress, and assumed juvenility of manner. I could not be angry—Did not I myself wear a mask? Why quarrel with hers, because it was less successful? I grieved deeply when I remembered that this was my Bertha, whom I had loved so fondly, and won with such transport—the dark eyed, dark-haired girl, with smiles of enchanting archness and a step like a fawn—this mincing, simpering, jealous old woman. I should have revered her gray locks and withered cheeks; but thus!—It was my, work, I knew; but I did not the less deplore this type of human weakness.

Her jealousy never slept. Her chief occupation was to discover that, in spite of outward appearances, I was myself growing old. I verily believe that the poor soul loved me truly in her heart, but never had woman so tormenting a mode of displaying fondness. She would discern wrinkles in my face and decrepitude in my walk, while I bounded along in youthful vigour, the youngest looking of twenty youths. I never dared address another woman: on one occasion, fancying that the *belle* of the village regarded me with favouring eyes, she bought me a gray wig. Her constant discourse among her acquaintances was, that though I looked so young, there was ruin at work within my frame; and she affirmed that the worst symptom about me was my apparent health.

My youth was a disease, she said, and I ought at all times to prepare, if not for a sudden and awful death, at least to awake some morning white-headed, and bowed down with all the marks of advanced years. I let her talk—I often joined in her conjectures. Her warnings chimed in with my never-ceasing speculations concerning my state, and I took an earnest, though painful, interest in listening to all that her quick wit and excited imagination could say on the subject.

Why dwell on these minute circumstances? We lived on for many long years. Bertha became bed-rid and paralytic: I nursed her as mother might a child. She grew peevish, and still harped upon one string—of how long I should survive her. It has ever been a source of consolation to me, that I performed my duty scrupulously towards her. She had been mine in youth, she was mine in age, and at last, when I heaped the sod over her corpse, I wept to feel that I had lost all that really bound me to humanity.

Since then how many have been my cares and woes, how few and empty my enjoyments! I pause here in my history—I will pursue it no further. A sailor without rudder or compass, tossed on a stormy sea—a traveller lost on a wide-spread heath, without landmark or star to him—such have I been: more lost, more hopeless than either. A nearing ship, a gleam from some far cot, may save them; but I have no beacon except the hope of death.

Death! mysterious, ill-visaged friend of weak humanity! Why alone of all mortals have you cast me from your sheltering fold? O, for the peace of the grave! the deep silence of the iron-bound tomb! that thought would cease to work in my brain, and my heart beat no more with emotions varied only by new forms of sadness!

Am I immortal? I return to my first question. In the first place, is it not more probable that the beverage of the alchymist was fraught rather with longevity than eternal life? Such is my hope.

And then be it remembered that I only drank half of the potion prepared by him. Was not the whole necessary to complete the charm? To have drained half the Elixir of Immortality is but to be half immortal—my Forever is thus truncated and null.

But again, who shall number the years of the half of eternity? I often try to imagine by what rule the infinite may be divided. Sometimes I fancy age advancing upon me. One gray hair I have found. Fool! Do I lament? Yes, the fear of age and death often creeps coldly into my heart; and the more I live, the more I dread death, even while I abhor life. Such an enigma is man—born to perish—when he wars, as I do, against the established laws of his nature.

But for this anomaly of feeling surely I might die: the medicine of the alchymist would not be proof against fire—sword—and the strangling waters. I have gazed upon the blue depths of many a placid lake, and the tumultuous rushing of many a mighty river, and have said, peace inhabits those waters; yet I have turned my steps away, to live yet another day. I have asked myself, whether suicide would be a crime in one to whom thus only the portals of the other world could be opened. I have done all, except presenting myself as a soldier or duellist, an object of destruction to my—no, not my fellow-mortals, and therefore I have shrunk away. They are not my fellows. The inextinguishable power of life in my frame, and their ephemeral existence, place us wide as the poles asunder. I could not raise a hand against the meanest or the most powerful among them.

Thus I have lived on for many a year—alone, and weary of myself—desirous of death, yet never dying—a mortal immortal. Neither ambition nor avarice can enter my mind, and the ardent love that gnaws at my heart, never to be returned—never to find an equal on which to expend itself—lives there only to torment me.

This very day I conceived a design by which I may end all—without self-slaughter, without making another man a Cain—an expedition, which mortal frame can never survive, even endued with the youth and strength that inhabits mine. Thus I shall put my immortality to the test, and rest for ever—or return, the wonder and benefactor of the human species.

Before I go, a miserable vanity has caused me to pen these pages. I would not die, and leave no name behind. Three centuries have passed since I quaffed the fatal beverage: another year shall not elapse before, encountering gigantic dangers—warring with the powers of frost in their home—beset by famine, toil, and tempest—I yield this body, too tenacious a cage for a soul which thirsts for freedom, to the destructive elements of air and water—or, if I survive, my name shall be recorded as one of the most famous among the sons of men; and, my task achieved, I shall adopt more resolute means, and, by scattering and annihilating the atoms that compose my frame, set at liberty the life imprisoned within, and so cruelly prevented from soaring from this dim earth to a sphere more congenial to its immortal essence.

Transformation

Forthwith this frame of min was wrench'd
With a woeful agony,
Which forced me to begin my tale,
And then it set me free.

Since then, at an uncertain hour,
That agony returns;
And till my ghastly tale is told
This heart within me burns.
                    —Coleridge's *Ancient Mariner.*

I have heard it said, that, when any strange, super natural, and necromantic adventure has occurred to a human being, that being, however desirous he may be to conceal the same, feels at certain periods torn up as it were by an intellectual earthquake, and is forced to bare the inner depths of his spirit to another. I am a witness of the truth of this. I have dearly sworn to myself never to reveal to human ears the horrors to which I once, in excess of fiendly pride, delivered myself over. The holy man who heard my confession, and reconciled me to the Church, is dead. None knows that once—

Why should it not be thus? Why tell a tale of impious tempting of Providence, and soul-subduing humiliation? Why? answer me, ye who are wise in the secrets of human nature! I only know that so it is; and in spite of strong resolve, of a pride that too much masters me of shame, and even of fear, so to render myself odious to my species, I must speak.

Genoa! my birthplace proud city! looking upon the blue

Mediterranean dost thou remember me in my boyhood, when thy cliffs and promontories, thy bright sky and gay vineyards, were my world? Happy time! when to the young heart the narrow-bounded universe, which leaves, by its very limitation, free scope to the imagination, enchains our physical energies, and, sole period in our lives, innocence and enjoyment are united.

Yet, who can look back to childhood, and not remember its sorrows and its harrowing fears? I was born with the most imperious, haughty, tameless spirit. I quailed before my father only; and he, generous and noble, but capricious and tyrannical, at once fostered and checked the wild impetuosity of my character, making obedience necessary, but inspiring no respect for the motives which guided his commands. To be a man, free, independent; or, in better words, insolent and domineering, was the hope and prayer of my rebel heart.

My father had one friend, a wealthy Genoese noble, who in a political tumult was suddenly sentenced to banishment, and his property confiscated. The Marchese Torella went into exile alone. Like my father, he was a widower: he had one child, the almost infant Juliet, who was left under my father's guardianship. I should certainly have been unkind to the lovely girl, but that I was forced by my position to become her protector. A variety of childish incidents all tended to one point, to make Juliet see in me a rock of defence; I in her, one who must perish through the soft sensibility of her nature too rudely visited, but for my guardian care. We grew up together.

The opening rose in May was not more sweet than this dear girl. An irradiation of beauty was spread over her face. Her form, her step, her voice—my heart weeps even now, to think of all of relying, gentle, loving, and pure, that she enshrined. When I was eleven and Juliet eight years of age, a cousin of mine, much older than either—he seemed to us a man—took great notice of my playmate; he called her his bride, and asked her to marry him. She refused, and he insisted, drawing her unwillingly towards him. With the countenance and emotions of a maniac I threw myself on him—I strove to draw his sword—I clung to his neck with the ferocious resolve to strangle him: he was obliged to call for assistance to disengage himself from me. On that night I led Juliet to the chapel of our house: I made her touch the sacred relics—I harrowed her child's heart, and profaned her child's lips with an oath, that she would be mine, and mine only.

Well, those days passed away. Torella returned in a few years, and became wealthier and more prosperous than ever. When I was seventeen, my father died; he had been magnificent to prodigality; Torella rejoiced that my minority would afford an opportunity for repairing my fortunes. Juliet and I had been affianced beside my father's deathbed—Torella was to be a second parent to me.

I desired to see the world, and I was indulged. I went to Florence, to Rome, to Naples; thence I passed to Toulon, and at length reached what had long been the bourne of my wishes, Paris. There was wild work in Paris then. The poor king, Charles the Sixth, now sane, now mad, now a monarch, now an abject slave, was the very mockery of humanity. The queen, the dauphin, the Duke of Burgundy, alternately friends and foes,—now meeting in prodigal feasts, now shedding blood in rivalry,—were blind to the miserable state of their country, and the dangers that impended over it, and gave themselves wholly up to dissolute enjoyment or savage strife. My character still followed me. I was arrogant and self-willed; I loved display, and above all, I threw off all control.

My young friends were eager to foster passions which furnished them with pleasures. I was deemed handsome—I was master of every knightly accomplishment. I was disconnected with any political party. I grew a favourite with all: my presumption and arrogance was pardoned in one so young: I became a spoiled child. Who could control me? not the letters and advice of Torella—only strong necessity visiting me in the abhorred shape of an empty purse. But there were means to refill this void. Acre after acre, estate after estate, I sold. My dress, my jewels, my horses and their caparisons, were almost unrivalled in gorgeous Paris, while the lands of my inheritance passed into possession of others.

The Duke of Orleans was waylaid and murdered by the Duke of Burgundy. Fear and terror possessed all Paris. The dauphin and the queen shut themselves up; every pleasure was suspended. I grew weary of this state of things, and my heart yearned for my boyhood's haunts. I was nearly a beggar, yet still I would go there, claim my bride, and rebuild my fortunes. A few happy ventures as a merchant would make me rich again. Nevertheless, I would not return in humble guise. My last act was to dispose of my remaining estate near Albaro for half its worth, for ready money.

Then I despatched all kinds of artificers, arras, furniture of regal splendour, to fit up the last relic of my inheritance, my palace in Genoa. I lingered a little longer yet, ashamed at the part of the prodigal returned, which I feared I should play. I sent my horses. One match less Spanish *jennet* I despatched to my promised bride: its *caparisons* flamed with jewels and cloth of gold. In every part I caused to be entwined the initials of Juliet and her Guido. My present found favour in hers and in her father's eyes.

Still to return a proclaimed spendthrift, the mark of impertinent wonder, perhaps of scorn, and to encounter singly the reproaches or taunts of my fellow-citizens, was no alluring prospect. As a shield between me and censure, I invited some few of the most reckless of my comrades to accompany me: thus I went armed against the world, hiding a rankling feeling, half fear and half penitence, by bravado.

I arrived in Genoa. I trod the pavement of my ancestral palace. My proud step was no interpreter of my heart, for I deeply felt that, though surrounded by every luxury, I was a beggar. The first step I took in claiming Juliet must widely declare me such. I read contempt or pity in the looks of all. I fancied that rich and poor, young and old, all regarded me with derision. Torella came not near me. No wonder that my second father should expect a son's deference from me in waiting first on him. But, galled and stung by a sense of my follies and demerit, I strove to throw the blame on others. We kept nightly orgies in Palazzo Carega.

To sleepless, riotous nights followed listless, supine mornings. At the *Ave Maria* we showed our dainty persons in the streets, scoffing at the sober citizens, casting insolent glances on the shrinking women. Juliet was not among them—no, no; if she had been there, shame would have driven me away, if love had not brought me to her feet.

I grew tired of this. Suddenly I paid the Marchese a visit. He was at his villa, one among the many which deck the suburb of San Pietro d Arena. It was the month of May, the blossoms of the fruit-trees were lading among thick, green foliage; the vines were shooting forth; the ground strewed with the fallen olive blooms; the firefly was in the myrtle hedge; heaven and earth wore a mantle of surpassing beauty. Torella welcomed me kindly, though seriously; and even his shade of displeasure soon wore away. Some resemblance to my father—some look and tone of youthful ingenuousness, softened the good old man's heart. He sent for his daughter—he presented me to her as her betrothed.

The chamber became hallowed by a holy light as she entered. Hers was that cherub look, those large, soft eyes, full dimpled cheeks, and mouth of infantine sweetness, that expresses the rare union of happiness and love. Admiration first possessed me; she is mine! was the second proud emotion, and my lips curled with haughty triumph. I had not been the *enfant gâté* of the beauties of France not to have learnt the art of pleasing the soft heart of woman. If towards men I was overbearing, the deference I paid to them was the more in contrast. I commenced my courtship by the display of a thousand gallantries to Juliet, who, vowed to me from infancy, had never admitted the devotion of others; and who, though accustomed to expressions of admiration, was uninitiated in the language of lovers.

For a few days all went well. Torella never alluded to my extravagance; he treated me as a favourite son. But the time came, as we discussed the preliminaries to my union with his daughter, when this fair face of things should be overcast. A contract had been drawn up in my father's lifetime. I had rendered this, in fact, void by having squandered the whole of the wealth which was to have been shared by Juliet and myself. Torella, in consequence, chose to consider this bond as cancelled, and proposed another, in which, though the wealth he bestowed was immeasurably increased, there were so many restrictions as to the mode of spending it, that I, who saw independence only in free career being given to my own imperious will, taunted him as taking advantage of my situation, and refused utterly to subscribe to his conditions. The old man mildly strove to recall me to reason. Roused pride became the tyrant of my thought: I listened with indignation—I repelled him with disdain.

"Juliet, thou art mine! Did we not interchange vows in our innocent childhood? Are we not one in the sight of God? and shall thy cold-hearted, cold-blooded father divide us? Be generous, my love, be just; take not away a gift, last treasure of thy Guido—retract not thy vows—let us defy the world, and, setting at nought the calculations of age, find in our mutual affection a refuge from every ill."

Fiend I must have been with such sophistry to endeavour to poison that sanctuary of holy thought and tender love. Juliet shrank from me affrighted. Her father was the best and kindest of men, and she strove to show me how, in obeying him, every good would follow. He would receive my tardy submission with warm affection, and generous pardon would follow my repentance;—profitless words for a young and gentle daughter to use to a man accustomed to make his will law, and to feel in his own heart a despot so terrible and stern that he could yield obedience to nought save his own imperious desires! My resentment grew with resistance; my wild companions were ready to add fuel to the flame. We laid a plan to carry off Juliet. At first it appeared to be crowned with success. Midway, on our return, we were overtaken by the agonized father and his attendants. A conflict ensued. Before the city guard came to decide the victory in favour of our antagonists, two of Torella's servitors were dangerously wounded.

This portion of my history weighs most heavily with me.

Changed man as I am, I abhor myself in the recollection. May none who hear this tale ever have felt as I. A horse driven to fury by a rider armed with barbed spurs was not more a slave than I to the violent tyranny of my temper. A fiend possessed my soul, irritating it to madness. I felt the voice of conscience within me; but if I yielded to it for a brief interval, it was only to be a moment after torn, as by a whirlwind, away—borne along on the stream of desperate rage—the plaything of the storms engendered by pride. I was imprisoned, and, at the instance of Torella, set free.

Again I returned to carry off both him and his child to France, which hapless country, then preyed on by free booters and gangs of lawless soldiery, offered a grateful refuge to a criminal like me. Our plots were discovered. I was sentenced to banishment; and, as my debts were already enormous, my remaining property was put in the hands of commissioners for their payment. Torella again offered his mediation, requiring only my promise not to renew my abortive attempts on himself and his daughter. I spurned his offers, and fancied that I triumphed when I was thrust out from Genoa, a solitary and penniless exile. My companions were gone: they had been dismissed the city some weeks before, and were already in France. I was alone—friendless, with neither sword at my side, nor *ducat* in my purse.

I wandered along the sea-shore, a whirlwind of passion possessing and tearing my soul. It was as if a live coal had been set burning in my breast. At first I meditated on what *I should do*. I would join a band of freebooters. Revenge!—the word seemed balm to me; I hugged it, caressed it, till, like a serpent, it stung me. Then again I would abjure and despise Genoa, that little corner of the world. I would return to Paris, where so many of my friends swarmed; where my services would be eagerly accepted; where I would carve out fortune with my sword, and make my paltry birthplace and the false Torella rue the day when they drove me, a new Coriolanus, from her walls. I would return to Paris—thus on foot—a beggar—and present myself in my poverty to those I had formerly entertained sumptuously?

There was gall in the mere thought of it.

The reality of things began to dawn upon my mind, bringing despair in its train. For several months I had been a prisoner: the evils of my dungeon had whipped my soul to madness, but they had subdued my corporeal frame. I was weak and wan. Torella had used a thousand artifices to administer to my comfort; I had detected and scorned them all, and I reaped the harvest of my obduracy. What was to be done? Should I crouch before my foe, and sue for forgiveness?—Die rather ten thousand deaths!- Never should they obtain that victory! Hate—I swore eternal hate! Hate from whom?—to whom?—From a wandering out- cast to a mighty noble! I and my feelings were nothing to them: already had they forgotten one so unworthy. And Juliet!—her angel face and sylph-like form gleamed among the clouds of my despair with vain beauty; for I had lost her—the glory and flower of the world! Another will call her his!—that smile of paradise will bless another!

Even now my heart fails within me when I recur to this rout of grim-visaged ideas. Now subdued almost to tears, now raving in my agony, still I wandered along the rocky shore, which grew at each step wilder and more desolate. Hanging rocks and hoar precipices overlooked the tideless ocean; black caverns yawned; and forever, among the seaworn recesses, murmured and dashed the unfruitful waters. Now my way was almost barred by an abrupt promontory, now rendered nearly impracticable by frag- ments fallen from the cliff.

Evening was at hand, when, seaward, arose, as if on the wav- ing of a wizard's wand, a murky web of clouds, blotting the late azure sky, and darkening and disturbing the till now placid deep. The clouds had strange, fantastic shapes, and they changed and mingled and seemed to be driven about by a mighty spell. The waves raised their white crests; the thunder first muttered, then roared from across the waste of waters, which took a deep pur- ple dye, necked with foam.

The spot where I stood looked, on one side, to the wide spread ocean; on the other, it was barred by a rugged promontory. Round this cape suddenly came, driven by the wind, a vessel. In vain the mariners tried to force a path for her to the open sea the gale drove her on the rocks. It will perish! all on board will perish! Would I were among them! And to my young heart the, idea of death came for the first time blended with that of joy. It was an awful sight to behold that vessel struggling with her fate. Hardly could I discern the sailors, but I heard them. It was soon all over! A rock, just covered by the tossing waves, and so unperceived, lay in wait for its prey.

A crash of thunder broke over my head at the moment that, with a frightful shock, the vessel dashed upon her unseen enemy. In a brief space of time she went to pieces. There I stood in safety; arid there were my fellow-creatures battling, how hopelessly, with annihilation. Methought I saw them struggling—too truly did I hear their shrieks, conquering the barking surges in their shrill agony. The dark breakers threw hither and thither the fragments of the wreck: soon it disappeared. I had been fascinated to gaze till the end: at last I sank on my knees—I covered my face with my hands. I again looked up; something was floating on the billows towards the shore. It neared and neared. Was that a human form? It grew more and more distinct; and at last a mighty wave, lifting the whole freight, lodged it upon a rock. A human being bestriding a sea-chest!—a human being! Yet was it one? Surely never such had existed before—a misshapen dwarf, with squinting eyes, distorted features, and body deformed, till it became a horror to behold. My blood, lately warming towards a fellow-being so snatched from a watery tomb, froze in my heart. The dwarf got off his chest; he tossed his straight, struggling hair from his odious visage.

"By St. Beelzebub!" he exclaimed, "I have been well bested." He looked round and saw me. "Oh, by the fiend! here is another ally of the mighty One. To what saint did you offer prayers, friend—if not to mine? Yet I remember you not on board."

I shrank from the monster and his blasphemy. Again he questioned me, and I muttered some inaudible reply. He continued:—

"Your voice is drowned by this dissonant roar. What a noise the big ocean makes! Schoolboys bursting from their prison are not louder than these waves set free to play. They disturb me. I will no more of their ill- timed brawling. Silence, hoary One!— Winds, *avaunt!*—to your homes!—Clouds, fly to the antipodes, and leave our heaven clear!"

As he spoke, he stretched out his two long, lank arms, that looked like spider's claws, and seemed to embrace with them the expanse before him. Was it a miracle? The clouds became broken and fled; the azure sky first peeped out, and then was spread a calm field of blue above us; the stormy gale was exchanged to the softly breathing west; the sea grew calm; the waves dwindled to riplets.

"I like obedience even in these stupid elements," said the dwarf. "How much more in the tameless mind of man! It was a well-got-up storm, you must allow—and all of my own making."

It was tempting Providence to interchange talk with this magician. But *Power*, in all its shapes, is respected by man. Awe, curiosity, a clinging fascination, drew me towards him.

"Come, don't be frightened, friend," said the wretch: "I am good humoured when pleased; and something does please me in your well-proportioned body and handsome face, though you look a little woe-begone. You have suffered a land—I, a sea wreck. Perhaps I can allay the tempest of your fortunes as I did my own. Shall we be friends?"—And he held out his hand; I could not touch it.

"Well, then, companions that will do as well. And now, while I rest after the buffeting I underwent just now, tell me why, young and gallant as you seem, you wander thus alone and downcast on this wild sea-shore."

The voice of the wretch was screeching and horrid, and his contortions as he spoke were frightful to behold. Yet he did gain a kind of influence over me, which I could not master, and I told him my tale. When it was ended, he laughed long and loud: the rocks echoed back the sound: hell seemed yelling around me.

"Oh, thou cousin of Lucifer!" said he; "so thou too hast fallen through thy pride; and, though bright as the son of Morning, thou art ready to give up thy good looks, thy bride, and thy well-being, rather than submit thee to the tyranny of good. I honour thy choice, by my soul!—So thou hast fled, and yield the day; and mean to starve on these rocks, and to let the birds peck out thy dead eyes, while thy enemy and thy betrothed rejoice in thy ruin. Thy pride is strangely akin to humility, methinks."

As he spoke, a thousand fanged thoughts stung me to the heart.

"What would you that I should do?" I cried.

"I!—Oh, nothing, but lie down and say your prayers before you die. But, were I you, I know the deed that should be done."

I drew near him. His supernatural powers made him an oracle in my eyes; yet a strange unearthly thrill quivered through my frame as I said, "Speak! teach me what act do you advise?"

"Revenge thyself, man!—humble thy enemies!—set thy foot on the old man's neck, and possess thyself of his daughter!"

"To the east and west I turn," cried I, "and see no means! Had I gold, much could I achieve; but, poor and single, I am powerless."

The dwarf had been seated on his chest as he listened to my story. Now he got off; he touched a spring; it flew open! What a mine of wealth of blazing jewels, beaming gold, and pale silver was displayed therein. A mad desire to possess this treasure was born within me.

"Doubtless," I said, "one so powerful as you could do all things."

"Nay," said the monster humbly, "I am less omnipotent than I seem. Some things I possess which you may covet; but I would give them all for a small share, or even for a loan of what is yours."

"My possessions are at your service," I replied bitterly—"my poverty, my exile, my disgrace—I make a free gift of them all."

"Good! I thank you. Add one other thing to your gift, and

my treasure is yours."

"As nothing is my sole inheritance, what besides nothing would you have?"

"Your comely face and well-made limbs."

I shivered. Would this all-powerful monster murder me? I had no dagger. I forgot to pray—but I grew pale.

"I ask for a loan, not a gift," said the frightful thing: "lend me your body for three days—you shall have mine to cage your soul the while, and, in payment, my chest. What say you to the bargain?—Three short days."

We are told that it is dangerous to hold unlawful talk; and well do I prove the same. Tamely written down, it may seem incredible that I should lend any ear to this proposition; but, in spite of his unnatural ugliness, there was something fascinating in a being whose voice could govern earth, air, and sea. I felt a keen desire to comply; for with that chest I could command the world. My only hesitation resulted from a fear that he would not be true to his bargain. Then, I thought, I shall soon die here on these lonely sands, and the limbs he covets will be mine no more:—it is worth the chance.

And, besides, I knew that, by all the rules of art-magic, there were formula and oaths which none of its practisers dared break. I hesitated to reply; and he went on, now displaying his wealth, now speaking of the petty price he demanded, till it seemed madness to refuse. Thus is it;—place our bark in the current of the stream, and down, over fall and cataract it is hurried; give up our conduct to the wild torrent of passion, and we are away, we know not whither.

He swore many an oath, and I adjured him by many a sacred name; till I saw this wonder of power, this ruler of the elements, shiver like an autumn leaf before my words; and as if the spirit spake unwillingly and per force within him, at last, he, with broken voice, revealed the spell whereby he might be obliged, did he wish to play me false, to render up the unlawful spoil. Our warm life-blood must mingle to make and to mar the charm.

Enough of this unholy theme. I was persuaded—the thing

was done. The morrow dawned upon me as I lay upon the shingles, and I knew not my own shadow as it fell from me. I felt myself changed to a shape of horror, and cursed my easy faith and blind credulity. The chest was there—there the gold and precious stones for which I had sold the frame of flesh which nature had given me. The sight a little stilled my emotions: three days would soon be gone.

They did pass. The dwarf had supplied me with a plenteous store of food. At first I could hardly walk, so strange and out of joint were all my limbs; and my voice—it was that of the fiend. But I kept silent, and turned my face to the sun, that I might not see my shadow, and counted the hours, and ruminated on my future conduct. To bring Torella to my feet—to possess my Juliet in spite of him all this my wealth could easily achieve. During dark night I slept, and dreamt of the accomplishment of my desires. Two suns had set—the third dawned. I was agitated, fearful.

Oh expectation, what a frightful thing art thou, when kindled more by fear than hope! How dost thou twist thyself round the heart, torturing its pulsations! How dost thou dart unknown pangs all through our feeble mechanism, now seeming to shiver us like broken glass, to nothingness—now giving us a fresh strength, which can *do* nothing, and so torments us by a sensation, such as the strong man must feel who cannot break his fetters, though they bend in his grasp. Slowly paced the bright, bright orb up the eastern sky; long it lingered in the zenith, and still more slowly wandered down the west: it touched the horizon's verge—it was lost! Its glories were on the summits of the cliff they grew dun and grey. The evening star shone bright. He will soon be here.

He came not!—By the living heavens, he came not!—and night dragged out its weary length, and, in its decaying age, "day began to grizzle its dark hair;" and the sun rose again on the most miserable wretch that ever upbraided its light. Three days thus I passed. The jewels and the gold—oh, how I abhorred them!

Well, well—I will not blacken these pages with demoniac ravings. All too terrible were the thoughts, the raging tumult of ideas that filled my soul. At the end of that time I slept; I had not before since the third sunset; and I dreamt that I was at Juliet's feet, and she smiled, and then she shrieked—for she saw my transformation—and again she smiled, for still her beautiful lover knelt before her. But it was not I—it was he, the fiend, arrayed in my limbs, speaking with my voice, winning her with my looks of love. I strove to warn her, but my tongue refused its office; I strove to tear him from her, but I was rooted to the ground—I awoke with the agony.

There were the solitary hoar precipices—there the plashing sea, the quiet strand, and the blue sky over all. What did it mean? was my dream but a mirror of the truth? was he wooing and winning my betrothed? I would on the instant back to Genoa—but I was banished. I laughed—the dwarf's yell burst from my lips—*I* banished! Oh no! they had not exiled the foul limbs I wore; I might with these enter, without fear of incurring the threatened penalty of death, my own, my native city.

I began to walk towards Genoa. I was somewhat accustomed to my distorted limbs; none were ever so ill-adapted for a straightforward movement; it was with infinite difficulty that I proceeded. Then, too, I desired to avoid all the hamlets strewed here and there on the sea-beach, for I was unwilling to make a display of my hideousness. I was not quite sure that, if seen, the mere boys would not stone me to death as I passed, for a monster; some ungentle salutations I did receive from the few peasants or fishermen I chanced to meet. But it was dark night before I approached Genoa. The weather was so balmy and sweet that it struck me that the Marchese and his daughter would very probably have quitted the city for their country retreat.

It was from Villa Torella that I had attempted to carry off Juliet; I had spent many an hour reconnoitring the spot, and knew each inch of ground in its vicinity. It was beautifully situated, embosomed in trees, on the margin of a stream. As I drew near, it became evident that my conjecture was right; nay, moreover, that the hours were being then devoted to feasting and merriment. For the house was lighted up; strains of soft and gay music were wafted towards me by the breeze. My heart sank within me. Such was the generous kindness of Torella's heart that I felt sure that he would not have indulged in public manifestations of rejoicing just after my unfortunate banishment, but for a cause I dared not dwell upon.

The country people were all alive and flocking about; it became necessary that I should conceal myself; and yet I longed to address some one, or to hear others discourse, or in any way to gain intelligence of what was really going on. At length, entering the walks that were in immediate vicinity to the mansion, I found one dark enough to veil my excessive frightfulness; and yet others as well as I were loitering in its shade. I soon gathered all I wanted to know—all that first made my very heart die with horror, and then boil with indignation. Tomorrow Juliet was to be given to the penitent, reformed, beloved Guido—tomorrow my bride was to pledge her vows to a fiend from hell! And I did this!—my accursed pride my demoniac violence and wicked self-idolatry had caused this act.

For if I had acted as the wretch who had stolen my form had acted—if, with a mien at once yielding and dignified, I had presented myself to Torella, saying, I have done wrong, forgive me; I am unworthy of your angel-child, but permit me to claim her hereafter, when my altered conduct shall manifest that I abjure my vices, and endeavour to become in some sort worthy of her. I go to serve against the infidels; and when my zeal for religion and my true penitence for the past shall appear to you to cancel my crimes, permit me again to call myself your son. Thus had he spoken; and the penitent was welcomed even as the prodigal son of Scripture: the fatted calf was killed for him; and he, still pursuing the same path, displayed such open-hearted regret for his follies, so humble a concession of all his rights, and so ardent a resolve to reacquire them by a life of contrition and virtue, that he quickly conquered the kind old man; and full pardon, and the gift of his lovely child, followed in swift succession.

Oh, had an angel from Paradise whispered to me to act thus! But now, what would be the innocent Juliet's fate? Would God permit the foul union—or, some prodigy destroying it, link the dishonoured name of Carega with the worst of crimes? Tomorrow at dawn they were to be married: there was but one way to prevent this—to meet mine enemy, and to enforce the ratification of our agreement. I felt that this could only be done by a mortal struggle. I had no sword—if indeed my distorted arms could wield a soldier's weapon—but I had a dagger, and in that lay my hope. There was no time for pondering or balancing nicely the question: I might die in the attempt; but besides the burning jealousy and despair of my own heart, honour, mere humanity, demanded that I should fall rather than not destroy the machinations of the fiend.

The guests departed—the lights began to disappear; it was evident that the inhabitants of the villa were seeking repose. I hid myself among the trees—the garden grow desert—the gates were closed—I wandered round and came under a window—ah! well did I know the same!—a soft twilight glimmered in the room—the curtains were half withdrawn. It was the temple of innocence and beauty. Its magnificence was tempered, as it were, by the slight disarrangements occasioned by its being dwelt in, and all the objects scattered around displayed the taste of her who hallowed it by her presence.

I saw her enter with a quick light step—I saw her approach the window—she drew back the curtain yet further, and looked out into the night. Its breezy freshness played among her ringlets, and wafted them from the transparent marble of her brow. She clasped her hands, she raised her eyes to heaven. I heard her voice. Guido! she softly murmured—mine own Guido! and then, as if overcome by the fullness of her own heart, she sank on her knees;—her upraised eyes—her graceful attitude—the beaming thankfulness that lighted up her face—oh, these are tame words! Heart of mine, thou imagest ever, though thou canst not portray, the celestial beauty of that child of light and love,

I heard a step—a quick firm step along the shady avenue. Soon I saw a cavalier, richly dressed, young and, methought, graceful to look on, advance. I hid myself yet closer. The youth approached; he paused beneath the window. She arose, and again looking out she saw him, and said—I cannot, no, at this distant time I cannot record her terms of soft silver tenderness; to me they were spoken, but they were replied to by him.

"I will not go," he cried: "here where you have been, where your memory glides like some heaven-visiting ghost, I will pass the long hours till we meet, never, my Juliet, again, day or night, to part. But do thou, my love, retire; the cold morn and fitful breeze will make thy cheek pale, and fill with languor thy love-lighted eyes. Ah, sweetest! could I press one kiss upon them, I could, methinks, repose.

And then he approached still nearer, and methought he was about to clamber into her chamber. I had hesitated, not to terrify her; now I was no longer master of myself. I rushed forward—I threw myself on him—I tore him away—I cried, "loathsome and foul-shaped wretch!"

I need not repeat epithets, all tending, as it appeared, to rail at a person I at present feel some partiality for. A shriek rose from Juliet's lips. I neither heard nor saw—I *felt* only mine enemy, whose throat I grasped, and my dagger's hilt; he struggled, but could not escape. At length hoarsely he breathed these words: "Do!—strike home! destroy this body—you will still live: may your life be long and merry!"

The descending dagger was arrested at the word, and he, feeling my hold relax, extricated himself and drew his sword, while the uproar in the house, and flying of torches from one room to the other, showed that soon we should be separated. In the midst of my frenzy there was much calculation: fall I might, and so that he did not survive, I cared not for the death-blow I might deal against myself. While still, therefore, he thought I paused, and while I saw the villainous resolve to take advantage of my hesitation, in the sudden thrust he made at me, I threw myself on his sword, and at the same moment plunged my dagger, with a true, desperate aim, in his side. We fell together, rolling over each other, and the tide of blood that flowed from the gaping wound of each mingled on the grass. More I know not—I fainted.

Again I return to life: weak almost to death, I found myself stretched upon a bed—Juliet was kneeling beside it. Strange! my first broken request was for a mirror. I was so wan and ghastly, that my poor girl hesitated, as she told me afterwards; but, by the mass! I thought myself a right proper youth when I saw the dear reflection of my own well-known features. I confess it is a weakness, but I avow it, I do entertain a considerable affection for the countenance and limbs I behold, whenever I look at a glass; and have more mirrors in my house, and consult them oftener, than any beauty in Genoa. Before you too much condemn me, permit me to say that no one better knows than I the value of his own body; no one, probably, except myself, ever having had it stolen from him.

Incoherently I at first talked of the dwarf and his crimes, and reproached Juliet for her too easy admission of his love. She thought me raving, as well she might; and yet it was some time before I could prevail on myself to admit that the Guido whose penitence had won her back for me was myself; and while I cursed bitterly the monstrous dwarf, and blest the well-directed blow that had deprived him of life, I suddenly checked myself when I heard her say, Amen! knowing that him whom she reviled was my very self. A little reflection taught me silence—a little practice enabled me to speak of that frightful night without any very excessive blunder.

The wound I had given myself was no mockery of one—it was long before I recovered—and as the benevolent and generous Torella sat beside me, talking such wisdom as might win friends to repentance, and mine own dear Juliet hovered near me, ad ministering to my wants, and cheering me by her smiles, the work of my bodily cure and mental reform went on together. I have never, indeed, wholly recovered my strength—my check is paler since—my person a little bent. Juliet sometimes ventures to allude bitterly to the malice that caused this change, but I kiss her on the moment, and tell her all is for the best. I am a fonder and more faithful husband, and true is this—but for that wound, never had I called her mine.

I did not revisit the seashore, nor seek for the fiend's treasure; yet, while I ponder on the past, I often think, and my confessor was not backward in favouring the idea, that it might be a good rather than an evil spirit, sent by my guardian angel, to show me the folly and misery of pride. So well at least did I learn this lesson, roughly taught as I was, that I am known now by all my friends and fellow-citizens by the name of Guido il Cortese.

Valerius: The Reanimated Roman

About eleven o'clock before noon in the month of September, two strangers landed in the little bay formed by the extreme point of Cape Miseno and the promontory of Bauli. The sky was of a deep serene blue, and the sea reflected its depth back with a darker tint. Through the clear water you saw the seaweed of various and beautiful colours as it grew on the remnants of the palaces of the Romans now buried under the waters. The sun shone bright causing an intolerable heat. The strangers on landing immediately sought a shady place where they might refresh themselves and remain until the sun should begin to descend towards the horizon. They sought the Elysian fields, and, winding among the poplars and mulberry trees festooned by the grapes which hung in rich and ripe clusters, they seated themselves under the shade of the tombs beside the Mare Morto.

One of these strangers was an Englishman of rank, as could easily be perceived by his noble carriage and manners full of dignity and freedom. His companion—I can compare him to nothing that now exists—his appearance resembled that of the statue of Marcus Aurelius in the Square of the Capitol at Rome. Placid and commanding, his features were Roman; except for his dress you would have imagined him to be a statue of one of the Romans animated with life. He wore the dress now common all over Europe, but it appeared unsuited to him and even as if he were unused to it. As soon as they were seated he began to speak thus:—

"I have promised to relate to you, my friend, what were my

sensations on my revival, and how the appearance of this world—fallen from what it once was—struck me when the light of the sun revisited my eyes after it had deserted them many hundred years. And how can I choose a better place for this relation. This is the spot which was chosen by our antient and venerable religion, as that which best represented the idea oracles had given or diviners received of the seats of the happy after death. These are the tombs of Romans. This place is much changed by the sacrilegious hand of man since those times, but still it bears the name of the Elysian fields. Avernus is but a short distance from us, and this sea which we perceive is the blue Mediterranean, unchanged while all else bears the marks of servitude and degradation.

"Pardon me—you are an Englishman, and they say you are free in your country—a country unknown when I lived—but the wretched Italians, who usurp the soil once trod by heroes, fill me with bitter disdain. Dare they usurp the name of Romans—dare they imagine that they descend from the Lords and Governors of the world? They forget that, when the republic died, every antient Roman family became by degrees extinct and that their followers might usurp the name, but were not and are not Romans.

"When I lived before, it was in the time of Cicero and of Cato. My rank was neither the highest nor the lowest in Rome: I was a Roman knight. I did not live to see my country enslaved by Caesar, who during my life was distinguished only by the debauchery of his manners. I died when I was nearly forty-five, defending my country against Catihine. At that time, the good men of Rome lamented bitterly the decline of morals in the city—Manius and Sulla had already taught us some of the miseries of tyranny, and I was accustomed to lament the day when the Senate appeared an assembly of demigods. But what men lived at that time?—The republic set gloriously as the sun of a bright and summer day. How could I despair of my country while such men as Cicero, Cato, Lucullus, and many others whom I knew as full of virtue and wisdom—who were my intimate and dearest friends—still existed.

"I need not trouble you with the history of my life—in modern times, domestic circumstances appear to be that part of a man's history most worth enquiring into. In Rome, the history of an individual was that of his country. We lived in the Forum and in the Senate House. My family had suffered by the civil wars: my father had been slain by Manius; and my uncle, who took care of me during my infancy, was proscribed by Sulla and murdered by his emissaries. My fortune was considerably diminished by these domestic misfortunes, but I lived frugally and filled with honour some of the highest offices of state—I was once consul.

"Nor will I now relate what would greatly interest you—all that I know concerning those great men with whose actions, even at this distance of time, you are intimately acquainted. These topics have formed and will form an inexhaustible source of conversation during the time we remain together, but at present I have promised to relate what I felt and saw when I revisited, now three years ago, this fallen Italy.

"As I approached Rome, I became agitated by a thousand emotions. I refused to see anything or to speak to anybody. Mute in a corner of the carriage, I hoarded my thoughts: sometimes thinking my companion unworthy my attention; at others still obstinately clinging, as a mother would to the memory of her lost child, to my loved country and doubting all that I had heard, all that these priests had told me. I believed in a conspiracy formed against me. I refused to speak to those we met on the road, lest their altered dialect should crush my last hope. I would visit no scenery. The eternal city survived in all its glory. It could not die—yet, still if it were dead, I would be silent till among the ruins of its Forum I should pour forth my last lament—and my words should awaken the dead to listen to me. 'Cicero—Gato—Pompey—were ye indeed dead—all trace of your path worn out. Still do ye haunt the Forum—awake—arise—welcome me!'

"The priest in vain endeavoured to draw me from my reverie. My countenance was impressed by sorrow, but I answered not. At length he exclaimed, 'Behold the Tiber!' Lovely river! Still and forever dost thou roll on thy eternal waters; thy waves glitter in the sun or are shadowed by the thunder cloud; thy name acted as a spell. Tears gushed from my eyes. I alighted from the carriage. I hastened to the banks and kneeling down I offered up to thee, sacred names of Jupiter and Pallas, vows which made my lips quiver and the light almost pass from my eyes: 'O Jupiter—Jupiter of the Capitol—thou who has beheld so many triumphs, still may thy temples exist, still may the victims be led to thy altars!—Minerva protect thy Rome.' In that moment of agonized prayer, the fate of my country seemed yet undecided—the sword was still suspended. Alas, I could not believe that all that is great and good had departed.

"In vain, my companion tried to tear me away from the banks of the divine river. I remained seated immovably by it; my eyes did not wander on the surrounding scenery that had changed, but they were fixed on the waters or raised to the blue bright sky above. 'These—these, at least are the same—ever, ever the same!' were the only words I uttered when, from time to time, the fall of my country with the fierce agony of fire rushed across my mind. The priest tried to soothe me—I was silent. At length, the strength of passion overcame me, and after many hours of insane contest I suffered myself to be led to the carriage and, drawing up the blinds, abandoned myself to a reverie whose bitterness was only diminished by my lost strength.

"It was night when we entered Rome. 'Tomorrow,' said my companion, 'we will visit the Forum.' I assented. I did not wish him to accompany me, and therefore retired early without disclosing my intentions. But as soon as I found myself free from importunity, I demanded a guide and hastened to visit the scene of all human greatness. The moon had risen and cast a bright light over the city of Rome—if I may call that Rome which in no way resembled the Queen of Nations as I remembered her. We passed along the Gorso, and I saw several magnificent obelisks, which seemed to tell me that the glory of my country had not passed away.

"I paused beside the Column of Antoninus, which sunk deep in the ground and, surrounded by the remains of forty columns, impressed the idea of decay upon my mind. My heart beat with fear and indignation as I approached the Forum by ways unknown to me. And the spell broke as I beheld the shattered columns and ruined temples of the Campo Vaccino—by that disgraceful name must now be designated the Roman Forum. I gazed round, but nothing there is as it was—I saw ruins of temples built after my time. The Coliseum was a stranger to me, and it appeared as if the altered state of these magnificent ruins suddenly quenched the enthusiasm of indignation which had before possessed my heart.

"I had never dared present to myself the image of the Roman Forum, degraded and debased; but a vague idea floated in my mind of broken columns, such as I remembered of the fallen images of the gods still left to decay in a spot where I had formerly worshipped them; but all was changed, and even the columns that remain of the temple erected by Camillus lost their identity surrounded by new candidates for immortality. I turned calmly to my guide and enquired, 'These are the ruins of the Roman Forum, and what is that immense building, whose shadow in the moonshine seems to bespeak something wonderful and magnificent, which I see at the end of the avenue of trees?'—'This is the Coliseum.'—'And what is Coliseum?'—'Do you not know? It is the renowned Circus built by Vespasian, Emperor of Rome.'-'Emperor of Rome, was he? Well, let us visit it.'

"We entered the Coliseum, that noble relict of imperial greatness—imperial it is true, but Roman. And that enthusiasm, which the broken columns of the Forum had extinguished, this wonderful pile again awakened. The moon shone through the broken arches and shed a glory around the fallen walls, crowned as they are by weeds and brambles. I looked around, and a holy awe seized me. I felt as if having deserted the Campo Vaccino, this had become the haunt of my noble compatriots. The seal of Eternity was on this building, and my heart heaved with the overpowering sensations under which it laboured. I said not a word.

"Alas! Alas! Such is the image of Rome fallen, torn, degraded by a hateful superstition; yet still commanding love honour; and still awakening in the imaginations of men all that can purify and ennoble the mind. The Coliseum is the Type of Rome. Its arches—its marbles—its noble aspect which must inspire all with awe, which, in the mind of man, is akin to adoration—its wonderful, its inexpressible beauty—all tell of its greatness. Its fallen walls—its weed-covered buttresses—and more than all, the insulting images with which it is filled tell its fall.

"I dismissed my guide. I would never quit the Coliseum; this should be my abode during my second residence on earth. I visited every part of it. From its height, I beheld Rome sleeping under the cold rays of the moon: the dome of St. Peter's and the various other domes and spires which make a second city, the habitations of gods above the habitations of men; the arch of Constantine at my feet; the Tiber and the great change in the situation of the city of modern times; all caught my attention, but they only awakened a vague and transitory interest. The Coliseum was to me henceforth the world, my eternal habitation. It is true that curiosity and importunity have dragged me from it now—but my absence will be short, and my heart is still there. I shall return. And in those hallowed precincts, I shall pour forth, before I die, my last awakening call to Romans and to Liberty.

"It is true that I was now convinced that Rome had fallen, that her consuls and triumphs were at an end, the temples of her Capitol destroyed. But the Coliseum had softened those sentiments whose energy must otherwise have destroyed me. Anger, despair, all human passion died within me. I devoted myself, a pilgrim for some years, to a world in whose shews I am a careless spectator. If Rome be dead, I fly from her remains, loathsome as those of human life. It is in the Coliseum alone that I recognise the grandeur of my country—that is the only worthy asylum for an antient Roman.

"Yet suddenly, the feeling so dreadful to the human mind, the feeling of utter solitude, operated a new change on my heart. I remembered as it were but of yesterday all the shews which antient Rome had presented. Seated under one of the arches of the building and hiding my face in my hands, I revived in my imagination the memory of what I had left, when I last lost the light of day. I had left the consuls in the full enjoyment of power. Some years before, the empire, torn by Manius and Sulla and unsupported by the virtue of any, seemed tottering on the edge of subjection.

"But during my life, a new spirit had arisen: men were again vivified by the sacred flame that burnt in the souls of Camillus and Fabricius, and I gloried with an excessive joy to be the friend of Cicero, Cato, and Lucullus; the younger men, the sons of my friends, Brutus, Cassius, were rising with the promise of equal virtue. When I died, I was possessed by the strong persuasion that, since philosophy and letters were now joined to a virtue unparalleled upon earth, Rome was approaching that perfection from which there was no fall; and that, although men still feared, it was a wholesome fear which awoke them to action and the better secured the triumph of Good.

"When I awoke, Rome was no longer. That light, which I had hailed as the forerunner of perfection, became the torches that added splendour to her funeral—and those men, whose souls were as the temples of perfection, were the victims sacrificed at her funeral pyre. Oh, never had a nation such a death, and her murderers celebrated such games round her tomb, as destroyed nearly half the world. They were not the combats of gladiators and beasts—but the fierce strife of contending passions, the war of millions.

"But that is now all over. The exultation of the tyrant has faded. The monument of Rome, so splendid through the course of ages and adorned by the spoils of kingdoms, is now degraded in the dust. Some scattered columns and arches live to tell her site, but her people are dead. The strangers that possess her have lost all the characteristics of Romans; they have fallen off from her holy religion. Modern Rome is the Capital of Christianity, and that title is that which is crown and top of my despair.

"But human language sinks under the endeavour to describe the tremendous change operated in the world, it is true, by the slow flow of many ages, but which appeared to me in my singular situation as the work of a few days. I cannot recollect the agony of those moments—without shuddering. It was not a train of bitter thought; it was not a despair that ate into the nerves but shewed no outward sign; it was not the first pang of grief for the loss of those we love. It was a fierce fire that enveloped forests and cities in its flame; it was a tremendous avalanche that bore down with it trees and rocks and turned the course of rivers; it was an earthquake that shakes the sea and overturns mountains and threatens to shew to the eyes of man the mysteries of the internal earth. Oh, it was more than all these! More than any words can express or any image portray!"

The Stranger paused in his narration, and a long silence ensued. His eyes were fixed on the dead waters before him, and his companion gazed on him with wonder and emotion. A breeze slightly passed over the sea and rippled it; its rustling was heard among the trees. The smallest change awakened the Roman from his reverie, and he continued.

"A year has passed since I stood for the first time within the Coliseum. The rich dark weeds seemed blacker under the moon's rays, and the fallen arches reared themselves in stillness and beauty. The air was silent: it was the dead of night, and no sound reached me from the city—but by degrees the moon sunk, and daylight dawned. The sounds of human life began, and my own thoughts, which during the night were conversant only with memories, now turned their courses to the mean and debased reality. I considered my present situation, for I wished to form some plan for my future life. I greatly disliked the priest, my companion.

"During my very short residence since my return to earth, I had conceived a great aversion to the class of men to which he belonged. I disliked the Catholic superstition and wished to have no commerce with its ministers and servants. The jewels and money which I had were sufficient for my maintenance, and I wished to cast off the subjection which his presence seemed to put me under. But although in my native Rome, I was in a strange city with unknown customs. I hardly understood their language, and the recollections of my former life would only cast me into ridiculous mistakes. It was then that a kind deity interfered and, sending my good genius to watch over me, extricated me from my difficulties.

"The old priest, when the next morning he found I had disappeared, sent the guide, who had conducted me the preceding night, to bring me back and himself commenced a round of visits to publish the curiosity which he had under his keeping. Among others, he visited Lord Harley who had long been resident at Rome and to whom he was perfectly well known. You know Lord Harley and his family. I need not, therefore, describe them to you—and you who know her character can easily imagine the interest and curiosity with which the old priest's account inspired his young wife. She ordered her carriage and, taking the priest with her, hastened to his hotel to see me. I had not returned—the guide who had been to seek me informed her that I refused to quit the Coliseum. She left the priest at the inn and, accompanied only by her little son, came to my retreat.

"I was seated under the ruined arches of the south side when I saw her approach, leading her child by the hand. She sat down beside me, and after a pause of a few seconds she addressed me in Italian. 'Forgive me if I interrupt you. I have seen Padre Giuseppe and know who you are. You are unhappy and are cast upon our modern world without friends or connections. Will you allow me to offer you my friendship?'—I was thrown into confusion by this speech, addressed to me by a beautiful girl perfectly a stranger to me, and paused before I could answer so kind but so uncommon an offer; she continued—'Consider me, I entreat you, as an old acquaintance—not a modern Italian, for indeed I am not one, but as one of those many strangers which your antient city drew to gaze on her. I come from a distant country and am, therefore, unknowing in your language and laws. You shall teach me to know all that was great and worthy in your days, and I will teach you the manners and customs of ours.'

"She talked to me thus and won me over by her sweet smiles and soft eloquence to confide myself entirely to her. 'You shall consider me as your daughter,' said she, 'if a Scotch girl may pretend to that honour. I come from that *Ultima Thule* discovered by Caesar, but unknown in your days. I am married to an Englishman a good deal older than I am, but he takes a pleasure in cultivating my mind. Come with me to our house; you will be cherished and honoured there, and we will try to soften the pangs which the fallen state of your country must inflict upon you.

"I followed her to her house and from that day began that friendship which is the only hope and comfort of my life. If on my return to earth my affections had never been awakened, I should not have lived long. But Isabell has softened my despair and nursed with angelic affection every wound of my heart. I cannot tell you how much I love her—how dear the sound of her voice is to me. Cicero did not love his Tullia as I do this divine creature. You cannot know half her virtues or half her wisdom. She is so frank-hearted, and yet so tender, that she wins my soul and binds it up in hers in a manner that I never experienced in my former life. She is Country, Friends—all, all, that I had lost is she to me.

"And now I have performed my promise in relating to you my first sensations upon awakening into life. I need not make a formal narration of what I have learnt since. In our proposed journey we shall have frequent opportunities of conversing and arguing. You have won me to a wish to see your country, and tomorrow we embark. I quit Rome—the Coliseum and Isabell—such is my restless nature. I want before I again die to examine the boasted improvements of modern times and to judge if, after the great fluctuation in human affairs, man is nearer perfection than in my days."

The sun had far descended when these friends rose and returned to the boat. As they rowed back to Naples, the sun set, leaving a rich orange tint in the sky which burned upon the waters, while Cape Miseno and the islands were marked by a black outline in the horizon. The moon rose on the other side of the bay and contrasted her silver light with the glowing colours of the Italian sunset. Night advanced, and the lights of the fisher boats glimmered across the sea, while one or two large ships seemed to pass like enormous shadows between the gazers and the moon. The brilliant spectacle of sunset and the soft light of the moon invited to reverie and forbade words to disturb the magic of the scene. The old Roman perhaps thought of the days he had formerly spent at Baiae, when the eternal sun had set as it now did, and he lived in other days with other men.

[The story ends at this point, but another and fragmentary version, told from Isabell Harley's point of view, follows in the manuscript.]

When I had drawn my singular friend from his solitude at the Coliseum, I, with the consent of Lord Harley, installed him in a room of our house. At first, he shunned all society and laboured under so great a depression of spirits that his health became affected. I found that I must make it my task to interest his feelings and to endeavour by whatever means to draw him from the apathy under which he was sunk. He appeared to regard everything around him as a spectacle in which he had no concern. He was indeed a being cut off from our world; the links that had bound him to it had been snapped many ages before; and, unless I could succeed in joining at least one of them again, he would soon perish. I wished to engage him to visit some of those mighty ruins which tell of the antient greatness of Rome.

I hesitated some time in my choice; the most majestic buildings had been built after his time, but I thought that their being situated in places familiar to his memory would give them that interest which otherwise, as unknown to him, they would want. I myself delighted to visit the baths of Antoninus, whose vast heaps of shattered walls and towers, clothed with ivy and the loveliest weeds, appear more like the natural scenery of a mountain than anything formed of human hands. To these noble ruins I determined to conduct him.

I visited him, therefore, one day; and leading the conversation to his former life and death, I said to him: "You were happy in dying before the fall of your country and in not witnessing its degradation under the Emperors. These Emperors, who succeeded to the power and glory of the republic, enjoyed an extent of dominion and a revenue unknown in times before or after. Wild and tremendous were the deeds and errors of the omnipotent men. Their enemy could not fly from them. They trampled at will on the necks of millions. Few used their dominion for uses of beneficence, but many, even of the most wicked, spent it for the purposes of magnificence.

They have left wonderful monuments behind, and I cannot regard these wonders as the acts of imperial greatness. They are the effects, although executed by unmeet hands, of republican virtue and power. When I visit them, I admire them as planned and modified by Camillus, by Fabricius, by the Scipios; and I regard Garacalla and Nero and even the more virtuous of the tribe, Titus and Adrian, as the mere workmen. When I visit the Coliseum, I do not think of Vespasian who built it or of the blood of gladiators and beasts which contaminated it, but I worship the spirit of antient Rome and of those noble heroes, who delivered their country from barbarians and who have enlightened the whole world by their miraculous virtue. I have heard you express a dislike of viewing the works of the oppressors of Rome, but visit them with me in this spirit, and you will find them strike you with that awe and reverence which power, acquired and accompanied by vice, can never give."

He suffered himself to be persuaded, and we passed under the Capitol and at the back of Mount Palatine on our way to the baths. The principal site of antient Rome is deserted, and we visit the Forum and the most populous of the hills of Rome through grassy lanes and across fields where few people ever come. This is fortunate; the ruins would lose half their beauty if surrounded by modern buildings, and we have only to regret that the Capitol has not been neglected as Mount Palatine and Mount Caelius are. I cannot tell what the feelings of Valenius were: his emotions were strong, but he was silent, but for ever cast his eyes up to the sky; and once he said, "I like to look at the heavens, and only at them, for they are not changed."

We entered the baths, and after visiting all the apartments, we ascended the shattered staircase and passed over the immense arches and the walls, which, when you are on them, appear like fields and glens and sloping hills. We were surrounded by fragrant weeds, and their height on each side of the path deceives you and adds still greater apparent extent to the ruins on which we walked. Sometimes, the top of some buttress is spread out into a field enamelled by the most beautiful flowers. And now winding about a difficult path, we reached the top of a turret and saw all Rome with the windings of the Tiber at but a short distance from us. This is of all others the place I delight most in Rome to visit: it joins the beauty and fragrance of Nature to the sublimest idea of human power; and when so united, they have an interest and feeling that sinks deep into my heart.

We seated ourselves on this pinnacle, and I sought in the eyes of my companion for an expression of wonder and delight with which mine were glistening. His were filled with tears. "You bring me here," he said, "to view the works of the Romans, and I behold nothing but destruction. What crowds of beautiful temples are fallen to the dust. My eyes wander over the seven hills, and all their glories are faded. When the columns of its Forum were broken, what could survive in Rome. The Capitol, less happy than most of the other hills who have returned to the solitude of Nature, is defiled by modern buildings.

And these ruins—they are grand, but how miserable a tale do they tell. These baths did not exist in my time. They existed in all their magnificence some hundred years after I had forgotten the world. But now their roofs have fallen; their pavements have disappeared; they are grass-grown, weed-grown, shattered yet still standing; and such is the immortality of Rome. The walls of Rome still stand, and they describe an immense circuit; the modern city is filled with the ruins of the antient. Strangers flock to it and wonder at the immensity of the remains. But to me it all appears void. The antient temples where I worshipped Quirinus and the protectors of what I then called the immortal city—alas, why do I wake to be undeceived."

"You dwell," I replied, "on the most mournful ideas. Rome is fallen, but she is still venerated. It is to me a singular and even a beautiful sight to see the care and pains with which her degenerate children preserve her reliques. Every one visits her with enthusiasm and quits her with bitter regret. All appears consecrated within her walls. When a stranger resides within their bounds, he feels as if he inhabited a sacred temple—sacred although defiled; and indignation and pity mingling with his admiration, he feels such sensations that soften his heart and can never even in age and affliction be forgotten. It seems to me that, if I were overtaken by the greatest misfortunes, I should be half consoled by the recollection of having dwelt in Rome. If a man of the age of Pericles were to revive in Athens, how much more reason would he have to lament over her fall, than you oven the age and decay of Rome."

As I wished to interest the feelings of Valerius and not so much to shew him all the remains of his country as to awaken in him by their sight a sentiment that he was still in some degree linked to the world, I chose as much as I could the most perfect and the most picturesque. He had not yet seen the Pantheon. I would not take him to it in the day, for I knew that its conversion to a Catholic Church, although it had probably preserved it, would be highly disgusting to him. I chose the time when the moon was yet in her encrease and when in her height she would shine over the open roof of the temple.

One evening about seven o'clock, without telling him where we were going, I took him out with me. We passed round the building to a back door—it was opened, and a man lighted us down a pair of narrow dirty stairs: as we descended I said to him,

"You are now going to see a temple built shortly after your time and dedicated to all the gods." He probably expected to see a ruin, but lo! we entered the most beautiful temple yet existing in the world. The bright moon shone directly over the aperture at top and lighted up the dome and the pavement—some bright stars twinkled by her side.

The columns shone dimly around. The spirit of beauty seemed to shed her rays over her favoured offspring and to penetrate everything—even the human mind—with a soft, still yet bright glory. In contemplating this scene, human admiration was unmingled with the deep feeling that it inspired—one seemed to enjoy the present god. If the work was human, the glory came from Nature; and Nature poured forth all her loveliness above this divine temple. The deep sky, the bright moon, and the twinkling stars were spread over it, and their light and beauty penetrated it. Why cannot human language express human thoughts? And how is it that there is a feeling inspired by the excess of beauty, which laps the heart in a gentle but eager flame, which may inspire virtue and love, but the feeling is far too intense for expression?

We were both silent. We walked round the temple, and then we seated ourselves on the steps of an altar and remained a long time in contemplation. It is at such a time when one feels the existence of that Pantheic Love with which Nature is penetrated—and when a strong sympathy with beauty, if such an expression may be allowed, is the only feeling which animates the soul. At length, as we rose to depart, Valenius said, "Why do they tell me that all is changed; does not this temple to our gods exist?"

I know not why—I ought not to have done it, for by the action I poisoned a moment of pure happiness—but I carelessly pointed to a cross that stood on the altar before which a solitary lamp burned. The cross did not alter my feelings, but those of my companion were embittered. The apple so fair to look at had turned to brackish dust. The cross told to him of change so great, so intolerable, that that one circumstance destroyed all that had arisen of love and pleasure in his heart. I tried in vain to bring him back to the deep feeling of beauty and of sacred awe with which he had been lately inspired. The spell was snapped. The moon-enlightened dome, the glittering pavement, the dim rows of lovely columns, the deep sky had lost to him their holiness. He hastened to quit the temple.

It was my first care to awaken in him a desire to know what of great and good had existed in his country after his death. He knew nothing of Virgil, Horace, Ovid, or Lucan—of Livy, Tacitus, or Seneca. You will have frequent opportunities of conversing with him, and he can tell you, much better than I can do, what the feelings were which this lecture excited in his mind. We used to visit an obscure nook of the Coliseum, where we scrambled with difficulty, and few would be inclined to follow us; or, on the walls of the baths of Caracalla or more frequently at the foot of the tomb of Cestius, that lovely spot where death appears to enjoy sunshine and the blue depth of the deep sky from which it is everywhere else shut out, we read together, and we discussed on what we read—our discussions were eternal.

The brilliant sun of Rome shone upon us, and the air and all the scene were invested by happiness and beauty. My heart was cheerful, and it was my constant endeavour to awaken similar feelings in the bosom of my companion. We read the Georgics here, and I felt a degree of happiness in reading them that I could not have believed that words had it in their power to bestow. It was an intoxicating pleasure, which this fine climate and the sunny beautiful poetry which it inspires can give and which in a clouded atmosphere I am convinced I never should have felt.

After reading, we visited some one of the galleries of Rome—Lord Harley's studious hours were then over, and he always accompanied us. The sight of the exquisite statues and paintings in Rome continued and often heightened this feeling of enjoyment. Did Valerius sympathize with me? Alas! no. There was a melancholy tint cast over all his thoughts; there was a sadness of demeanour, which the sun of Rome and the verses of Virgil could not dissipate. He felt deeply, but little joy mingled with his sentiments. With my other feelings towards him, I had joined to them an inexplicable one that my companion was not a being of the earth. I often paused anxiously to know whether he respired the air, as I did, or if his form cast a shadow at his feet. His semblance was that of life, yet he belonged to the dead. I did not feel fear or terror; I loved and revered him. I was warmly interested in his happiness, but there was mingled with these commoner sensations an awe—I cannot call it dread, yet it had something slightly allied to that repulsive feeling—a sentiment for which I can find no name, which mingled with all my thoughts and strangely characterised all my intercourse with him.

Often when borne on in discourse by my thoughts, I encountered the glance of his bright yet placid eye; although it beamed only in sympathy, yet it checked me. If he put his hand upon mine, I did not shudder, but, as it were, my thoughts paused in their course and my heart heaved with something of an involuntary uneasiness until it was removed. Yet this was all very slight; I hardly noticed it, and it could not diminish my love and interest for him; perhaps if I would own all the truth, my affection was encreased by it; and not by endeavour but spontaneously I strove to repay by interest and intellectual sympathy the earthly barrier there seemed placed between us.

Ferdinando Eboli

During this quiet time of peace we are fast forgetting the exciting and astonishing events of the Napoleonic wars; and the very names of Europe's conquerors are becoming antiquated to the ears of our children. Those were more romantic days than these; for the revulsions occasioned by revolution or invasion were full of romance; and travellers in those countries in which these scenes had place hear strange and wonderful stories, whose truth so much resembles fiction, that, while interested in the narration, we never give implicit credence to the narrator. Of this kind is a tale I heard at Naples. The fortunes of war perhaps did not influence its actors, yet it appears improbable that any circumstances so out of the usual routine could have had place under the garish daylight that peace sheds upon the world.

When Murat, then called Gioacchino, king of Naples, raised his Italian regiments, several young nobles, who had before been scarcely more than vine-dressers on the soil, were inspired with a love of arms, and presented themselves as candidates for military honours. Among these was the young Count Eboli. The father of this youthful noble had followed Ferdinand to Sicily; but his estates lay principally near Salerno, and he was naturally desirous of preserving them; while the hopes that the French government held out of glory and prosperity to his country made him often regret that he had followed his legitimate but imbecile king to exile.

When he died, therefore, he recommended his son to return to Naples, to present himself to his old and tried friend, the

Marchese Spina, who held a high office in Murat's government, and through his means to reconcile himself to the new king.' All this was easily achieved. The young and gallant Count was permitted to possess his patrimony; and, as a further pledge of good fortune, he was betrothed to the only child of the Marchese Spina. The nuptials were deferred till the end of the ensuing campaign.

Meanwhile the army was put in motion, and Count Eboli only obtained such short leave of absence as permitted him to visit for a few hours the villa of his future father-in-law, there to take leave of him and his affianced bride. The villa was situated on one of the Appennines to the north of Salerno, and looked down, over the plain of Calabria, in which Pæstum is situated, on to the blue Mediterranean. A precipice on one side, a brawling mountain torrent, and a thick grove of ilex, added beauty to the sublimity of its site. Count Eboli ascended the mountain-path in all the joy of youth and hope. His stay was brief. An exhortation and a blessing from the *Marchese*, a tender farewell, graced by gentle tears, from the fair Adalinda, were the recollections he was to bear with him, to inspire him with courage and hope in danger and absence. The sun had just sunk behind the distant isle of Istria, when, kissing his lady's hand, he said a last "*Addio*," and with slower steps, and more melancholy mien, rode down the mountain on his road to Naples.

That same night Adalinda retired early to her apartment, dismissing her attendants; and then, restless from mingled fear and hope, she threw open the glass-door that led to a balcony looking over the edge of the hill upon the torrent, whose loud rushing often lulled her to sleep, but whose waters were concealed from sight by the ilex trees, which lifted their topmost branches above the guarding parapet of the balcony.

Leaning her cheek upon her hand, she thought of the dangers her lover would encounter, of her loneliness the while, of his letters, and of his return. A rustling sound now caught her ear. Was it the breeze among the ilex trees! Her own veil was unwaved by every wind, her tresses even, heavy in their own rich beauty only, were not lifted from her cheek. Again those sounds. Her blood retreated to her heart, and her limbs trembled. What could it mean? Suddenly the upper branches of the nearest tree were disturbed; they opened, and the faint starlight showed a man's figure among them. He prepared to spring from his hold on to the wall. It was a feat of peril. First the soft voice of her lover bade her "Fear not," and on the next instant he was at her side, calming her terrors, and recalling her spirits, that almost left her gentle frame, from mingled surprise, dread, and joy. He encircled her waist with his arm, and pouring forth a thousand passionate expressions of love, she leant on his shoulder, and wept from agitation, while he covered her hands with kisses, and gazed on her with ardent adoration.

Then in calmer mood they sat together; triumph and joy lighted up his eyes, and a modest blush glowed on her cheek: for never before had she sat alone with him, nor heard unrestrained his impassioned assurances of affection. It was, indeed. Love's own hour. The stars trembled on the roof of his eternal temple; the dashing of the torrent, the mild summer atmosphere, and the mysterious aspect of the darkened scenery, were all in unison to inspire security and voluptuous hope. They talked of how their hearts, through the medium of divine nature, might hold commune during absence; of the joys of reunion, and of their prospect of perfect happiness.

The moment at last arrived when he must depart. "One tress of this silken hair," said he, raising one of the many curls that clustered on her neck. "I will place it on my heart, a shield to protect me against the swords and balls of the enemy." He drew his keen-edged dagger from its sheath. "Ill weapon for so gentle a deed," he said, severing the lock, and at the same moment many drops of blood fell fast on the fair arm of the lady. He answered her fearful inquiries by showing a gash he had awkwardly inflicted on his left hand. First he insisted on securing his prize, and then he permitted her to bind his wound, which she did half laughing, half in sorrow, winding round his hand a riband loosened from her own arm.

"Now, farewell," he cried; "I must ride twenty miles ere dawn, and the descending Bear shows that midnight is past." His descent was difficult, but he achieved it happily, and the stave of a song—whose soft sounds rose like the smoke of incense from an altar—from the dell below, to her impatient ear, assured her of his safety.

As is always the case when an account is gathered from eye-witnesses, I never could ascertain the exact date of these events. They occurred, however, while Murat was king of Naples; and when he raised his Italian regiments, Count Eboli, as aforesaid, became a junior officer in them, and served with much distinction, though I cannot name either the country or the battle in which he acted so conspicuous a part that he was on the spot promoted to a troop.

Not long after this event, and while he was stationed in the north of Italy, Gioacchino, sending for him to headquarters late one evening, entrusted him with a confidential mission, across a country occupied by the enemy's troops, to a town possessed by the French. It was necessary to undertake the expedition during the night, and he was expected to return on that succeeding the following day. The king himself gave him his despatches and the word; and the noble youth, with modest firmness, protested that he would succeed, or die, in the fulfilment of his trust.

It was already night, and the crescent moon was low in the west, when Count Ferdinando Eboli, mounting his favourite horse, at a quick gallop cleared the streets of the town; and then, following the directions given him, crossed the country among the fields planted with vines, carefully avoiding the main road. It was a beauteous and still night; calm and sleep occupied the earth; war, the blood-hound, slumbered; the spirit of love alone had life at that silent hour. Exulting in the hope of glory, our young hero commenced his journey, and visions of aggrandizement and love formed his reveries.

A distant sound roused him: he checked his horse and listened; voices approached. When recognising the speech of a German, he turned from the path he was following, to a still straighter way. But again the tone of an enemy was heard, and the trampling of horses. Eboli did not hesitate; he dismounted, tied his steed to a tree, and, skirting along the enclosure of the field, trusted to escape thus unobserved. He succeeded after an hour's painful progress, and arrived on the borders of a stream, which, as the boundary between two states, was the mark of his having finally escaped danger.

Descending the steep bank of the river, which, with his horse, he might perhaps have forded, he now prepared to swim. He held his despatch in one hand, threw away his cloak, and was about to plunge into the water, when from under the dark shade of the *argine*, which had concealed them, he was suddenly arrested by unseen hands, cast on the ground, bound, gagged, and blinded, and then placed into a little boat, which was sculled with infinite rapidity down the stream.

There seemed so much of premeditation in the act that it baffled conjecture, yet he must believe himself a prisoner to the Austrian. While, however, he still vainly reflected, the boat was moored, he was lifted out, and the change of atmosphere made him aware that they entered some house. With extreme care and celerity, yet in the utmost silence, he was stripped of his clothes, and two rings he wore drawn from his fingers; other *habiliments* were thrown over him; and then no departing footstep was audible, but soon he heard the splash of a single oar, and he felt himself alone. He lay perfectly unable to move, the only relief his captor or captors had afforded him being the exchange of the gag for a tightly-bound handkerchief.

For hours he thus remained, with a tortured mind, bursting with rage, impatience, and disappointment; now writhing as well as he could in his endeavours to free himself, now still in despair. His despatches were taken away, and the period was swiftly passing when he could by his presence have remedied in some degree this evil. The morning dawned, and, though the full glare of the sun could not visit his eyes, he felt it play upon his limbs. As the day advanced, hunger preyed on him, and, though amidst the visitation of mightier, he at first disdained this minor, evil, towards evening it became, in spite of himself, the predominant sensation.

Night approached, and the fear that he should remain, and even starve, in this unvisited solitude had more than once thrilled through his frame, when feminine voices and a child's gay laugh met his ear. He heard persons enter the apartment, and he was asked in his native language, while the ligature was taken from his mouth, the cause of his present situation. He attributed it to *banditti*. His bonds were quickly cut, and his banded eyes restored to sight. It was long before he recovered himself. Water brought from the stream, however, was some refreshment, and by degrees he resumed the use of his senses, and saw that he was in a dilapidated shepherd's cot, with no one near him save the peasant girl and a child, who had liberated him. They rubbed his ankles and wrists, and the little fellow offered him some bread and eggs, after which refreshment and an hour's repose Ferdinando felt himself sufficiently restored to revolve his adventure in his mind, and to determine on the conduct he was to pursue.

He looked at the dress which had been given him in exchange for that which he had worn. It was of the plainest and meanest description. Still no time was to be lost; and he felt assured that the only step he could take was to return with all speed to the headquarters of the Neapolitan army, and inform the king of his disasters and his loss.

It were long to follow his backward steps, and to tell all of indignation and disappointment that swelled his heart. He walked painfully but resolutely all night, and by three in the morning entered the town where Gioacchino then was. He was challenged by the sentinels; he gave the word confided to him by Murat, and was instantly made prisoner by the soldiers. He declared to them his name and tank, and the necessity he was under of immediately seeing the king. He was taken to the guardhouse, and the officer on duty there listened with contempt to his representations, telling him that Count Ferdinando Eboli had returned three hours before, ordering him to be confined for further examination as a spy. Eboli loudly insisted that some impostor had taken his name; and while he related the story of his capture, another officer came in, who recognised his person; other individuals acquainted with him joined the party; and as the impostor had been seen by none but the officer of the night, his tale gained ground.

A young Frenchman of superior rank, who had orders to attend the king early in the morning, carried a report of what was going forward to Murat himself. The tale was so strange that the king sent for the young Count; and then, in spite of having seen and believed in counterfeit a few hours before, and having received from him an account of his mission, which had been faithfully executed, the appearance of the youth staggered him, and he commanded the presence of him who, as Count Eboli, had appeared before him a few hours previously. As Ferdinand stood beside the king, his eye glanced at a large and splendid mirror. His matted hair, his bloodshot eyes, his haggard looks, and torn and mean dress, derogated from the nobility of his appearance; and still less did he appear like the magnificent Count Eboli, when, to his utter confusion and astonishment, his counterfeit stood beside him.

He was perfect in all the outward signs that denoted high birth; and so like him whom he represented, that it would have been impossible to discern one from the other apart. The same chestnut hair clustered on his brow; the sweet and animated hazel eyes were the same; the one voice was the echo of the other. The composure and dignity of the pretender gained the suffrages of those around. When he was told of the strange appearance of another Count Eboli, he laughed in a frank good-humoured manner, and, turning to Ferdinand, said, "You honour me much in selecting me for your personation; but there are two or three things I like about myself so well, that you must excuse my unwillingness to exchange myself for you."

Ferdinand would have answered, but the false Count, with greater haughtiness, turning to the king, said, "Will your majesty decide between us? I cannot bandy words with a fellow of this sort." Irritated by scorn, Ferdinand demanded leave to challenge the pretender; who said, that if the king and his brother-officers did not think that he should degrade himself and disgrace the army by going out with a common vagabond, he was willing to chastise him, even at the peril of his own life. But the king, after a few more questions, feeling assured that the unhappy noble was an impostor, in severe and menacing terms reprehended him for his insolence, telling him that he owed it to his mercy alone that he was not executed as a spy, ordering him instantly to be conducted without the walls of the town, with threats of weighty punishment if he ever dared to subject his impostures to further trial.

It requires a strong imagination, and the experience of much misery, fully to enter into Ferdinand's feelings. From high rank, glory, hope, and love, he was hurled to utter beggary and disgrace. The insulting words of his triumphant rival, and the degrading menaces of his so lately gracious sovereign, rang in his ears; every nerve in his frame writhed with agony. But, fortunately for the endurance of human life, the worst misery in early youth is often but a painful dream, which we cast off when slumber quits our eyes.

After a struggle with intolerable anguish, hope and courage revived in his heart. His resolution was quickly made. He would return to Naples, relate his story to the Marchese Spina, and through his influence obtain at least an impartial bearing from the king. It was not, however, in his peculiar situation, an easy task to put his determination into effect. He was penniless; his dress bespoke poverty; he had neither friend nor kinsman near, but such as would behold in him the most impudent of swindlers. Still his courage did not fail him.

The kind Italian soil, in the autumnal season now advanced, furnished him with chesnuts, arbutus berries, and grapes. He took the moat direct road over the hills, avoiding towns, and indeed every habitation; travelling principally in the night, when, except in cities, the officers of government had retired from their stations. How he succeeded in getting from one end of Italy to the other it is difficult to say; but certain it is, that, after the interval of a few weeks, he presented himself at the Villa Spina.

With considerable difficulty he obtained admission to the presence of the *Marchese*, who received him standing, with an inquiring look, not at all recognising the noble youth. Ferdinand requested a private interview, for there were several visitors present. His voice startled the *Marchese*, who complied, taking him into another apartment. Here Ferdinand disclosed himself, and, with rapid and agitated utterance, was relating the history of his misfortunes, when the tramp of horses was heard, the great bell rang, and a domestic announced "Count Ferdinando Eboli."

"It is himself," cried the youth, turning pale. The words were strange, and they appeared still more so when the person announced entered; the perfect semblance of the young noble, whose name he assumed, as he had appeared when last at his departure, he trod the pavement of the hall. He inclined his head gracefully to the baron, turning with a glance of some surprise, but more disdain, towards Ferdinand, exclaiming, "Thou here!"

Ferdinand drew himself up to his full height. In spite of fatigue, ill-fare, and coarse garments, his manner was full of dignity. The *Marchese* looked at him fixedly, and started as he marked his proud mien, and saw in his expressive features the very face of Eboli. But again he was perplexed when he turned and discerned, as in a mirror, the same countenance reflected by the newcomer, who underwent this scrutiny somewhat impatiently. In brief and scornful words he told the *Marchese* that this was a second attempt in the intruder to impose himself as Count Eboli; that the trick had failed before, and would again; adding, laughing, that it was hard to be brought to prove himself to be himself, against the assertion of a *briccone*, whose likeness to him, and matchless impudence, were his whole stock-in-trade.

"Why, my good fellow," continued he, sneeringly, "you put me out of conceit with myself, to think that one, apparently so like me, should get on no better in the world."

The blood mounted into Ferdinand's cheeks on his enemy's

bitter taunts; with difficulty he restrained himself from closing with his foe, while the words "traitorous impostor!" burst from his lips. The baron commanded the fierce youth to be silent, and, moved by a look that he remembered to be Ferdinand's, he said gently, "By your respect for me, I adjure you to be patient; fear not but that I will deal impartially."

Then turning to the pretended Eboli, he added that he could not doubt but that he was the true Count, and asked excuse for his previous indecision. At first the latter appeared angry, but at length he burst into a laugh, and then, apologising for his ill-breeding, continued laughing heartily at the perplexity of the *Marchese*. It is certain his gaiety gained more credit with his auditor than the indignant glances of poor Ferdinand. The false Count then said that, after the king's menaces, he had entertained no expectation that the farce was to be played over again. He had obtained leave of absence, of which he profited to visit his future father-in-law, after having spent a few days in his own *palazzo* at Naples. Until now Ferdinand had listened silently, with a feeling of curiosity, anxious to learn all he could of the actions and motives of his rival; but at these last words be could no longer contain himself.

"What!" cried he, "hast thou usurped my place in my own father's house, and dared assume my power in my ancestral halls?"

A gush of tears overpowered the youth; he hid his face in his hands. Fierceness and pride lit up the countenance of the pretender.

"By the eternal God and the sacred cross, I swear," he exclaimed, "that palace is my father's palace; those halls the halls of my ancestors"

Ferdinand looked up with surprise; "And the earth opens not," he said, "to swallow the perjured man."

He then, at the call of the *Marchese*, related his adventures, while scorn mantled on the features of his rival. The *Marchese*, looking at both, could not free himself from doubt. He turned from one to the other: in spite of the wild and disordered appearance of poor Ferdinand, there was something in him that forbade his friend to condemn him as the impostor; but then it was utterly impossible to pronounce such the gallant and noble-looking youth, who could only be acknowledged as the real Count by the disbelief of the other's tale. The *Marchese*, calling an attendant, sent for his fair daughter.

"This decision," said he, "shall be made over to the subtle judgement of a woman, and the keen penetration of one who loves."

Both the youths now smiled—the same smile; the same expression—that of anticipated triumph. The baron was more perplexed than ever.

Adalinda had heard of the arrival of Count Eboli, and entered, resplendent in youth and happiness. She turned quickly towards him who resembled most the person she expected to see; when a well-known voice pronounced her name, and she gazed aghast on the double appearance of the lover. Her father, taking her hand, briefly explained the mystery, and bade her assure herself which was her affianced husband.

"*Signorina*," said Ferdinand, "disdain me not because I appear before you thus in disgrace and misery. Your love, your goodness will restore me to prosperity and happiness."

"I know not by what means," said the wondering girl, "but surely you are Count Eboli."

"Adalinda," said the rival youth, "waste not your words on a villain. Lovely and deceived one, I trust, trembling I say it, that I can with one word assure you that I am Eboli"

"Adalinda," said Ferdinand, "I placed the nuptial ring on your finger; before God your vows were given to me."

The false Count approached the lady and, bending one knee, took from heart a locket, enclosing hair tied with a green riband, which she recognised to have worn, and pointed to a slight scar on his left hand.

Adalinda blushed deeply, and, turning to her father, said, motioning towards the kneeling youth,—

"He is Ferdinand."

All protestations now from the unhappy Eboli were vain. The *Marchese* would have cast him into a dungeon; but at the earnest request of his rival, he was not detained, but thrust ignominiously from the villa. The rage of a wild beast newly chained was less than the tempest of indignation that now tilled the heart of Ferdinand. Physical suffering, from the fatigue and fasting, was added to his internal anguish; for some hours madness, if that were madness which never forgets its ill, possessed him. In a tumult of feelings there was one predominant idea: it was to take possession of his father's house, and to try, by ameliorating the fortuitous circumstances of his lot, to gain the upper hand of his adversary. He expended his remaining strength in reaching Naples, entered his family palace, and was received and acknowledged by his astonished domestics.

One of his first acts was to take from a cabinet a miniature of his father encircled with jewels, and to invoke the aid of the paternal spirit. Refreshment and a bath restored him to some of his usual strength; and he looked forward with almost childish delight to one night to be spent in peace under the roof of his father's house. This was not permitted, ere midnight the great bell sounded: his rival entered as master, with the Marchese Spina. The result may be divined. The *Marchese* appeared more indignant than the false Eboli. He insisted that the unfortunate youth should be imprisoned. The portrait, whose setting was costly, found on him, proved him guilty of robbery. He was given into the hands of the police, and thrown into a dungeon. I will not dwell on the subsequent scenes. He was tried by the tribunal, condemned as guilty, and sentenced to the galleys for life.

On the eve of the day when he was to be removed from the Neapolitan prison to work on the roads in Calabria, his rival visited him in his dungeon. For some moments both looked at the other in silence. The impostor gazed on the prisoner with mingled pride and compassion: there was evidently a struggle in his heart. The answering glance of Ferdinand was calm, free, and dignified. He was not resigned to his hard fate, but he disdained to make any exhibition of despair to his cruel and successful foe.

A spasm of pain seemed to wrench the bosom of the false one; and he turned aside, striving to recover the hardness of heart which had hitherto supported him in the prosecution of his guilty enterprise. Ferdinand spoke first.

"What would the triumphant criminal with his innocent victim?"

His visitant replied haughtily, "Do not address such epithets to me, or I leave you to your fate: I am that which I say I am."

"To me this boast!" cried Ferdinand scornfully; "but perhaps these walls have ears."

"Heaven, at least, is not deaf," said the deceiver; "favouring Heaven, which knows and admits my claim. But a truce to this idle discussion. Compassion—a distaste to see one so very like myself in such ill condition—a foolish whim, perhaps, on which you may congratulate yourself—has led me hither. The bolts of your dungeon are drawn; here is a purse of gold; fulfil one easy condition, and you are free."

"And that condition?"

"Sign this paper,"

He gave to Ferdinand a writing, containing a confession of his imputed crimes. The hand of the guilty youth trembled as he gave it; there was confusion in his mien, and a restless uneasy rolling of his eye. Ferdinand wished in one mighty word, potent as lightning, loud as thunder, to convey his burning disdain of this proposal: but expression is weak, and calm is more full of power than storm. Without a word, he tore the paper in two pieces and threw them at the feet of his enemy.

With a sudden change of manner, his visitant conjured him, in voluble and impetuous terms, to comply. Ferdinand answered only by requesting to be left alone. Now and then a half word broke uncontrollably from his lips; but he curbed himself. Yet he could not hide his agitation when, as an argument to make him yield, the false Count assured him that he was already married to Adalinda, Bitter agony thrilled poor Ferdinand's frame; but he preserved a calm mien, and an unaltered resolution. Having exhausted every menace and every persuasion, his rival left him, the purpose for which he came unaccomplished. On the morrow, with many others, the refuse of mankind, Count Ferdinando Eboli was led in chains to the unwholesome plains of Calabria, to work there at the roads.

I must hurry over some of the subsequent events, for a detailed account of them would fill volumes. The assertion of the usurper of Ferdinand's right, that he was already married to Adalinda, was, like all else he said, false. The day was, however, fixed for their union, when the illness and the subsequent death of the Marchese Spina delayed its celebration. Adalinda retired during the first months of mourning to a castle belonging to her father not far from Arpino, a town of the kingdom of Naples, in the midst of the Appennines, about 50 miles from the capital.

Before she went, the deceiver tried to persuade her to consent to a private marriage. He was probably afraid that, in the long interval that was about to ensue before he could secure her, she would discover his imposture. Besides, a rumour had gone abroad that one of the fellow-prisoners of Ferdinand, a noted bandit, had escaped, and that the young count was his companion in flight. Adalinda, however, refused to comply with her lover's entreaties, and retired to her seclusion with an old aunt, who was blind and deaf, but an excellent *duenna*. The false Eboli seldom visited his mistress; but he was a master in his art, and subsequent events showed that he must have spent all his time, disguised, in the vicinity of the castle. He contrived by various means, unsuspected at the moment, to have all Adalinda's servants changed for creatures of his own; so that, without her being aware of the restraint, she was, in fact, a prisoner in her own house.

It is impossible to say what first awakened her suspicions concerning the deception put upon her. She was an Italian, with all the habitual quiescence and lassitude of her countrywomen in the ordinary routine of life, and with all their energy and passion when roused. The moment the doubt darted into her mind she resolved to be assured. A few questions relative to scenes that had passed between poor Ferdinand and herself sufficed for this.

They were asked so suddenly and pointedly that the pretender was thrown off his guard; he looked confused, and stammered in his replies. Their eyes met; he felt that he was detected, and she saw that he perceived her now confirmed suspicions. A look such as is peculiar to an impostor—a glance that deformed his beauty, and filled his usually noble countenance with the hideous lines of cunning and cruel triumph—completed her faith in her own discernment.

"How," she thought, "could I have mistaken this man for my own gentle Eboli?" Again their eyes met. The peculiar expression of his terrified her, and she hastily quitted the apartment.

Her resolution was quickly formed. It was of no use to attempt to explain her situation to her old aunt. She determined to depart immediately for Naples, throw herself at the feet of Gioacchino, and to relate and obtain credit for her strange history. But the time was already lost when she could have executed this design. The contrivances of the deceiver were complete—she found herself a prisoner. Excess of fear gave her boldness, if not courage. She sought her jailor. A few minutes before she had been a young and thoughtless girl, docile as a child, and as unsuspecting; now she felt as if she had suddenly grown old in wisdom, and that the experience of years had been gained in that of a few seconds.

During their interview she was wary and firm, while the instinctive power of innocence over guilt gave majesty to her demeanour. The contriver of her ills for a moment cowered beneath her eye. At first he would by no means allow that he was not the person he pretended to be, hut the energy and eloquence of truth bore down his artifice, so that, at length driven into a comer, he turned—a stag at bay. Then it was her turn to quail, for the superior energy of a man gave him the mastery. He declared the truth: he was the elder brother of Ferdinand, a natural son of the old Count Eboli. His mother, who had been wronged, never forgave her injurer, and bred her son in deadly hate for his parent, and a belief that the advantages enjoyed by his more fortunate brother were rightfully his own. His education was rude; but he had an Italian's subtle talents, swiftness of perception, and guileful arts.

"It would blanch your cheek," he said to his trembling auditress, "could I describe all that I have suffered to achieve my purpose, I would trust to none—I executed all myself. It was a glorious triumph, but due to my perseverance and my fortitude, when I and my usurping brother stood—I, the noble, he, the degraded outcast—before our sovereign."

Having rapidly detailed his history, he now sought to the favourable ear of Adalinda, who stood with averted angry looks. He tried by the varied shows of passion and tenderness to move her heart. Was he not, in truth, the object of her love? Was it not he who scaled her balcony at Villa Spina? He recalled scenes of mutual overflow of feeling to her mind, thus urging arguments the most potent with a delicate woman. Pure blushes tinged her cheek, but horror of the deceiver predominated over every other sentiment. He swore that as soon as they should he united he would free Ferdinand, and bestow competency, nay, if so she willed it, half his possessions on him. She coldly replied, that she would rather share the chains of the innocent, and misery, than link herself with imposture and crime.

She demanded her liberty; but the untamed and even ferocious nature that had borne the deceiver through his career of crime now broke forth, and he invoked fearful imprecations on his head if she ever quitted the castle except as his wife, His look of conscious power and unbridled wickedness terrified her; her flashing eyes spoke abhorrence. It would have been far easier for her to have died than have yielded the smallest point to a man who had made her feel for one moment his irresistible power, arising from her being an unprotected woman, wholly in his hands, She left him, feeling as if she had just escaped from the impending sword of an assassin.

One hour's deliberation suggested to her a method of escape from her terrible situation. In a wardrobe at the castle lay, in their pristine gloss, the *habiliments* of a page of her mother, who had died suddenly, leaving these unworn relics of his station.

Dressing herself in these, she tied up her dark shining hair, and even, with a somewhat bitter feeling, girded on the slight sword that appertained to the costume. Then through a private passage leading from her own apartment to the chapel of the castle, she glided with noiseless steps, long after the *Ave Maria*, sounded at four o'clock, had, on a November night, given token that half an hour had passed since the setting of the sun.

She possessed the key of the chapel door—it opened at her touch; she closed behind her, and she was free. The pathless hills were around her, the starry heavens above, and a, cold wintry breeze murmured around the castle walls; but fear of her enemy conquered every other fear, and she tripped lightly on in a kind of ecstasy for many a long hour over the stony mountain path—she, who had never before walked more than a mile or two from home at any time in her life—till her feet were blistered, her slight shoes cut through, her way utterly lost At morning's dawn she found herself in the midst of the wild ilex-covered Appennines, and neither habitation nor human being apparent.

She was hungry and weary. She had brought gold and jewels with her; but here were no means of exchanging these for food. She remembered stories of *banditti*, but none could be so ruffian-like and cruel as him from whom she fled. This thought, a little rest, and a draught of water from a pure mountain-spring, restored her to some portion of courage, and she continued her journey. Noonday approached; and, in the south of Italy, the noonday sun, when unclouded, even in November, is oppressively warm, especially to an Italian woman, who never exposes herself to its beams.

Faintness came over her. There appeared recesses in the mountain sides along which she was travelling, grown over with bay and arbutus: she entered one of these, there to repose. It was deep, and led to another that opened into a spacious cavern lighted from above: there were cates, grapes, and a flagon of wine on a rough-hewn table. She looked fearfully around, but no inhabitant appeared. She placed herself at the table, and, half in dread, ate of the food presented to her; and then sat, her elbow on the table, her head resting on her little snow-white hand, her dark hair shading her brow and clustering round her throat.

An appearance of languor and fatigue was diffused through her attitude, while her soft black eyes filled at intervals with large tears as, pitying herself, she recurred to the cruel circumstances of her lot. Her fanciful but elegant dress, her feminine form, her beauty and her grace, as she sat pensive and alone in the rough unhewn cavern, formed a picture a poet would describe with delight, an artist love to paint.

"She seemed a being of another world; a *seraph*, all light and beauty: a Ganymede, escaped from his thrall above to his natal Ida. It was long before I recognised, looking down on her from the opening hill, my lost Adalinda." Thus spoke the young Count Eboli, when he related this story; for its end was as romantic as its commencement.

When Ferdinando had arrived, a galley-slave in Calabria, he found himself coupled with a bandit, a brave fellow, who abhorred his chains, from love of freedom, as much as his fellow-prisoner did, from all the combination of disgrace and misery they brought upon him. Together they devised a plan of escape, and succeeded in effecting it. On their road, Ferdinand related his story to the outlaw, who encouraged him to hope for a favourable turn of fate; and meanwhile invited and persuaded the desperate man to share his fortunes as a robber among the wild hills of Calabria.

The cavern where Adalinda had taken refuge was one of their fastnesses, whither they betook themselves at periods of imminent danger for safety only, as no booty could be collected in that unpeopled solitude; and there, one afternoon, returning from the chase, they found the wandering, fearful, solitary, fugitive girl and never was lighthouse more welcome to tempest-tossed sailor than was her own Ferdinand to his lady-love.

Fortune, now tired of persecuting the young noble, favoured him still further. The story of the lovers interested the bandit chief, and promise of reward secured him. Ferdinand persuaded

Adalinda to remain one night in the cave, and on the following morning they prepared to proceed to Naples; but at the moment of their departure they were surprised by an unexpected visitant: the robbers brought in a prisoner—it was the impostor. Missing on the morrow her who was the pledge of his safety and success, but assured that she could not have wandered far, he despatched emissaries in all directions to seek her; and himself, joining in the pursuit, followed the road she had taken, and was captured by these lawless men, who expected rich ransom from one whose appearance denoted rank and wealth. When they discovered who their prisoner was, they generously delivered him up into his brother's hands,

Ferdinand and Adalinda proceeded to Naples. On their arrival, she presented herself to Queen Caroline; and, through her, Murat heard with astonishment the device that had been practised on him. The young Count was restored to his honours and possessions, and within a few months afterwards was united to his betrothed bride.

The compassionate nature of the Count and Countess led them to interest themselves warmly in the fate of Ludovico, whose subsequent career was more honourable but less fortunate. At the intercession of his relative, Gioacchino permitted him to enter the army, where he distinguished himself, and obtained promotion. The brothers were at Moscow together, and mutually assisted each other during the horrors of the retreat. At one time overcome by drowsiness, the mortal symptom resulting from excessive cold, Ferdinand lingered behind his comrades; but Ludovico, refusing to leave him, dragged him on in spite of himself, till, entering a village, food and fire restored him, and his life was saved.

On another evening, when wind and sleet added to the horror of their situation, Ludovico, after many ineffective struggles, slid from his horse lifeless; Ferdinand was at his side, and, dismounting, endeavoured by every means in his power to bring back pulsation to his stagnant blood. His comrades went forward, and the young Count was left alone with his dying brother in the white boundless waste.

Once Ludovico opened his eyes and recognised him; he pressed his hand, and his lips moved to utter a blessing as he died. At that moment the welcome sounds of the enemy's approach roused Ferdinand from the despair into which his dreadful situation plunged him. He was taken prisoner, and his life was thus saved. When Napoleon went to Elba, he, with many others of his countrymen, was liberated, and returned to Naples.

The Mourner

One fatal remembrance, one sorrow that throws
Its bleak shade alike o'er our joys and our woes,
To which life nothing darker or brighter can bring,
For which joy has no balm, and affliction no sting!
                                        —Moore

A gorgeous scene of kingly pride is the prospect now before us!—the offspring of art, the nursling of nature—where can the eye rest on a landscape more deliciously lovely than the fair expanse of Virginia Water, now an open mirror to the sky, now shaded by umbrageous banks, which wind into dark recesses, or are rounded into soft promontories? Looking down on it, now that the sun is low in the west, the eye is dazzled, the soul oppressed, by excess of beauty. Earth, water, air drink to overflowing the radiance that streams from yonder well of light; the foliage of the trees seems dripping with the golden flood; while the lake, filled with no earthly dew, appears but an imbasining of the sun-tinctured atmosphere; and trees and gay pavilion float in its depth, more clear, more distinct than their twins in the upper air.

Nor is the scene silent: strains more sweet than those that lull Venus to her balmy rest, more inspiring than the song of Tiresias which awoke Alexander to the deed of ruin, more solemn than the chantings of St. Cecilia, float along the waves and mingle with the lagging breeze, which ruffles not the lake. Strange, that a few dark scores should be the key to this fountain of sound; the unconscious link between unregarded noise and harmonies

296

which unclose paradise to our entranced senses!

The sun touches the extreme boundary, and a softer, milder light mingles a roseate tinge with the fiery glow. Our boat has floated long on the broad expanse; now let it approach the umbrageous bank. The green tresses of the graceful willow dip into the waters, which are checked by them into a ripple. The startled teal dart from their recess, skimming the waves with splashing wing. The stately swans float onward; while innumerable water fowl cluster together out of the way of the oars. The twilight is blotted by no dark shades; it is one subdued, equal receding of the great tide of day. We may disembark, and wander yet amid the glades, long before the thickening shadows speak of night.

The plantations are formed of every English tree, with an old oak or two standing out in the walks. There the glancing foliage obscures heaven, as the silken texture of a veil a woman's lovely features. Beneath such fretwork we may indulge in light-hearted thoughts; or, if sadder meditations lead us to seek darker shades, we may pass the cascade towards the large groves of pine, with their vast undergrowth of laurel, reaching up to the Belvidere; or, on the opposite side of the water, sit under the shadow of the silver-stemmed birch, or beneath the leafy pavilions of those fine old beeches, whose high fantastic roots seem formed in nature's sport; and the near jungle of sweet-smelling myrica leaves no sense unvisited by pleasant ministration.

Now this splendid scene is reserved for the royal possessor; but in past years, while the lodge was called the Regent's Cottage, or before, when the under-ranger inhabited it, the mazy paths of Chapel Wood were open, and the iron gates enclosing the plantations and Virginia Water were guarded by no Cerebus untamable by sops.

It was here, on a summer's evening, that Horace Neville and his two fair cousins floated idly on the placid lake,

In that sweet mood when pleasant thoughts
Bring sad thoughts to the mind.

Seville had been eloquent in praise of English scenery. "In

distant climes," he said, "we may find landscapes grand in barbaric wildness, or rich in the luxuriant vegetation of the south, or sublime in Alpine magnificence. We may lament, though it is ungrateful to say so on such a night as this, the want of a more genial sky; but where find scenery to be compared to the verdant, well-wooded, well-watered groves of our native land; the clustering cottages, shadowed by fine old elms; each garden blooming with early flowers, each lattice gay with geraniums and roses; the blue-eyed child devouring his white bread, while he drives a cow to graze; the hedge redolent with summer blooms; the enclosed cornfields, seas of golden grain, weltering in the breeze; the stile, the track across the meadow, leading through the copse, under which the path winds, and the meeting branches overhead, which give, by their dimming tracery, a cathedral-like solemnity to the scene; the river, winding 'with sweet inland murmur;' and, as additional graces, spots like these oases of taste—gardens of Eden—the works of wealth, which evince at once the greatest power and the greatest will to create beauty?

"And yet," continued Neville, "it was with difficulty that I persuaded myself to reap the best fruits of my uncle's will, and to inhabit this spot, familiar to my boyhood, associated with unavailing regrets and recollected pain."

Horace Neville was a man of birth—of wealth; but he could hardly be termed a man of the world. There was in his nature a gentleness, a sweetness, a winning sensibility, allied to talent and personal distinction, that gave weight to his simplest expressions, and excited sympathy for all his emotions. His younger cousin, his junior by several years, was attached to him by the tenderest sentiments—secret long—but they were now betrothed to each other—a lovely, happy pair. She looked inquiringly, but he turned away. "No more of this," he said, and, giving a swifter impulse to their boat, they speedily reached the shore, landed, and walked through the long extent of Chapel Wood. It was dark night before they met their carriage at Bishopsgate.

A week or two after, Horace received letters to call him to a distant part of the country. A few days before his departure, he requested his cousin to walk with him. They bent their steps across several meadows to Old Windsor Churchyard. At first he did not deviate from the usual path; and as they went they talked cheerfully—gaily. The beauteous sunny day might well exhilarate them; the dancing waves sped onwards at their feet; the country church lifted its rustic spire into the bright pure sky.

There was nothing in their conversation that could induce his cousin to think that Neville had led her hither for any saddening purpose; but when they were about to quit the churchyard, Horace, as if he had suddenly recollected himself, turned from the path, crossed the greensward, and paused beside a grave near the river. No stone was there to commemorate the being who reposed beneath—it was thickly grown with grass, starred by a luxuriant growth of humble daisies: a few dead leaves, a broken bramble twig, defaced its neatness. Neville removed these, and then said, "Juliet, I commit this sacred spot to your keeping while I am away."

"There is no monument," he continued; "for her commands were implicitly obeyed by the two beings to whom she addressed them. One day another may lie near, and his name will be her epitaph. I do not mean myself," he said, half-smiling at the terror his cousin s countenance expressed; "but promise me, Juliet, to preserve this grave from every violation. I do not wish to sadden you by the story; yet, if I have excited your interest, I will satisfy it; but not now—not here."

It was not till the following day, when, in company with her sister, they again visited Virginia Water, that, seated under the shadow of its pines, whose melodious swinging in the wind breathed unearthly harmony, Neville, unasked, commenced his story.

"I was sent to Eton at eleven years of age. I will not dwell upon my sufferings there; I would hardly refer to them, did they not make a part of my present narration. I was a fag to a hard taskmaster; every labour he could invent—and the youthful tyrant was ingenious—he devised for my annoyance; early and late, I was forced to be in attendance, to the neglect of my school duties, so incurring punishment. There were worse things to bear than these: it was his delight to put me to shame, and, finding that I had too much of my mother in my blood,—to endeavour to compel me to acts of cruelty from which my nature revolted,—I refused to obey. Speak of West Indian slavery! I hope things may be better now; in my days, the tender years of aristocratic childhood were yielded up to a capricious, unrelenting, cruel bondage, far beyond the measured despotism of Jamaica.

"One day—I had been two years at school, and was nearly thirteen—my tyrant, I will give him no other name, issued a command, in the wantonness of power, for me to destroy a poor little bullfinch I had tamed and caged. In a hapless hour he found it in my room, and was indignant that I should dare to appropriate a single pleasure. I refused, stubbornly, dauntlessly, though the consequence of my disobedience was immediate and terrible. At this moment a message came from my tormentor's tutor—his father had arrived. 'Well, old lad, he cried, I shall pay you off some day!' Seizing my pet at the same time, he wrung its neck, threw it at my feet, and, with a laugh of derision, quitted the room.

"Never before—never may I again feel the same swelling, boiling fury in my bursting heart;—the sight of my nursling expiring at my feet—my desire of vengeance—my impotence, created a Vesuvius within me, that no tears flowed to quench. Could I have uttered—acted—my passion, it would have been less torturous: it was so when I burst into a torrent of abuse and imprecation. My vocabulary—it must have been a choice collection—was supplied by him against whom it was levelled. But words were air. I desired to give more substantial proof of my resentment—I destroyed everything in the room belonging to him; I tore them to pieces, I stamped on them, crushed them with more than childish strength.

"My last act was to seize a timepiece, on which my tyrant infinitely prided himself, and to dash it to the ground. The sight of this, as it lay shattered at my feet, recalled me to my senses, and something like an emotion of fear allayed the tumult in my heart. I began to meditate an escape: I got out of the house, ran down a lane, and across some meadows, far out of bounds, above Eton. I was seen by an elder boy, a friend of my tormentor. He called to me, thinking at first that I was performing some errand for him; but seeing that I *shirked*, he repeated his '*Come up!*' in an authoritative voice. It put wings to my heels; he did not deem it necessary to pursue.

"But I grow tedious, my dear Juliet; enough that fears the most intense, of punishment both from my masters and the upper boys, made me resolve to run away. I reached the banks of the Thames, tied my clothes over my head, swam across, and, traversing several fields, entered Windsor Forest, with a vague childish feeling of being able to hide myself for ever in the unexplored obscurity of its immeasurable wilds. It was early autumn; the weather was mild, even warm; the forest oaks yet showed no sign of winter change, though the fern beneath wore a yellowy tinge. I got within Chapel Wood; I fed upon chestnuts and beech nuts; I continued to hide myself from the gamekeepers and woodmen. I lived thus two days.

"But chestnuts and beechnuts were sorry fare to a growing lad of thirteen years old. A day's rain occurred, and I began to think myself the most unfortunate boy on record. I had a distant, obscure idea of starvation: I thought of the Children in the Wood, of their leafy shroud, gift of the pious robin; this brought my poor bullfinch to my mind, and tears streamed in torrents down my cheeks. I thought of my father and mother; of you, then my little baby cousin and playmate; and I cried with renewed fervour, till, quite exhausted, I curled myself up under a huge oak among some dry leaves, the relics of a hundred summers, and fell asleep.

"I ramble on in my narration as if I had a story to tell; yet I have little except a portrait—a sketch—to present, for your amusement or interest. When I awoke, the first object that met my opening eyes was a little foot, delicately clad in silk and soft kid. I looked up in dismay, expecting to behold some gaily dressed appendage to this indication of high-bred elegance; but I saw a girl, perhaps seventeen, simply clad in a dark cotton dress, her face shaded by a large, very coarse straw hat; she was pale even to marmoreal whiteness; her chestnut-coloured hair was parted in plain tresses across a brow which wore traces of extreme suffering; her eyes were blue, full, large, melancholy, often even suffused with tears; but her mouth had an infantine sweetness and innocence in its expression, that softened the otherwise sad expression of her countenance.

"She spoke to me. I was too hungry, too exhausted, too unhappy, to resist her kindness, and gladly permitted her to lead me to her home. We passed out of the wood by some broken palings on to Bishopsgate Heath, and after no long walk arrived at her habitation. It was a solitary, dreary-looking cottage; the palings were in disrepair, the garden waste, the lattices unadorned by flowers or creepers; within, all was neat, but sombre, and even mean. The diminutiveness of a cottage requires an appearance of cheerfulness and elegance to make it pleasing; the bare floor,-clean, it is true,—the rush chairs, deal table, checked curtains of this cot, were beneath even a peasant's rusticity; yet it was the dwelling of my lovely guide, whose little white hand, delicately gloved, contrasted with her unadorned attire, as did her gentle self with the clumsy appurtenances of her too humble dwelling.

"Poor child! she had meant entirely to hide her origin, to degrade herself to a peasant's state, and little thought that she forever betrayed herself by the strangest incongruities. Thus, the arrangements of her table were mean, her fare meagre for a hermit; but the linen was matchlessly fine, and wax lights stood in candlesticks which a beggar would almost have disdained to own. But I talk of circumstances I observed afterwards; then I was chiefly aware of the plentiful breakfast she caused her single attendant, a young girl, to place before me, and of the sweet soothing voice of my hostess, which spoke a kindness with which lately I had been little conversant. When my hunger was appeased, she drew my story from me, encouraged me to write to my father, and kept me at her abode till, after a few days, I returned to school pardoned. No long time elapsed before I got into the upper forms, and my woeful slavery ended.

"Whenever I was able, I visited my disguised nymph. I no longer associated with my schoolfellows; their diversions, their pursuits appeared vulgar and stupid to me; I had but one object in view—to accomplish my lessons, and to steal to the cottage of Ellen Burnet.

"Do not look grave, love! true, others as young as I then was have loved, and I might also; but not Ellen. Her profound, her intense melancholy, sister to despair—her serious, sad discourse—her mind, estranged from all worldly concerns, forbade that; but there was an enchantment in her sorrow, a fascination in her converse, that lifted me above commonplace existence; she created a magic circle, which I entered as holy ground: it was not akin to heaven, for grief was the presiding spirit; but there was an exaltation of sentiment, an enthusiasm, a view beyond the grave, which made it unearthly, singular, wild, enthralling. You have often observed that I strangely differ from all other men; I mingle with them, make one in their occupations and diversions, but I have a portion of my being sacred from them:—a living well, sealed up from their contamination, lies deep in my heart—it is of little use, but there it is; Ellen opened the spring, and it has flowed ever since.

"Of what did she talk? She recited no past adventures, alluded to no past intercourse with friend or relative; she spoke of the various woes that wait on humanity, on the intricate mazes of life, on the miseries of passion, of love, remorse, and death, and that which we may hope or fear beyond the tomb; she spoke of the sensation of wretchedness alive in her own broken heart, and then she grew fearfully eloquent, till, suddenly pausing, she reproached herself for making me familiar with such wordless misery. 'I do you harm,' she often said; 'I unfit you for society; I have tried, seeing you thrown upon yonder distorted miniature of a bad world, to estrange you from its evil contagion; I fear that I shall be the cause of greater harm to you than could spring from association with your fellow-creatures in the ordinary course of things. This is not well avoid the stricken deer.'

"There were darker shades in the picture than those which I have already developed. Ellen was more miserable than the imagination of one like you, dear girl, unacquainted with woe, can portray. Sometimes she gave words to her despair—it was so great as to confuse the boundary between physical and mental sensation—and every pulsation of her heart was a throb of pain. She has suddenly broken off in talking of her sorrows, with a cry of agony—bidding me leave her—hiding her face on her arms, shivering with the anguish some thought awoke. The idea that chiefly haunted her, though she earnestly endeavoured to put it aside, was self-destruction—to snap the silver cord that bound together so much grace, wisdom, and sweetness—to rob the world of a creation made to be its ornament.

"Sometimes her piety checked her; oftener a sense of unendurable suffering made her brood with pleasure over the dread resolve. She spoke of it to me as being wicked; yet I often fancied this was done rather to prevent her example from being of ill effect to me, than from any conviction that the Father of all would regard angrily the last act of His miserable child. Once she had prepared the mortal beverage; it was on the table before her when I entered; she did not deny its nature, she did not attempt to justify herself; she only besought me not to hate her, and to soothe by my kindness her last moments.—'I cannot live!' was all her explanation, all her excuse; and it was spoken with such fervent wretchedness that it seemed wrong to attempt to persuade her to prolong the sense of pain.

"I did not act like a boy; I wonder I did not; I made one simple request, to which she instantly acceded, that she should walk with me to this Belvidere. It was a glorious sunset; beauty and the spirit of love breathed in the wind, and hovered over the softened hues of the landscape. 'Look, Ellen,' I cried, if only such loveliness of nature existed, it were worth living for!

"True, if a latent feeling did not blot this glorious scene with murky shadows. Beauty is as we see it—my eyes view all things deformed and evil. She closed them as she said this; but, young and sensitive, the visitings of the soft breeze already began to minister consolation. 'Dearest Ellen,' I continued, 'what do I not owe to you? I am your boy, your pupil; I might have gone on blindly as others do, but you opened my eyes; you have given me a sense of the just, the good, the beautiful and have you done this merely for my misfortune? If you leave me, what can become of me? The last words came from my heart, and tears gushed from my eyes. 'Do not leave me, Ellen,' I said; 'I cannot live without you—and I cannot die, for I have a mother—a father.'

"She turned quickly round, saying, 'You are blessed sufficiently.' Her voice struck me as unnatural; she grew deadly pale as she spoke, and was obliged to sit down. Still I clung to her, prayed, cried; till she—I had never seen her shed a tear before—burst into passionate weeping. After this she seemed to forget her resolve. We returned by moonlight, and our talk was even more calm and cheerful than usual. When in her cottage, I poured away the fatal draught. Her 'goodnight' bore with it no traces of her late agitation; and the next day she said, 'I have thoughtlessly, even wickedly, created a new duty to myself, even at a time when I had forsworn all; but I will be true to it. Pardon me for making you familiar with emotions and scenes so dire; I will behave better—I will preserve myself, if I can, till the link between us is loosened, or broken, and I am free again.'

"One little incident alone occurred during our intercourse that appeared at all to connect her with the world. Sometimes I brought her a newspaper, for those were stirring times; and though, before I knew her, she had forgotten all except the world her own heart enclosed, yet, to please me, she would talk of Napoleon—Russia, from whence the emperor now returned overthrown and the prospect of his final defeat. The paper lay one day on her table; some words caught her eye; she bent eagerly down to read them, and her bosom heaved with violent palpitation; but she subdued herself, and after a few moments told me to take the paper away.

"Then, indeed, I did feel an emotion of even impertinent inquisitiveness; I found nothing to satisfy it—though afterwards I became aware that it contained a singular advertisement, saying, 'If these lines meet the eye of any one of the passengers who were on board the *St. Mary*, bound for Liverpool from Barbadoes, which sailed on the third of May last, and was destroyed by fire in the high seas, a part of the crew only having been saved by His Majesty's frigate the *Bellerophon*, they are entreated to communicate with the advertiser; and if anyone be acquainted with the particulars of the Hon. Miss Eversham's fate and present abode, they are earnestly requested to disclose them, directing to L. E., Stratton Street, Park Lane.

"It was after this event, as winter came on, that symptoms of decided ill-health declared themselves in the delicate frame of my poor Ellen. I have often suspected that, without positively attempting her life, she did many things that tended to abridge it and to produce mortal disease. Now, when really ill, she refused all medical attendance; but she got better again, and I thought her nearly well when I saw her for the last time, before going home for the Christmas holidays. Her manner was full of affection: she relied, she said, on the continuation of my friendship; she made me promise never to forget her, though she refused to write to me, and forbade any letters from me.

"Even now I see her standing at her humble doorway. If an appearance of illness and suffering can ever be termed lovely, it was in her. Still she was to be viewed as the wreck of beauty. What must she not have been in happier days, with her angel expression of face, her nymph-like figure, her voice, whose tones were music? So young—so lost! was the sentiment that burst even from me, a young lad, as I waved my hand to her as a last *adieu*. She hardly looked more than fifteen, but none could doubt that her very soul was impressed by the sad lines of sorrow that rested so unceasingly on her fair brow. Away from her, her figure forever floated before my eyes;—I put my hands before them, still she was there: my day, my night dreams were filled by my recollections of her.

"During the winter holidays, on a fine soft day, I went out to hunt: you, dear Juliet, will remember the sad catastrophe; I fell and broke my leg. The only person who saw me fall was a young man who rode one of the most beautiful horses I ever saw, and I believe it was by watching him as he took a leap, that I incurred my disaster: he dismounted, and was at my side in a minute. My own animal had fled; he called his; it obeyed his voice; with ease he lifted my light figure on to the saddle, contriving to support my leg, and so conducted me a short distance to a lodge situated in the woody recesses of Elmore Park, the seat of the Earl of D——, whose second son my preserver was. He was my sole nurse for a day or two, and during the whole of my illness passed many hours of each day by my bedside. As I lay gazing on him, while he read to me, or talked, narrating a thousand strange adventures which had occurred during his service in the Peninsula, I thought—is it forever to be my fate to fall in with the highly gifted and excessively unhappy?

"The immediate neighbour of Lewis family was Lord Eversham. He had married in very early youth, and became a widower young. After this misfortune, which passed like a deadly blight over his prospects and possessions, leaving the gay view utterly sterile and bare, he left his surviving infant daughter under the care of Lewis' mother, and travelled for many years in far distant lands. He returned when Clarice was about ten, a lovely sweet child, the pride and delight of all connected with her. Lord Eversham, on his return—he was then hardly more than thirty—devoted himself to her education.

"They were never separate: he was a good musician, and she became a proficient under his tutoring. They rode—walked—read together. When a father is all that a father may be, the sentiments of filial piety, entire dependence, and perfect confidence being united, the love of a daughter is one of the deepest and strongest, as it is the purest passion of which our natures are capable. Clarice worshipped her parent, who came, during the transition from mere childhood to the period when reflection and observation awaken, to adorn a commonplace existence with all the brilliant adjuncts which enlightened and devoted affection can bestow. He appeared to her like an especial gift of Providence, a guardian angel—but far dearer, as being akin to her own nature. She grew, under his eye, in loveliness and refinement both of intellect and heart. These feelings were not divided almost strengthened, by the engagement that had taken place between her and Lewis:—Lewis was destined for the army, and, after a few years service, they were to be united.

"It is hard, when all is fair and tranquil, when the world, opening before the ardent gaze of youth, looks like a well-kept demesne, unencumbered by let or hindrance for the annoyance of the young traveller, that we should voluntarily stray into desert wilds and tempest-visited districts. Lewis Elmore was ordered to Spain; and, at the same time, Lord Eversham found it necessary to visit some estates he possessed in Barbadoes. He was not sorry to revisit a scene, which had dwelt in his memory as an earthly paradise, nor to show to his daughter a new and strange world, so to form her understanding and enlarge her mind.

"They were to return in three months, and departed as on a summer tour. Clarice was glad that, while her lover gathered experience and knowledge in a distant land, she should not remain in idleness; she was glad that there would be some diversion for her anxiety during his perilous absence; and in every way she enjoyed the idea of travelling with her beloved father, who would fill every hour, and adorn every new scene, with pleasure and delight. They sailed. Clarice wrote home, with enthusiastic expressions of rapture and delight from Madeira:—yet, without her father, she said, the fair scene had been blank to her. More than half her letter was filled by the expressions of her gratitude and affection for her adored and revered parent. While he, in his, with fewer words, perhaps, but with no less energy, spoke of his satisfaction in her improvement, his pride in her beauty, and his grateful sense of her love and kindness.

"Such were they, a matchless example of happiness in the dearest connection in life, as resulting from the exercise of their reciprocal duties and affections. A father and daughter; the one all care, gentleness, and sympathy, consecrating his life for her happiness; the other fond, duteous, grateful:—such had they been,—and where were they now,—the noble, kind, respected parent, and the beloved and loving child? They had departed from England as on a pleasure voyage down an inland stream; but the ruthless car of destiny had overtaken them on their unsuspecting way, crushing them under its heavy wheels—scattering love, hope, and joy as the bellowing avalanche overwhelms and grinds to mere spray the streamlet of the valley. They were gone; but whither? Mystery hung over the fate of the most helpless victim; and my friend's anxiety was, to penetrate the clouds that hid poor Clarice from his sight.

"After an absence of a few months, they had written, fixing their departure in the St. Mary, to sail from Barbadoes in a few days. Lewis, at the same time, returned from Spain: he was invalided, in his very first action, by a bad wound in his side. He arrived, and each day expected to hear of the landing of his friends, when that common messenger, the newspaper, brought him tidings to fill him with more than anxiety—with fear and agonizing doubt. The *St. Mary* had caught fire, and had burned in the open sea. A frigate, the *Bellerophon*, had saved a part of the crew. In spite of illness and a physician's commands, Lewis set out the same day for London to ascertain as speedily as possible the fate of her he loved.

"There he heard that the frigate was expected in the Downs. Without alighting from his travelling chaise, he posted thither, arriving in a burning fever. He went on board, saw the commander, and spoke with the crew. They could give him few particulars as to whom they had saved; they had touched at Liverpool, and left there most of the persons, including all the passengers rescued from the *St. Mary*. Physical suffering for awhile disabled Mr. Elmore; he was confined by his wound and consequent fever, and only recovered to give himself up to his exertions to discover the fate of his friends;—they did not appear nor write; and all Lewis' inquiries only tended to confirm his worst fears; yet still he hoped, and still continued indefatigable in his perquisitions.

He visited Liverpool and Ireland, whither some of the passengers had gone, and learnt only scattered, incongruous details of the fearful tragedy, that told nothing of Miss Eversham's present abode, though much that confirmed his suspicion that she still lived.

"The fire on board the *St. Mary* had raged long and fearfully before the *Bellerophon* hove in sight, and boats came off for the rescue of the crew. The women were to be first embarked; but Clarice clung to her father, and refused to go till he should accompany her. Some fearful presentiment that, if she were saved, he would remain and die, gave such energy to her resolve, that not the entreaties of her father, nor the angry expostulations of the captain, could shake it. Lewis saw this man, after the lapse of two or three months, and he threw most light on the dark scene. He well remembered that, transported with anger by her obstinacy, he had said to her, 'You will cause your father's death and be as much a parricide as if you put poison into his cup; you are not the first girl who has murdered her father in her wilful mood.'

"Still Clarice passionately refused to go—there was no time for long parley—the point was yielded, and she remained pale, but firm, near her parent, whose arm was around her, supporting her during the awful interval. It was no period for regular action and calm order; a tempest was rising, the scorching waves blew this way and that, making a fearful day of the night which veiled all except the burning ship. The boats returned with difficulty, and one only could contrive to approach; it was nearly full; Lord Eversham and his daughter advanced to the deck's edge to get in. 'We can only take one of you,' vociferated the sailors; 'keep back on your life! throw the girl to us—we will come back for you if we can.' Lord Eversham cast with a strong arm his daughter, who had now entirely lost her self-possession, into the boat; she was alive again in a minute; she called to her father, held out her arms to him, and would have thrown herself into the sea, but was held back by the sailors.

"Meanwhile Lord Eversham, feeling that no boat could again

approach the lost vessel, contrived to heave a spar overboard, and threw himself into the sea, clinging to it. The boat, tossed by the huge waves, with difficulty made its way to the frigate; and as it rose from the trough of the sea, Clarice saw her father struggling with his fate—battling with the death that at last became the victor; the spar floated by, his arms had fallen from it; were those his pallid features? She neither wept nor fainted, but her limbs grew rigid, her face colourless, and she was lifted as a log on to the deck of the frigate.

"The captain allowed that on her homeward voyage the people had rather a horror of her, as having caused her father's death; her own servants had perished, few people remembered who she was; but they talked together with no careful voices as they passed her, and a hundred times she must have heard herself accused of having destroyed her parent. She spoke to no one, or only in brief reply when addressed; to avoid the rough remonstrances of those around, she appeared at table, ate as well as she could; but there was a settled wretchedness in her face that never changed.

"When they landed at Liverpool, the captain conducted her to an hotel; he left her, meaning to return, but an opportunity of sailing that night for the Downs occurred, of which he availed himself, without again visiting her. He knew, he said, and truly, that she was in her native country, where she had but to write a letter to gather crowds of friends about her; and where can greater civility be found than at an English hotel, if it is known that you are perfectly able to pay your bill!

"This was all that Mr. Elmore could learn, and it took many months to gather together these few particulars. He went to the hotel at Liverpool. It seemed that as soon as there appeared some hope of rescue from the frigate, Lord Evershain had given his pocket-book to his daughter's care, containing bills on a banking-house at Liverpool to the amount of a few hundred pounds. On the second day after Clarice's arrival there, she had sent for the master of the hotel, and showed him these. He got the cash for her; and the next day she quitted Liverpool in a little coasting vessel. In vain Lewis endeavoured to trace her. Apparently she had crossed to Ireland; but whatever she had done, wherever she had gone, she had taken infinite pains to conceal herself, and all clue was speedily lost.

"Lewis had not yet despaired; he was even now perpetually making journeys, sending emissaries, employing every possible means for her discovery. From the moment he told me this story, we talked of nothing else. I became deeply interested, and we ceaselessly discussed the probabilities of the case, and where she might be concealed. That she did not meditate suicide was evident from her having possessed herself of money; yet, unused to the world, young, lovely, and inexperienced, what could be her plan? What might not have been her fate?

"Meanwhile I continued for nearly three months confined by the fracture of my limb; before the lapse of that time, I had begun to crawl about the ground, and now I considered myself as nearly recovered. It had been settled that I should not return to Eton, but be entered at Oxford; and this leap from boyhood to man's estate elated me considerably. Yet still I thought of my poor Ellen, and was angry at her obstinate silence.

"Once or twice I had, disobeying her command, written to her, mentioning my accident, and the kind attentions of Mr. Elmore. Still she wrote not; and I began to fear that her illness might have had a fatal termination. She had made me vow so solemnly never to mention her name, never to inquire about her during my absence, that, considering obedience the first duty of a young inexperienced boy to one older than himself, I resisted each suggestion of my affection or my fears to transgress her orders.

"And now spring came, with its gift of opening buds, odoriferous flowers, and sunny genial days. I returned home, and found my family on the eve of their departure for London; my long confinement had weakened me; it was deemed inadvisable for me to encounter the bad air and fatigues of the metropolis, and I remained to rusticate. I rode and hunted, and thought of Ellen; missing the excitement of her conversation, and feeling a vacancy in my heart which she had filled.

"I began to think of riding across the country from Shrop-shire to Berks for the purpose of seeing her. The whole land-scape haunted my imagination—the fields round Eton—the sil-ver Thames—the majestic forest—this lovely scene of Virginia Water—the heath and her desolate cottage—she herself pale, slightly bending from weakness of health, awakening from dark abstraction to bestow on me a kind smile of welcome. It grew into a passionate desire of my heart to behold her, to cheer her as I might by my affectionate attentions, to hear her, and to hang upon her accents of inconsolable despair as if it had been celes-tial harmony. As I meditated on these things, a voice seemed for ever to repeat, Now go, or it will be too late; while another yet more mournful tone responded, You can never see her more!

"I was occupied by these thoughts, as, on a summer moon-light night, I loitered in the shrubbery, unable to quit a scene of entrancing beauty, when I was startled at hearing myself called by Mr. Elmore. He came on his way to the coast; he had received a letter from Ireland, which made him think that Miss Eversham was residing near Enniscorthy,—a strange place for her to select, but as concealment was evidently her object, not an improbable one. Yet his hopes were not high; on the contrary, he performed this journey more from the resolve to leave nothing undone, than in expectation of a happy result. He asked me if I would accompany him; I was delighted with the offer, and we departed together on the following morning.

"We arrived at Milford Haven, where we were to take our passage. The packet was to sail early in the morning—we walked on the beach, and beguiled the time by talk. I had never men-tioned Ellen to Lewis; I felt now strongly inclined to break my vow, and to relate my whole adventure with her; but restrained myself, and we spoke only of the unhappy Clarice—of the de-spair that must have been hers, of her remorse and unavailing regret.

"We retired to rest; and early in the morning I was called to prepare for going on board. I got ready, and then knocked at

Lewis door; he admitted me, for he was dressed, though a few of his things were still unpacked, and scattered about the room. The morocco case of a miniature was on his table; I took it up. 'Did I never show you that?' said Elmore; 'poor dear Clarice! she was very happy when that was painted!'

"I opened it;—rich, luxuriant curls clustered on her brow and the snow-white throat; there was a light zephyr appearance in the figure; an expression of unalloyed exuberant happiness in the countenance; but those large dove's eyes, the innocence that dwelt on her mouth, could not be mistaken, and the name of Ellen Burnet burst from my lips.

"There was no doubt: why had I ever doubted? the thing was so plain! Who but the survivor of such a parent, and she the apparent cause of his death, could be so miserable as Ellen? A torrent of explanation followed, and a thousand minute circumstances, forgotten before, now assured us that my sad hermitess was the beloved of Elmore. No more sea voyage—not a second of delay—our chaise, the horses heads turned to the east, rolled on with lightning rapidity, yet far too slowly to satisfy our impatience.

"It was not until we arrived at Worcester that the tide of expectation, flowing all one way, ebbed. Suddenly, even while I was telling Elmore some anecdote to prove that, in spite of all, she would be accessible to consolation, I remembered her ill-health and my fears. Lewis saw the change my countenance underwent; for some time I could not command my voice; and when at last I spoke, my gloomy anticipations passed like an electric shock into my friend's soul.

"When we arrived at Oxford we halted for an hour or two, unable to proceed; yet we did not converse on the subject so near our hearts, nor until we arrived in sight of Windsor did a word pass between us; then Elmore said, Tomorrow morning, dear Neville, you shall visit Clarice; we must not be too precipitate.

"The morrow came. I arose with that intolerable weight at my breast, which it is grief's worst heritage to feel. A sunny day it was; yet the atmosphere looked black to me; my heart was dead within me. We sat at the breakfast-table, but neither ate, and after some restless indecision, we left our inn, and (to protract the interval) walked to Bishopsgate. Our conversation belied our feelings: we spoke as if we expected all to be well; we felt that there was no hope. We crossed the heath along the accustomed path.

"On one side was the luxuriant foliage of the forest, on the other the widespread moor; her cottage was situated at one extremity, and could hardly be distinguished, until we should arrive close to it. When we drew near, Lewis bade me go on alone; he would wait my return. I obeyed, and reluctantly approached the confirmation of my fears. At length it stood before me, the lonely cot and desolate garden; the unfastened wicket swung in the breeze; every shutter was closed.

"To stand motionless and gaze on these symbols of my worst forebodings was all that I could do. My heart seemed to me to call aloud for Ellen,—for such was she to me,—her other name might be a fiction—but silent as her own life-deserted lips were mine. Lewis grew impatient, and advanced. My stay had occasioned a transient ray of hope to enter his mind; it vanished when he saw me and *her* deserted dwelling. Slowly we turned away, and were directing our steps back again, when my name was called by a child. A little girl came running across some fields towards us, whom at last I recognised as having seen before with Ellen. 'Mr. Neville, there is a letter for you!' cried the child. 'A letter; where?—who?' 'The lady left a letter for you. You must go to Old Windsor, to Mr. Cooke's; he has got it for you.'

"She had left a letter: was she then departed on an earthly journey? 'I will go for it immediately. Mr. Cooke! Old Windsor! where shall I find him? who is he?'

"'Oh, sir, everybody knows him,' said the child; 'he lives close to the churchyard; he is the sexton. After the burial, Nancy gave him the letter to take care of.'

"Had we hoped? had we for a moment indulged the expectation of ever again seeing our miserable friend? Never! never!

Our hearts had told us that the sufferer was at peace—the unhappy orphan with her father in the abode of spirits! Why, then, were we here? Why had a smile dwelt on our lips, now wreathed into the expression of anguish? Our full hearts demanded one consolation—to weep upon her grave; her sole link now with us, her mourners. There at last my boy's grief found vent in tears, in lamentation. You saw the spot; the grassy mound rests lightly on the bosom of fair Clarice, of my own poor Ellen. Stretched upon this, kissing the scarcely springing turf; for many hours no thought visited me but the wretched one, that she had lived, and was lost to me forever!

"If Lewis had ever doubted the identity of my friend with her he loved, the letter put into our hands undeceived him; the handwriting was Miss Eversham's, it was directed to me, and contained words like these:—

'April 11.

'I have vowed never to mention certain beloved names, never to communicate with beings who cherished me once, to whom my deepest gratitude is due; and, as well as poor bankrupt can, is paid. Perhaps it is a mere prevarication to write to you, dear Horace, concerning them; but Heaven pardon me! my disrobed spirit would not repose, I fear, if I did not thus imperfectly bid them a last farewell. 'You know him, Neville; and know that he forever laments her whom he has lost. Describe your poor Ellen to him, and he will speedily see that *she* died on the waves of the murderous Atlantic. Ellen had nothing in common with *her*, save love for, and interest in him. Tell him it had been well for him, perhaps, to have united himself to the child of prosperity, the nursling of deep love; but it had been destruction, even could he have meditated such an act, to wed the *parrici*—.

'I will not write that word. Sickness and near death have taken the sting from my despair. The agony of woe which you witnessed is melted into tender affliction and pious hope. I am not miserable now. Now! When you read these

316

words, the hand that writes, the eye that sees, will be a little dust, becoming one with the earth around it. You, perhaps he, will visit my quiet retreat, bestow a few tears on my fate, but let them be secret; they may make green my grave, but do not let a misplaced feeling adorn it with any other tribute. It is my last request; let no stone, no name, mark that spot.

'Farewell, dear Horace! Farewell to one other whom I may not name. May the God to whom I am about to resign my spirit in confidence and hope, bless your earthly career! Blindly, perhaps, you will regret me for your own sakes; but for mine, you will be grateful to the Providence which has snapt the heavy chain binding me to unutterable sorrow, and which permits me from my lowly grass-grown tomb to say to you. I am at peace.

'Ellen.'

Roger Dodsworth: The Reanimated Englishman

It may be remembered, that on the fourth of July last,[1] a paragraph appeared in the papers importing that Dr. Hotham, of Northumberland, returning from Italy, over Mount St. Gothard, a score or two of years ago, had dug out from under an avalanche, in the neighbourhood of the mountain, a human being whose animation had been suspended by the action of the frost. Upon the application of the usual remedies, the patient was resuscitated, and discovered himself to be Mr. Dodsworth, the son of the antiquary Dodsworth, who perished in the reign of Charles I. He was thirty-seven years of age at the time of his inhumation, which had taken place as he was returning from Italy, in 1654.

It was added that as soon as he was sufficiently recovered he would return to England, under the protection of his preserver. We have since heard no more of him, and various plans for public benefit, which have started in philanthropic minds on reading the statement, have already returned to their pristine nothingness. The antiquarian society had eaten their way to several votes for medals, and had already begun, in idea, to consider what prices it could afford to offer for Mr. Dodsworth's old clothes, and to conjecture what treasures in the way of pamphlet, old song, or autographic letter his pockets might contain.

Poems from all quarters, of all kinds, elegiac. congratulatory, burlesque and allegoric, were half written. Mr. Godwin had sus-

---

1. 1826

pended for the sake of such authentic information the history of the Commonwealth he had just begun. It is hard not only that the world should be baulked of these destined gifts from the talents of the country, but also that it should be promised and then deprived of a new subject of romantic wonder and scientific interest. A novel idea is worth much in the commonplace routine of life, but a new fact, an astonishment, a miracle, a palpable wandering from the course of things into apparent impossibilities, is a circumstance to which the imagination must cling with delight, and we say again that it is hard, very hard, that Mr. Dodsworth refuses to appear, that the believers in his resuscitation are forced to undergo the sarcasms and triumphant arguments of those sceptics who always keep on the safe side of the hedge.

Now we do not believe that any contradiction or impossibility is attached to the adventures of this youthful antique. Animation (I believe physiologists agree) can as easily be suspended for an hundred or two years, as for as many seconds. A body hermetically sealed up by the frost, is of necessity preserved in its pristine entireness. That which is totally secluded from the action of external agency, can neither have anything added to nor taken away from it, no decay can take place, for something can never become nothing; under the influence of that state of being which we call death, change but not annihilation removes from our sight the *corporeal atoma*; the earth receives sustenance from them, the air is fed by them, each element takes its own, thus seizing forcible repayment of what it had lent.

But the elements that hovered round Mr. Dodsworth's icy shroud had no power to overcome the obstacle it presented. No zephyr could gather a hair from his head, nor could the influence of the dewy night or genial morn penetrate his more than adamantine panoply. The story of the *Seven Sleepers* rests on a miraculous interposition—they slept. Mr. Dodsworth did not sleep his breast never heaved, his pulses were stopped; death had his finger pressed on his lips which no breath might pass. He has removed it now, the grim shadow is vanquished, and stands

319

wondering. His victim has cast from him the frosty spell, and arises as perfect a man as he had lain down an hundred and fifty years before.

We have eagerly desired to be furnished with some particulars of his first conversations, and the mode in which he has learnt to adapt himself to his new scene of life. But since facts are denied to us, let us be permitted to indulge in conjecture. What his first words were may be guessed from the expressions used by people exposed to shorter accidents of the like nature. But as his powers return, the plot thickens. His dress had already excited Doctor Hotham's astonishment—the peaked beard—the love locks—the frill, which, until it was thawed, stood stiff under the mingled influence of starch and frost; his dress fashioned like that of one of Vandyke's portraits, or (a more familiar similitude) Mr. Saplo's costume in Winter's *Opera of the Oracle*, his pointed shoes—all spoke of other times. The curiosity of his preserver was keenly awake, that of Mr. Dodsworth was about to be roused.

But to be enabled to conjecture with any degree of likelihood the tenor of his first inquiries, we must endeavour to make out what part he played in his former life. He lived at the most interesting period of English History—he was lost to the world when Oliver Cromwell had arrived at the summit of his ambition, and in the eyes of all Europe the commonwealth of England appeared so established as to endure forever. Charles I. was dead; Charles II. was an outcast, a beggar, bankrupt even in hope.

Mr. Dodsworth's father, the antiquary, received a salary from the republican general, Lord Fairfax, who was himself a great lover of antiquities, and died the very year that his son went to his long, but unending sleep, a curious coincidence this, for it would seem that our frost-preserved friend was returning to England on his father's death, to claim probably his inheritance—how short lived are human views! Where now is Mr. Dodsworth's patrimony? Where his co-heirs, executors, and fellow legatees? His protracted absence has, we should suppose, given the present possessors to his estate—the world's chronology is an hundred and seventy years older since he seceded from the busy scene, hands after hands have tilled his acres, and then become clods beneath them; we may be permitted to doubt whether one single particle of their surface is individually the same as those which were to have been his—the youthful soil would of itself reject the antique clay of its claimant.

Mr. Dodsworth, if we may judge from the circumstance of his being abroad, was no zealous commonwealth's man, yet having chosen Italy as the country in which to make his tour and his projected return to England on his father's death, renders it probable that he was no violent loyalist. One of those men he seems to be (or to have been) who did not follow Cato's advice as recorded in the *Pharsalia*; a party, if to be of no party admits of such a term, which Dante recommends us utterly to despise, and which not unseldom falls between the two stools, a seat on either of which is so carefully avoided.

Still Mr. Dodsworth could hardly fail to feel anxious for the latest news from his native country at so critical a period; his absence might have put his own property in jeopardy; we may imagine therefore that after his limbs had felt the cheerful return of circulation, and after he had refreshed himself with such of earth's products as from all analogy he never could have hoped to live or eat, after he had been told from what peril he had been rescued, and said a prayer thereon which even appeared enormously long to Dr. Hotham—we may imagine, we say, that his first question would be: 'if any news had arrived lately from England.'

"I had letters yesterday," Dr. Hotham may well be supposed to reply.

"Indeed," cries Mr. Dodsworth, "and pray, sir, has any change for better or worse occurred in that poor distracted country?"

Dr. Hotham suspects a Radical, and coldly replies: "Why, sir, it would be difficult to say in what its distraction consists. People talk of starving manufacturers, bankruptcies, and the fall of the Joint Stock Companies—excrescences these, excrescences which will attach themselves to a state of full health. England, in fact, was never in a more prosperous condition."

Mr. Dodsworth now more than suspects the Republican, and, with what we have supposed to be his accustomed caution, sinks for a while his loyalty, and in a moderate tone asks: "Do our governors look with careless eyes upon the symptoms of over-health?"

"Our governors," answers his preserver, "if you mean our ministry, are only too alive to temporary embarrassment." (We beg Doctor Hotham's pardon if we wrong him in making him a high Tory; such a quality appertains to our pure anticipated cognition of a Doctor, and such is the only cognisance that we have of this gentleman.) "It were to be wished that they showed themselves more firm—the king, God bless him!"

"Sir!" exclaims Mr. Dodsworth.

Dr. Hotham continues, not aware of the excessive astonishment exhibited by his patient: "The king, God bless him, spares immense sums from his privy purse for the relief of his subjects, and his example has by all the aristocracy and wealth of England."

"The King!" ejaculates Mr. Dodsworth.

"Yes, sir," emphatically rejoins his preserver; "the king, and I am happy to say that the prejudices that so unhappily and unwarrantably possessed the English people with regard to His Majesty are now, with a few" (with added severity) "and I may say contemptible exceptions, exchanged for dutiful love and such reverence as his talents, virtues, and paternal care deserve."

"Dear sir, you delight me," replies Mr. Dodsworth, while his loyalty late a tiny bud suddenly expands into full flower; "yet I hardly understand; the change is so sudden; and the man-Charles Stuart, King Charles, I may now call him, his murder is I trust execrated as it deserves?"

Dr. Hotham put his hand on the pulse of his patient—he feared an access of delirium from such a wandering from the subject. The pulse was calm, and Mr. Dodsworth continued: "That unfortunate martyr looking down from heaven is, I trust, appeased by the reverence paid to his name and the prayers dedicated to his memory. No sentiment, I think I may venture to assert, is so general in England as the compassion and love in which the memory of that hapless monarch is held."

"And his son, who now reigns?—"

"Surely, sir, you forget; no son; that of course is impossible. No descendant of his fills the English throne, now worthily occupied by the house of Hanover. The despicable race of the Stuarts, long outcast and wandering, is now extinct, and the last days of the last Pretender to the crown of that family justified in the eyes of the world the sentence which ejected it from the kingdom forever."

Such must have been Mr. Dodsworth's first lesson in politics. Soon, to the wonder of the preserver and preserved, the real state of the case must have been revealed; for a time, the strange and tremendous circumstance of his long trance may have threatened the wits of Mr. Dodsworth with a total overthrow. He had, as he crossed Mount Saint Gothard, mourned a father—now every human being he had ever seen is "lapped in lead,"[2] is dust, each voice he had ever heard is mute.

The very sound of the English tongue is changed, as his experience in conversation with Dr. Hotham assures him. Empires, religions, races of men, have probably sprung up or faded; his own patrimony (the thought is idle, yet without it, how can he live?) is sunk into the thirsty gulph that gapes ever greedy to swallow the past; his learning, his acquirements, are probably obsolete; with a bitter smile he thinks to himself, I must take to my father's profession, and turn antiquary. The familiar objects, thoughts, and habits of my boyhood, are now antiquities. He wonders where the hundred and sixty folio volumes of MS. that his father had compiled, and which, as a lad, he had regarded with religious reverence, now are—where—ah, where? His favourite playmate, the friend of his later years, his destined and lovely bride, tears long frozen are uncongealed, and flow down his young cheeks.

But we do not wish to be pathetic; surely since the days of

2. Shakespeare, *The passionate Pilgrim*, 1, 396

the patriarchs, no fair lady had her death mourned by her lover so many years after it had taken place. Necessity, tyrant of the world, in some degree reconciles Mr. Dodsworth to his fate. At first he is persuaded that the later generation of man is much more deteriorated from his contemporaries; he begins to doubt his first impression. The ideas that had taken possession of his brain before his accident, and which had been frozen up for many years, begin to thaw and dissolve away, making room for others. He dresses himself in the modern style, and does not object much to anything except the neck-cloth and hardboarded hat.

He admires the texture of his shoes and stockings, and looks with admiration on a small Genevese watch, which he often consults, as if he were not yet assured that time had made progress in its accustomed manner, and as if he should find on its dial plate ocular demonstration that he had exchanged his thirty-seventh year for his two hundredth and upwards, and had left *a.d.* 1654 far behind to find himself suddenly a beholder of the ways of men in this enlightened nineteenth century. His curiosity is insatiable; when he reads, his eyes cannot purvey fast enough to his mind, and every now and then he lights upon some inexplicable passage, some discovery and knowledge familiar to us, but undreamed of in his days, that throws him into wonder and interminable reverie.

Indeed, he may be supposed to pass much of his time in that state, now and then interrupting himself with a royalist song against old Noll and the Roundheads, breaking off suddenly, and looking round fearfully to see who were his auditors, and on beholding the modern appearance of his friend the Doctor, sighing to think that it is no longer of import to any, whether he sings a cavalier catch or a puritanic psalm.

It were an endless task to develop all the philosophic ideas to which Mr. Dodsworth's resuscitation naturally gives birth. We should like much to converse with this gentleman, and still more to observe the progress of his mind, and the change of his ideas in his very novel situation. If he be a sprightly youth, fond of the shows of the world, careless of the higher human pursuits, he may proceed summarily to cast into the shade all trace of his former life, and endeavour to merge himself at once into the stream of humanity now flowing. It would be curious enough to observe the mistakes he would make, and the medley of manners which would thus be produced. He may think to enter into an active life, become Whig or Tory as his inclinations lead, and get a seat in the, even to him, once called chapel of St. Stephens.

He may content himself with turning contemplative philosopher, and find sufficient food for his mind in tracing the march of the human intellect, the changes which have been wrought in the dispositions, desires, and powers of mankind. Will he be an advocate for perfectibility or deterioration? He must admire our manufactures, the progress of science, the diffusion of knowledge, and the fresh spirit of enterprise characteristic of our countrymen. Will he find any individuals to be compared to the glorious spirits of his day? Moderate in his views as we have supposed him to be, he will probably fall at once into the temporising tone of mind now so much in vogue. He will be pleased to find a calm in politics; he will greatly admire the ministry who have succeeded in conciliating almost all parties—to find peace where he left feud. The same character which he bore a couple of hundred years ago, will influence him now; he will still be the moderate, peaceful, unenthusiastic Mr. Dodsworth that he was in 1647.

For notwithstanding education and circumstances may suffice to direct and form the rough material of the mind, it cannot create, nor give intellect, noble aspiration, and energetic constancy where dullness, wavering of purpose, and grovelling desires are stamped by nature. Entertaining this belief we have (to forget Mr. Dodsworth for a while) often made conjectures how such and such heroes of antiquity would act, if they were reborn in these times: and then awakened fancy has gone on to imagine that some of them are reborn; that according to the theory explained by Virgil in his sixth *Æneid,* every thousand years the dead return to life, and their souls endued with the same sensibilities and capacities as before, are turned naked of knowledge into this world, again to dress their skeleton powers in such *habiliments* as situation, education, and experience will furnish.

Pythagoras, we are told, remembered many transmigrations of this sort, as having occurred to himself, though for a philosopher he made very little use of his anterior memories. It would prove an instructive school for kings and statesmen, and in fact for all human beings, called on as they are, to play their part on the stage of the world, could they remember what they had been. Thus we might obtain a glimpse of heaven and of hell, as, the secret of our former identity confined to our bosoms, we winced or exulted in the blame or praise bestowed on our former selves.

While the love of glory and posthumous reputation is as natural to man as his attachment to life itself, he must be, under such a state of things, tremblingly alive to the historic records of his honour or shame. The mild spirit of Fox would have been soothed by the recollections that he had played a worthy part as Marcus Antoninus—the former experiences of Alcibiades or even of the emasculated Steeny of James I. might have caused Sheridan to have refused to tread over again the same path of dazzling but fleeting brilliancy. The soul of our modern Corinna would have been purified and exalted by a consciousness that once it had given life to the form of Sappho.

If at the present moment the witch, memory, were in a freak, to cause all the present generation to recollect that some ten centuries back they had been somebody else, would not several of our free thinking martyrs wonder to find that they had suffered as Christians under Domitian, while the judge as he passed sentence would suddenly become aware, that formerly he had condemned the saints of the early church to torture, for not renouncing the religion he now upheld—nothing but benevolent actions and real goodness would come pure out of the ordeal.

While it would be whimsical to perceive how some great men in parish affairs would strut under the consciousness that their hands had once held a sceptre, an honest artisan or pilfering domestic would find that he was little altered by being transformed into an idle noble or director of a joint stock company; in every way we may suppose that the humble would be exalted, and the noble and the proud would feel their stars and honours dwindle into baubles and child's play when they called to mind the lowly stations they had once occupied. If philosophical novels were in fashion, we conceive an excellent one might be written on the development of the same mind in various stations, in different periods of the world's history.

But to return to Mr. Dodsworth, and indeed with a few more words to bid him farewell. We entreat him no longer to bury himself in obscurity; or if he modestly decline publicity, we beg him to make himself known personally to us. We have a thousand inquiries to make, doubts to clear up, facts to ascertain. If any fear that the old habits and strangeness of appearance will make him ridiculous to those accustomed to associate with modern exquisites, we beg to assure him that we are not given to ridicule mere outward shows, and that worth and intrinsic excellence will always claim our respect.

This we say, if Mr. Dodsworth is alive. Perhaps he is again no more. Perhaps he opened his eyes only to shut them again more obstinately; perhaps his ancient clay could not thrive on the harvests of these latter days. After a little wonder; a little shuddering to find himself the dead alive—finding no affinity between himself and the present state of things—he has bidden once more an eternal farewell to the sun. Followed to his grave by his preserver and the wondering villagers, he may sleep the true death-sleep in the same valley where he so long reposed. Doctor Hotham may have erected a simple tablet over his twice-buried remains inscribed—

To the Memory of R. Dodsworth,
An Englishman,
Born April 1, 1617; Died July 16, 1826; Aged 209.

An inscription which, if it were preserved during any terrible convulsion that caused the world to begin its life again, would occasion many learned disquisitions and ingenious theories concerning a race which authentic records showed to have secured the privilege of attaining so vast an age.

The Bride of Modern Italy

My heart is fixt
This is the sixt.—Elia

On a serene winter morning two young ladies, Clorinda and
Teresa, walked up and down the garden of the convent of St.
S——, at Rome. If my reader has never seen a convent, or if he
has only seen the better kind, let him dismiss from his mind all
he may have heard or imagined of such abodes, or he can never
transport himself into the garden of St. S——. he must figure it
to himself as bounded by a long, low, straggling, white washed,
weather-stained building, with grated windows, the lower ones
glassless. It is a kitchen garden, but the refuse of the summer
stock alone remained, except a few cabbages, which perfumed
the air with their rank exhalations.

The walks were neglected, not yet overgrown, but strewed
with broken earthen-ware, ashes, cabbage-stalks, orange-peel,
bones, and all that marks the vicinity of a much frequented,
but disorderly mansion. The beds were intersected by these
paths, and the whole was surrounded by a high wall. This common scene was, however, unlike what it would have been in
this country. You saw the decayed and straggling boughs of the
passion-flower against the walls of the convent; here and there
a geranium, its luxuriant foliage starred by scarlet flowers, grew
unharmed by frost among the cabbages; the lemon plants had
been removed to shelter, but orange trees were nailed against
the wall, the golden fruit peeping out from the amidst the dark
leaves; the wall itself variegated by a thousand rich hues; and

thick and pointed aloes grew beneath it. Under the highest wall, opposite the back door of the convent, a corner of ground was enclosed; this was the burial place of the nuns; and in the path that led from the door to this enclosure Clorinda and Teresa walked up and down.

"He will never come!" exclaimed Clorinda.

"I fear the dinner bell will ring and interrupt us, if he does come," observed Teresa.

"Some cruel obstacle doubtless prevents him," continued Clorinda, sighing—"and I have prayed to St. Giacomo, and vowed to give him the best flowers and a candle a foot long next Easter."

Teresa smiled: "I remember," she said, "that at Christmas you fulfilled such a vow to San Francesco,—was not that for the sake of Cieco Magni? For you change your saint as your lover changes name;—tell me sweet Clorinda, how many saints have benefited by your piety?"

Clorinda looked angry, and then sorrowful; the large drops gathered in her dark eyes: "You are unkind to taunt me thus. Teresina;—when did I love truly until now? Believe me, never; and if heaven bestows Giacomo upon me—oh! That is his bell!—naughty Teresa, you will cause me to meet him with tears in my eyes."

Away they ran to the parlour of the convent, and were joined there by an old woman purblind and nearly deaf, who was present at the visit of Giacomo de' Tolomei, the brother of Teresa. He kissed the hands of the young ladies, and they commenced a conversation, which, by the lowness of their tones, and an occasional intermixture of French, was quite incomprehensible to their Argus, who was busily employed in knitting a large green worsted shawl

"Well?"—said Clorinda, in a tone of inquiry.

"Well, dear Clorinda, I have executed our design, though I hope little from it. I have written a proposal of marriage; if you approve of it, I will send it to your parents. Here it is."

"What is that paper?" cried the Argus.

Teresa bawled in her ear: "Only the history of the late miracle performed at Asisa" (Italians, male or female, are not great patronisers of truth), "look at it, dear Eusta." (Eusta could not read.) "I will read it to you by and bye." Eusta went on with her knitting.

The two girls looking over one another, read the proposal of marriage, which Giacomo de' Tolomei made to the parents of Clorinda Saviani. The paper was divided into two columns, one headed "The Proposal,"—the other "Observations to be made thereon"—and this latter column was left blank. The proposal itself was divided into several heads and numbered. It premised that a noble family of Sienna wishing to ally themselves to the family of the Saviani of Rome, in the persons of their eldest son and Clorinda, they presented the following considerations to the heads of that house first, that the young man was well-made, good-looking, healthy, studiously inclined, and of irreproachable morals.

The circumstances of his fortune were then detailed, and the claims of dowry: it concluded by saying, that if the parents of Clorinda approved of the terms proposed, the young people might be introduced to each other, and if mutually pleased at their interview, the nuptials might be celebrated in the course of a few months. When Clorinda had finished reading, the tears that had gathered in her eyes fell drop after drop upon the paper.—"Wherefore do you weep?" asked Giacomo, "why do you distress me thus?"

"This proposal will never be accepted. You have asked twelve thousand crowns in dowry; my parents will not give me more than six."

"And yet," replied Giacomo, "I have named a sum to which I am convinced my father will never agree; he will require twenty thousand at least; even if your parents accede I shall have to win his consent; but if prayers and tears can move him, I will not be chary of either."

The bell rang for dinner, old Eusta arose, and Giacomo retired. Dinner!—what dainty feast of convent-like confectionaries does the reader picture?—Let him see, in truth, a long, brick-paved floor, with long deal tables, and benches *ditto*; the tables covered with not white cloths; cellars of black salt; bottles of sour wine, and small loaves of bitter bread. Then came the *minestra*, consisting (for it was fast day) of what we call macaroni, water, oil, and cheese; then a few vegetables swimming in oil; a concluding dish of eggs fried with garlic, and the repast of one of the most highborn and loveliest girls in Rome was finished.

Clorinda Saviani was indeed handsome, and all her fine features expressed the *bisogna d'amare* which ruled her heart. She was just eighteen, and had been five years in this convent, waiting until her father should find a husband of noble birth, who would be content with a slender dowry. During this time she had formed several attachments for various youths, who, under different pretexts, had visited the convent. She had written letters, prayed and wept, and then yielding to insurmountable difficulties she had changed her idol, though she had never ceased to love.

The fastidious English must not be disgusted with this picture. It is, perhaps, only a coarse representation of what takes place at every ball-room with us. And if it went beyond;—the nature of the Catholic religion, which crushes the innate conscience by giving a false one in its room; the system of artifice and heartlessness that subsists in a convent; the widely spread maxim in Italy, that dishonour attaches itself to the discovered not the concealed fault—all this forms the excuse why with a tender heart and much native talent, there was neither constancy in Clorinda's love, nor dignity in her conduct.

After their repast the friends retired to Clorinda's cell; a small, though high room, floored with brick, miserably furnished, and neither clean nor orderly. A *prie-dieu* was beside the little bed with a crucifix over it, together with two or three prints (like our penny children's prints) of saints, among which St. Giacomo appeared with the freshest and cleanest face; besides these was a glass (resembling a bird's drinking vessel) containing holy water, rather the worse for long standing; in a closet, with the door ajar, among tattered books and female apparel, hung a glass-case enclosing a waxen Gesu Bambino, and some flowers, gathered for this holy dedication and drooping for want of light, were placed beneath him; some mignionette, basil, and heliotrope, weeds o'ergrown, flowered in a wooden trough at the window; a broken looking glass; a leaden inkstand—such was Clorinda's *boudoir.*

"I despair," she exclaimed—"I see no end to my evils—and but one road open flight"

"Which would ruin my brother."

"How?—he is of another state."

"And your honour?"

"Honour in this dungeon!—O, let me breathe the fresh air of heaven; let me no longer see this prison room; these high walls and all the circumstances of my convent life, and I care not for the rest."

"But how? You may get people into the convent—but to get out yourself is a different affair."

"I have many plans:—if this proposal of your brother fail, as it will, I will disclose them to him."

A lay sister now came in to ask the young ladies if they would take coffee with the Superior. They found her alone; a little, squat, snuff-taking old woman; she was in high ill-humour: "Body of Bachus!" she began, "you introduce strange laws in St. S——!—This coffee is detestable—Your brother, Teresina, is here every day—I detest coffee without rum—Clorinda sees him, and it begins to be talked of—when he comes tomorrow, you only must receive him, and request him to discontinue his visits."

Clorinda's tears mingled with her coffee—"The old witch!" she said, when they had retired, "she is fishing for a present."—

"And must have one; what shall Giacomo bring her?"

"Let him send some rum. Did you not see the faces she made over her coffee? Yet she is too niggardly to buy it herself."

A note was hastily dispatched to Giacomo by Teresa, to inform him of the necessary oblation. He came the next day well provided; for the waiter of a neighbouring inn accompanied him bearing six bottles of what bore the name of *Bomme*. Teresa was called and dispatched to solicit the presence of the Superior. She came; Giacomo took off his hat: "*Signora*," said he, "it is winter time, and I bring you a wintry gift.—Will you favour me by accepting this rum?"

"*Signor*, you are too courteous."

"The courtesy is yours, *Signora*, in honouring me by receiving my present. I hope that you will find it good."—He uncorked a bottle; Teresa ran for a glass; Giacomo filled it, and the Superior emptied it. Clorinda at the same moment tripped into the room. She started with a natural air, and after saluting Giacomo was going away, but he detained her, and they all sat down together, until the Superior was called away to give out bread for supper, and the three young people remained together.

The girls turned to Giacomo with inquiring looks: his were sorrowful. "My proposal has not been received. Your parents replied that they have proposed you to someone, and cannot break off the treaty."

"And thus I am to be sacrificed!" cried Clorinda, casting up her beautiful eyes.

"Will you consent?" said Giacomo reproachfully.

"What means have I? I have talked of flight" (Giacomo's countenance fell); "and that, although difficult, is not impossible."

"How?"

"Why, my cell adjoins that of the Superior. She is fond of sweet things; on the next holiday I will—make some cakes for her, filled with sugar and a little opium. I can then steal away the keys, make an impression on wax (I have a large piece already), and you can easily get them counterfeited."

"You would engage my brother in a dangerous enterprise," said Teresa.

"My dear, dear Clorinda, my sweet friend," said Giacomo. "you are ignorant of the world's ways. I would sacrifice my life to you; but you would thus lose your honour, I should be imprisoned, and you would be sent to some dreary convent among the mountains, till forced to marry some boor who would render you miserable for life."

"What is to be done then?" asked Clorinda discontentedly.

"It requires thought. Something must, something shall, be done; do you be faithful to me, and refuse your parents' offer, and I do not despair. In the meantime I will set out for Sienna tomorrow and see my father."

Giacomo had formed an intimacy with a young English artist residing at Rome, and he left the cares of his love in the hands of this gentleman, while he by short days' journeys, and with a heavy heart, proceeded towards Sienna. The following day brought a letter of five pages, in a nearly illegible hand, to be delivered to Clorinda. Our Englishman had been a year in Rome, but he had never yet been within a convent. As he passed the prison-like building of St. S——, and measured with his eye the lofty walls of its garden, he had peopled it with nuns of all ages, states, and dispositions;—the solemn and demure, the ambitious, the bigoted, and those who, repenting of their vows, wetted their pallet with their midnight tears, and then, prostrate on the damp marble before the crucifix, prayed God to pardon them for being human.

And then he thought of the novices fearful as brides, but not so hopeful; and of the boarders who dreamt of the world outside, as we of Paradise beyond the grave. He pictured echoing corridors, painted windows, the impenetrable grate, the religious cloister, and the garden, that most immaculate of asylums, with grassy walks, majestic trees, and veiled forms flitting under their shade. Well, thought he, I am now in for it; and if I do not lose my heart, I shall at least gain some excellent hints for my picture of the Profession of Eloisa.

He crossed the outer hall, rang at the bell, and the old tottering portress came towards the door. He asked for "the Signora Teresa de' Tolomei." He was shown into the parlour—a vaulted room, the floor bricked, the furniture mean, without fire or chimney, though the cold east wind covered the ground with hoar frost. In a few minutes the two friends tripped into the room, followed by Eusta, who instead of her knitting, carried a fire-pot filled with wood ashes, over which she held her withered hands and her blue nose frost bitten. The girls were somewhat startled on seeing the stranger, who advanced, and announcing himself as Signor Marcott Alleyn, a friend of the brother of Teresa, delivered a little packet, together with a note which bade his sister confide implicitly in the Englishman.

The conversation became animated. No bashfulness intruded to prevent Clorinda from discoursing eloquently of her passion, especially when she observed the deep interest which her account excited. Alleyn was a man of infinitely pleasing manners; he had a soft tone of voice and eyes full of expression. Italian ladies are not accustomed to the English system of gallantry; since in that country either downright love is made, or the most distant coldness preserved between the sexes.

Alleyn's compassion was excited in various ways. He heard that Clorinda had been imprisoned in that convent for five years; he saw the desolate garden, he felt the bitter cold, which was unalleviated by anything except fire-pots; he had a glance at the blank corridors and squalid cells, and he saw in the victim an elegance of manners and a delicate sensitiveness that ill accorded with such dreary privations.

Several visits ensued, and Alleyn became a favourite in the convent. He was only seventeen; his spirits were high; he diverted the friends, brought presents of rum and confectionary to the nuns, kissed some of the least ugly, made covert game of the Superior, and established himself with greater freedom in this seclusion in a week than Giacomo had done in a year. At first he sympathised with Clorinda, now he did more—he amused her. If she wept for the absence of Giacomo, he made her laugh at some story told *apropos*, which diverted her. If she complained of the petty tyranny of the nuns, he laid some plot of droll revenge, which she executed. He introduced a system of English jokes and hoaxes, at which the poor Italians were perfectly aghast, and to which no experience prevented their becoming victims; so utterly unable were they to comprehend the meaning of such machinations; and then, when their loud voices pealed through the arched passages in wonder and anger, they were appeased by soft words and well-timed gifts.

But this sunshine could not last forever. Clorinda was at first more happy and gay than she had ever been. She in vain endeavoured to lament the absence of her lover. Alleyn prevented every emotion except gaiety from finding a place in her heart. She looked forward with delight for the hour of his visit, and the merriment that he excited left its traces on the rest of the day. Her step was light; and the cold of her cheerless cell was unfelt, since it had been adorned with caricatures of the Superior and nuns; their tyranny was either laid asleep or revenged, and Giacomo was, alas! Forgotten. Her love-breathing letters lost their fire, and the writing them became an irksome task; her sighs were changed into smiles—but suddenly these again vanished, and Clorinda became more pensive and sad than ever.

She avoided Teresa, and passed most of her time in lonely walks up and down the straight paths of the garden. She was fretful if Alleyn did not come; when he was announced, she would blush, sit silent in his presence, and if any of his sallies provoked her with laughter, it was quickly quenched by her tears. Her devotions even lost their accustomed warmth; Alleyn had no tutelary saint; no Marcott had ever been honoured with canonisation, nor had any of the bones found in the catacombs been baptised with that transalpine name. "Marry, this is *miching Mallecho*; it means mischief,"—the brief mischief of inconstancy, new love, and all the evils attendant on such a change.

Alleyn did not suspect this turn in the tide, left *tête-à-tête* one morning, some slight attentions on his part painted her cheeks with blushes; the confession was not far behind, he heard with mingled surprise and delight, and one kiss sealed their infidelity to the absent Giacomo just as Teresa and Eusta entered.

Alleyn was only seventeen. At that age men look on women living as Edens which they dare not imagine they can ever enjoy; they love, and dream not of being loved; they seek, and their wildest fancies do not picture themselves as sought: so it was small wonder that the heart of Alleyn beat with exultation, that his step was light and his eyes sparkling as he left the convent on that day. His visits were now more frequent; Teresa was confined to her room by illness, and the lovers (though that sacred name is prophaned by such an application) were left together unwatched. Clorinda's thoughts turned wholly upon escape, and this Alleyn heedlessly fostered such thoughts, until one day she said: "If I quit the convent this night, will you be under the walls to receive me?"

"My sweet Clorinda, are you serious?"

"Alas! No, I cannot. But in a few nights I trust that I shall be able to execute my project. Look, here is wax with an impression of the keys of the convent; you must get others made from it. The sisters shall sleep well that night, and before morning we will be far on our journey towards your happy country. Fear not; my disguise is ready—all will go well."

"The devil it will!" thought Alleyn, as he quitted St. S——, and carefully placing the waxen impression he had received against a sunny wall, he paced up the Corso,—"and the devil take me if ever I go within those walls again! I have sown a pretty crop, but I am not mad enough to reap it; and, as the fates will have it, here is Tolomei returned to tax me with my false proceedings. I wish all convents and women—."

Tolomei now accosted him. They walked together towards the Coliseum, talking of indifferent things. They climbed to the highest part of the ruin, and then seated amid leafy shrubs and fragrant violets and wallflowers, looking over the desert lanes and violated Forum of Rome, Giacomo asked—"What news of Clorinda?"

Alleyn wished himself hanged, and, with a look that almost indicated that his wish was about to be fulfilled, replied briefly to his friend's questions, and then began a sting himself, that he might escape his keen, lover-like looks—more painful than his words. Giacomo's hopes were nearly dead. His father was inexorable; and had learnt, besides, that the person selected by her parents as a husband for Clorinda had arrived in Rome, and this accomplished his misery. He shed abundance of tears as he related this, and ended by declaring that if he still found Clorinda faithful and affectionate, the contrariety of his destiny would urge him to some desperate measure. They separated at length, having appointed to go together to St. S—— on the following day.

Alleyn broke this appointment. He sent an excuse to Giacomo, who accordingly went alone. In the evening he received a note from Clorinda. She lamented his absence; declared her utter aversion for Giacomo; bewailed her hard fate, and having acquainted him that she was to spend the following day with her parents, entreated him to call on the succeeding one. Alleyn passed the intermediate time at Tivoli, that he might avoid his injured friend, and at the appointed hour went to the convent. Teresa and Clorinda were together; they both looked disturbed and angry; when Alleyn appeared, Teresa arose, and casting a disdainful look on the conscious pair, left the parlour.

Clorinda burst into tears. "Oh, my beloved friend," she cried, "I have gone through heart-breaking scenes since I last saw you. This cruel Teresa is constantly upbraiding me, and Giacomo's silent looks of grief are a still greater reproach. Yet I am innocent. This heart has escaped from my control; its overwhelming sensations defy all the efforts of my reason, and I passionately love without hope, almost without a return—nor is this all."

She then related that during her visit of the day before, she had been introduced to the person on whom her parents had resolved to bestow her. "At first," she continued, "I was ignorant of the design on foot, and saw him with indifference. Presently my mother took me aside; she began with a torrent of reproaches; told me that all my artifices were discovered, and then showed me a letter of mine to Giacomo which had been intercepted by that artful monster the Superior, and concluded by telling me that I must agree instantly to marry the personage to whom I had been introduced. 'Not that you shall be forced,' she said; 'beware therefore of spreading that report; but your conduct necessitates the strongest measures. If you refuse this match, which is in every way suitable to you, you must prepare to be sent to a convent of Carthusian Nuns at Benevento, where if you do not take the veil, you will be strictly guarded, and your plots, letters, and lovers, will be of no avail.' Without permitting me to reply, this cruel mother led me back to the drawing-room; this personage, whose name is Romani, came near me, and presently took an opportunity of asking whether I agreed to the arrangement of my parents.

"What could I say? I gave an ungracious assent, and they consider the matter settled. His estate is near Spoleto, and he is gone to prepare for my reception. The writings are drawing up; the time will soon arrive when I shall change my cage and be miserable for life. You alone, Alleyn, you generous and brave Englishman, can aid me; take me hence; bear me away to freedom and love, let me not be sacrificed to this unknown bridegroom, whose person I hardly know, and the idea of whom fills my heart with despair." Alleyn replied as he best might, with expressions of real sorrow, but of small consolation, and the inexorable dinner-bell rang and separated them just as he concluded his reply.

The same evening Alleyn received a note from her:

"My horror of this marriage," she wrote, "increases in proportion as the period of its accomplishment approaches. I hear today that my parents have already given my *corrèdo* to Romani, which he is to expend in jewels and dresses for me, and thus my fate is nearly sealed. I shall be banished from Rome and my friends; I shall live with a stranger—I must be miserable. Giacomo is better than this. But as union with him is impossible, and you refuse to aid me, and to liberate one whom you say you love, listen to a plan I have formed; some years ago I was addressed by one, who at that time gained my heart, and of whom I still regard with tenderness. The smallness of my dowry caused his father to break off the treaty; this father is now dead. Go to this gentleman—find out whether he still loves me. Married to him, I should be united to one whose merits I know—I should live at Rome, and there would be some alleviation to my cruel fate. At least come tomorrow to the convent, and endeavour to console your miserable friend."

Alleyn, as may easily be supposed, did not pay the required visit to the quondam lover of Clorinda. Perhaps she expected this; for the same night she wrote to him herself. Her letter was long and eloquent. Its expressions seemed to proceed from the overflowings of a passionate and loving heart. She referred to Alleyn as a common friend, and urged expedition in every measure that was to be pursued. This letter was intercepted and carried to her parents. On the following day Alleyn received a despairing note, entreating him not to come to the convent.

"Alas!" she wrote, "how truly miserable I am! What a fate! I suffer and am the cause of a thousand griefs to others. Oh heaven! I were better dead; then I should cease to lament, or at least to occasion wretchedness to others. Now I am hated by others, and even by myself—Oh my incomparable friend! Angel of my heart! Can I be the cause of misery even to you? See Giacomo, my beloved friend; tell him how deeply I pity him, but counsel him in my name to desist from all further pursuit. He must permit me to obey my parents, and they will never consent. My sole aim now is to escape from this prison."

Another and another letter came; and she earnestly begged him not to go the convent. Thus nearly a month passed, when one morning early Alleyn was surprised by a visit from the Superior of the convent of St. S———. The old lady seemed very full of matter. She drank the *rosoglio* presented to her, took snuff, and opened her budget. She talked of the trouble she had ever had with poor Clorinda; inveighed against Giacomo; during her long discourse she praised her own sagacity, the tender affection of Clorinda's parents, and related how she had always opposed the entrance of young men into the convent and their free communication with Clorinda, except his own; but that his politeness and known integrity had in this particular caused her to relax her discipline; and she concluded by inviting him to visit the convent whenever it should be agreeable to him. She then took her leave.

Alleyn was much disturbed. He wished not to go to St. S——; he knew that he ought not to see Clorinda again. He resolved not to go out at all, and sat thinking of her beauty, love, and unaffected manners, until he resolved to walk that he might get rid of such thoughts. He hurried down the Corso, and before he was aware found himself before the door of the convent of St. S——. He paused, again he moved, and entered the outer hall-his hand was on the bell, when the door opened and Giacomo came out. Seeing Alleyn, he threw himself into his arms, shedding a torrent of tears. This exordium startled our Englishman; the conclusion was soon told: Clorinda had married Romani the day before, and on the same evening had quitted Rome for Spoleto.

This news sobered Alleyn at once; he shuddered almost to think of the folly he had been about to commit, feeling as one who is stayed by a friendly hand when about to place his foot beyond the brink of a high precipe. They turned from the convent door. "And yet," said Alleyn as he walked on, "are you secure of the truth of your account? The Superior called on me yesterday and invited me to visit St. S——. Why should she do this if Clorinda were gone? I have half a mind to go and fathom this mystery."

"Ay, go by all means," replied Giacomo bitterly, "you will be welcome; fill your pockets with sugar plums; dose the old lady with *rosoglio*, and kiss the gentle nuns, the youngest of whom bears the weight of sixty years under the fillet on her brow. They miss your good cheer, and who knows, Clorinda gone, what other nets they may weave to secure so valuable a prize. True, you are an Englishman and a heretic; words which, interpreted into pure Tuscan, mean an untired prodigal, and one, pardon me, whose conscience will no more stickle at violating yon sanctuary than at eating flesh on Fridays. Go by all means, and make the best of your good fortune among those *Houris*."

"Rather say, take post horses for Spoleto, friend Giacomo. And yet neither—it is all vanity and vexation of spirit. I will go paint my Profession of Eloisa."

The Sisters of Albano

And near Albano's scarce divided waves
Shine from a sister valley;—and afar
The Tiber winds, and the broad ocean laves
The Italian coast where sprang the Epic war,
'Arms and the Man,' whose re-ascendiing star
Rose o'er an empire; but beneath thy right
Tully reposed from Rome; and where yon bar
Of girdling mountains intercepts the sight
The Sabine farm was till'd, the weary bard's delight.

It was to see this beautiful lake that I made my last excursion
before quitting Rome. The spring had nearly grown into summer, the trees were all in full but fresh green foliage, the vine-
dresser was singing, perched among them, training his vines: the
cicala had not yet begun her song, the heats therefore had not
commenced; but at evening the fire-flies gleamed among the
hills, and the cooing *aziola* assured us of what in that country
needs no assurance—fine weather for the morrow. We set out
early in the morning to avoid the heats, breakfasted at Albano,
and till ten o'clock passed our time in visiting the Mosaic, the
villa of Cicero, and other curiosities of the place.

We reposed during the middle of the day in a tent elevated
for us at the hill-top, whence we looked on the hill-embos-
omed lake, and the distant eminence crowned by a town with
its church. Other villages and cottages were scattered among the
foldings of mountains, and beyond we saw the deep blue sea of
the southern poets, which received the swift and immortal Ti-

ber, rocking it to repose among its devouring waves. The Coliseum falls and the Pantheon decays,—the very hills of Rome are perishing,—but the Tiber lives forever, flows forever, and forever feeds the land-encircled Mediterranean with fresh waters.

Our summer and pleasure-seeking party consisted of many: to me the most interesting person was the Countess Atanasia D——, who was as beautiful as an imagination of Raphael, and good as the ideal of a poet. Two of her children accompanied her, with animated looks and gentle manners, quiet, yet enjoying, I sat near her, watching the changing shadows of the landscape before us. As the sun descended, it poured a tide of light into the valley of the lake, deluging the deep bank formed by the mountain with liquid gold. The domes and turrets of the far town flashed and gleamed, the trees were dyed in splendour; two or three slight clouds, which had drunk the radiance till it became their essence, floated golden islets in the lustrous empyrean. The waters, reflecting the brilliancy of the sky and the fire-tinted banks, beamed a second heaven, a second irradiated earth, at our feet.

The Mediterranean, gazing on the sun,—as the eyes of a mortal bride fail and are dimmed when reflecting her lover's glance,—was lost, mixed in his light, till it had become one with him.—Long (our souls, like the sea, the hills, and lake, drinking in the supreme loveliness) we gazed, till the too full cup overflowed, and we turned away with a sigh. At our feet there was a knoll of ground, that formed the foreground of our picture; two trees lay basking against the sky, glittering with the golden light, which the dew seemed to hang amid their branches; a rock closed the prospect on the other side, twined round by creepers, and redolent with blooming myrtle; a brook, crossed by huge stones, gushed through the turf, and on the fragments of rock that lay about, sat two or three persons, peasants, who attracted our attention.

One was a hunter, as his gun, lying on a bank not far off, demonstrated, yet he was a tiller of the soil; his rough straw hat, and his picturesque but coarse dress, belonged to that class. The

other was some *contadina*, in the costume of her country, returning, her basket on her arm, from the village to her cottage home.
They were regarding the stores of a pedlar, who with doffed
hat stood near: some of these consisted of pictures and prints—
views of the country, and portraits of the Madonna. Our peasants regarded these with pleased attention.

"One might easily make out a story for that pair," I said: "his
gun is a help to the imagination, and we may fancy him a bandit with his *contadina* love, the terror of all the neighbourhood,
except of her, the most defenceless being in it."

"You speak lightly of such a combination," said the lovely
countess at my side, "as if it must not in its nature be the cause
of dreadful tragedies. The mingling of love with crime is a dread
conjunction, and lawless pursuits are never followed without
bringing on the criminal, and all allied to him, ineffable misery.
I speak with emotion, for your observation reminds me of an
unfortunate girl, now one of the Sisters of Charity in the convent of Santa Chiara at Rome, whose unhappy passion for a
man, such as you mention, spread destruction and sorrow widely around her."

I entreated my lovely friend to relate the history of the nun.
For a long time she resisted my entreaties, as not willing to depress the spirit of a party of pleasure by a tale of sorrow. But I
urged her, and she yielded. Her sweet Italian phraseology now
rings in my ears, and her beautiful countenance is before me. As
she spoke, the sun set, and the moon bent her silver horn in the
ebbing tide of glory he had left. The lake changed from purple
to silver, and the trees, before so splendid, now in dark masses,
just reflected from their tops the mild moonlight. The fire-flies
flashed among the rocks; the bats circled round us: meanwhile
thus commenced the Countess Atanasia:—

The nun of whom I speak had a sister older than herself; I can
remember them when as children they brought eggs and fruit
to my father's villa, Maria and Anina were constantly together.
With their large straw hats to shield them from the scorching
sun, they were at work in their father's *podere* all day, and in the

evening, when Maria, who was the elder by four years, went to the fountain for water, Anina ran at her side. Their cot—the folding of the hill conceals it—is at the lakeside opposite; and about a quarter of a mile up the hill is the rustic fountain of which I speak. Maria was serious, gentle, and considerate; Anina was a laughing, merry little creature, with the face of a cherub.

When Maria was fifteen, their mother fell ill, and was nursed at the convent of Santa Chiara at Rome. Maria attended her, never leaving her bedside day or night. The nuns thought her an angel, she deemed them saints; her mother died, and they persuaded her to make one of them; her father could not but acquiesce in her holy intention, and she became one of the Sisters of Charity, the nun-nurses of Santa Chiara, Once or twice a year she visited her home, gave sage and kind advice to Anina, and sometimes wept to part from her; but her piety and her active employments for the sick reconciled her to her fate. Anina was more sorry to lose her sister's society. The other girls of the village did not please her: she was a good child, and worked hard for her father, and her sweetest recompense was the report he made of her to Maria, and the fond praises and caresses the latter bestowed on her when they met.

It was not until she was fifteen that Anina showed any diminution of affection for her sister. Yet I cannot call it diminution, for she loved her perhaps more than over, though her holy calling and sage lectures prevented her from reposing confidence, and made her tremble lest the nun, devoted to heaven and good works, should read in her eyes, and disapprove of the earthly passion that occupied her. Perhaps a part of her reluctance arose from the reports that were current against her lover's character, and certainly from the disapprobation and even hatred of him that her father frequently expressed.

Ill-fated Anina! I know not if in the north your peasants love as ours; but the passion of Anina was entwined with the roots of her being, it was herself: she could die, but not cease to love. The dislike of her father for Domenico made their intercourse clandestine. He was always at the fountain to fill her pitcher, and lift it on her head. He attended the same mass; and when her father went to Albano, Velletri, or Rome, he seemed to learn by instinct the exact moment of his departure, and joined her in the *podere*, labouring with her and for her, till the old man was seen descending the mountain-path on his return. He said he worked for a *contadino* near Nemi. Anina sometimes wondered that he could spare so much time for her; but his excuses were plausible, and the result too delightful not to blind the innocent girl to its obvious cause.

Poor Domenico! the reports spread against him were too well founded: his sole excuse was that his father had been a robber before him, and he had spent his early years among these lawless men. He had better things in his nature, and yearned for the peace of the guiltless. Yet he could hardly be called guilty, for no dread crime stained him. Nevertheless, he was an outlaw and a bandit; and now that he loved Anina, these names were the stings of an adder to pierce his soul. He would have fled from his comrades to a far country, but Anina dwelt amid their very haunts. At this period also the police established by the French Government, which then, possessed Rome, made these bands more alive to the conduct of their members; and rumours of active measures to be taken against those who occupied the hills near Albono, Nemi, and Veiletri, caused them to draw together in tighter bonds. Domenico would not, if he could, desert his friends in the hour of danger.

On a *festa* at this time—it was towards the end of October—Anina strolled with her father among the villagers, who all over Italy make holiday by congregating and walking in one place. Their talk was entirely of the *ladri* and the French, and many terrible stories were related of the extirpation of *banditti* in the kingdom of Naples, and the mode by which the French succeeded in their undertaking was minutely described. The troops scoured the country, visiting one haunt of the robbers after the other, and dislodging them, tracked them ns in those countries they hunt the wild beasts of the forest, till, drawing the circle narrower, they enclosed them in one spot.

They then drew a cordon round the place, which they guarded with the utmost vigilance, forbidding any to enter it with provisions, on pain of instant death. And as this menace was rigorously executed, in a short time the besieged bandits were starved into a surrender. The French troops were now daily expected, for they had been seen at Velletri and Nemi; at the same time it was affirmed that several outlaws had taken up their abode at Rocca Giovano, a deserted village on the summit of one of these hills, and it was supposed that they would make that place the scene of their final retreat.

The next day, as Anina worked in the *podere*, a party of French horse passed by along the road that separated her garden from the lake. Curiosity made her look at them; and her beauty was too great not to attract. Their observations and address soon drove her away; for a woman in love consecrates herself to her lover, and deems the admiration of others to be profanation. She spoke to her father of the impertinence of these men; and he answered by rejoicing at their arrival, and the destruction of the lawless bands that would ensue.

When in the evening Anina went to the fountain, she looked timidly around, and hoped that Domenico would be at his accustomed post, for the arrival of the French destroyed her feeling of security. She went rather later than usual, and a cloudy evening made it seem already dark; the wind roared among the trees, bending hither and thither even the stately cypresses; the waters of the lake were agitated into high waves, and dark masses of thunder-cloud lowered over the hilltops, giving a lurid tinge to the landscape.

Anina passed quickly up the mountain-path. When she came in sight of the fountain, which was rudely hewn in the living rock, she saw Domenico leaning against a projection of the hill, his hat drawn over his eyes, his *tabaro* fallen from his shoulders, his arms folded in an attitude of dejection. He started when he saw her; his voice and phrases were broken and unconnected; yet he never gazed on her with such ardent love, nor solicited her to delay her departure with such impassioned tenderness.

"How glad I am to find you here!" she said; "I was fearful of meeting one of the French soldiers: I dread them even more than the *banditti*."

Domenico cast a look of eager inquiry on her, and then turned away, saying, "Sorry am I that I shall not be here to protect you. I am obliged to go to Rome for a week or two. You will be faithful, Anina *mia*; you will love me, though I never see you more?"

The interview, under these circumstances, was longer than usual. He led her down the path till they nearly came in sight of her cottage; still they lingered. A low whistle was heard among the myrtle under-wood at the lakeside; he started; it was repeated; and be answered it by a similar note. Anina, terrified, was about to ask what this meant, when, for the first time, he pressed her to his heart, kissed her roseate lips, and, with a muttered "*Carissima addio*," left her, springing down the bank; and as she gazed in wonder, she thought she saw a boat cross a line of light made by the opening of a cloud. She stood long absorbed in reverie, wondering and remembering with thrilling pleasure the quick embrace and impassioned farewell of her lover. She delayed so long that her father came to seek her.

Each evening after this, Anina visited the fountain at the *Ave Maria*; he was not there: each day seemed an age; and incomprehensible fears occupied her heart. About a fortnight after, letters arrived from Maria. They came to say that she had been ill of the malaria fever, that she was now convalescent, but that change of air was necessary for her recovery, and that she had obtained leave to spend a month at home at Albano. She asked her father to come the next day to fetch her.

Those were pleasant tidings for Anina; she resolved to disclose everything to her sister, and during her long visit she doubted not but that she would contrive her happiness. Old Andrea departed the following morning, and the whole day was spent by the sweet girl in dreams of future bliss. In the evening Maria arrived, weak and wan, with all the marks of that dread illness about her, yet, as she assured her sister, feeling quite well.

As they sat at their frugal supper, several villagers came in to inquire for Maria; but all their talk was of the French soldiers and the robbers, of whom a band of at least twenty was collected in Rocca Giovane, strictly watched by the military.

"We may be grateful to the French," said Andrea, "for this good deed; the country will be rid of these ruffians."

"True, friend," said another; "but it is horrible to think what these men suffer: they have, it appears, exhausted all the food they brought with them to the village, and are literally starving. They have not an ounce of *maccaroni* among them; and a poor fellow who was taken and executed yesterday was a mere anatomy: you could tell every bone in his skin."

"There was a sad story the other day," said another, "of an old man from Nemi, whose son, they say, is among them at Rocca Giovane: he was found within the lines with some *baccallà* under his *pastrano*, and shot on the spot."

"There is not a more desperate gang," observed the first speaker, "in the states and the *regno* put together. They have sworn never to yield but upon good terms. To secure these, their plan is to waylay passengers and make prisoners, whom they keep as hostages for mild treatment from the Government. But the French are merciless; they are better pleased that the bandits wreak their vengeance on these poor creatures than spare one of their lives."

"They have captured two persons already," said another; "and there is old Betta Tossi half frantic, for she is sure her son is taken: he has not been at home these ten days."

"I should rather guess," said an old man, "that he went there with goodwill: the young scapegrace kept company with Domenico Baldi of Nemi."

"No worse company could he have kept in the whole country," said Andrea; "Domenico is the bad son of a bad race. Is he in the village with the rest?"

"My own eyes assured me of that," replied the other. "When I was up the hill with eggs and fowls to the *piquette* there, I saw the branches of an ilex move; the poor fellow was weak perhaps, and could not keep his hold; presently he dropped to the ground; every musket was levelled at him, but he started up and was away like a hare among the rocks. Once he turned, and then I saw Domenico as plainly, though thinner, poor lad, by much than he was,—as plainly as I now see—*Santa Virgine*! what is the matter with Nina?"

She had fainted. The company broke up, and she was left to her sister's care. When the poor child came to herself she was fully aware of her situation, and said nothing, except expressing a wish to retire to rest. Maria was in high spirits at the prospect of her long holiday at home; but the illness of her sister made her refrain from talking that night, and blessing her, as she said good night, she soon slept. Domenico starving!—Domenico trying to escape and dying through hunger, was the vision of horror that wholly possessed poor Anina.

At another time, the discovery that her lover was a robber might have inflicted pangs as keen as those which she now felt; but this at present made a faint impression, obscured by worse wretchedness. Maria was in a deep and tranquil sleep, Anina rose, dressed herself silently, and crept downstairs. She stored her market-basket with what food there was in the house, and, un-latching the cottage-door, issued forth, resolved to reach Rocca Giovane, and to administer to her lover's dreadful wants.

The night was dark, but this was favourable, for she know every path and turn of the hills, every bush and knoll of ground between her home and the deserted village which occupies the summit of that hill. You may see the dark outline of some of its houses about two hours' walk from her cottage. The night was dark, but still; the *libeccio* brought the clouds below the moun-tain-tops, and veiled the horizon in mist; not a leaf stirred; her footsteps sounded loud in her ears, but resolution overcame fear. She had entered yon ilex grove, her spirits rose with her success, when suddenly she was challenged by a sentinel; no time for es-cape; fear chilled her blood; her basket dropped from her arm; its contents rolled out on the ground; the soldier fired his gun, and brought several others round him; she was made prisoner.

In the morning, when Maria awoke she missed her sister from her side. I have overslept myself, she thought, and Nina would not disturb me. But when she came downstairs and met her father, and Anina did not appear, they began to wonder. She was not in the *podere*; two hours passed, and then Andrea went to seek her. Entering the near village, he saw the *contadini* crowding together, and a stifled exclamation of "*Ecco il padre!*" told him that some evil had betided.

His first impression was that his daughter was drowned; but the truth, that she had been taken by the French carrying provisions within the forbidden line, was still more terrible. He returned in frantic desperation to his cottage, first to acquaint Maria with what had happened, and then to ascend the hill to save his child from her impending fate. Maria heard his tale with horror; but an hospital is a school in which to learn self-possession and presence of mind. "Do you remain, my father," she said; "I will go. My holy character will awe these men, my tears move them: trust me; I swear that I will save my sister." Andrea yielded to her superior courage and energy.

The nuns of Santa Chiara when out of their convent do not usually wear their monastic habit, but dress simply in a black gown. Maria, however, had brought her nun's *habiliments* with her, and, thinking thus to impress the soldiers with respect, she now put them on. She received her father's benediction, and, asking that of the Virgin and the saints, she departed on her expedition. Ascending the hill, she was soon stopped by the sentinels. She asked to see their commanding officer, and being conducted to him, she announced herself as the sister of the unfortunate girl who had been captured the night before. The officer, who had received her with carelessness, now changed countenance: his serious look frightened Maria, clasped her hands, exclaiming, "You have not injured the child I she is safe!"

"She is safe—now," he replied with hesitation; "but there is no hope of pardon."

"Holy Virgin, have mercy on her! What will be done to her?"

"I have received strict orders: in two hours she dies."

"No! no!" exclaimed Maria impetuously, "that cannot be! You cannot be so wicked as to murder a child like her."

"She is old enough, *madame*," said the officer, "to know that she ought not to disobey orders; mine are so strict, that were she but nine years old, she dies."

These terrible words stung Maria to fresh resolution: she entreated for mercy; she knelt; she vowed that she would not depart without her sister; she appealed to Heaven and the saints. The officer, though cold-hearted, was good-natured and courteous, and he assured her with the utmost gentleness that her supplications were of no avail; that wore the criminal his own daughter he must enforce his orders. As a sole concession, he permitted her to see her sister. Despair inspired the nun with energy; she almost ran up the hill, out-speeding her guide: they crossed a folding of the hills to a little sheep-cot, where sentinels paraded before the door.

There was no glass to the windows, so the shutters were shut; and when Maria first went in from the bright daylight she hardly saw the slight figure of her sister leaning against the wall, her dark hair fallen below her waist, her head sunk on her bosom, over which her arms were folded. She started wildly as the door opened, saw her sister, and sprang with a piercing shriek into her arms. They were left alone together: Anina uttered a thousand frantic exclamations, beseeching her sister to save her, and shuddering at the near approach of her fate. Maria had felt herself, since their mother's death, the natural protectress and support of her sister, and she never deemed herself so called on to fulfil this character as now that the trembling girl clasped her neck,—her tears falling on her cheeks, and her choked voice entreating her to save her.

The thought—could I suffer instead of you! was in her heart, and she was about to express it, when it suggested another idea, on which she was resolved to act. First she soothed Anina by her promises, then glanced round the cot; they were quite alone: she went to the window, and through a crevice saw the soldiers conversing at some distance. "Yes, dearest sister," she cried, "I will—I can save you—quick—we must change dresses—there is no time to be lost!—you must escape in my habit."

"And you remain to die??"

"They dare not murder the innocent, a nun! Fear not for me—I am safe."

Anina easily yielded to her sister, but her fingers trembled; every string she touched she entangled. Maria was perfectly self-possessed, pale, but calm. She tied up her sister's long hair, and adjusted her veil over it so as to conceal it; she unlaced her bodice, and arranged the folds of her own habit on her with the greatest care—then more hastily she assumed the dress of her sister, putting on, after a lapse of many years, her native *contadina* costume. Anina stood by, weeping and helpless, hardly hearing her sister's injunctions to return speedily to their father, and under his guidance to seek sanctuary. The guard now opened the door. Anina clung to her sister in terror, while she, in soothing tones, entreated her to calm herself.

The soldier said they must delay no longer, for the priest had arrived to confess the prisoner. To Anina the idea of confession associated with death was terrible; to Maria it brought hope. She whispered in a smothered voice, "The priest will protect me—fear not—hasten to our father!"

Anina almost mechanically obeyed: weeping, with her handkerchief placed unaffectedly before her face, she passed the soldiers; they closed the door on the prisoner, who hastened to the window, and saw her sister descend the hill with tottering steps, till she was lost behind some rising ground. The nun fell on her knees—cold dew bathed her brow, instinctively she feared; the French had shown small respect for the monastic character; they destroyed the convents and desecrated the churches. Would they be merciful to her, and spare the innocent? Alas! was not Anina innocent also? Her sole crime had been disobeying an arbitrary command, and she had done the same.

"Courage!" cried Maria; "perhaps I am fitter to die than my sister is, Gesu, pardon me my sins, but I do not believe that I shall outlive this day!"

In the meantime, Anina descended the hill slowly and trembling. She feared discovery,—she feared for her sister,—and above all, at the present moment, she feared the reproaches and anger of her father. By dwelling on this last idea, it became exaggerated into excessive terror, and she determined, instead of returning to her home, to make a circuit among the hills, to find her way by herself to Albano, where she trusted to find protection from her pastor and confessor. She avoided the open paths, and following rather the direction she wished to pursue than any beaten road, she passed along nearer to Rocca Giovane than she anticipated. She looked up at its ruined houses and bell-tops steeple, straining her eyes to catch a glimpse of him, the author of all her ills.

A low but distinct whistle reached her ear, not far off; she started,—she remembered that on the night when she last saw Domenico a note like that had called him from her side; the sound was echoed and re-echoed from other quarters; she stood aghast, her bosom heaving, her hands clasped. First she saw a dark and ragged head of hair, shadowing two fiercely gleaming eyes, rise from beneath a bush. She screamed, but before she could repeat her scream three men leapt from behind a rock, secured her arms, threw a cloth over her face, and hurried her up the acclivity. Their talk, as she went along, informed her of the horror and danger of her situation.

Pity, they said, that the holy father and some of his red stockings did not command the troops: with a nun in their hands, they might obtain any terms. Coarse jests passed as they dragged their victim towards their ruined village. The paving of the street told her when they arrived at Rocca Giovane, and the change of atmosphere that they entered a house. They unbandaged her eyes: the scene was squalid and miserable, the walls ragged and black with smoke, the floor strewn with offals and dirt; a rude table and broken bench was all the furniture; and the leaves of Indian corn, heaped high in one corner, served, it seemed, for a bed, for a man lay on it, his head buried in his folded arms.

Anina looked round on her savage hosts: their countenances expressed every variety of brutal ferocity, now rendered more dreadful from gaunt famine and suffering.

"Oh, there is none who will save me!" she cried. The voice startled the man who was lying on the floor; he leapt up—it was Domenico: Domenico, so changed, with sunk cheeks and eyes, matted hair, and looks whose wildness and desperation differed little from the dark countenances around him. Could this be her lover?

His recognition and surprise at her dress led to an explanation. When the robbers first heard that their prey was no prize, they were mortified and angry; but when she related the danger she had incurred by endeavouring to bring them food, they swore with horrid oaths that no harm should befall her, but that if she liked she might make one of them in all honour and equality. The innocent girl shuddered. "Let me go," she cried; "let me only escape and hide myself in a convent forever!"

Domenico looked at her in agony, "Yes, poor child," he said; "go save yourself; God grant no evil befall you; the ruin is too wide already." Then turning eagerly to his comrades, he continued: "You hear her story. She was to have been shot for bringing food to us: her sister has substituted herself in her place. We know the French; one victim is to them as good as another: Maria dies in their hands. Let us save her. Our time is up; we must fall like men, or starve like dogs: we have still ammunition, still some strength left. To arms! let us rush on the poltroons, free their prisoner, and escape or die!"

There needed but an impulse like this to urge the outlaws to desperate resolves. They prepared their arms with looks of ferocious determination. Domenico, meanwhile, led Anina out of the house, to the verge of the hill, inquiring whether she intended to go. On her saying to Albano, he observed, "That were hardly safe; be guided by me, I entreat you: take these *piastres*, hire the first conveyance you find, hasten to Rome, to the convent of Santa Chiara: for pity's sake, do not linger in this neighbourhood."

"I will obey your injunctions, Domenico," she replied, "but I cannot take your money; it has cost you too dear: fear not, I shall arrive safely at Rome without that ill-fated silver."

Domenico's comrades now called loudly to him; he had no time to urge his request; he threw the despised dollars at her feet.

"Nina, *adieu* forever," he said: "may you love again more happily!"

"Never!" she replied. "God has saved me in this dress; it were sacrilege to change it: I shall never quit Santa Chiara."

Domenico had led her a part of the way down the rock; his comrades appeared at the top, calling to him.

"Gesu save you!" cried he: "reach the convent—Maria shall join you there before night. Farewell!" He hastily kissed her hand, and sprang up the acclivity to rejoin his impatient friends.

The unfortunate Andrea had waited long for the return of his children. The leafless trees and bright clear atmosphere permitted every object to be visible, but he saw no trace of them on the hillside; the shadows of the dial showed noon to be passed, when, with uncontrollable impatience, he began to climb the hill, towards the spot where Anina had been taken. The path he pursued was in part the same that this unhappy girl had taken on her way to Rome. The father and daughter met: the old man saw the nun's dress, and saw her unaccompanied: she covered her face with her hands in a transport of fear and shame; but when, mistaking her for Maria, he asked in a tone of anguish for his youngest darling, her arms fell—she dared not raise her eyes, which streamed with tears.

"Unhappy girl!" exclaimed Andrea, "where is your sister?"

She pointed to the cottage prison, now discernible near the summit of a steep acclivity. "She is safe," she replied: "she saved me; but they dare not murder her."

"Heaven bless her for this good deed!" exclaimed the old man fervently; "but you hasten on your way, and I will go in search of her."

Each proceeded on an opposite path. The old man wound

up the hill, now in view, and now losing sight of the hut where his child was captive: he was aged, and the way was steep. Once, when the closing of the hill hid the point towards which he forever strained his eyes, a single shot was fired in that direction: his staff fell from his hands, his knees trembled and failed him; several minutes of dead silence elapsed before he recovered himself sufficiently to proceed: full of fears he went on, and at the next turn saw the cot again.

A party of soldiers were on the open space before it, drawn up in a line as if expecting an attack. In a few moments from above them shots were fired, which they returned, and the whole was enveloped and veiled in smoke. Still Andrea climbed the hill, eager to discover what had become of his child; the firing continued quick and hot. Now and then, in the pauses of musketry and the answering echoes of the mountains, he heard a funeral chant; presently, before he was aware, at a turning of the hill, be met a company of priests and *contadini*, carrying a large cross and a bier. The miserable father rushed forward with frantic impatience; the awestruck peasants set down their load—the face was uncovered, and the wretched man fell helpless on the corpse of his murdered child.

The Countess Atanasia paused, overcome by the emotions inspired by the history she related. A long pause ensued: at length one of the party observed, "Maria, then, was the sacrifice to her goodness."

"The French," said the countess, "did not venerate her holy vocation; one peasant girl to them was the same as another. The immolation of any victim suited their purpose of awe-striking the peasantry. Scarcely, however, had the shot entered her heart, and her blameless spirit been received by the saints in Paradise, when Domenico and his followers rushed down the hill to avenge her and themselves. The contest was furious and bloody; twenty French soldiers fell, and not one of the *banditti* escaped,—Domenico, the foremost of the assailants, being the first to fall."

I asked, "And where are now Anina and her father?"

"You may see them, if you will," said the countess, "on your return to Rome. She is a nun of Santa Chiara. Constant acts of benevolence and piety have inspired her with calm and resignation. Her prayers are daily put up for Domenico's soul, and she hopes, through the intercession of the Virgin, to rejoin him in the other world. "Andrea is very old; he has outlived the memory of his sufferings; but he derives comfort from the filial attentions of his surviving daughter. But when I look at his cottage on this lake, and remember the happy laughing face of Anina among the vines, I shudder at the recollection of the passion that has made her cheeks pale, her thoughts for ever conversant with death, her only wish to find repose in the grave."

The Heir of Mondolfo

In the beautiful and wild country near Sorrento, in the Kingdom of Naples, at the time it was governed by monarchs of the
house of Anjou, there lived a territorial noble, whose wealth and
power overbalanced that of the neighbouring nobles. His castle, itself a stronghold, was built on a rocky eminence, toppling
over the blue and lovely Mediterranean. The hills around were
covered with ilex-forests, or subdued to the culture of the olive
and vine. Under the sun no spot could be found more favored
by nature.

If at eventide you had passed on the placid wave beneath the
castellated rock that bore the name of Mondolfo, you would
have imagined that all happiness and bliss must reside within
its walls, which, thus nestled in beauty, overlooked a scene of
such surpassing loveliness; yet if by chance you saw its lord issue from the portal, you shrunk from his frowning brow, you
wondered what could impress on his worn cheek the combat
of passions. More piteous sight was it to behold his gentle lady,
who, the slave of his unbridled temper, the patient sufferer of
many wrongs, seemed on the point of entering upon that only
repose "where the wicked cease from troubling and the weary
are at rest."[1]

The Prince Mondolfo had been united early in life to a princess of the regal family of Sicily. She died in giving birth to a son.
Many years subsequently, after a journey to the northern Italian
states, he returned to his castle, married. The speech of his bride

---

1. The quotation is from *Job* 3, 17

declared her to be a Florentine. The current tale was that he married her for love, and then hated her as the hindrance of his ambitious views. She bore all for the sake of her only child—a child born to its father's hate; a boy of gallant spirit, brave even to wildness.

As he grew up, he saw with anger the treatment his mother received from the haughty Prince. He dared come forward as her defender; he dared oppose his boyish courage to his father's rage: the result was natural—he became the object of his father's dislike. Indignity was heaped on him; the vassals were taught to disobey him, the menials to scorn him, his very brother to despise him as of inferior blood and birth. Yet the blood of Mondolfo was his; and, though tempered by the gentle Isabel's more kindly tide, it boiled at the injustice to which he was a victim. A thousand times he poured forth the overflowings of his injured spirit in eloquent complaints to his mother.

As her health decayed, he nurtured the project, in case of her death, of flying his paternal castle, and becoming a wanderer, a soldier of fortune. He was now thirteen. The Lady Isabel soon, with a mother's penetration, discovered his secret, and on her deathbed made him swear not to quit his father's protection until he should have attained the age of twenty. Her heart bled for the wretchedness that she foresaw would be his lot; but she looked forward with still greater horror to the picture her active fancy drew of her son at an early age wandering forth in despair, alone and helpless, suffering all the extremities of famine and wretchedness; or, almost worse, yielding to the temptations that in such a situation would be held out to him. She extracted this vow, and died satisfied that he would keep it. Of all the world, she alone knew the worth of her Ludovico—had penetrated beneath the rough surface, and become acquainted with the rich store of virtue and affectionate feeling that lay like unsunned ore in his sensitive heart.

Fernando hated his son. From his earliest boyhood he had felt the sentiment of aversion, which, far from endeavouring to quell, he allowed to take deep root, until Ludovico's most innocent action became a crime, and a system of denial and resistance was introduced that called forth all of sinister that there was in the youth's character, and engendered an active spirit of detestation in his father's mind. Thus Ludovico grew, hated and hating. Brought together through their common situation, the father and son, lord and vassal, oppressor and oppressed, the one was continually ready to exert his power of inflicting evil, the other perpetually on the alert to resist even the shadow of tyranny. After the death of his mother, Ludovico's character greatly changed.

The smile that, as the sun, had then often irradiated his countenance, now never shone; suspicion, irritability, and dogged resolution, seemed his master-feelings. He dared his father to the worst, endured that worst, and prevented from flying by his sacred observance of his vow, nurtured all angry and even revengeful feelings till the cup of wrath seemed ready to overflow. He was loved by none, and loving none his good qualities expired, or slept as if they would never more awaken.

His father had intended him for the Church; and Ludovico, until he was sixteen, wore the priestly garb. That period past, be cast it aside, and appeared habited as a cavalier of those days, and in short words told his parent that he refused to comply with his wishes; that he should dedicate himself to arms and enterprise. All that followed this declaration—menace, imprisonment, and even ignominy—he bore, but he continued firm; and the haughty Fernando was obliged to submit his towering will to the firmer will of a stripling. And now, for the first time, while rage seemed to burst his heart, he felt to its highest degree the sentiment of hatred; he expressed this passion—words of contempt and boundless. detestation were heaped upon Ludovico's head. The boy replied; and the bystanders feared that a personal encounter would ensue. Once Fernando put his hand on his sword, and the unarmed Ludovico drew in and collected himself, as if ready to spring and seize the arm that might be uplifted against him.

Fernando saw and dreaded the mad ferocity his son's eye expressed. In all personal encounters of this kind the victory rests not with the strong, but the most fearless. Fernando was not ready to stake his own life, or even with his own hand to shed his son's blood; Ludovico, not as aggressor, but in self-defense, was careless of the consequences of an attack—he would resist to the death; and this dauntless feeling gave him an ascendency his father felt and could not forgive.

From this time Fernando's conduct toward his son changed. He no longer punished, imprisoned, or menaced him. This was usage for a boy, but the Prince felt that they were man to man, and acted accordingly. He was the gainer by the change; for he soon acquired all the ascendency that experience, craft, and a court education, must naturally give him over a hot-headed youth, who, nerved to resist all personal violence, neither saw nor understood a more covert mode of proceeding.

Fernando hoped to drive his son to desperation. He set spies over him, paid the tempters that were to lead him to crime, and by a continued system of restraint and miserable thwarting hoped to reduce him to such despair that he would take refuge in any line of conduct that promised freedom from so irksome and degrading a slavery. His observance of his vow saved the youth; and this steadiness of purpose gave him time to read and understand the motives of the tempters. He saw his father's master-hand in all, and his heart sickened at the discovery.

He had reached his eighteenth year. The treatment he had endured and the constant exertion of fortitude and resolution had already given him the appearance of manhood, He was tall, well made, and athletic. His person and demeanor were more energetic than graceful, and his manners were haughty and reserved. He had few accomplishments, for his father had been at no pains for his education; feats of horsemanship and arms made up the whole catalogue. He hated books, as being a part of a priest's insignia; he was averse to all occupation that brought bodily repose with it. His complexion was dark—hardship had even rendered it sallow; his eyes, once soft, now glared with fierceness; his lips, formed to express tenderness, were now habitually curled in contempt; his dark hair, clustering in thick curls round his throat, completed the wild but grand and interesting appearance of his person.

It was winter, and the pleasures of the chase began. Every morning the huntsmen assembled to attack the wild-boars or stags which the dogs might arouse in the fastnesses of the Apennines.

This was the only pleasure that Ludovico ever enjoyed. During these pursuits he felt himself free. Mounted on a noble horse, which he urged to its full speed, his blood danced in his veins, and his eyes shone with rapture as he cast his eagle glance to Heaven; with a smile of ineffable disdain, he passed his false friends or open tormentors, and gained a solitary precedence in the pursuit.

The plain at the foot of Vesuvius and its neighbouring hills was stripped bare by winter; the full stream rushed impetuously from the hills; and there was mingled with it the baying of the dogs and the cries of the hunters; the sea, dark under a lowering sky, made a melancholy dirge as its waves broke on the shore; Vesuvius groaned heavily, and the birds answered it by wailing shrieks; a heavy *sirocco* hung upon the atmosphere, rendering it damp and cold. This wind seems at once to excite and depress the human mind: it excites it to thought, but colors those thoughts, as it does the sky, with black. Ludovico felt this; but he tried to surmount the natural feelings with which the ungenial air filled him.

The temperature of the air changed as the day advanced. The clouded sky spent itself in snow, which fell in abundance; it then became clear, and sharp frost succeeded. The aspect of earth was changed. Snow covered the ground and lay on the leafless trees, sparkling, white, and untrod.

Early in the morning a stag had been roused, and, as he was coursed along the plain skirting the hills, the hunters went at speed. All day the chase endured. At length the stag, who from the beginning had directed his course toward the hills, began to ascend them, and, with various windings and evolutions, almost put the hounds to fault. Day was near its close when Ludovico alone followed the stag, as it made for the edge of a kind of platform of the mountain, which, isthmus-like, was connected with the hill by a small tongue of land, and on three sides was precipitous to the plain below.

Ludovico balanced his spear, and his dogs drew in, expecting that the despairing animal would there turn to bay. He made one bound, which conducted him to the very brow of the precipice—another, and he was seen no more. He sprang downward, expecting more pity from the rocks beneath than from his human adversary. Ludovico was fatigued by the chase and angry at the escape of his prey. He sprang from his horse, tied him to a tree, and sought a path by which he might safely descend to the plain. Snow covered and hid the ground, obliterating the usual traces that the flocks or herds might have left as they descended from their pastures on the hills to the hamlets beneath; but Ludovico had passed his boyhood among mountains: while his hunting-spear found sure rest on the ground, he did not fear, or while a twig afforded him sufficient support as he held it, he did not doubt to secure his passage; but the descent was precipitous, and necessary caution obliged him to be long.

The sun approached the horizon, and the glow of its departure was veiled by swift-rising clouds which the wind blew upward from the sea—a cold wind, which whirled the snow from its resting-place and shook it from the trees. Ludovico at length arrived at the foot of the precipice. The snow reflected and enhanced the twilight, and he saw four deep marks that must have been made by the deer. The precipice was high above, and its escape appeared a miracle. It must have escaped; but those were the only marks it had left.

Around lay a forest of ilex, beset by thick, entangled underwood, and it seemed impossible that any animal so large as the stag in pursuit could have broken its way through the apparently impenetrable barrier it opposed. The desire to find his quarry became almost a passion in the heart of Ludovico. He walked round to seek for an opening, and at last found a narrow pathway through the forest, and some few marks seemed to indicate that the stag must have sought for refuge up the glen. With a swiftness characteristic even of his prey, Ludovico rushed up the pathway, and thought not of how far he ran, until, breathless, he stopped before a cottage that opposed itself to his further progress. He stopped and looked around.

There was something singularly mournful in the scene. It was not dark, but the shades of evening seemed to descend from the vast woof of cloud that climbed the sky from the West. The black and shining leaves of the ilex and those of the laurel and myrtle underwood were strongly contrasted with the white snow that lay upon them. A breeze passed among the boughs, and scattered the drift that fell in flakes, and disturbed by fits the silence around; or, again, a bird twittered, or flew with melancholy flap of wing, beneath the trees to its nest in some hollow trunk.

The house seemed desolate; its windows were glassless, and small heaps of snow lay upon the sills. There was no print of footing on the equal surface of the path that led right up to the door, yet a little smoke now and then struggled upward from its chimney, and, on paying fixed attention, Prince Ludovico thought he heard a voice. He called, but received no answer. He put his hand on the latch; it yielded, and he entered.

On the floor, strewed with leaves, lay a person sick and dying; for, though there was a slight motion in the eyes that showed that life had not yet deserted his throne, the paleness of the visage was that of death only. It was an aged woman, and her white hair showed that she descended to no untimely grave. But a figure knelt beside her which might have been mistaken for the angel of heaven waiting to receive and guide the departing soul to eternal rest, but for the sharp agony that was stamped on the features, and the glazed but earnest gaze of her eye.

She was very young, and beautiful as the star of evening. She had apparently despoiled herself to bestow warmth on her dying friend, for her arms and neck were bare but for the quantity of dark and flowing hair that clustered on her shoulders. She was absorbed in one feeling, that of watching the change in the sick person. Her cheeks, even her lips, were pale; her eyes seemed to gaze as if her whole life reigned in their single perception.

She did not hear Ludovico enter, or, at least, she made no sign that indicated that she was conscious of it. The sick person murmured; as she bent her head down to catch the sound, she replied, in an accent of despair:

"I can get no more leaves, for the snow is on the ground; nor have I any other earthly thing to place over you."

"Is she cold?" said Ludovico, creeping near, and bending down beside the afflicted girl.

"Oh, very cold!" she replied, "and there is no help."

Ludovico had gone to the chase in a silken mantle lined with the choicest furs: he had thrown it off, and left it with his horse that it might not impede his descent. He hastened from the cottage, he ran down the lane, and, following the marks of his footsteps, he arrived where his steed awaited him. He did not again descend by the same path, reflecting that it might be necessary for him to seek assistance for the dying woman. He led his horse down the bill by a circuitous path, and, although he did this with all possible speed, night closed in, and the glare of the snow alone permitted him to see the path that he desired to follow.

When he arrived at the lane he saw that the cottage, before so dark, was illuminated, and, as he approached, he heard the solemn hymn of death as it was chanted by the priests who filled it. The change had taken place, the soul had left its mortal mansion, and the deserted ruin was attended with more of solemnity than had been paid to the mortal struggle. Amid the crowd of priests Ludovico entered unperceived, and he looked around for the lovely female he had left She sat, retired from the priests, on a heap of leaves in a corner of the cottage. Her clasped hands lay on her knees, her head was bent downward, and every now and then she wiped away her fast-falling tears with her hair. Ludovico threw his cloak over her. She looked up, and drew the covering round her, more to hide her person than for the sake of warmth, and then, again turning away, was absorbed in her melancholy thoughts.

Ludovico gazed on her in pity. For the first time since his mother's death, tears filled his eyes, and his softened countenance beamed with tender sympathy. He said nothing, but he continued to look on as a wish arose in his mind that he might wipe the tears that one by one fell from the shrouded eyes of the unfortunate girl. As he was thus engaged, he heard his name called by one of the attendants of the castle, and, throwing the few pieces of gold he possessed into the lap of the sufferer, he suddenly left the cottage, and, joining the servant who had been in search of him, rode rapidly toward his home.

As Ludovico rode along, and the first emotions of pity having, as it were, ceased to throb in his mind, these feelings merged into the strain of thought in which he habitually indulged, and turned its course to something new.

"I call myself wretched," he cried—"I, the well-clad and fed, and this lovely peasant-girl, half famished, parts with her necessary clothing to cover the dying limbs of her only friend. I also have lost my only friend, and that is my true misfortune, the cause of all my real misery—sycophants would assume that name—spies and traitors usurp that office. I have cast these aside—shaken them from me as yon bough shakes to earth its incumbrance of snow, not as cold as their iced hearts, but I am alone—solitude gnaws my heart and makes me savage—miserable—worthless."

Yet, although he thought in this manner, the heart of Ludovico was softened by what he had seen, and milder feelings pressed upon him. He had felt sympathy for one who needed it; he had conferred a benefit on the necessitous; tenderness molded his lips to a smile, and the pride of utility gave dignity to the fire of his eye. The people about him saw the change, and, not meeting with the usual disdain of his manner, they also became softened, and the alteration apparent in his character seemed ready to effect as great a metamorphosis in his external situation. But the time was not come when this change would become permanent.

On the day that succeeded to this hunt, Prince Fernando

removed to Naples, and commanded his son to accompany him. The residence at Naples was peculiarly irksome to Ludovico. In the country he enjoyed comparative freedom. Satisfied that he was in the castle, his father sometimes forgot him for days together; but it was otherwise here. Fearful that he should form friends and connections, and knowing that his commanding figure and peculiar manners excited attention and often curiosity, he kept him ever in sight; or, if he left him for a moment, he first made himself sure of the people around him, and left such of his own confidants whose very presence was venom to the eye of Ludovico. Add to which, Prince Mondolfo delighted to insult and browbeat his son in public, and, aware of his deficiencies in the more elegant accomplishments, he exposed him even to the derision of his friends. They remained two months at Naples, and then returned to Mondolfo.

It was spring; the air was genial and spirit-stirring. The white blossoms of the almond-trees and the pink ones of the peach just began to be contrasted with the green leaves that shot forth among them. Ludovico felt little of the exhilarating effects of spring. Wounded in his heart's core, he asked nature why she painted a sepulcher; he asked the airs why they fanned the sorrowful and the dead. He wandered forth to solitude. He rambled down the path that led to the sea; he sat on the beach, watching the monotonous flow of the waves; they danced and sparkled; his gloomy thoughts refused to imbibe cheerfulness from wave or sun.

A form passed near him—a peasant-girl, who balanced a pitcher, urn-shaped, upon her head; she was meanly clad, but she attracted Ludovico's regard, and when, having approached the fountain, she took her pitcher and turned to fill it, he recognized the cottager of the foregoing winter. She knew him also, and, leaving her occupation, she approached him and kissed his hand with that irresistible grace that southern climes seem to instill into the meanest of their children.

At first she hesitated, and began to thank him in broken accents, but words came as she spoke, and Ludovico listened to her eloquent thanks—the first he had heard addressed to him by any human being. A smile of pleasure stole over his face—a smile whose beauty sank deep into the gazer's heart. In a minute they were seated on the bank beside the fountain, and Viola told the story of her poverty-stricken youth—her orphan lot—the death of her best friend—and it was now only the benign climate which, in diminishing human wants, made her appear less wretched than then. She was alone in the world—living in that desolate cottage—providing for her daily fare with difficulty. Her pale cheek, the sickly languor that pervaded her manner, gave evidence of the truth of her words; but she did not weep, she spoke words of good heart, and it was only when she alluded to the benefaction of Ludovico that her soft dark eyes swam with tears.

The youth visited her cottage the next day. He rode up the lane, now grass-grown and scented by violets, which Viola was gathering from the banks. She presented her nosegay to him. They entered the cottage together. It was dilapidated and miserable. A few flowers placed in a broken vase was a type only of poor Viola herself—a lovely blossom in the midst of utter poverty; and the rose-tree that shaded the window could only tell that sweet Italy, even in the midst of wretchedness, spares her natural wealth to adorn her children.

Ludovico made Viola sit down on a bench by the window, and stood opposite to her, her flowers in his hand, listening. She did not talk of her poverty, and it would be difficult to recount what was said. She seemed happy and smiled and spoke with a gleeful voice, which softened the heart of her friend, so that he almost wept with pity and admiration. After this, day by day, Ludovico visited the cottage and bestowed all his time on Viola. He came and talked with her, gathered violets with her, consoled and advised her, and became happy.

The idea that he was of use to a single human being instilled joy into his heart; and yet he was wholly unconscious how entirely he was necessary to the happiness of his *protégée*. He felt happy beside her, he was delighted to bestow benefits on her, and to see her profit by them; but he did not think of love, and his mind, unawakened to passion, reposed from its long pain without a thought for the future. It was not so with the peasant-girl. She could not see his eyes bent in gentleness on her, his mouth lighted by its tender smile, or listen to his voice as he bade her trust in him, for that he would be father, brother, all to her, without deeply, passionately loving him. He became the sun of her day, the breath of her life—her hope, joy, and sole posses-sion. She watched for his coming, she watched him as he went, and for a long time she was happy. She would not repine that he replied to her earnest love with calm affection only—she was a peasant, he a noble—and she could claim and expect no more; he was a god—she might adore him; and it were blasphemy to hope for more than a benign acceptation of her worship.

Prince Mondolfo was soon made aware of Ludovico's visits to the cottage of the forest, and he did not doubt that Viola had become the mistress of his son. He did not endeavour to interrupt the connection, or put any bar to his visits. Ludovico, indeed, enjoyed more liberty than ever, and his cruel father con-fined himself alone to the restricting of him more than ever in money. His policy was apparent: Ludovico had resisted every temptation of gambling and other modes of expense thrown in his way.

Fernando had long wished to bring his son to a painful sense of his poverty and dependence, and to oblige him to seek the necessary funds in such a career as would necessitate his deser-tion of the paternal roof. He had wound many snares around the boy, and all were snapped by his firm but almost unconscious resistance; but now, without seeking, without expectation, the occasion came of itself which would lead him to require far more than his father had at any time allowed him, and now that allowance was restricted, yet Ludovico did not murmur—and until now he had had enough.

A long time Fernando abstained from all allusion to the con-nection of his son; but one evening, at a banquet, gayety over-came his caution—a gayety which ever led him to sport with his son's feelings, and to excite a pain which might repress the smile that his new state of mind ceased to make frequent visits to his countenance.

"Here," cried Fernando, as he filled a goblet—"here, Ludovico, is to the health of your violet-girl!" and he concluded his speech with some indecorous allusion that suffused Ludovico's cheek with red. Without replying he arose to depart.

"And whither are you going, sir?" cried his father. "Take yon cup to answer my pledge, for, by Bacchus! none that sit at my table shall pass it uncourteously by."

Ludovico, still standing, filled his cup and raised it as he was about to speak and retort to his father's speech, but the memory of his words and the innocence of Viola pressed upon him and filled his heart almost to bursting. He put down his cup, pushed aside the people who sought to detain him, and left the castle, and soon the laughter of the revelers was no more heard by him, though it had loudly rung and was echoed through the lofty halls. The words of Fernando had awakened a strange spirit in Ludovico. "Viola! Can she love me? Do I love her?"

The last question was quickly answered. Passion, suddenly awake, made every artery tingle by its thrilling presence. His cheeks burned and his heart danced with strange exultation as he hastened toward the cottage, unheeding all but the universe of sensation that dwelt within him. He reached its door. Blank and dark the walls rose before him, and the boughs of the wood waved and sighed over him.

Until now he had felt impatience alone—the sickness of fear—fear of finding a cold return to his passion's feeling now entered his heart; and, retreating a little from the cottage, he sat on a bank, and hid his face in his hands, while passionate tears gushed from his eyes and trickled from between his fingers. Viola opened the door of her cottage; Ludovico had failed in his daily visit, and she was unhappy. She looked on the sky—the sun had set, and Hesperus glowed in the West; the dark ilex-trees made a deep shade, which was broken by innumerable fire-flies, which flashed now low on the ground, discovering the flowers as they slept hushed and closed in night, now high among the branches, and their light was reflected by the shining leaves of ilex and laurel.

Viola's wandering eye unconsciously selected one and followed it as it flew, and ever and anon cast aside its veil of darkness and shed a wide pallor around its own form. At length it nestled itself in a bower of green leaves formed by a clump of united laurels and myrtles; and there it stayed, flashing its beautiful light, which, coming from among the boughs, seemed as if the brightest star of the heavens had wandered from its course, and, trembling at its temerity, sat panting on its earthly perch.

Ludovico sat near the laurel—Viola saw him—her breath came quick—she spoke not—but stepped lightly to him—and looked with such mazed ecstasy of thought that she felt, nay, almost heard, her heart beat with her emotion. At length she spoke—she uttered his name, and he looked up on her gentle face, her beaming eyes and her sylph-like form bent over him. He forgot his fears, and his hopes were soon confirmed. For the first time he pressed the trembling lips of Viola, and then tore himself away to think with rapture and wonder on all that had taken place.

Ludovico ever acted with energy and promptness. He returned only to plan with Viola when they might be united. A small chapel in the Apennines, sequestered and unknown, was selected; a priest was easily procured from a neighbouring convent and easily bribed to silence. Ludovico led back his bride to the cottage in the forest. There she continued to reside; for worlds he would not have had her change her habitation; all his wealth was expended in decorating it; yet his all only sufficed to render it tolerable. But they were happy. The small circlet of earth's expanse that held in his Viola was the universe to her husband. His heart and imagination widened and filled it until it encompassed all of beautiful, and was inhabited by all of excellent, this world contains.

She sang to him; he listened, and the notes built around him a magic bower of delight. He trod the soil of paradise, and its winds fed his mind to intoxication. The inhabitants of Mondolfo could not recognize the haughty, resentful Ludovico in the benign and gentle husband of Viola.

His father's taunts were unheeded, for he did not hear them. He no longer trod the earth, but, angel-like, sustained by the wings of love, skimmed over it, so that he felt not its inequalities nor was touched by its rude obstacles. And Viola, with deep gratitude and passionate tenderness, repaid his love. She thought of him only, lived for him, and with unwearied attention kept alive in his mind the first dream of passion.

Thus nearly two years passed, and a lovely child appeared to bind the lovers with closer ties, and to fill their humble roof with smiles and joy.

Ludovico seldom went to Mondolfo; and his father, continuing his ancient policy, and glad that in his attachment to a peasant-girl he had relieved his mind from the fear of brilliant connections and able friends, even dispensed with his attendance when he visited Naples. Fernando did not suspect that his son had married his low-born favorite; if he had, his aversion for him would not have withheld him from resisting so degrading an alliance; and, while his blood flowed in Ludovico's veins, he would never have avowed offspring who were contaminated by a peasant's less highly-sprung tide.

Ludovico had nearly completely his twentieth year when his elder brother died. Prince Mondolfo at that time spent four months at Naples, endeavouring to bring to a conclusion a treaty of marriage he had entered into between his heir and the daughter of a noble Neapolitan house, when this death overthrew his hopes, and he retired in grief and mourning to his castle. A few weeks of sorrow and reason restored him to himself. He had loved even this favoured eldest son more as the heir of his name and fortune than as his child; and the web destroyed that he had woven for him, he quickly began another.

Ludovico was summoned to his father's presence. Old habit yet rendered such a summons momentous; but the youth, with a proud smile, threw off these boyish cares, and stood with a gentle dignity before his altered parent.

"Ludovico," said the Prince, "four years ago you refused to take a priest's vows, and then you excited my utmost resentment; now I thank you for that resistance."

A slight feeling of suspicion crossed Ludovico's mind that his father was about to cajole him for some evil purpose. Two years before he would have acted on such a thought, but the habit of happiness made him unsuspicious. He bent his head gently.

"Ludovico," continued his father, while pride and a wish to conciliate disturbed his mind and even his countenance, "my son, I have used you hardly; but that time is now past."

Ludovico gently replied:

"My father, I did not deserve your ill-treatment; I hope I shall merit your kindness when I know—"

"Yes, yes," interrupted Fernando, uneasily, "you do not understand—you desire to know why—in short, you, Ludovico, are now all my hope—Olympio is dead—the house of Mondolfo has no support but you—"

"Pardon me," replied the youth. "Mondolfo is in no danger; you, my lord, are fully able to support and even to augment its present dignity."

"You do not understand. Mondolfo has no support but you. I am old, I feel my age, and these gray hairs announce it to me too glaringly. There is no collateral branch, and my hope must rest in your children"—

"My children, my lord!" replied Ludovico. "I have only one; and if the poor little boy"—

"What folly is this?" cried Fernando, impatiently. "I speak of your marriage and not"—

"My lord, my wife is ever ready to pay her duteous respects to you"—

"Your wife, Ludovico! But you speak without thought. How? Who?"

"The violet-girl, my lord."

A tempest had crossed the countenance of Fernando. That his son, unknown to him, should have made an unworthy alliance, convulsed every fiber of his frame, and the lowering of his brows and his impatient gesture told the intolerable anguish of such a thought. The last words of Ludovico restored him. It was not his wife that he thus named—he felt assured that it was not.

He smiled somewhat gloomily, still it was a smile of satisfaction.

"Yes," he replied, "I understand; but you task my patience-you should not trifle with such a subject or with me. I talk of your marriage. Now that Olympio is dead, and you are, in his place, heir of Mondolfo, you may, in his stead, conclude the advantageous, nay, even princely, alliance I was forming for him."

Ludovico replied with earnestness:

"You are pleased to misunderstand me. I am already married. Two years ago, while I was still the despised, insulted Ludovico, I formed this connection, and it will be my pride to show the world how, in all but birth, my peasant-wife is able to follow the duties of her distinguished situation."

Fernando was accustomed to command himself. He felt as if stabbed by a poniard; but he paused till calm and voice returned, and then he said:

"You have a child?"

"An heir, my lord," replied Ludovico, smiling—for his father's mildness deceived him—"a lovely, healthy boy."

"They live near here?"

"I can bring them to Mondolfo in an hour's space. Their cottage is in the forest, about a quarter of a mile east of the convent of Santa Chiara."

"Enough, Ludovico; you have communicated strange tidings, and I must consider of them. I will see you again this evening."

Ludovico bowed and disappeared. He hastened to his cottage, and related all that he remembered or understood of this scene, and bade Viola prepare to come to the castle at an instant's notice. Viola trembled; it struck her that all was not so fair as Ludovico represented; but she hid her fears, and even smiled as her husband with a kiss hailed his boy as heir of Mondolfo.

Fernando had commanded both look and voice while his

son was within hearing. He had gone to the window of his chamber, and stood steadily gazing on the drawbridge until Ludovico crossed it and disappeared. Then, unrestrained, he strode up and down the apartment, while the roof rang with his impetuous tread. He uttered cries and curses, and struck his head with his clenched fist.

It was long ere he could think—he felt only, and feeling was torture. The tempest at length subsided, and he threw himself in his chair. His contracted brows and frequently-convulsed lips showed how entirely he was absorbed in consideration. All at first was one frightful whirl; by degrees, the motion was appeased; his thoughts flowed with greater calmness; they subsided into one channel whose course he warily traced until he thought that he saw the result, Hours passed during this contemplation. When he arose from his chair, as one who had slept and dreamed uneasily, his brows became by degrees smooth; he stretched out his arm, and, spreading his hand, cried:

"So it is! and I have vanquished him!"

Evening came, and Ludovico was announced. Fernando feared his son. He had ever dreaded his determined and fearless mode of action. He dreaded to encounter the boy's passions with his own, and felt in the clash that his was not the master-passion. So, subduing all of hate, revenge, and wrath, he received him with a smile. Ludovico smiled also; yet there was no similarity in their look: one was a smile of frankness, joy, and affection—the other the veiled grimace of smothered malice. Fernando said:

"My son, you have entered lightly into a marriage as if it were a child's game, but, where principalities and noble blood are at stake, the loss or gain is too momentous to be trifled with.

Silence, Ludovico! Listen to me, I entreat. You have made a strange marriage with a peasant, which, though I may acknowledge, I cannot approve, which must be displeasing to your sovereign, and derogatory to all who claim alliance with the house of Mondolfo."

Cold dew stood on the forehead of Fernando as he spoke; he paused, recovered his self-command, and continued:

"It will be difficult to reconcile these discordant interests, and a moment of rashness might cause us to lose our station, fortune, everything! Your interests are in my hands. I will be careful of them. I trust, before the expiration of a very few months, the future Princess Mondolfo will be received at the court of Naples with due honor and respect. But you must leave it to me. You must not move in the affair. You must promise that you will not, until I permit, mention your marriage to any one, or acknowledge it if you are taxed with it."

Ludovico, after a moment's hesitation, replied:

"I promise that, for the space of six months, I will not mention my marriage to anyone. I will not be guilty of falsehood, but for that time I will not affirm it or bring it forward in any manner so as to annoy you."

Fernando again paused; but prudence conquered, and he said no more. He entered on other topics with his son; they supped together, and the mind of Ludovico, now attuned to affection, received all the marks of his father's awakening love with gratitude and joy. His father thought that he held him in his toils, and was ready to sweeten the bitterness of his intended draft by previous kindness.

A week passed thus in calm. Ludovico and Viola were perfectly happy. Ludovico only wished to withdraw his wife from obscurity from that sensation of honest pride which makes us desire to declare to the whole world the excellence of a beloved object. Viola shrank from such an exhibition; she loved her humble cottage—humble still though adorned with all that taste and love could bestow on it. The trees bent over Its low roof and shaded its windows, which were filled with flowering shrubs; its floor shone with marble, and vases of antique shape and exquisite beauty stood in the niches of the room.

Every part was consecrated by the memory of their first meeting and their loves—the walks in snow and violets; the forest of ilex with its underwood of myrtle and its population of fireflies; the birds; the wild and shy animals that sometimes came in sight, and, seen, retreated; the changes of the seasons, of the hues of nature influenced by them; the alterations of the sky; the walk of the moon; and the moving of the stars—all were dear, known, and commented on by this pair, who saw the love their own hearts felt reflected in the whole scene around, and in their child, their noisy but speechless companion, whose smiles won hopes, and whose bright form seemed as if sent from Heaven to reward their constant affection.

A week passed, and Fernando and Ludovico were riding together, when the Prince said:

"Tomorrow, early, my son, you must go to Naples. It is time that you should show yourself there as my heir, and the best representative of a princely house. The sooner you do this the quicker will arrive the period for which, no doubt, you long, when the unknown Princess Mondolfo will be acknowledged by all. I cannot accompany you. In fact, circumstances which you may guess make me desire that you should appear at first without me. You will be distinguished by your sovereign, courted by all, and you will remember your promise as the best means of accomplishing your object. In a very few days I will join you."

Ludovico readily assented to this arrangement, and went the same evening to take leave of Viola. She was seated beneath the laurel tree where first they had made their mutual vows; her child was in her arms, gazing with wonder and laughter on the light of the flies. Two years had passed. It was summer again, and as the beams from their eyes met and mingled each drank in the joyous certainty that they were still as dear to one another as when he, weeping from intense emotion, sat under that tree.

He told her of his visit to Naples which his father had settled for him, and a cloud passed over her countenance, but she dismissed it. She would not fear; yet again and again a thrilling sense of coming evil made her heart beat, and each time was resisted with greater difficulty. As night came on, she carried the sleeping child into the cottage, and placed him on his bed, and then walked up and down the pathway of the forest with Ludovico until the moment of his departure should arrive, for the heat of the weather rendered it necessary that he should travel by night.

Again the fear of danger crossed her, and again she with a smile shook off the thought; but, when he turned to give her his parting embrace, it returned with full force on her. Weeping bitterly, she clung to him, and entreated him not to go. Startled by her earnestness, he eagerly sought an explanation, but the only explanation she could give excited a gentle smile as he caressed and bade her to be calm; and then, pointing to the crescent moon that gleamed through the trees and checkered the ground with their moving shades, he told her he would be with her ere its full, and with one more embrace left her weeping.

And thus it is a strange prophecy often creeps about, and the spirit of Cassandra inhabits many a hapless human heart, and utters from many lips unheeded forebodings of evils that are to be: the hearers heed them not—the speaker hardly gives them credit—the evil comes which, if it could have been avoided, no Cassandra could have foretold, for if that spirit were not a sure harbinger so would it not exist; nor would these half revealings have place if the to come did not fulfill and make out the sketch.

Viola beheld him depart with hopeless sorrow, and then turned to console herself beside the couch of her child. Yet, gazing on him, her fears came thicker; and in a transport of terror she rushed from the cottage, ran along the pathway, calling on Ludovico's name, and sometimes listening if she might hear the tread of his horse, and then again shrieking aloud for him to return.

But he was far out of hearing, and she returned again to her cot, and, lying down beside her child, clasping his little hand in hers, at length slept peacefully.

Her sleep was light and short. She arose before the sun, and hardly had he begun to cast long shadows on the ground when, attiring herself in her veil, she was about to go with the infant to the neighbouring chapel of Santa Chiara, when she heard the trampling of horses come up the pathway; her heart beat quick, and still quicker when she saw a stranger enter the cottage. His form was commanding, and age, which had grizzled his hair, had not tempered the fire of his eye nor marred the majesty of his carriage; but every lineament was impressed by pride and even cruelty. Self-will and scorn were even more apparent.

He was somewhat like what Ludovico had been, and so like what he then was that Viola did not doubt that his father stood before her. She tried to collect her courage, but the surprise, his haughty mien, and, above all, the sound of many horses, and the voices of men who had remained outside the cottage, so disturbed and distracted her that her heart for a moment failed her, and she leaned trembling and ashy white against the wall, straining her child to her heart with convulsive energy. Fernando spoke:

"You are Viola Amaldi, and you call yourself, I believe, the wife of Ludovico Mandolfo?"

"I am so"—her lips formed themselves to these words, but the sound died away.

Fernando continued:

"I am Prince Mondolfo, father of the rash boy who has entered into this illegal and foolish contract. When I heard of it my plan was easily formed, and I am now about to put it into execution. I could easily have done so without coming to you, without enduring the scene which, I suppose, I shall endure; but benevolence has prompted me to the line of conduct I adopt, and I hope that I shall not repent it."

Fernando paused; Viola had heard little of what he had said. She was employed in collecting her scattered spirits, in bidding her heart be still, and arming herself with the pride and courage of innocence and helplessness. Every word he spoke was thus of use to her, as it gave her time to recollect herself. She only bowed her head as he paused, and he continued:

"While Ludovico was a younger son, and did not seek to obtrude his misalliance into notice, I was content that he should enjoy what he termed happiness unmolested; but circumstances have changed. He has become the heir of Mondolfo, and must support that family and title by a suitable marriage. Your dream has passed. I mean you no ill. You will be conducted hence with your child, placed on board a vessel, and taken to a town in Spain. You will receive a yearly stipend, and, as long as you seek no communication with Ludovico, or endeavour to leave the asylum provided for you, you are safe; but the slightest movement, the merest yearning for a station you may never fill, shall draw upon you and that boy the vengeance of one whose menaces are but the uplifted arm—the blow quickly follows!"

The excess of danger that threatened the unprotected Viola gave her courage. She replied:

"I am alone and feeble, you are strong, and have ruffians waiting on you to execute such crimes as your imagination suggests. I care not for Mondolfo, nor the title, nor the possession, but I will never, oh! never, never! renounce my Ludovico—never do aught to derogate from our plighted faith. Torn from him, I will seek him, though it be barefoot and a-hungered, through the wide world. He is mine by that love be has been pleased to conceive for me; I am his by the sentiment of devotion and eternal attachment that now animates my voice. Tear us asunder, yet we shall meet again, and, unless you put the grave between us, you cannot separate us."

Fernando smiled in scorn.

"And that boy," he said, pointing to the infant, "will you lead him, innocent lamb, a sacrifice to the altar of your love, and plant the knife yourself in the victim's heart?"

Again the lips of Viola became pale as she clasped her boy and exclaimed, in almost inarticulate accents:

"There is a God in Heaven!" Fernando left the cottage, and it was soon filled by men, one of whom threw a cloak over Viola and her boy, and, dragging them from the cottage, placed them in a kind of litter, and the cavalcade proceeded silently. Viola had uttered one shriek when she beheld her enemies, but, knowing their power and her own impotence, she stifled all further cries. When in the litter she strove in vain to disengage herself from the cloak that enveloped her, and then tried to hush her child, who, frightened at his strange situation, uttered piercing cries. At length he slept; and Viola, darkling and fearful, with nothing to sustain her spirits or hopes, felt her courage vanish.

She wept long with despair and misery. She thought of Ludovico and what his grief would be, and her tears were redoubled. There was no hope, for her enemy was relentless, her child torn from her, a cloister her prison. Such were the images constantly before her. They subdued her courage, and filled her with terror and dismay.

The cavalcade entered the town of Salerno, and the roar of the sea announced to poor Viola that they were on its shores.

"O bitter waves!" she cried. "My tears are as bitter as ye, and they will soon mingle!"

Her conductors now entered a building. It was a watch-tower at some distance from the town, on the sea-beach. They lifted Viola from the litter and led her to one of the dreary apartments of the tower. The window, which was not far from the ground, was grated with iron; it bore the appearance of a guardroom. The chief of her conductors addressed her, courteously asked her to excuse the rough lodging; the wind was contrary, he said, but change was expected, and the next day he hoped they would be able to embark. He pointed to the destined vessel in the offing.

Viola, excited to hope by his mildness, began to entreat his compassion, but he immediately left her. Soon after another man brought in food, with a flask of wine and a jug of water. He also retired; her massive door was locked, the sound of retreating footsteps died away.

Viola did not despair; she felt, however, that it would need all her courage to extricate herself from her prison. She ate a part of the food which had been provided, drank some water, and then, a little refreshed, she spread the cloak her conductors had left on the floor, placed her child on it to play, and then stationed herself at the window to see if any one might pass whom she might address, and, if he were not able to assist her in any other way, he might at least bear a message to Ludovico, that her fate might not be veiled in the fearful mystery that threatened it; but probably the way past her window was guarded, for no one drew near.

As she looked, however, and once advanced her head to gaze more earnestly, it struck her that her person would pass between the iron grates of her window, which was not high from the ground. The cloak, fastened to one of the stanchions, promised a safe descent. She did not dare make the essay; nay, she was so fearful that she might be watched, and that, if she were seen near the window, her jailers might be struck with the same idea, that she retreated to the farther end of the room, and sat looking at the bars with fluctuating hope and fear, that now dyed her cheeks with crimson, and again made them pale as when Ludovico had first seen her.

Her boy passed his time in alternate play and sleep. The ocean still roared, and the dark clouds brought up by the *sirocco* blackened the sky and hastened the coming evening. Hour after hour passed; she, heard no clock; there was no sun to mark the time, but by degrees the room grew dark, and at last the *Ave Maria* tolled, heard by fits between the howling of the winds and the dashing of the waves. She knelt, and put up a fervent prayer to the Madonna, protector of innocence—prayer for herself and her boy—no less innocent than the Mother and Divine Child, to whom she made her orisons. Still she paused. Drawing near to the window, she listened for the sound of any human being: that sound, faint and intermittent, died away, and with darkness came rain that poured in torrents, accompanied by thunder and lightning that drove every creature to shelter.

Viola shuddered. Could she expose her child during such a night? Yet again she gathered courage. It only made her meditate on some plan by which she might get the cloak as a shelter for her boy after it had served for their descent. She tried the bars, and found that, with some difficulty, she could pass, and, gazing downward from the outside, a flash of lightning revealed the ground not far below. Again she commended herself to divine protection; again she called upon and blessed her Ludovico; and then, not fearless but determined, she began her operations.

She fastened the cloak by means of her long veil, which,

hanging to the ground, was tied by a slip-knot, and gave way when pulled. She took her child in her arms, and, having got without the bars, bound him with the sash to her waist, and then, without accident, she reached the ground.

Having then secured the cloak, and enveloped herself and her child in its dark and ample folds, she paused breathlessly to listen. Nature was awake with its loudest voice—the sea roared—and the incessant flashes of lightning that discovered that solitude around her were followed by such deafening peals as almost made her fear. She crossed the field, and kept the sight of the white sea-foam to her right hand, knowing that she thus proceeded in an opposite direction from Mondolfo. She walked as fast as her burden permitted her, keeping the beaten road, for the darkness made her fear to deviate.

The rain ceased, and she walked on, until, her limbs falling under her, she was fain to rest, and refresh herself with the bread she had brought with her from the prison. Action and success had inspired her with unusual energy. She would not fear—she believed herself free and secure. She wept, but it was the over-flowing emotion that found no other expression. She doubted not that she should rejoin Ludovico. Seated thus in the dark night—having for hours been the sport of the elements, which now for an instant paused in their fury—seated on a stone by the roadside—a wide, dreary, unknown country about her—her helpless child in her arms—herself having just finished eating the only food she possessed—she felt triumph, and joy, and love, descend into her heart, prophetic of future reunion with her beloved.

It was summer, and the air consequently warm. Her cloak had protected her from the wet, so her limbs were free and un-numbed. At the first ray of dawn she arose, and at the nearest pathway she struck out of the road, and took her course nearer the bordering Apennines. From Salerno as far south as the eye could reach, a low plain stretched itself along the seaside, and the hills at about the distance of ten miles bound it in. These mountains are high and singularly beautiful in their shape; their crags point to Heaven and streams flow down their sides and water the plain below.

After several hours' walking, Viola reached a pine forest, which descended from the heights and stretched itself in the plain. She sought its friendly shelter with joy, and, penetrating its depths until she saw trees only on all sides of her, she again reposed. The *sirocco* had been dissipated by the thunderstorm, and the sun, vanquishing the clouds that at first veiled its splendor, glowed forth in the clear majesty of noon. Southern born, Viola did not fear the heat.

She collected pine nuts, she contrived to make a fire, and ate them with appetite; and then, seeking a covert, she lay down and slept, her boy in her arms, thanking Heaven and the Virgin for her escape. When she awoke, the triumph of her heart somewhat died away. She felt the solitude, she felt her helplessness, she feared pursuers, yet she dashed away the tears, and then reflecting that she was too near Salerno—the sun being now at the sea's verge—she arose and pursued her way through the intricacies of the wood. She got to the edge of it so far as to be able to direct her steps by the neighbouring sea.

Torrents intercepted her path, and one rapid river threatened to impede it altogether; but, going somewhat lower down, she found a bridge; and then, approaching still nearer to the sea, she passed through a wide and desolate kind of pasture-country, which seemed to afford neither shelter nor sustenance to any human being. Night closed in, and she was fearful to pursue her way, but, seeing some buildings dimly in the distance, she directed her steps thither, hoping to discover a hamlet where she might get shelter and such assistance as would enable her to retrace her steps and reach Naples without being discovered by her powerful enemy.

She kept these high buildings before her, which appeared like vast cathedrals, but that they were untopped by any dome or spire; and she wondered much what they could be, when suddenly they disappeared. She would have thought some rising ground had intercepted them, but all before her was plain. She paused, and at length resolved to wait for dawn. All day she had seen no human being; twice or thrice she had heard the bark of a dog, and once the whistle of a shepherd, but she saw no one. Desolation was around her; this, indeed, had lulled her into security at first. Where no men were, there was no danger for her. But at length the strange solitude became painful-she longed to see a cottage, or to find some peasant, however uncouth, who might answer her inquiries and provide for her wants. She had viewed with surprise the buildings which had been as beacons to her. She did not wish to enter a large town, and she wondered how one could exist in such a desert; but she had left the wood far behind her, and required food.

Night passed—balmy and sweet night—the breezes fanned her, the glowing atmosphere encompassed her, the fire-flies flitted round her, bats wheeled about in the air, and the heavy-winged owl hooped anigh, while the beetle's constant hum filled the air. She lay on the ground, her babe pillowed on her arm, looking upon the starry heavens. Many thoughts crowded upon her: the thought of Ludovico, of her reunion with him, of joy after sorrow; and she forgot that she was alone, half-famished, encompassed by enemies in a desert plain of Calabria[2]—she slept.

She awoke not until the sun had risen high—it had risen above the temples of Pastum,[3] and the columns threw short shadows on the ground. They were near her, unseen during night, and were now revealed as the edifices that had attracted her the evening before. They stood on a rugged plain, despoiled of all roof, their columns and cornices encompassing a space of high and weed-grown grass; the deep-blue sky canopied them and filled them with light and cheerfulness. Viola looked on them with wonder and reverence; they were temples to some god who still seemed to deify them with his presence; he clothed them still with beauty, and what was called their ruin might, in its picturesque wildness and sublime loneliness, be more adapted

---

2. Part of the Kingdom of Naples, a peninsula forming the heel of the Italian boot. Today it is the southern part of Apulia.
3. In Southern Italy, modern Pesto..

to his nature than when, roofed and gilded, they stood in pristine strength; and the silent worship of air and happy animals might be more suited to him than the concourse of the busy and heartless.

The most benevolent of spirit-gods seemed to inhabit that desert, weed-grown area; the spirit of beauty flitted between those columns embrowned by time, painted with strange color, and raised a genial atmosphere on the deserted altar. Awe and devotion filled the heart of lonely Viola; she raised her eyes and heart to Heaven in thanksgiving and prayer—not that her lips formed words, or her thoughts suggested connected sentences, but the feeling of worship and gratitude animated her; and, as the sunlight streamed through the succession of columns, so did joy, dove-shaped, fall on and illumine her soul.

With such devotion as seldom before she had visited a saint-dedicated church, she ascended the broken and rude steps of the larger temple, and entered the plot that it in-closed. An inner circuit of smaller columns formed a smaller area, which she entered, and, sitting on a huge fragment of the broken cornice that had fallen to the ground, she silently waited as if for some oracle to visit her sense and guide her.

Thus sitting, she heard the near bark of a dog, followed by the bleating of sheep, and she saw a little flock spread itself in the field adjoining the farther temple. They were shepherded by a girl clothed in rags, but the season required little covering; and these poor people, moneyless, possessing only what their soil gives them, are in the articles of clothing poor even to nakedness.

In inclement weather they wrap rudely-formed clothes of undressed sheepskin around them—during the heats of summer they do little more than throw aside these useless garments. The shepherd-girl was probably about fifteen years of age; a large black straw hat shaded her head from the intense rays of the sun; her feet and legs were bare; and her petticoat, tucked up, Diana-like, above one knee, gave a picturesque appearance to her rags, which, bound at her waist by a girdle, bore some resemblance to the costume of a Greek maiden. Rags have a costume of their own, as fine in their way, in their contrast of rich colors and the uncouth boldness of their drapery, as kingly robes. Viola approached the shepherdess and quietly entered into conversation with her; without making any appeal to her charity or feelings, she asked the name of the place where she was, and her boy, awake and joyous, soon attracted attention.

The shepherd-girl was pretty, and, above all, good-natured; she caressed the child, seemed delighted to have found a companion for her solitude, and, when Viola said that she was hungry, unloaded her scrip of roasted pine nuts, boiled chestnuts, and coarse bread. Viola ate with joy and gratitude. They remained together all day; the sun went down, the glowing light of its setting faded, and the shepherdess would have taken Viola home with her. But she dreaded a human dwelling, still fearing that, wherever there appeared a possibility of shelter, there her pursuers would seek her.

She gave a few small silver-pieces, part of what she had about her when seized, to her new friend, and, bidding her bring sufficient food for the next day, entreated her not to mention her adventure to anyone. The girl promised, and, with the assistance of her dog, drove the flock toward their fold. Viola passed the night within the area of the larger temple.

Not doubting the success of his plan, on the very evening that followed its execution, Prince Mondolfo had gone to Naples. He found his son at the Mondolfo Palace. Despising the state of a court, and careless of the gaieties around him, Ludovico longed to return to the cottage of Viola.

So, after the expiration of two days, he told his father that he should ride over to Mondolfo, and return the following morning. Fernando did not oppose him, but, two hours after his departure, followed him, and arrived at the castle just after Ludovico, leaving his attendants there, quitted it to proceed alone to his cottage. The first person Prince Mondolfo saw was the chief of the company who had had the charge of Viola. His story was soon told: the unfavorable wind, the imprisonment in a room barricaded with the utmost strength, her incomprehensible escape, and the vain efforts that had subsequently been made to find her.

Fernando listened as if in a dream; convinced of the truth, he saw no clue to guide him—no hope of recovering possession of his prisoner. He foamed with rage, then endeavoured to suppress as useless his towering passion. He overwhelmed the bearer of the news with execrations; sent out parties of men in pursuit in all directions, promising every reward, and urging the utmost secrecy, and then, left alone, paced his chamber in fury and dismay. His solitude was of no long duration. Ludovico burst into his room, his countenance lighted up with rage.

"Murderer!" he cried. "Where is my Viola?"

Fernando remained speechless.

"Answer!" said Ludovico. "Speak with those lips that pronounced her death-sentence—or raise against me that hand from which her blood is scarcely washed—Oh, my Viola! thou and my angel-child, descend with all thy sweetness into my heart, that this hand write not parricide on my brow!"

Fernando attempted to speak.

"No!" shrieked the miserable Ludovico; "I will not listen to her murderer. Yet—is she dead? I kneel—I call you father—I appeal to that savage heart—I take in peace that hand that often struck me, and now has dealt the death-blow—oh, tell me, does she yet live?"

Fernando seized on this interval of calm to relate his story. He told the simple truth; but could such a tale gain belief? It awakened the wildest rage in poor Ludovico's heart. He doubted not that Viola had been murdered; and, after every expression of despair and hatred, he bade his father seek his heir among the clods of the earth, for that such he should soon become, and rushed from his presence.

He wandered to the cottage, he searched the country round, he heard the tale of those who had witnessed any part of the carrying off of his Viola. He went to Salerno. He heard the tale there told with the most determined incredulity. It was the tale, he doubted not, that his father forged to free himself from accusation, and to throw an impenetrable veil over the destruction of Viola.

His quick imagination made out for itself the scene of her death. The very house in which she had been confined had at the extremity of it a tower jutting out over the sea; a river flowed at its base, making its confluence with the ocean deep and dark. He was convinced that the fatal scene had been acted there. He mounted the tower; the higher room was windowless, the iron grates of the windows had for some cause been recently taken out. He was persuaded that Viola and her child had been thrown from that window into the deep and gurgling waters below.

He resolved to die! In those days of simple Catholic faith, suicide was contemplated with horror. But there were other means almost as sure. He would go a pilgrim to the Holy Land, and fight and die beneath the walls of Jerusalem. Rash and energetic, his purpose was no sooner formed than he hastened to put it in execution. He procured a pilgrim's weeds at Salerno, and at midnight, advising none of his intentions, he left that city, and proceeded southward.

Alternate rage and grief swelled his heart. Rage at length died away. She whose murderer he execrated was an angel in Heaven, looking down on him, and he in the Holy Land would win his right to join her. Tender grief dimmed his eyes. The world's great theatre closed before him-of all its trappings his pilgrim's cloak was alone gorgeous, his pilgrim's staff the only sceptre—they were the symbols and signs of the power he possessed beyond the earth, and the pledges of his union with Viola. He bent his steps toward Brundusium.[4] He walked on fast, as if he grudged all space and time that lay between him and his goal.

Dawn awakened the earth and he proceeded on his way. The sun of noon darted its ray upon him, but his march was uninterrupted. He entered a pine wood, and, following the track of flocks, he heard the murmurs of a fountain. Oppressed with thirst, he hastened toward it. The water welled up from the

4. On the east-southeast coast of Italy

ground and filled a natural basin; flowers grew on its banks and looked on the waters unreflected, for the stream paused not, but whirled round and round, spending its superabundance in a small rivulet that, dancing over stones and glancing in the sun, went on its way to its eternity—the sea. The trees had retreated from the mountain, and formed a circle about it; the grass was green and fresh, starred with summer flowers.

At one extremity was a silent pool that formed a strange contrast with the fountain that, ever in motion, showed no shape, and reflected only the color of the objects around it. The pool reflected the scene with greater distinctness and beauty than its real existence. The trees stood distinct, the ambient air between, all grouped and pictured by the hand of a divine artist. Ludovico drank from the fount, and then approached the pool. He looked with half wonder on the scene depicted there. A bird now flitted across in the air, and its form, feathers, and motion, were shown in the waters. An ass emerged from among the trees, where in vain it sought herbage, and came to grass near these waters; Ludovico saw it depicted therein, and then looked on the living animal, almost appearing less real, less living, than its semblance in the stream.

Under the trees from which the ass had come lay someone on the ground, enveloped in a mantle, sleeping. Ludovico looked carelessly—he hardly at first knew why his curiosity was roused; then an eager thought, which he deemed madness, yet resolved to gratify, carried him forward.

Rapidly he approached the sleeper, knelt down, and drew aside the cloak, and saw Viola, her child within her arms, the warm breath issued from her parted lips, her lovebeaming eyes hardly veiled by the transparent lids, which soon were lifted up.

Ludovico and Viola, each too happy to feel the earth they trod, returned to their cottage-their cottage dearer than any palace—yet only half believing the excess of their own joy. By turns they wept, and gazed on each other and their child, holding each other's hands as if grasping reality and fearful it would vanish.

Prince Mondolfo heard of their arrival. He had long suffered keenly from the fear of losing his son. The dread of finding himself childless, heirless, had tamed him. He feared the world's censure, his sovereign's displeasure—perhaps worse accusation and punishment. He yielded to fate. Not daring to appear before his intended victim, he sent his confessor to mediate for their forgiveness, and to entreat them to take up their abode at Mondolfo. At first, little credit was given to these offers. They loved their cottage, and had small inclination to risk happiness, liberty, and life, for worthless luxury. The Prince, by patience and perseverance, at length convinced them. Time softened painful recollections; they paid him the duty of children, and cherished and honored him in his old age; while he caressed his lovely grandchild, he did not repine that the violet-girl should be the mother of the heir of Mondolfo.

Euphrasia

A Tale of Greece

It was not long after the breaking out of the Greek Revolution that Harry Valency visited Greece. Many an Englishman was led thither at that time by the spirit of adventure, and
many perished. Valency was not nineteen; his spirit was wild and
reckless;—thought or care had never touched his brow; his heart
was too light for love. Restless and energetic, he longed to try
his powers, with the instinct that leads the young deer to butt
against trees, or to wrestle with each other in the forest-dells. He
was the only son of a widowed mother, whose life was wrapped
in his, and he loved her fondly; yet left her, impelled by a desire for adventure, unable to understand what anxiety and fear
meant; and in his own person eager to meet even misfortune, so
that it came in a guise to call forth manly and active struggles.

He longed to have the pages of his young life written over
by deeds that would hereafter be memories, to which he could
turn with delight. The cause of Greece warmed his soul. He
was in a transport of ecstasy when he touched the shores of that
antique land, and looked around on mountain and mountain-
stream, whose names were associated with the most heroic acts,
and the most sublime poetry man ever achieved or wrote. Yes, he
was now in Greece. He was about to fight in her cause against
the usurping Turk. He had prepared himself by a sedulous study
of Romaic; he was on his way to the seat of Government, to
offer his services.

To proceed thither from the spot where he had disembarked

was a matter of some difficulty; the Turkish troops being then in possession of many of the passes. At length he heard that a band of about fifty Greek soldiers, headed by a young but brave and renowned chief, was about to pursue the same road; he asked, and obtained leave to accompany them.

How delightful was the commencement of the journey! How beautiful the country—defile and steep hill-side, by which they proceeded; where the grey olive clothed the upland, or vines, embracing elms, red now with late summer tints, varied the scene. The mountain-tops were bare, or crowned with pines, and torrents ran down the sides and fed a stream in the dell. The air was balmy; the *cicala* loud and merry—to live was to be happy. Valency was mounted on a spirited horse; he made it leap and *caracole*. He threw a spear against a tree, and dashed after to recover it. He fired at a mark as he hurried on at full gallop; every feat was insufficient to tame his exhaustless spirits.

The chief marked him with eyes, whose deep melancholy expression darkened as he gazed. He was known as bravest among the brave; yet gentle as a woman. He was young and singularly handsome; his countenance was stamped with traces of intellectual refinement, while his person was tall, muscular, and strong, but so gracefully formed, that every attitude reminded you of some Praxitilean shape of his own native land.

Once he had been more beautiful; joy, as well as tenderness, and a soldier's ardour had lighted up his dark eye; his lip had been the home of smiles, and the thoughts, which pre sided in his brow, had been as clear and soft and glad some as that godlike brow itself. Now this was changed. Grief had become a master passion: his cheeks were sunken; his eye seemed to brood eternally over melancholy regrets; his measured harmonious voice was attuned to the utterance of no light fancy or gay sallies; he spoke only the necessary words of direction to his followers, and then silence and gloom gathered over his face.

His sorrow was respected; for it was known to be well founded, and to spring from a recent disaster. If any of his troop desired to indulge in merriment, they withdrew from his vicinity. It was strange to them to hear the light laugh of the English youth ring through the grove, and to catch the tones of his merry voice, as he sang some of their own gayest songs. The chief gazed with interest. There was a winning frankness in the boy; he was so very young, and all he did was in graceful accordance with his age. We are alike mere youths, thought the chief, and how different! Yet soon he may become like me. He soars like an eagle; but the eagle may be wounded, and stoop to earth; because earth contains its secret and its regret.

Suddenly Valency, who was some hundred yards in advance, was encountered by a Greek, riding at full speed towards the advancing troop.

"Back! back! silence!" the man cried. He was a scout, who had been sent on before, and now brought tidings that a troop of three or four hundred of the Turkish army were entering the defile, and would soon advance on the handful of men which Valency accompanied. The scout rode directly up to the leader, and made his report, adding,—

"We have yet time. If we fall back but a quarter of a mile, there is a path I know, by which I can guide you across the mountain; on the other side we shall be safe."

A smile of scorn for a moment wreathed the lip of the chief at the word safety, but his face soon reassumed its usual sad composure. The troop had halted; each man bent his eye on the leader. Valency, in particular, marked the look of scorn, and felt that he would never retreat before danger.

"Comrades!" the chief thus addressed his men, "it shall never be said that Greeks fell back to make way for the destroyers; we will betake ourselves to our old war fare. Before we entered this olive wood, we passed a thick cover, where the dark jutting mountain-side threw a deep shadow across our path, and the torrent drowned all sound of voice or hoof. There we shall find ambush; there the enemy will meet death."

He turned his horse's head, and in a few minutes reached the spot he named; the men were mostly eager for the fray—while one or two eyed the mountain-side, and then the path that led to the village, which they had quitted that morning. The chief saw their look, and he glanced also at the English youth, who had thrown himself from his horse, and was busy loading and priming his arms. The chief rode up to him.

"You are our guest and fellow-traveller," he said, "but not our comrade in the fight. We are about to meet danger—it may be that not one of us shall escape. You have no injuries to avenge, no liberty to gain; you have friends—probably a mother—in your native land. You must not fall with us. I am going to send a message to warn the village we last passed through—do you accompany my messengers."

Valency had listened attentively at first; but as the chief continued, his attention reverted to his task of loading his pistols. The last words called a blush into his cheek.

"You treat me as a boy," he cried; "I may be one in aspect, but you shall find me a man in heart this day. You also young, I have not deserved your scorn!"

The chief caught the youth's flashing eye. He held out his hand to him, saying, "Forgive me."

"I will," said Valency, "on one condition;—give me a post of danger—of honour. You owe it to me in reparation of the insult you offered."

"Be it so," said the chief; "your place shall be at my side." A few minutes more and his dispositions were made;—two of the most downhearted of the troop were despatched to alarm the village, the rest were placed behind the rocks; beneath the bushes, wherever broken ground, or tuft of underwood, or fragment from the cliff, afforded shelter and concealment, a man was placed; while the chief himself took his stand on an elevated platform, and, sheltered by a tree, gazed upon the road. Soon the tramp of horses, the busy sound of feet and voices were heard, overpowering the rushing of the stream; and turban and musket could be distinguished as the enemy's troop threaded the defile.

The shout of battle—the firing—the clash of weapons were over. Above the crest of the hill, whose side had afforded ambush to the Greeks, the crescent moon hung, just about to dip behind;

the stars in her train burnt bright as lamps floating in the firmament; while the fire flies flashed among the myrtle underwood and up the mountainside; and sometimes the steel of the arms strewn around, dropped from the hand of the dead, caught and reflected the flashes of the celestial or earthly stars. The ground was strewn with the slain. Such of the enemy as had cut their way through were already far—the sound of their horses hoofs had died away. The Greeks who had fled across the mountain had reached a place of safety—none lay there but the silent dead—cold as the moonbeam that rested for a moment on their pale faces. All were still and motionless; some lay on the hillside among the underwood—some on the open road—horses and men had fallen, pell-mell—none moved—none breathed.

Yet there was a sigh—it was lost in the murmur of the stream; a groan succeeded, and then a voice feeble and broken, "My mother, my poor mother!"—the pale lips that spoke these words could form no other, a gush of tears followed. The cry seemed to awake another form from among the dead. One of the prostrate bodies raised itself slowly and painfully on its arm, the eyes were filmy, the countenance pallid from approaching death, the voice was hollow, yet firm, that said, "Who speaks?—who lives?—who weeps?"

The question struck shame to the wounded man; he checked his overflow of passionate sobbings. The other spoke again, "It was not the voice of a Greek—yet I thought I had saved that gallant boy—the ball meant for him is now in my side.—Speak again, young Englishman—on whom do you call?"

"On her who will weep my death too bitterly—on my mother," replied Valency, and tears would follow the loved name.

"Art thou wounded to death?" asked the chief.

"Thus unaided I must die," he replied; "yet, could I reach those waters, I might live—I must try." And Valency rose; he staggered a few steps, and fell heavily at the feet of the chief. He had fainted. The Greek looked on the ghastly pallor of his face; he half rose—his own wound did not bleed, but it was mortal, and a deadly sickness had gathered round his heart, and chilled his brow, which he strove to master, that he might save the English boy. The effort brought cold drops on his brow, as he rose on his knees and stooped to raise the head of Valency; he shuddered to feel the warm moisture his hand encountered.

It is his blood; his life-blood he thought; and again he placed his head on the earth, and continued a moment still, summoning what vitality remained to him to animate his limbs. Then with a determined effort he rose, and staggered to the banks of the stream. He held a steel cap in his hand—and now he stooped down to fill it; but with the effort the ground slid from under him, and he fell. There was a ringing in his ears—a cold dew on his brow—his breath came thick—the cap had fallen from his hand—he was dying.

The bough of a tree, shot off in the morning's *mêlée*, lay near;—the mind, even of a dying man, can form swift, unerring combinations of thought;—it was his last chance—the bough was plunged in the waters, and he scattered the grateful, reviving drops over his face; vigour returned with the act, and he could stoop and fill the cap, and drink a deep draught, which for a moment restored the vital powers. And now he carried water to Valency; he dipped the unfolded turban of a Turk in the stream, and bound the youth's wound, which was a deep sabre cut in the shoulder, that had bled copiously.

Valency revived—life gathered warm in his heart—his cheeks, though still pale, lost the ashy hue of death—his limbs again seemed willing to obey his will—he sat up, but he was too weak, and his head dropped. As a mother tending her sick first-born, the Greek chief hovered over him; he brought a cloak to pillow his head; as he picked up this, he found that some careful soldier had brought a small bag at his saddle-bow, in which was a loaf and a bunch or two of grapes; he gave them to the youth, who ate. Valency now recognised his saviour; at first he wondered to see him there, tending on him, apparently unhurt; but soon the chief sank to the ground, and Valency could mark the rigidity of feature, and ghastliness of aspect, that portended death.

In his turn he would have assisted his friend; but the chief stopped him—"You die if you move," he said; "your wound will bleed afresh, and you will die, while you cannot aid me. My weakness does not arise from mere loss of blood. The messenger of death has reached a vital part—yet a little while and the soul will obey the summons. It is slow, slow is the deliverance; yet the long creeping hour will come at last, and I shall be free."

"Do not speak thus," cried Valency; "I am strong now—I will go for help."

"There is no help for me," replied the chief, "save the death I desire. I command you, move not."

Valency had risen, hut the effort was vain: his knees bent under him, his head spun round; before he could save himself he had sunk to the ground.

"Why torture yourself?" said the chief. "A few hours and help will come: it will not injure you to pass this interval beneath this calm sky. The cowards who fled will alarm the country; by dawn succour will be here: you must wait for it. I too must wait—not for help, but for death. It is soothing even to me to die here beneath this sky, with the murmurs of yonder stream in my ear, the shadows of my native mountains thrown athwart. Could aught save me, it would be the balmy airs of this most blessed night; my soul feels the bliss, though my body is sick and fast stiffening in death. Such was not the hour when she died whom soon I shall meet, my Euphrasia, my own sweet sister, in heaven!"

It was strange, Valency said, that at such an hour, but half saved from death, and his preserver in the grim destroyer's clutches, that he should feel curiosity to know the Greek chief's story. His youth, his beauty, his valour—the act, which Valency well remembered, of his springing forward so as to shield him with his own person—his last words and thoughts devoted to the soft recollection of a beloved sister,—awakened an interest beyond even the present hour, fraught as it was with the chances of life and death. He questioned the chief.

Probably fever had succeeded to his previous state of weakness, imparted a deceitful strength, and even inclined him to talk; for thus dying, unaided and unsheltered, with the starry sky overhead, he willingly reverted to the years of his youth and to the miserable event which a few months before had eclipsed the sun of his life and rendered death welcome.

They—brother and sister, Constantino and Euphrasia—were the last of their race. They were orphans; their youth was passed under the guardianship of the brother by adoption of their father, whom they named father, and who loved them. He was a glorious old man, nursed in classic lore, and more familiar with the deeds of men who had glorified his country several thousand years before than with any more modern names. Yet all who had ever done and suffered for Greece were embalmed in his memory, and honoured as martyrs in the best of causes. He had been educated in Paris, and travelled in Europe and America, and was aware of the progress made in the science of politics all over the civilised world.

He felt that Greece would soon share the benefits to arise from the changes then operating, and he looked forward at no distant day to its liberation from bondage. He educated his young ward for that day. Had he believed that Greece would have continued hopelessly enslaved, he had brought him up as a scholar and a recluse: but, assured of the impending struggle, he made him a warrior; he implanted a detestation of the oppressor, a yearning love for the sacred blessings of freedom, a noble desire to have his name enrolled among the deliverers of his country.

The education he bestowed on Euphrasia was yet more singular. He knew that though liberty must be bought and maintained by the sword, yet that its dearest bless ings must be derived from civilisation and knowledge; and he believed women to be the proper fosterers of these. They cannot handle a sword nor endure bodily labour for their country, but they could refine the manners, exalt the souls—impart honour, and truth, and wisdom to their relatives and their children. Euphrasia, therefore, he made a scholar.

By nature she was an enthusiast and a poet. The study of the classic literature of her country corrected her taste and exalted her love of the beautiful. While a child, she improvised passionate songs of liberty; and as she grew in years and loveliness, and her heart opened to tenderness, and she became aware of all the honour and happiness that a woman must derive from being held the friend of man, not his slave, she thanked God that she was a Greek and a Christian; and holding fast by the advantages which these names conferred, she looked forward eagerly to the day when Mohammedanism should no longer contaminate her native land, and when her countrywomen should be awakened from ignorance and sloth in which they were plunged, and learn that their proper vocation in the creation was that of mothers of heroes and teachers of sages.

Her brother was her idol, her hope, her joy. And he who had been taught that his career must be that of deeds, not words, yet was fired by her poetry and eloquence to desire glory yet more eagerly, and to devote himself yet more entirely and with purer ardour to the hope of one day living and dying for his country. The first sorrow the orphans knew was the death of their adopted father. He descended to the grave full of years and honour. Constantine was then eighteen; his fair sister had just entered her fifteenth year.

Often they spent the night beside the revered tomb of their lost friend, talking of the hopes and aspirations he had implanted. The young can form such sublime, such beautiful dreams. No disappointment, no evil, no bad passion shadows their glorious visions. To dare and do greatly for Greece was the ambition of Constantine. To cheer and watch over her brother, to regulate his wilder and more untaught soul, to paint in celestial colours the bourne he tended towards by action, were Euphrasia's tasks.

"There is a heaven," said the dying man as he told his tale,— "there is a paradise for those who die in the just cause. I know not what joys are there prepared for the blest; but they can scarcely transcend those that were mine as I listened to my own sweet sister, and felt my heart swell with patriotism and fond, warm affection."

At length there was a stir through the land, and Constantine made a journey of some distance, to confer with the *capitani* of the mountains, and to prepare for the outbreak of the revolution. The moment came, sooner even than he expected. As an eagle chained when the iron links drop from him, and with clang of wing and bright undazzled eye he soars to heaven, so did Constantine feel when freedom to Greece became the war-cry. He was still among the mountains when first the echoes of his native valleys repeated that animating, that sacred word. Instead of returning, as he intended, to his Athenian home, he was hurried off to Western Greece, and became a participator in a series of warlike movements, the promised success of which filled him with transport.

Suddenly a pause came in the delirium of joy which possessed his soul. He received not the accustomed letters from his sister—missives which had been to him angelic messengers, teaching him patience with the unworthy—hope in disappointment—certainty of final triumph. Those dear letters ceased; and he thought he saw in the countenances of his friends around a concealed knowledge of evil. He questioned them: their answers were evasive. At the same time, they endeavoured to fill his mind with the details of some anticipated exploit in which his presence and co-operation was necessary.

Day after day passed; he could not leave his post without injury to the cause, without even the taint of dishonour. He belonged to a band of Albanians, by whom he had been received as a brother, and he could not desert them in the hour of danger. But the suspense grew too terrible; and at length, finding that there was an interval of a few days which he might call his own, he left the camp, resting neither day nor night; dismounting from one horse only to bestride another, in forty-eight hours he was in Athens, before his vacant, desecrated home. The tale of horror was soon told. Athens was still in the hands of the Turks; the sister of a rebel had become the prey of the oppressor. She had none to guard her. Her matchless beauty had been seen and marked by the son of the pasha; she had for the last two months been immured in his harem.

"Despair is a cold, dark feeling," said the dying warrior; "if I may name that despair which had a hope—a certainty—an aim. Had Euphrasia died I had wept. Now my eyes were horn—my heart stone. I was silent. I neither expressed resentment nor revenge. I concealed myself by day; at night I wandered round the tyrant's dwelling. It was a pleasure-palace, one of the most luxurious in our beloved Athens. At this time it was carefully guarded: my character was known, and Euphrasia's worth; and the oppressor feared the result of his deed. Still, under shadow of darkness I drew near. I marked the position of the women's apartments I learned the number the length of the watch the orders they received, and then I returned to the camp. I revealed my project to a few select spirits. They were fired by my wrongs, and eager to deliver my Euphrasia."—

Constantine broke off—a spasm of pain shook his body. After this had passed he lay motionless for a few minutes; then starting up, as fever and delirium, excited by the exertion of speaking, increased by the agonies of recollection, at last fully possessed him.

"What is this?" he cried. "Fire! Yes, the palace burns. Do you not hear the roaring of the flames, and thunder too—the artillery of Heaven levelled against the unblest? Ha! a shot—he falls—they are driven back—now fling the torches—the wood crackles—there, there are the women's rooms—ha! poor victims! lo! you shudder and fly! Fear not; give me only my Euphrasia!—my own Euphrasia! No disguise can hide thee, dressed as a Turkish bride crowned with flowers, thy lovely face, the seat of unutterable woe—still, my sweet sister, even in this smoke and tumult of this house, thou art the angel of my life!

"Spring into my arms, poor, frightened bird; cling to me—it is herself—her voice—her fair arms are round my neck—what ruin—what flame—what choking smoke—what driving storm can stay me? Soft! the burning breach is passed—there are steps—gently—dear one, I am firm—fear not!—what eyes glare?—fear not, Euphrasia, he is dead—the miserable retainers of the tyrant fell beneath our onset—ha! a shot—gracious Panargia, is this thy protection?"

Thus did he continue to rave: the onset, the burning of the palace, the deliverance of his sister, all seemed to pass again vividly as if in present action. His eyes glared; he tossed up his arms; he shouted as if calling his followers around him; and then in tones of heartfelt tenderness he addressed the fair burden he fancied that he bore—till, with a shriek, he cried again, "A shot!" and sank to the ground as if his heartstrings had broken.

An interval of calm succeeded; he was exhausted; his voice was broken.

"What have I told thee?" he continued feebly; "I have said how a mere handful of men attacked the palace, and drove back the guards—how we strove in vain to make good our entrance— fresh troops were on their way—there was no alternative; we fired the palace. Deep in the seclusion of the harem the women had retreated, a herd of frightened deer. One alone stood erect. Her eyes bent on the intruders—a dagger in her hand—majestic and fearless, her face was marked with traces of passed suffering, but at the moment the stern resolution her soft features expressed was more than human. The moment she saw me, all was changed; the angel alone beamed in her countenance.

"Her dagger fell from her hand—she was in my arms—I bore her from the burning roof—the rest you know; have I not said it! Some miscreant, who survived the slaughter, and yet lay as dead on the earth, aimed a deadly shot. She did not shriek At first she clung closer to my neck, and then I felt her frame shiver in my arms and her hold relax. I trusted that fear alone moved her; but she knew not fear—it was death. Horses had been prepared, and were waiting; a few hours more and I hoped to be on our way to the west, to that portion of Greece that was free. But I felt her head fall on my shoulder. I heard her whisper, I die, my brother! carry me to our father's tomb.

"My soul yearned to comply with her request; but it was impossible. The city was alarmed; troops gathering from all quarters. Our safety lay in flight, for still I thought that her wound was not mortal. I bore her to the spot where we had left our horses. Here two or three of my comrades speedily joined me;

they had rescued the women of the harem from the flames, but the various sounds denoting the advance of the Turkish soldiery caused them to hurry from the scene. I leapt on my horse, and placed my sweet sister before me, and we fled amain through desert streets, I well knew how to choose, and along the lanes of the suburbs into the open country, where, deviating from the high-road, along which I directed my companions to proceed in all haste—alone with my beloved burden, I sought a solitary, unsuspected spot among the neighbouring hills.

"The storm which had ceased for a time, now broke afresh; the deafening thunder drowned every other sound, while the frequent glare of the lightning showed us our path; my horse did not quail before it. Euphrasia still lay clinging to me; no complaint escaped her; a few words of fondness, of encouragement, of pious resignation, she now and then breathed forth. I knew not she was dying, till at last entering a retired valley, where an olive wood afforded shelter, and still better the *portico* of a fallen ancient temple, I dismounted and bore her to the marble steps, on which I placed her.

"Then indeed I felt how near the beloved one was to death, from which I could not save her. The lightning showed me her face—pale as the marble which pillowed it. Her dress was dabbled in warm blood, which soon stained the stones on which she lay. I took her hand; it was deathly cold. I raised her from the marble; I pillowed her cheek upon my heart. I repressed my despair, or rather my despair in that hour was mild and soft as herself. There was no help—no hope. The life-blood oozed fast from her side; scarce could she raise her heavy eyelids to look on me; her voice could no longer articulate my name. The burden of her fair limbs grew heavier and more chill; soon it was a corpse only that I held.

"When I knew that her sufferings were over, I raised her once more in my arms, and once more I placed her before me on my horse, and betook me to my journey. The storm was over now, and the moon bright above. Earth glittered under the rays, and a soft breeze swept by, as if heaven itself became clear and peaceful to receive her stainless soul, and present it to its Maker. By morning's dawn, I stopped at a convent gate, and rang. To the holy maidens within I consigned my own fair Euphrasia. I kissed but once again her dear brow, which spoke of peace in death; and then saw her placed upon a bier, and was away, back to my camp, to live and die for Greece."

He grew more silent as he became weaker. Now and then he spoke a few words to record some other of Euphrasia's perfections, or to repeat some of her dying words; to speak of her magnanimity, her genius, her love, and his own wish to die.

"I might have lived," he said, "till her image had faded in my mind, or been mingled with less holy memories. I die young, all her own."

His voice grew more feeble after this; he complained of cold. Valency continued: "I contrived to rise, and crawl about, and to collect a *capote* or two, and a *pelisse* from among the slain, with some of which I covered him; and then I drew one over myself, for the air grew chill, as midnight had passed away and the morning hour drew near. The warmth which the coverings imparted calmed the aching of my wound, and, strange to say, I felt slumber creep over me. I tried to watch and wake. At first the stars above and the dark forms of the mountains mingled with my dreamy feelings; but soon I lost all sense of where I was, and what I had suffered, and slept peacefully and long.

"The morning sunbeams, as creeping down the hill side they at last fell upon my face, awoke me. At first I had forgotten all thought of the events of the past night, and my first impulse was to spring up, crying aloud, where am I? but the stiffness of my limbs and their weakness, soon revealed the truth. Gladly I now welcomed the sound of voices, and marked the approach of a number of peasants along the ravine.

"Hitherto, strange to say, I had thought only of myself; but with the ideas of succour came the recollection of my companion, and the tale of the previous night. I glanced eagerly to where he lay; his posture disclosed his state; he was still, and stiff, and dead. Yet his countenance was calm and beautiful. He had died in the dear hope of meeting his sister, and her image had shed peace over the last moment of life.

"I am ashamed to revert to myself. The death of Constantino is the true end of my tale. My wound was a severe one. I was forced to leave Greece, and for some months remained between life and death in Cefalonia, till a good constitution saved me, when at once I returned to England."

A Tale of the Passions; or,
The Death of Despina

After the death of Manfred, King of Naples, the Ghibellines
lost their ascendency throughout Italy. The exiled Guelphs returned to their native cities; and, not contented with resuming
the reins of government, they prosecuted their triumph until the
Ghibellines in their turn were obliged to fly, and to mourn in
banishment over the violent party spirit which had before occasioned their bloody victories, and now their irretrievable defeat. After an obstinate contest, the Florentine Ghibellines were
forced to quit their native town; their estates were confiscated;
their attempts to reinstate themselves frustrated; and receding
from castle to castle, they at length took refuge in Lucca, and
awaited with impatience the arrival of Corradino from Germany, through whose influence they hoped again to establish
the Imperial supremacy.

The first of May was ever a day of rejoicing and festivity at
Florence. The youth of both sexes, and of all ranks, paraded the
streets, crowned with flowers, and singing the canzonets of the
day. In the evening they assembled in the *Piazza del Duomo*,
and spent the hours in dancing. The *Carroccio* was led through
the principal streets, the ringing of its bell drowned in the peals
that rang from every belfry in the city, and in the music of fifes
and drums which made a part of the procession that followed
it. The triumph of the reigning party in Florence caused them
to celebrate the anniversary of the first of May, 1268, with peculiar splendour. They had indeed hoped that Charles d Anjou,

King of Naples, the head of the Guelphs in Italy, and then *Vicare* (President) of their republic, would have been there to adorn the festival by his presence.

But the expectation of Corradino had caused the greater part of his newly-conquered and oppressed kingdom to revolt, and he had hastily quitted Tuscany to secure by his presence those con quests of which his avarice and cruelty endangered the loss. But although Charles somewhat feared the approaching contest with Corradino, the Florentine Guelphs, newly reinstated in their city and possessions, did not permit a fear to cloud their triumph. The principal families vied with each other in the display of their magnificence during the festival.

The knights followed the *Carroccio* on horseback, and the windows were filled with ladies who leant upon gold-inwoven carpets, while their own dresses, at once simple and elegant, their only ornaments, flowers, contrasted with the glittering tapestry and the brilliant colours of the flags of the various communities. The whole population of Florence poured into the principal streets, and none were left at home, except the decrepit and sick, unless it were some discontented Ghibelline, whose fear, poverty, or avarice had caused him to conceal his party when it had been banished from the city.

It was not the feeling of discontent which prevented Monna Gegia de' Becari from being among the first of the revellers; and she looked angrily on what she called her "Ghibelline leg," which fixed her to her chair on such a day of triumph, The sun shone in all its glory in an unclouded sky, and caused the fair Florentines to draw their *fazioles* (veils) over their dark eyes, and to bereave the youth of those beams more vivifying than the sun's rays. The same sun poured its full light into the lonely apartment of Monna Gegia, and almost extinguished the fire which was lighted in the middle of the room, over which hung the pot of *minestra*, the dinner of the dame and her husband. But she had deserted the fire, and was seated by her window, holding her beads in her hand, while every now and then she peeped from her lattice (five storeys high) into the narrow lane below;

but no creature passed. She looked at the opposite window; a cat slept there beside a pot of heliotrope, but no human being was heard or seen, they had all gone to the *Piazza del Duomo*.

Monna Gegia was an old woman, and her dress of green *calrasio* (stuff) showed that she belonged to one of the *Arli Minori* (working classes). Her head was covered by a red kerchief, which, folded triangularly, hung loosely over it; her grey hairs were combed back from her high and wrinkled brow. The quickness of her eye spoke the activity of her mind, and the slight irritability that lingered about the corners of her lips might be occasioned by the continual war maintained between her bodily and mental faculties.

"Now, by St. John!" she said, "I would give my gold cross to make one of them; though by giving that I should appear on a *festa*, without that which no *festa* yet ever found me wanting." And as she spoke she looked with great complacency on a large but thin gold cross which was tied round her withered neck by a ribbon, once black, now of a rusty brown.

"Methinks this leg of mine is bewitched; and it may well be that my Ghibelline husband has used the black art to hinder me from following the *Carroccio* with the best of them."—A slight sound, as of footsteps in the street far below, interrupted the good woman's soliloquy.—"Perhaps it is Monna Lisabetta, or Messer Giani dei Agli, the weaver, who mounted the breach first when the castle of Pagibonzi was taken."—She looked down, but could see no one, and was about to relapse into her old train of thoughts, when her attention was again attracted by the sound of steps ascending the stairs: they were slow and heavy, but she did not doubt who her visitant was when a key was applied to the hole of the door; the latch was lifted up, and a moment after, with an unassured mien and downcast eyes, her husband entered.

He was a short, stunted man, more than sixty years of age; his shoulders were broad and high; his lank hair was still coal-black; his brows were overhanging and bushy; his eyes black and quick; his lips as it were contradicted the sternness of the upper part of

his face, for their gentle curve betokened even delicacy of sentiment, and his smile was inexpressibly sweet. He had on a low-
crowned, red cloth cap, which he drew over his eyes, and, seating
himself on a low bench by the fire, he heaved a deep sigh. He
appeared disinclined to enter into any conversation, but Monna
Gegia was resolved that he should not enjoy his melancholy
mood uninterrupted.

"Have you been to mass, Cincolo?" she asked, beginning
by a question sufficiently removed from the point she longed
to approach.—He shrugged his shoulders uneasily, but did not
reply.—"You are too early for your dinner," continued Gegia;
"do you not go out again?"

Cincolo answered "No!" in an accent that denoted his disin-
clination to further questioning. But this very impatience only
served to feed the spirit of contention that was fermenting in
the bosom of Gegia.

"You are not used," she said, "to pass your May days under
your chimney."—No answer.—"Well," she continued, "if you
will not speak, I have done!"—meaning that she intended to
begin—"but by that lengthened face of thine I see that some
good news is stirring abroad, and I bless the Virgin for it, whatever it may be. Come, tell me what happy tidings make thee so
woe-begone."

Cincolo remained silent for awhile, then turning half round,
but not looking at his wife, he replied, "What if old Marzio the
lion be dead?"

Gegia turned pale at the idea, but a smile that lurked in the
good-natured mouth of her husband reassured her.

"Nay, St. John defend us!" she began, "but that is not true.
Old Marzio's death would not drive you within these four walls,
except it were to triumph over your old wife. By the blessing
of St. John, not one of our lions have died since the eve of the
battle of Monte Aperto; and I doubt not that they were poisoned; for Mari, who fed them that night, was more than half
a Ghibelline in his heart. Besides, the bells are still ringing, and
the drums still beating, and all would be silent enough if old

413

Marzio were to die. On the first of May too! Santa Reparata is too good to us to allow such ill-luck;—and she has more favour, I trust, in the seventh heaven than all the Ghibelline saints in your calendar. No, good Cincolo, Marzio is not dead, nor the Holy Father, nor Messer Carlo of Naples; but I would bet my gold cross against the wealth of your banished men, that Pisa is taken—or Corradino—or"—

"And I here! No, Gegia, old as I am, and much as you need my help (and that last is why I am here at all), Pisa would not be taken while this old body could stand in the breach; or Corradino die, till this lazy blood were colder on the ground than it is in my body. Ask no more questions, and do not rouse me: there is no news, no good or ill luck, that I know. But when I saw the Neri, the Pulci, the Buondelmonti, and the rest of them, ride like kings through the streets, whose very hands are hardly dry from the blood of my kindred; when I saw their daughter crowned with flowers, and thought how the daughter of Arrigo del Elisei was mourning for her murdered father, with ashes on her head, by the hearth of a stranger,—my spirit must be more dead than it is if such a sight did not make me wish to drive among them; and methought I could scatter their pomp with my awl for a sword. But I remembered thee, and am here unstained with blood."

"That thou wilt never be!" cried Monna Gegia, the colour rising in her wrinkled cheeks. "Since the battle of Monte Aperto thou hast never been well washed of that shed by thee and thy confederates; and how could ye? for the Arno has never since run clear of the blood then spilt."

And if the sea were red with that blood, still, while there is any of the Guelphs to spill, I am ready to spill it, were it not for thee. Thou dost well to mention Monte Aperto, and thou wouldst do better to remember over whom its grass now grows."

Peace, Cincolo; a mother's heart has more memory in it than thou thinkest; and I well recollect who spurned me as I knelt, and dragged my only child, but sixteen years of age, to die in the cause of that misbeliever Manfred. Let us indeed speak no more.

Woe was the day when I married thee! but those were happy times when there was neither Guelph nor Ghibelline;—they will never return."

"Never,—until, as thou sayest, the Arno run clear of the blood shed on its banks;—never while I can pierce the heart of a Guelph;—never till both parties are cold under one bier."

"And thou and I, Cincolo?"

"Are two old fools, and shall be more at peace underground than above it. Rank Guelph as thou art, I married thee before I was a Ghibelline; so now I must eat from the same platter with the enemy of Manfred, and make shoes for Guelphs, instead of following the fortunes of Dorradino, and sending them, my battle-axe in my hand, to buy their shoes in Bologna."

"Hush! hush! good man, talk not so loud of thy party; nearest thou not that someone knocks?"

Cincolo went to open the door with the air of a man who thinks himself ill-used at being interrupted in his discourse, and is disposed to be angry with the intruder, however innocent he might be of any intention of breaking in upon his eloquent complaint. The appearance of his visitor calmed his indignant feelings. He was a youth whose countenance and person showed that he could not be more than sixteen; but there was a self-possession in his demeanour, and a dignity in his physiognomy, that belonged to a more advanced age. His figure was slight, and his countenance, though beautiful, was pale as monumental marble; the thick and curling locks of his chestnut hair clustered over his brow and round his fair throat; his cap was drawn far down on his forehead. Cincolo was about to usher him with deference into his humble room, but the youth stayed him with his hand, and uttered the words "*Swabia, Cavalieri!*" the words by which the Ghibellines were accustomed to recognise each other. He continued in a low and hurried tone: "Your wife is within?"

"She is."

"Enough. Although I am a stranger to you, I come from an old friend. Harbour me until nightfall; we will then go out, and I will explain to you the motives of my intrusion. Call me Ricciardo de' Rossini of Milan, travelling to Rome. I leave Florence this evening."

Having said these words, without giving Cincolo time to reply, he motioned that they should enter the room. Monna Gegia had fixed her eyes on the door from the moment he had opened it, with a look of impatient curiosity; when she saw the youth enter, she could not refrain from exclaiming, "*Gesu Maria!*"—so different was he from any one she had expected to see.

"A friend from Milan," said Cincolo.

"More likely from Lucca," replied his wife, gazing on her visitant. "You are doubtless one of the banished men, and you are more daring than wise to enter this town; however, if you be not a spy, you are safe with me."

Ricciardo smiled and thanked her in a low, sweet voice. "If you do not turn me out," he said, "I shall remain under your roof nearly all the time I remain in Florence, and I leave it soon after dusk."

Gegia again gazed on her guest, nor did Cincolo scrutinize him with less curiosity. His black cloth tunic reached below his knees, and was confined by a black leather girdle at the waist. He had on trousers of coarse scarlet stuff, over which were drawn short boots; a cloak of common fox's fur, unlined, hung from his shoulder. But, although his dress was thus simple, it was such as was then worn by the young Florentine nobility. At that time the Italians were simple in their private habits: the French army led by Charles d Anjou into Italy, first introduced luxury into the palaces of the Cisalpines. Manfred was a magnificent prince, but it was his saintly rival who was the author of that trifling foppery of dress and ornaments which degrades a nation, and is a sure precursor of their downfall.

But of Ricciardo—his countenance had all the regularity of a Grecian head; and his blue eyes, shaded by very long, dark eyelashes, were soft, yet full of expression. When he looked up, the heavy lids, as it were, unveiled the gentle light beneath, and then again closed over them, as shading what was too brilliant to behold. His lips expressed the deepest sensibility, and something perhaps of timidity, had not the placid confidence of his demeanour forbidden such an idea.

His host and hostess were at first silent; but he asked some natural questions about the buildings of their city, and by degrees led them into discourse. When midday struck, Cincolo looked towards his pot of *minestra*, and Ricciardo followed his look, asked if that was not the dinner. "You must entertain me," he said, "for I have not eaten today."

A table was drawn near the window, and the *minestra*, poured out into one plate, was placed in the middle of it, a spoon was given to each, and a jug of wine filled from a barrel. Ricciardo looked at the two old people, and seemed somewhat to smile at the idea of eating from the same plate with them; he ate, however, though sparingly, and drank of the wine, though with still greater moderation. Cincolo, however, under pretence of serving his guest, filled his jug a second time, and was about to rise for the third measure, when Ricciardo, placing his small white hand on his arm, said, "Are you a German, my friend, that you cease not after so many draughts? I have heard that you Florentines were a sober people."

Cincolo was not much pleased with this reproof, but he felt that it was timely; so, conceding the point, he sat down again, and, somewhat heated with what he had already drank, he asked his guest the news from Germany, and what hopes for the good cause? Gegia bridled at these words, and Ricciardo replied, "Many reports are abroad, and high hopes entertained, especially in the north of Italy, for the success of our expedition. Corradino is arrived at Genoa, and it is hoped that, although the ranks of his army were much thinned by the desertion of his German troops, they will be quickly filled by Italians, braver and truer than those foreigners, who, strangers to our soil, could not fight for his cause with our ardour?"

"And how does he bear himself?"

"As beseems one of the house of Swabia, and the nephew of Manfred. He is inexperienced and young. He is not more than sixteen. His mother would hardly consent to this expedition, but wept at the fear of all he might endure; for he has been nursed in every luxury, and habituated to the tender care of a woman, who, although she be a princess, has waited on him with anxious solicitude. But Corradino is of good heart; docile, but courageous; obedient to his wiser friends, gentle to his inferiors, but noble of soul, the spirit of Manfred seems to animate his unfolding mind; and surely, if that glorious prince now enjoys the reward of his surpassing virtues, he looks down with joy and approbation on him who is, I trust, destined to fill his throne."

The enthusiasm with which Ricciardo spoke suffused his pale countenance with a slight blush, while his eyes swam in the lustre of the dew that filled them. Gegia was little pleased with this harangue, but curiosity kept her silent, while her husband proceeded to question his guest. "You seem to be well acquainted with Corradino?"

"I saw him at Milan, and was closely connected with his most intimate friend there. As I have said, he has arrived at Genoa, and perhaps has even now landed at Pisa; he will find many friends in that town. Every man there will be his friend; but during his journey southward he will have to contend with our Florentine army, commanded by the Marshals of the usurper Charles, and assisted by his troops. Charles himself has left us, and is gone to Naples to prepare for this war. But he is detested there, as a tyrant and a robber, and Corradino will be received in the Regno as a saviour; so that if he once surmount the obstacles which oppose his entrance, I do not doubt his success, and trust that he will be crowned within a month at Rome, and the week after sit on the throne of his ancestors in Naples."

"And who will crown him?" cried Gegia, unable to contain herself. "Italy contains no heretic base enough to do such a deed, unless it be a Jew; or he send to Constantinople for a Greek, or to Egypt for a Mohammedan. Cursed may the race of the Frederics ever be! Thrice cursed one who has affinity to the miscreant Manfred! And little do you please me, young man, by holding such discourse in my house."

Cincolo looked at Ricciardo, as if he feared that so violent a partisan for the house of Swabia would be irritated at his wife's attack; but he was looking on the aged woman with a regard of the most serene benignity; no contempt even was mingled with the gentle smile that played round his lips. "I will restrain myself," he said, and, turning to Cincolo, he conversed on more general subjects, describing the various cities of Italy that he had visited; discussing their modes of government, and relating anecdotes concerning their inhabitants, with an air of experience that, contrasted with his youthful appearance, greatly impressed Cincolo, who looked on him at once with admiration and respect.

Evening came on. The sound of bells died away after the *Ave Maria* had ceased to ring, but the distant sound of music was wafted to them by the night air. Ricciardo was about to address Cincolo, when a knocking at the gate interrupted him. It was Buzeccha, the Saracen, a famous chess-player, who was used to parade about under the colonnades of the Duomo, and challenge the young nobles to play; and sometimes much stress was laid on these games, and the gain and loss became the talk of Florence. Buzeccha was a tall and ungainly man, with all that good-natured consequence of manner which the fame he had acquired by his proficiency in so trifling a science, and the familiarity with which he was permitted to treat those superior to him in rank, who were pleased to measure their forces with him, might well bestow. He was beginning with "*Eh, Messere!*" when perceiving Ricciardo, he cried, "Who have we here?"

"A friend to good men," replied Ricciardo , smiling.

"Then, by Mahomet, thou art my friend, my stripling."

"Thou shouldst be a Saracen, by thy speech?" said Ricciardo.

"And through the help of the Prophet, so am I. One who in Manfred's time—but no more of that. We won't talk of Manfred, eh, Monna Gegia? I am Buzeccha, the chess-player, at your service, Messer lo Forestiere."

The introduction thus made, they began to talk of the procession of the day. After a while, Buzeccha introduced his favourite subject of chess-playing; he recounted some wonderfully good strokes he had achieved, and related to Ricciardo how before the *Palagio del Popolo*, in the presence of Count Guido Novelle de' Giudi, then *Vicare* of the city, he had played an hour at three chess-boards with three of the best chess-players in Florence, playing two by memory and one by sight; and out of three games which made the board, he had won two.

This account was wound up by a proposal to play with his host. "Thou art a hard-headed fellow, Cincolo, and make better play than the nobles. I would swear that thou thinkest of chess only as thou cobblest thy shoes; every hole of your awl is a square of the board, every stitch a move, and a finished pair paid for checkmate to your adversary; eh, Cincolo? Bring out the field of battle, man."

Ricciardo interposed: "I leave Florence in two hours, and before I go, Messer Cincolo promised to conduct me to the *Piazza del Duomo*"

"Plenty of time, good youth," cried Buzeccha, arranging his men; "I only claim one game, and my games never last more than a quarter of an hour; and *then* we will both escort you, and you shall dance a set into the bargain with a black-eyed *houri*, all Nazarine as thou art. So stand out of my light, good youth, and shut the window, if you have heeding, that the torch flare not so."

Ricciardo seemed amused by the authoritative tone of the chess-player; he shut the window and trimmed the torch which, stuck against the wall, was the only light they had, and stood by the table, overlooking the game. Monna Gegia had replaced the pot for supper, and sat somewhat uneasily, as if she were displeased that her guest did not talk with her. Cincolo and Buzeccha were deeply intent on their game, when a knock was heard at the door. Cincolo was about to rise and open it, but Ricciardo saying, "Do not disturb yourself," opened it himself, with the manner of one who does humble offices as if ennobling them, so that no one action can be more humble to them than another.

The visitant was welcomed by Gegia alone, with "Ah! Messer Beppe, this is kind, on May Day night."

Ricciardo glanced slightly on him, and then resumed his stand by the players. There was little in Messer Beppe to attract a favourable regard. He was short, thin, and dry; his face long-drawn and liny; his eyes deep-set and scowling, his lips straight, his nose hooked, and his head covered by a close skull-cap, his hair cut close all round. He sat down near Gegia, and began to discourse in a whining, servile, voice, complimenting her on her good looks, launching forth into praise of the magnificence of certain Guelph Florentines, and concluded by declaring that he was hungry and tired.

"Hungry, Beppe?" said Gegia, "that should have been your first word, friend. Cincolo, wilt thou give thy guest to eat? Cincolo, art thou deaf? Art thou blind? Dost thou not hear? Wilt thou not see?—Here is Messer Giuseppe de Bosticchi."

Cincolo slowly, his eyes still fixed on the board, was about to rise. But the name of the visitant seemed to have the effect of magic on Ricciardo.

"Bosticchi! "he cried—"Giuseppe Bosticchi! I did not expect to find that man beneath thy roof, Cincolo, all Guolph as thy wife is; for she also has eaten of the bread of Elisei. Farewell! thou will find me in the street below; follow me quickly."

He was about to go, but Bosticchi placed himself before the door, saying in a tone whose whine expressed mingled rage and servility, "In what have I offended this young gentleman? Will he not tell me my offence?"

"Dare not to stop my way," cried Ricciardo , passing his hand before his eyes, "nor force me again to look on thee. Begone!"

Cincolo stopped him. "Thou art too hasty, and far too passionate, my noble guest," said he; "however this man may have offended thee, thou art too violent."

"Violent!" cried Ricciardo, almost suffocated by passionate emotion. "Ay, draw thy knife, and show the blood of Arrigo dei Elisei, with which it is still stained."

A dead silence followed. Bosticchi slunk out of the room;

Ricciardo hid his face in his hands and wept. But soon he calmed his passion, and said: "This is indeed childish. Pardon me; that man is gone; excuse and forget my violence. Resume thy game, Cincolo, but conclude it quickly, for time gains on us. Hark! an hour of night sounds from the Campanile."

"The game is already concluded," said Buzeccha sorrowfully; "thy cloak overthrew the best checkmate this head ever planned—so God forgive thee!"

"Checkmate!" cried the indignant Cincolo—"Checkmate! and my queen mowing you down, rank and file!"

"Let us begone!" exclaimed Ricciardo. "Messer Buzeccha, you will play out your game with Monna Gegia. Cincolo will return ere long. So taking his host by the arm, he drew him out of the room, and descended the narrow high stairs with the air of one to whom those stairs were not unknown.

When in the street he slackened his pace, and, first looking round to assure himself that none overheard their conversation, he addressed Cincolo:"Pardon me, my dear friend; I am hasty, and the sight of that man made every drop of my blood cry aloud in my veins. But I do not come here to indulge in private sorrows or private revenge, and my design ought alone to engross me. It is necessary for me to see speedily and secretly Messer Guielmo Lostendardo, the Neapolitan commander. I bear a message to him from the Countess Elizabeth, the mother of Corradino, and I have some hope that its import may induce him to take at least a neutral part during the impending conflict.

"I have chosen you, Cincolo, to aid me in this, for not only you are of that little note in your town that you may act for me without attracting observation, but you are brave and true, and I may confide to your known worth. Lostendardo resides at *the Palagio del Governo*. When I enter its doors I am in the hands of my enemies, and its dungeons may alone know the secret of my destiny. I hope better things. But if after two hours I do not appear or let you hear of my welfare, carry this packet to Corradino at Pisa. You will then learn who I am; and if you feel any indignation at my fate, let that feeling attach you still more strongly to the cause for which I live and die."

As Ricciardo spoke, he still walked on, and Cincolo observed that, without his guidance, he directed his steps towards the *Palagio del Governo.*

"I do not understand this," said the old man. "By what argument, unless you bring one from the other world, do you hope to induce Messer Guielmo to aid Corradino? He is so bitter an enemy of Manfred, that although that prince is dead, yet when he mentions his name he grasps the air as it were a dagger. I have heard him with horrible imprecations curse the whole house of Swabia."

A tremor shook the frame of Ricciardo, but he replied, "Lostendardo was once the firmest support of that house, and the friend of Manfred. Strange circumstances gave birth in his mind to this unnatural hatred, and he became a traitor. But, perhaps, now that Manfred is in Paradise, the youth, the virtues, and the inexperience of Corradino may inspire him with more generous feelings, and reawaken his ancient faith. At least I must make this last trial. This cause is too holy, too sacred, to admit of common forms of reasoning or action. The nephew of Manfred must sit upon the throne of his ancestors; and to achieve that I will endure what I am about to endure."

They entered the palace; Messer Guielmo was carousing in the great hall.

"Bear this ring to him, good Cincolo, and say that I wait. Be speedy, that my courage, my life, do not desert me at the moment of trial."

Cincolo, casting one more inquisitive glance on his extraordinary companion, obeyed his orders, while the youth leant against one of the pillars of the court and passionately cast up his eyes to the clear firmament.

"Oh, ye stars!" he cried in a smothered voice, "ye are eternal; let my purpose, my will, be as constant as ye!"

Then, more calm, he folded his arms in his cloak, and with strong inward struggle endeavoured to repress his emotion. Several servants approached him, and bade him follow them. Again he looked at the sky and said, "Manfred," and then he walked on with slow but firm steps. They led him through several halls and corridors to a large apartment hung with tapestry, and well lighted by numerous torches; the marble of the floor reflected their glare, and the arched roof echoed the footsteps of one who paced the apartment as Ricciardo entered. It was Lostendardo. He made a sign that the servants should retire; the heavy door closed behind them, and Ricciardo stood alone with Messer Guielmo; his countenance pale but composed, his eyes cast down as in expectation, not in fear; and but for the convulsive motion of his lips, you would have guessed that every faculty was almost suspended by intense agitation.

Lostendardo approached. He was a man in the prime of life, tall and athletic; he seemed capable with a single exertion to crush the frail being of Ricciardo. Every feature of his countenance spoke of the struggle of passions, and the terrible egotism of one who would sacrifice even himself to the establishment of his will: his black eyebrows were scattered, his grey eyes deep set and scowling, his look at once stern and haggard. A smile seemed never to have disturbed the settled scorn which his lips expressed; his high forehead, already becoming bald, was marked by a thousand contradictory lines. His voice was studiously restrained as he said: "Wherefore do you bring that ring?"

Ricciardo looked up and met his eye, which glanced fire as he exclaimed, "Despina!"—He seized her hand with a giant's grasp: "I have prayed for this night and day, and thou art now here! Nay, do not struggle; you are mine; for by my salvation I swear that thou shalt never again escape me."

Despina replied calmly: "Thou mayest well believe that in thus placing myself in thy power I do not dread any injury thou canst inflict upon me, or I were not here. I do not fear thee, for I do not fear death. Loosen then thy hold, and listen to me. I come in the name of those virtues that were once thine; I come in the name of all noble sentiment, generosity, and ancient faith, and I trust that in listening to me your heroic nature will second my voice, and that Lostendardo will no longer rank with those

424

whom the good and great never name but to condemn."

Lostendardo appeared to attend little to what she said. He gazed on her with triumph and malignant pride; and if he still held her his motive appeared rather the delight he felt in displaying his power over her, than any fear that she would escape. You might read in her pale check and glazed eye, that if she feared, it was herself alone that she mistrusted; that her design lifted her above mortal dread, and that she was as impassive as the marble she resembled to any event that did not either advance or injure the object for which she came. They were both silent, until Lostendardo leading her to a seat, and then standing opposite to her, his arms folded, every feature dilated by triumph, and his voice sharpened by agitation, he said: "Well, speak! What wouldst thou with me?"

"I come to request, that if you cannot be induced to assist Prince Corradino in the present struggle, you will, at least, stand neutral, and not oppose his advance to the kingdom of his ancestors."

Lostendardo laughed. The vaulted roof repeated the sound, but the harsh echo, though it resembled the sharp cry of an animal of prey whose paw is on the heart of its enemy, was not so discordant and dishuman as the laugh itself. "How," he asked, "dost thou pretend to induce me to comply? This dagger"—and he touched the hilt of one that was half concealed in his vesture—"is yet stained by the blood of Manfred; ere long it will be sheathed in the heart of that foolish boy."

Despina conquered the feeling of horror these words inspired, and replied: "Will you give a few minutes patient hearing?"

"I will give you a few minutes hearing, and if I be not so patient as in the Palagio Reale, fair Despina must excuse me. Forbearance is not a virtue to which I aspire."

"Yes, it was in the Palagio Reale at Naples, the palace of Manfred, that you first saw me. You were then the bosom friend of Manfred, selected by him as his confidant and counsellor. Why did you become a traitor? Start not at that word: if you could hear the united voice of Italy, and even of those who call themselves your friends, they would echo that name. Why did you thus degrade and belie yourself? You call me the cause, yet I am most innocent. You saw me at the Court of your master, an attendant on Queen Sibilla, and one who, unknown to herself, had already parted with her heart, her soul, her will, her entire being, an involuntary sacrifice at the shrine of all that is noble and divine in human nature. My spirit worshipped Manfred as a saint, and my pulses ceased to beat when his eye fell upon me. I felt this, but I knew it not.

"You awoke me from my dream. You said that you loved me, and you reflected in too faithful a mirror my own emotions: I saw myself and shuddered. But the profound and eternal nature of my passion saved me. I loved Manfred. I loved the sun because it enlightened him; I loved the air that fed him; I deified myself, for that my heart was the temple in which he resided. I devoted myself to Sibilla, for she was his wife, and never in thought or dream degraded the purity of my affection towards him. For this you hated him. He was ignorant of my passion: my heart contained it as a treasure, which you having discovered came to rifle. You could more easily deprive me of life than my devotion for your king, and therefore you were a traitor.

"Manfred died, and you thought that I had then forgotten him. But love would indeed be a mockery if death were not the most barefaced cheat. How can he die who is immortalized in my thoughts—my thoughts, that comprehend the universe, and contain eternity in their grasping? What though his earthly vesture is thrown as a despised weed beside the *verde*, he lives in my soul as lovely, as noble, as entire, as when his voice awoke the mute air; nay, his life is more entire, more true. For before, that small shrine that encased his spirit was all that existed of him; but now, he is a part of all things; his spirit surrounds me, interpenetrates; and divided from him during his life, his death has united me to him forever."

The countenance of Lostendardo darkened fearfully. When she paused, he looked black as the sea before the heavily charged thunder-clouds that canopy it dissolve themselves into rain. The tempest of passion that arose in his heart seemed too mighty to admit of swift manifestation; it came slowly up from the profoundest depths of his soul, and emotion was piled upon emotion before the lightning of his anger sped to its destination. "Your arguments, eloquent Despina," he said, "are indeed unanswerable. They work well for your purpose. Corradino is, I hear, at Pisa: you have sharpened my dagger; and before the air of another night rust it, I may, by deeds, have repaid your insulting words."

"How far do you mistake me! And is praise and love of all heroic excellence insult to you! Lostendardo, when you first knew me, I was an inexperienced girl; I loved, but knew not what love was, and circumscribing my passion in narrow bounds, I adored the being of Manfred as I might love an effigy of stone, which, when broken, has no longer an existence. I am now much altered. I might before have treated you with disdain or anger, but now these base feelings have expired in my heart. I am animated but by one feeling—an aspiration to another life, another state of being.

"All the good depart from this strange earth; and I doubt not that when I am sufficiently elevated above human weaknesses, it will also be my turn to leave this scene of woe. I prepare myself for that moment alone; and in endeavouring to fit myself for a union with all the brave, generous, and wise, that once adorned humanity, and have now passed from it, I consecrate myself to the service of this most righteous cause. You wrong me, therefore, if you think there is aught of disdain in what I say, or that any degrading feelings are mingled with my devotion of spirit when I come and voluntarily place myself in your power.

"You can imprison me forever in the dungeons of this palace, as a returned Ghibelline and spy, and have me executed as a criminal. But before you do this, pause for your own sake; reflect on the choice of glory or ignominy that you are now about to make. Let your old sentiments of love for the house of Swabia have some sway in your heart; reflect, that as you are the despised enemy, so you may become the chosen friend of its last descendant, and receive from every heart the .praise of having restored Corradino to the honours and power to which he was born.

"Compare this prince to the hypocritical, the bloody and mean-spirited Charles. When Manfred died I went to Germany, and have resided at the court of the Countess Elizabeth; I have therefore been an hourly witness of the great and good qualities of Corradino. The bravery of his spirit makes him rise above the weakness of youth and inexperience; he possesses all the nobility of spirit that belongs to the family of Swabia, and, in addition, a purity and gentleness that attracts the respect and love of the old and wary courtiers of Frederic and Conrad.

"You are brave, and would be generous, did not the fury of your passions, like a consuming fire, destroy in their violence every generous sentiment: how then can you become the tool of Chariest His scowling eyes and sneering lips betoken the selfishness of his mind. Avarice, cruelty, meanness, and artifice are the qualities that characterize him, and render him unworthy of the majesty he usurps. Let him return to Provence, and reign with paltry despotism over the luxurious and servile Trench; the freeborn Italians require another lord. They are not fit to bow to one whose palace is the change-house of money-lenders, whose generals are usurers, whose courtiers are milliners or monks, and who basely vows allegiance to the enemy of freedom and virtue, Clement, the murderer of Manfred.

"Their king, like them, should be clothed in the armour of valour and simplicity; his ornaments, his shield and spear; his treasury, the possessions of his subjects; his army, their unshaken lover. Charles will treat you as a tool; Corradino as a friend. Charles will make you the detested tyrant of a groaning province; Corradino, the governor of a prosperous and happy people. I cannot tell by your manner if what I have said has in any degree altered your determination. I cannot forget the scenes that passed between us at Naples. I might then have been disdainful; I am not so now.

"Your execrations of Manfred excited every angry feeling in my mind; but, as I have said, all but the feeling of love expired in my heart when Manfred died, and methinks that where love is, excellence must be its companion. You said you loved me; and though, in other times, that love was twin-brother to hate,—though then, poor prisoner in your heart, jealousy, rage, contempt, and cruelty, were its handmaids,—yet if it were love, methinks that its divinity must have purified your heart from baser feelings; and now that I, the bride of Death, am removed from your sphere, gentler feelings may awaken in your bosom, and you may incline mildly to my voice.

"If indeed you loved me, will you not now be my friend? Shall we not hand in hand pursue the same career? Return to your ancient faith; and now that death and religion have placed the seal upon the past, let Manfred's spirit, looking down, behold his repentant friend the firm ally of his successor, the best and last scion of the house of Swabia."

She ceased; for the glare of savage triumph which, as a rising fire at night-time, enlightened with growing and fearful radiance the face of Lostendardo, made her pause in her appeal. He did not reply; but when she was silent he quitted the attitude in which he had stood immovably opposite to her, and pacing the hall with measured steps, his head declined, he seemed to ruminate on some project. Could it be that he weighed her reasonings? If he hesitated, the side of generosity and old fidelity would certainly prevail. Yet she dared not hope; her heart beat fast; she would have knelt, but she feared to move, lest any motion should disturb his thoughts, and curb the flow of good feeling which she fondly hoped had arisen within him: she looked up and prayed silently as she sat.

Notwithstanding the glare of the torches, the beams of one small star struggled through the dark window pane; her eye resting on it, her thoughts were at once elevated to the eternity and space which that star symbolized; it seemed to her the spirit of Manfred, and she inwardly worshipped it, as she prayed that it would shed its benign influence on the soul of Lostendardo.

Some minutes elapsed in this fearful silence, and then he approached her. "Despina, allow me to reflect on your words; tomorrow I will answer you. You will remain in this palace until the morning, and then you shall see and judge of my repentance and returning faith."

He spoke with studious gentleness. Despina could not see his face, for the lights shone behind him. When she looked up to reply, the little star twinkled just above his head, and seemed with its gentle lustre to reassure her. Our minds, when highly wrought, are strangely given to superstition, and Despina lived in a superstitious age. She thought that the star bade her comply, and assured her of protection from Heaven;—from where else could she expect it? She said, therefore, "I consent. Only let me request that you acquaint the man who gave you my ring that I am safe, or he will fear for me."

"I will do as you desire."

"And I will confide myself to your care. I cannot, dare not, fear you. If you would betray me, still I trust in the heavenly saints that guard humanity."

Her countenance was so calm,—it beamed with so angelic a self-devotion and a belief in good, that Lostendardo dared not look on her. For one moment—as she, having ceased to speak, gazed upon the star—he felt impelled to throw himself at her feet, to confess the diabolical scheme he had forged, and to commit himself body and soul to her guidance, to obey, to serve, to worship her. The impulse was momentary; the feeling of revenge returned on him. From the moment she had rejected him, the fire of rage had burned in his heart, consuming all healthy feeling, all human sympathies, and gentleness of soul. He had sworn never to sleep on a bed, or to drink aught but water, until his first cup of wine was mingled with the blood of Manfred. He had fulfilled this vow.

A strange alteration had worked within him from the moment he had drained that unholy cup. The spirit, not of a man, but of a devil, seemed to live within him, urging him to crime, from which his long protracted hope of more complete revenge had alone deterred him. But Despina was now in his power, and it seemed to him as if fate had preserved him so long only that he might now wreak his full rage upon her. When she spoke of love, he thought how from that he might extract pain. He formed his plan; and this slight human weakness now conquered, he bent his thoughts to its completion. Yet he feared to stay longer with her; so he quitted her, saying that he would send attendants who would show her an apartment where she might repose.

He left her, and several hours passed; but no one came. The torches burnt low, and the stars of heaven could now with twinkling beams conquer their feebler light. One by one these torches went out, and the shadows of the high windows of the hall, before invisible, were thrown upon its marble pavement. Despina looked upon the shade, at first unconsciously, until she found herself counting one, two, three, the shapes of the iron bars that lay so placidly on the stone.

"Those grates are thick," she said; "this room would be a large but secure dungeon." As by inspiration, she now felt that she was a prisoner. No change, no word, had intervened since she had walked fearlessly in the room, believing herself free. But now no doubt of her situation occurred to her mind; heavy chains seemed to fall around her; the air to feel thick and heavy as that of a prison; and the star-beams that had before cheered her, became the dreary messengers of fearful danger to herself, and of the utter defeat of all the hopes she had dared nourish of success to her beloved cause.

Cincolo waited, first with impatience, and then with anxiety, for the return of the youthful stranger. He paced up and down before the gates of the palace; hour after hour passed on; the stars arose and descended, and ever and anon meteors shot along the sky. They were not more frequent than they always are during a clear summer night in Italy; but they appeared strangely numerous to Cincolo, and portentous of change and calamity. Midnight struck, and at that moment a procession of monks passed, bearing a corpse and chanting a solemn *De Profundis*.

Cincolo felt a cold tremor shake his limbs when he reflected how ill an augury this was for the strange adventurer he had guided to that palace. The sombre cowls of the priests, their hollow voices, and the dark burden they carried, augmented his agitation even to terror. Without confessing the cowardice to himself, he was possessed with fear lest he should be included in the evil destiny that evidently awaited his companion. Cincolo was a brave man; he had often been foremost in a perilous assault; but the most courageous among us sometimes feel our hearts fail within us at the dread of unknown and fated danger.

He was struck with panic;—he looked after the disappearing lights of the procession, and listened to their fading voices; his knees shook, a cold perspiration stood on his brow; until, unable to resist the impulse, he began slowly to withdraw himself from the Palace of Government, and to quit the circle of danger which seemed to hedge him in if he remained on that spot.

He had hardly quitted his post by the gate of the palace, when he saw lights issue from it, attendant on a company of men, some of whom were armed, as appeared from the reflection their lances heads cast; and some of them carried a litter, hung with black and closely drawn. Cincolo was rooted to the spot. He could not render himself any reason for his belief, but he felt convinced that the stranger youth was there, about to be carried out to death. Impelled by curiosity and anxiety, he followed the party as they went towards the Porta Romana: they were challenged by the sentinels at the gate; they gave the word and passed.

Cincolo dared not follow, but he was agitated by fear and compassion. He remembered the packet confided to his care; he dared not draw it from his bosom, lest any Guelph should be near to overlook and discover that it was addressed to Corradino; he could not read, but ho wished to look at the arms of the seal, to see whether they bore the imperial ensigns. He returned back to the *Palagio del Governo*: all there was dark and silent; he walked up and down before the gates, looking up at the windows, but no sign of life appeared. He could not tell why he was thus agitated, but he felt as if all his future peace depended on the fate of this stranger youth. He thought of Gegia, her helplessness and age; but he could not resist the impulse that impelled him, and he resolved that very night to commence his journey to Pisa, to deliver the packet, to learn who the stranger was, and what hopes he might entertain for his safety.

He returned home, that he might inform Gegia of his journey. This was a painful task, but he could not leave her in doubt. He ascended his narrow stairs with trepidation. At the head of them a lamp twinkled before a picture of the Virgin. Evening after evening it burnt there, guarding through its influence his little household from all earthly or supernatural dangers. The sight of it inspired him with courage; he said an *Ave Maria* before it; and then looking around him to assure himself that no spy stood on the narrow landing-place, he drew the packet from his bosom and examined the seal.

All Italians in those days were conversant in heraldry, since from ensigns of the shields of the knights they learned, better than from their faces or persons, to what family and party they belonged. But it required no great knowledge for Cincolo to decipher these arms; he had known them from his childhood; they were those of the Elisei, the family to whom he had been attached as a partisan during all these civil contests. Arrigo de Elisei had been his patron, and his wife had nursed his only daughter, in those happy days when there was neither Guelph nor Ghibelline. The sight of these arms re awakened all his anxiety. Could this youth belong to that house? The seal showed that he really did; and this discovery confirmed his determination of making every exertion to save him, and inspired him with sufficient courage to encounter the remonstrances and fears of Monna Gegia.

He unlocked his door; the old dame was asleep in her chair, but awoke as he entered. She had slept only to refresh her curiosity, and she asked a thousand questions in a breath, to which Cincolo did not reply: he stood with his arms folded looking at the fire, irresolute how to break the subject of his departure. Monna Gegia continued to talk.

"After you went, we held a consultation concerning this hot-brained youth of this morning: I, Buzeccha, Beppe de' Bosticchi who returned, and Monna Lissa from the Mercato Nuovo. We all agreed that he must be one of two persons; and be it one or the other, if he have not quitted Florence, the Stinchi [1] will be his habitation by sunrise. Eh, Cincolo, man! you do not speak; where did you part with your prince?"

"Prince, Gegia! Are you mad?—what prince?"

"Nay, he is either a prince or a baker; either Corradino himself, or Ricciardo, the son of Messer Tommaso de Manelli; he that lived o'th' Arno, and baked for all that Sesto, when Count Guido de Giudi was *Vicario*. By this token, that Messer Tommaso went to Milan with Ubaldo de Gargalandi, and Ricciardo, who went with his father, must now be sixteen. He had the fame of kneading with as light a hand as his father, but he liked better to follow arms with the Gargalandi. He was a fair, likely youth, they said; and so, to say the truth, was our youngster of this morning. But Monna Lissa will have it that it must be Corradino himself."

Cincolo listened as if the gossip of two old women could unravel his riddle. He even began to doubt whether the last conjecture, extravagant as it was, had not hit the truth. Every circumstance forbade such an idea; but he thought of the youth and exceeding beauty of the stranger, and he began to doubt. There was none among the Elisei who answered to his appearance. The flower of their youth had fallen at Monte Aperto; the eldest of the new generation was but ten; the other males of that house were of a mature age. Gegia continued to talk of the anger that Beppe de' Bosticchi evinced at being accused of the murder of Arrigo de Elisei.

"If he had done that deed," she cried, "never more should he have stood on my hearth; but he swore his innocence; and truly, poor man, it would be a sin not to believe him." Why, if the stranger were not an Elisei, should he have shown such horror on viewing the supposed murderer of the head of that family? Cincolo turned from the fire; he examined whether his knife hung safely in his girdle, and he exchanged his sandal-like

---

1. The name of the common prison at Florence.

shoes for stronger boots of common undressed fur. This last act attracted the attentions of Gegia.

"What are you about, good man?" she cried. "This is no hour to change your dress, but to come to bed. Tonight you will not speak; but tomorrow I hope to get it all out from you. What are you about?"

"I am about to leave you, my dear Gegia; and Heaven bless and take care of you! I am going to Pisa."

Gegia uttered a shriek, and was about to remonstrate with great volubility, while the tears rolled down her aged cheeks. Tears also filled the eyes of Cincolo, as he said, "I do not go for the cause you suspect. I do not go into the army of Corradino, though my heart will be with it. I go but to carry a letter, and will return without delay."

"You will never return," cried the old woman: "the Commune will never let you enter the gates of this town again, if you set foot in that traitorous Pisa. But you shall not go; I will raise the neighbours; I will declare you mad"—

"Gegia, no more of this! Here is all the money I have. Before I go, I will send your Cousin 'Nunziata to you. I must go. It is not the Ghibelline cause, or Corradino, that obliges me to risk your ease and comforts; but the life of one of the Elisei is at stake; and if I can save him, would you have me rest here, and afterwards curse you and the hour when I was born?"

"What! is he ——? But no; there is none among the Elisei so young as he; and none so lovely, except her whom these arms carried when an infant—but she is a female. No, no; this is a tale trumped up to deceive me and gain my consent; but you shall never have it. Mind that! you will never have it! and I prophesy that if you do go, your journey will be the death of both of us." She wept bitterly. Cincolo kissed her aged cheek, and mingled his tears with hers; and then recommending her to the care of the Virgin and the saints, he quitted her; while grief choked her utterance, the name of the Elisei had deprived her of all energy to resist his purpose.

It was four in the morning before the gates of Florence were opened and Cincolo could leave the city. At first he availed himself of the carts of the *contadini* to advance on his journey; but as he drew near Pisa, all modes of conveyance ceased, and he was obliged to take by-roads, and act cautiously, not to fall into the hands of the Florentine outposts, or of some fierce Ghibelline, who might suspect him, and have him carried before the *Podesta* of the village; for if once suspected and searched, the packet addressed to Corradino would convict him, and he would pay for his temerity with his life.

Having arrived at Vico Pisano, he found a troop of Pisan horse there on guard; he was known to many of the soldiers, and he obtained a conveyance for Pisa; but it was night before he arrived. He gave the Ghibelline watchword, and was admitted within the gates. He asked for Prince Corradino: he was in the city, at the palace of the Lanfranchi. He crossed the Arno, and was admitted into the palace by the soldiers who guarded the door.

Corradino had just returned from a successful skirmish in the Lucchese states, and was reposing; but when Count Gherardo Doneratico, his principal attendant, saw the seal of the packet, he immediately ushered the bearer into a small room, where the prince lay on a fox's skin thrown upon the pavement. The mind of Cincolo had been so bewildered by the rapidity of the events of the preceding night, by fatigue and want of sleep, that he had overwrought himself to believe that the stranger youth was indeed Corradino; and when he had heard that that prince was in Pisa, by a strange disorder of ideas he still imagined that he and Ricciardo were the same; that the black litter was a phantom, and his fears ungrounded.

The first sight of Corradino, his fair hair and round Saxon features, destroyed this idea: it was replaced by a feeling of deep anguish, when Count Gherardo, announcing him, said, "One who brings a letter from Madonna Despina dei Elisei, waits upon your Highness."

The old man sprang forward, uncontrolled by the respect he would otherwise have felt for one of so high lineage as Corradino. "From Despina! Did you say from her? Oh! unsay your words! Not from my beloved, lost foster-child."

Tears rolled down his cheeks. Corradino, a youth of fascinating gentleness, attempted to reassure him. "Oh! my gracious Lord," cried Cincolo, "open that packet, and see if it be from my blessed child—if in the disguise of Ricciardo I led her to destruction." He wrung his hands. Corradino, pale as death with fear for the destiny of his lovely and adventurous friend, broke the seal. The packet contained an inner envelope without any direction, and a letter, which Corradino read, while horror convulsed every feature. He gave it to Gherardo. "It is indeed from her. She says that the bearer can relate all that the world will probably know of her fate. And you old man, who weep so bitterly, you to whom my best and lovely friend refers me, tell me what you know of her?"

Cincolo told his story in broken accents. "May these eyes be forever blinded!" he cried, when he had concluded, "that knew not Despina in those soft looks and heavenly smiles. Dotard that I am! When my wife railed at your family and princely self, and the sainted Manfred, why did I not read her secret in her forbearance? Would she have forgiven those words in any but her who had nursed her infancy, and been a mother to her when Madonna Pia died? And when she taxed Bosticchi with her father's death, I, blind fool, did not see the spirit of the Elisei in her eyes. My Lord, I have but one favour to ask you. Let me hear her letter, that I may judge from that what hopes remain;—but there are none—none."

"Read to him, my dear count," said the prince; "I will not fear as he fears. I dare not fear that one so lovely and beloved is sacrificed for my worthless cause." Gherardo read the letter.

Cincolo de Becari, my foster-father, will deliver this letter into your hands, my respected and dear Corradino. The Countess Elizabeth has urged me to my present undertaking; I hope nothing from it, except to labour for your cause, and perhaps, through its event, to quit somewhat earlier a life which is but a grievous trial to my weak mind. I go to endeavour to arouse the feelings of fidelity and generosity in the soul of the traitor Lostendardo; I go to place myself in his hands, and I do not hope to escape from them again. Corradino, my last prayer will be for your success. Mourn not for one who goes home after a long and weary exile. Burn the enclosed packet, without opening it. The Mother of God protect thee!

Despina.

Corradino had wept as this epistle was reading, but then, starting up, he said, "To revenge or death! we may yet save her!"

A blight had fallen on the house of Swabia, and all their enterprises were blasted. Beloved by their subjects, noble, and with every advantage of right on their side, except those the Church bestowed, they were defeated in every attempt to defend themselves against a foreigner and a tyrant, who ruled by force of arms, and those in the hands of a few only, over an extensive and warlike territory. The young and daring Corradino was also fated to perish in this contest. Having overcome the troops of his adversary in Tuscany, he advanced towards his kingdom with the highest hopes.

His arch-enemy, Pope Clement IV., had shut himself up in Viterbo, and was guarded by a numerous garrison. Corradino passed in triumph and hope before the town, and proudly drew out his troops before it, to display to the Holy Father his forces, and humiliate him by this show of success. The cardinals, who beheld the lengthened line and good order of the army, hastened to the papal palace. Clement was in his oratory praying. The frightened monks, with pale looks, related how the excommunicated heretic dared to menace the town where the Holy Father himself resided; adding, that if the insult were carried to the pitch of an assault, it might prove dangerous warfare.

The pope smiled contemptuously. "Do not fear," he said; "the projects of these men will dissipate in smoke." He then went on the ramparts, and saw Corradino and Frederic of Austria, who defiled the line of knights in the plain below. He watched them for a time; then turning to his cardinals, he said, "They are victims, who permit themselves to be led to sacrifice."

His words were a prophecy. Notwithstanding the first successes of Corradino, and the superior numbers of his army, he was defeated by the artifice of Charles in a pitched battle. He escaped from the field, and, with a few friends, arrived at a tower called Asturi, which belonged to the family of Frangipani, of Koine. Here he hired a vessel, embarked, and put out to sea, directing his course for Sicily, which, having rebelled against Charles, would, he hoped, receive him with joy. They were already under weigh, when one of the family of the Frangipani, seeing a vessel filled with Germans making all sail from shore, suspected that they were fugitives from the battle of Taglicozzo. He followed them in other vessels, and took them all prisoners. The person of Corradino was a rich prey for him; he delivered him into the hands of his rival, and was rewarded by the donation of a fief near Benevento.

The dastardly spirit of Charles instigated him to the basest revenge; and the same tragedy was acted on those shores which has been renewed in our days. A daring and illustrious prince was sacrificed with the mock forms of justice, at the sanguinary altar of tyranny and hypocrisy. Corradino was tried. One of his judges alone, a Provençal, dared to condemn him, and he paid with his life the forfeit of his baseness. For scarcely had he, solitary among his fellows, pronounced the sentence of death against this prince, than Robert of Flanders, the brother-in-law of Charles himself, struck him on the breast with a staff, crying, "It behoves not thee, wretch, to condemn to death so noble and worthy a knight." The judge fell dead in the presence of the king, who dared not avenge his creature.

On the 26th of October Corradino and his friends were led out to die in the market-place of Naples, by the sea side. Charles was present with all his court, and an immense multitude surrounded the triumphant king, and his more royal adversary, about to suffer an ignominious death. The funereal procession approached its destination. Corradino, agitated, but controlling his agitation, was drawn in an open car. After him came a close litter, hung with black, with no sign to tell who was within.

The Duke of Austria and several other illustrious victims followed. The guard that conducted them to the scaffold was headed by Lostendardo; a malicious triumph laughed in his eyes, and he rode near the litter, looking from time to time first at it and then at Corradino, with the dark look of a tormenting fiend. The procession stopped at the foot of the scaffold, and Corradino looked at the flashing light which every now and then arose from Vesuvius, and threw its reflection on the sea. The sun had not yet risen, but the halo of its approach illuminated the bay of Naples, its mountains, and its islands. The summits of the distant hills of Baiæ gleamed with its first beams.

Corradino thought, "By the time those rays arrive here, and shadows are cast from the persons of these men—princes and peasants—around me, my living spirit will be shadowless." Then he turned his eyes on the companions of his fate, and for the first time he saw the silent and dark litter that accompanied them. At first he thought, "It is my coffin." But then he recollected the disappearance of Despina, and would have sprang towards it. His guards stopped him; he looked up, and his glance met that of Lostendardo, who smiled—a smile of dread but the feeling of religion which had before calmed him again descended on him; he thought that her sufferings, as well as his, would soon be over.

They were already over; and the silence of the grave is upon those events which had occurred since Cincolo beheld her carried out of Florence, until now that she was led by her fierce enemy to behold the death of the nephew of Manfred. She must have endured much; for when, as Corradino advanced to the front of the scaffold, the litter being placed opposite to it, Lostendardo ordered the curtains to be withdrawn, the white hand that hung inanimate from the side was thin as a winter leaf, and her fair face, pillowed by the thick knots of her dark hair, was sunken and ashy pale, while you could see the deep blue of her eyes struggle through the closed eyelids. She was still in the attire in which she had presented herself at the house of Cincolo.

Perhaps her tormentor thought that her appearance as a youth would attract less compassion than if a lovely woman were thus dragged to so unnatural a scene.

Corradino was kneeling and praying when her form was thus exposed. He saw her, and saw that she was dead! About to die himself; about, pure and innocent, to die ignominiously, while his base conqueror, in pomp and glory, was spectator of his death, he did not pity those who were at peace; his compassion belonged to the living alone; and as he arose from his prayer he exclaimed, "My beloved mother, what profound sorrow will the news thou art about to hear cause thee!"

He looked upon the living multitude around him, and saw that the hard-visaged partisans of the usurper wept; he heard the sobs of his oppressed and conquered subjects; so he drew his glove from his hand and threw it among the crowd, in token that he still held his cause good, and submitted his head to the axe.

During many years after those events, Lostendardo enjoyed wealth, rank, and power. When suddenly, while at the summit of glory and prosperity, he withdrew from the world, took the vows of a severe order in a convent in one of the desolate and unhealthy plains by the sea shore in Calabria; and after having gained the character of a saint, through a life of self-inflicted torture, he died murmuring the names of Corradino, Manfred, and Despina.

The Pole

It was near the close of day that a travelling *calèche*, coming from Rome, was seen approaching at full gallop towards Mola di Gaeta. The road leading to the inn is rocky and narrow; on one side is an orange grove, extending to the sea; on the other, an old Roman wall, overgrown by blossoming shrubs, enormous aloes, floating tangles of vines, and a thousand species of parasite plants peculiar to the South. Scarcely had the *calèche* Entered this defile, when the careless postillion drove one of the wheels over a protruding ledge of rock, and overturned it; and, in the next moment, a crowd of people came running to the spot. Not one of them, however, thought of relieving the traveller within the fallen vehicle; but, with violent gestures and loud outcries, be-gan to examine what damage the *calèche* had sustained, and what profit they might derive from it.

The wheelwright declared every wheel was shattered; the carpenter that the shafts were splintered; whilst the blacksmith, passing and repassing under the carriage, tugged at every clamp and screw and nail, with all the violence necessary to ensure himself a handsome job. The traveller it contained having qui-etly disengaged himself from various cloaks, books, and maps, now slowly descended, and for a moment the busy crowd forgot their restlessness, to gaze upon the noble figure of the stranger. He seemed to be scarcely two-and-twenty. In stature he was tall, and his form was moulded in such perfect propor-tions, that it presented a rare combination of youthful lightness and manly strength. His countenance, had you taken from it its deep thoughtfulness and its expression of calm intrepid bravery, might have belonged to the most lovely woman, so transparently blooming was his complexion, so regular his features, so blond and luxuriant his hair. Of all those present, he seemed the least concerned at the accident; he neither looked at the *calèche*, nor paid any attention to the offers of service that were screamed from a dozen mouths; but, drawing out his watch, asked his servant if the carriage was broken.

"*Pann*, [1] the shafts are snapped, two of the springs are injured, and the linch-pin has flown."

"How long will it take to repair them?"

"Twenty-four hours."

"It is now four o clock. See that everything be in order again by to-morrow's daybreak."

"*Pann*, with these lazy Italians, I fear it will be impossible"—

"*Ya paswalam*," [2] replied the traveller coldly, but decidedly. "Pay what you will, but let all be ready for the hour I have mentioned."

Without another word, he walked towards the inn, followed by the crowd, teasing for alms. A few seconds ago they had all been active and healthy beings, so full of employment they could not afford to mend his *calèche* unless tempted by some extraordinary reward; now the men declared themselves cripples and invalids, the children were orphans, the women helpless widows, and they would all die of hunger if his *Eccellenza* did not bestow a few *grani*. "What a tedious race!" exclaimed the traveller, casting a handful of coins upon the ground, which caused a general scramble, and enabled him to proceed unmolested.

At the inn new torments awaited him; a fresh crowd, composed of the landlord, the landlady, and their waiters and hostlers, gathered round, and assailed him with innumerable questions. The landlord hoped none of his limbs were broken, and begged him to consider himself master of the house; the waiters desired to know at what hour he would sup, what fare he chose,

---

1. My Lord, in Polish
2. I will it, in Polish.

how long he intended to stay, where he came from, whither he was going; and the landlady led him, ostentatiously, through all the rooms of the inn, expatiating endlessly upon the peculiar and indescribable advantages of each. Ineffably weary of their officiousness, the traveller at last traversed a long and spacious hall, and took refuge in a balcony that looked upon the bay of Gaeta.

The inn is built upon the site of Cicero's Villa. Beneath the balcony, and on each side, along the whole curve of the bay, stretched a thick grove of orange-trees, which sloped down to the very verge of the Mediterranean. Balls of golden fruit, and blossoms faint with odour, and fair as stars, studded this amphitheatre of dark foliage; and at its extremity the liquid light of the waves pierced the glossy leaves, mingling their blue splendour with earth's green paradise. Every rock and mountain glowed with a purple hue, so intense and soft, they resembled violet vapours dissolving into the pale radiance of the evening sky. Far away in the deep broad flood of the ocean rose the two mountain islands of Ischia and Procida, between which Vesuvius thrust in his jagged form, and his floating banner of snow-white smoke. The solitary heaven was without sun or moon, without a star or cloud, but smiled in that tender vestal light which speaks of eternal, immutable peace.

It would be difficult to define the feelings of the traveller as he gazed on this scene: his countenance, uplifted to heaven, was animated with a profound and impassioned melancholy, with an expression of an earnest and fervid pleading against some vast and inevitable wrong. He was thinking of his country; and whilst he contrasted its ruined villages and devastated fields with the splendour and glow of the fair land before him, was breathing inwardly a passionate appeal against that blind and cruel destiny which had consigned Poland to the desolating influence of Russian despotism. His reverie was interrupted by the sound of a female voice singing in Polish among the orange trees at his feet. The singer was invisible; but the sweetness of her voice, and the singular reference of the words (the following prose translation conveys their meaning) to the thoughts of his own mind, filled the traveller with surprise:—

"When thou gazest upon the azure heaven, so mighty in its calm, do not say, bright enchantment, hast thou no pity, that thou dawnest thus in unattainable loveliness upon my world-wearied eyes.

"When the southern wind softly breathes, do not say reproachfully, Thy cradle is the ether of the morning sun, thou drinkest the odorous essence of myrtle and lemon blossoms; thou shouldst bear upon thy wings all sweet emotions, all soft desires; why bringest thou then no healing to the anguish I endure?

"Neither in the dark hour, when thou thinkest upon thy country and thy friends, say not with grief, They are lost! They are not! Say rather with joy, They were illustrious! and it is bliss to know that they have been! "

It were wise in me to obey thy lesson, sweet song stress, thought the traveller; and revolving in his mind the singularity of the serenade, he continued to gaze upon the trees below. There was no rustling amid their branches, no sound which told a human being was concealed beneath their foliage; nothing was heard beyond the almost imperceptible breathings of the evening air. Did such things exist anywhere but in the imagination of the poet? He could almost have believed that the spirit of that divine scene had assumed a human voice and human words to soothe his melancholy, so floating and airy had been the strain, so deep the silence that succeeded it.

One moment more, and there arose from the same spot cries for help uttered in Italian, and shrieks of distress so piercing, they made the traveller fly with the speed of lightning through the great hall, down the staircase into the garden. The first object that met his eyes was the figure of a girl about sixteen, her one arm tightly embracing the stem of a tree, her other angrily repelling a young man who was endeavouring to drag her away.

"I will not go with you—I love you no longer, Giorgio—and go with you, I will not," shrieked the girl, in tones of mingled violence and fear.

"You must—you shall," retorted her aggressor in a voice of thunder.

"I have found you again, and I won't be duped by your fooleries, Marietta.—And who are you, and who begged you to interfere?" added he, turning fiercely upon the traveller, whose strong grasp had torn him from Marietta.

"An officer, as it should seem by your dress;—be pleased to know that I am also an officer, and risk my displeasure no further."

"No officer would ill-treat a defenceless girl," the Pole replied with quiet contempt

At this taunt Giorgio quivered with rage. His features, handsome and regular as those of Italians generally are, became quite distorted. His hands with convulsive movements sought about his breast for the dagger that was concealed there, his dark flashing eyes fixed intently at the same time upon his adversary, as if he hoped the fiendish spirit that burned within them might previously annihilate him.

"Be on your guard—he is a perfect wretch," cried Marietta, rushing towards her protector.

The arrival of several servants from the inn dispelled all idea of present danger: they dragged off Giorgio, telling him that, although the girl was his sister, he had no right to separate her from the *corps d'opera*, with whom she was travelling through Gaeta.

"*E vero—verissimo*" cried Marietta with joyful triumph.

"What is it to him if I like my liberty, and prefer wandering about, singing here and there."

"Marietta! beware! dare not to speak ill of me!" screamed the retiring Giorgio, looking back over his shoulder, and accompanying his words with a look of such frightful menace as completely subdued his sister.

She watched in anxious silence till he had disappeared, and then, with affectionate humility and a graceful quickness that allowed not of its prevention, knelt lightly down, and pressed the stranger's hand to her lips.

"You have more than repaid me for the song I sang to you," she said, rising and leading the way to the inn; "and, if you like it, I will sing others to you whilst you sup."

"Are you a Pole?" inquired the traveller.

"A fine demand! how can I be a Pole? Did you not say yourself there was no longer any such country as Poland?"

"I? not that I recollect."

"If you did not say it, confess at least that you thought it. The Poles are all become Russians, and for nothing in the world, *Signor*, would I be a Russian. Why in all their language they have no word that expresses *honour*.[3] No! rather than be a Russian, much as I hate it, I would go with Giorgio."

"Are you an Italian?"

"No—not exactly."

"What are you, then?"

"Um! I am. what I am; who can be more? But, *Signor*, one thing I must beg of you, do not ask me any questions about myself, nor any about Giorgio. I will sing to you, talk to you, wait upon—you anything of that kind you please, but I will not answer questions on those subjects."

Seating herself upon a stool, in a dark corner of the traveller's apartment, as far removed as possible from him, and all other interruptions, Marietta passed the evening in playing on her guitar and singing. She was a most accomplished singer, possessing and managing all the intricacies of the art with perfect ease, but this scarcely excited admiration in comparison with the natural beauty of her voice. There was a profound melancholy in its intense sweetness, that dissolved the soul of the traveller in grief.

All that was dear to him in the memory of the past,—the joys of home and child hood, the tenderness and truth of his first friendships, the glow of patriotism; every cherished hour, every endeared spot, all that he had loved, and all that he had lost upon earth, seemed again to live and again to fade, as he listened to her strains. "Without paying any attention to him, and apparently

---

3. This is true. The Russian language is without that word.

447

without any effort to herself, she breathed forth melody after melody for her own pleasure, like some lone nightingale, that, in a home of green leaves, sings to cheer its solitude with sweet sounds. Her countenance and figure would have been beautiful had they been more fully developed. They resembled those sketches of a great artist in which there are only a few lightly-traced lines, but those so full of spirit and meaning, that you easily imagine what a masterpiece it would have been when finished.

The first visit of our traveller, on arriving, next day, at Naples was to the Princess Dashkhoff. She was a Russian lady, whose high birth, immense wealth, and talents for intrigue, had procured for her the intimacy of half the crowned heads of Europe, and had made her all-powerful at the Court of St. Petersburg. Detesting the cold barbarism of her native country, she had established herself at Naples, in a splendid mansion, near the Strada Nuova; and affecting an extravagant admiration for Italy, by her munificent patronage of the arts and artists, and by perpetual exhibitions of her own skill, in drawing and singing, dancing and acting, had obtained the name of the Corinna of the North. Her *salon* was the evening resort of the wise, the idle, the witty, and the dissipated. Not to know Corinna was to be yourself unknown; and not to frequent her *conversazioni* was, as far as society was concerned, to be banished from all that was fashionable or delightful in Naples.

It was the hour of evening reception. The Pole burned with impatience to speak to the Princess, for on her influence, at Petersburg, depended the fate of his only brother. A splendid suite of apartments, blazing with lights, crowded with company, lay open before him; without allowing himself to be announced, he entered them. When a highly imaginative mind is absorbed by some master feeling, all opposing contrasts, all glowing extremes, serve but to add depth and intensity to that feeling.

The festal scene of marble columns garlanded by roses, the walls of Venetian mirror, reflecting the light of innumerable tapers, and the forms of lovely women and gay youths floating in the mazy dance, seemed to him deceitful shows that veiled some frightful sorrow; and with eager, rapid steps, as if borne along by the impulse of his own thoughts, he hurried past them. Scarcely knowing how he had arrived there, he at length found himself standing beside the Princess, in a marble colonnade, open above to the moonlight and the stars of heaven, and admitting at its sides the odours of the blossoming almond trees of the adjacent gardens.

"Ladislas!" exclaimed the lady, starting; "is it possible—to see you here almost exceeds belief."

After remaining some moments in deep silence, collecting and arranging his thoughts, the Pole replied. A conversation ensued, in so low a voice as to be only audible to themselves; from their attitudes and gestures it might be inferred that Ladislas was relating some tale of deep anguish, mixed with solemn and impressive adjurations, to which the Princess listened with a consenting tranquillizing sympathy.

They issued from the recess, walked up the colonnade, and entered a small temple that terminated it. From the centre of its airy dome hung a lighted alabaster lamp of a boat-like shape, beneath which a youthful female was seated alone sketching a range of moonlight hills that appeared between the columns. "Idalie," said the Princess, "I have brought you a new subject for your pencil—and such a subject, my love—one whose fame has already made him dear to your imagination; no less a person than the hero of Ostrolenka [4] and the Vistula. So call up one of those brightest, happiest moods of your genius, in which all suc-

---

4. At Ostrolenka, the Russian and Polish armies were in sight of one another. The destruction of the Poles seemed inevitable; not expecting the attack, their lines were not formed, and the Russians were triple in number, and advancing in the most perfect order. In this emergency, three hundred students from the University of Warsaw drew hastily up in a body, and, devoting themselves willingly to death, marched forward to meet the onset of the enemy. They were headed by a young man, who distinguished himself by the most exalted courage, and was the only one of their numbers who escaped. He stationed his band in a small wood that lay directly in the path of the Russians, and checked their progress for the space of three hours. Every tree of that wood now waves above a patriot's grave. In the meantime the Polish army formed, bore down, and gained a brilliant victory.

ceeds to you, and enrich my album with his likeness," spreading it before her.

It is difficult to refuse any request to a person who has just granted us an important favour. Ladislas suffered himself to be seated, and as soon as the Princess had quitted them, the gloom which had shadowed his brow at the names of Ostrolenka and the Vistula vanished. The surpassing beauty of the young artist would have changed the heaviest penance into a pleasure. She was lovely as one of Raffaelle's Madonnas; and, like them, there was a silent beauty in her presence that struck the most superficial beholder with astonishment and satisfaction. Her hair, of a golden and burnished brown (the colour of the autumnal foliage illuminated by the setting sun), fell in gauzy wavings round her face, throat, and shoulders.

Her small, clear forehead, gleaming with gentle thought; her curved, soft, and rosy lips; the delicate moulding of the lower part of the face, expressing purity and integrity of nature, were all perfectly Grecian. Her hazel eyes, with their arched lids and dark arrowy lashes, pierced the soul with their full and thrilling softness. She was clad in long and graceful drapery, white as snow; but, pure as this garment was, it seemed a rude disguise to the resplendent softness of the limbs it enfolded. The delicate light that gleamed from the alabaster lamp above them was a faint simile of the ineffable spirit of love that burned within Idaho's fair, transparent frame; and the one trembling, shining star of evening that palpitates responsively to happy lovers, never seemed more divine or more beloved than she did to Ladislas, as she sat there, now fixing a timid but attentive gaze upon his countenance, and then dropping it upon the paper before her.

And not alone for Ladislas was this hour the dawn of passionate love. The same spell was felt in the heart of Idalie. One moment their eyes met and glanced upon each other, the look of exalted, eternal love—mute, blessed, and inexpressible. Their lids fell and were raised no more. Rapture thrilled their breasts and swelled their full hearts; for, motionless, and in deep silence, as if every outward faculty were absorbed in reverence, they continued, each inwardly knowing, hearing, seeing nothing but the divine influence and attraction of the other.

I know not if the portrait was finished. I believe it was not. Noiselessly Idalie arose and departed to seek the Princess, and Ladislas followed. "Who is that lovely being? "inquired an English traveller some time afterward, pointing out Idalie from a group of ladies.

"A Polish girl—a *protégée* of mine," was the reply of the Princess; "a daughter of one of Kosciusko's unfortunate followers, who died here, poor and unknown. She has a great genius for drawing and painting, but she is so different in her nature from the generality of people, that I am afraid she will never get on in the world. All the family are wild and strange. There is a brother who they say is a complete ruffian; brave as a Pole and as unprincipled as an Italian! a villain quite varnished in picturesque, like one of your Lord Byron's *corsairs* and *giaours*. Then there is a younger sister; the most uncontrollable little creature, who chose to pretend my house was insupportable, and ran away into Calabria or Campagna, and set up as a *prima donna*. But these, to be sure, are the children of a second wife, an Italian; and Idalie, I must confess, has none of their lawlessness, but is remarkably gentle and steady."

Disgusted with this heartless conversation, which disturbed his ecstasy, Ladislas hastily quitted the Dashkhoff palace, and entered the Villa Reale, whose embowering trees promised solitude. Not one straggler of the gay crowds that frequent this luxurious garden from morning till midnight was now to be seen. With its straight walks buried in gloom and shadow; its stone fonts of sleeping water; its marble statues, its heaven-pointing obelisks, and its midnight air, it was silent as a deserted oratory, when the last strain of the vesper hymn has died away, the last taper has ceased to burn, the last censer has been flung, and both priests and worshippers have departed. Ladislas cast himself upon a stone seat in the ilex grove that skirts the margin of the bay.

"I dreamt not of love," he exclaimed; "I sought her not! I had renounced life and all its train of raptures, hopes, and joys. Cold, and void of every wish, the shadow of death lay upon my heart; suddenly she stood before me, lovely as an angel that heralds departed spirits to the kingdom of eternal bliss. Fearless, but mild, she poured the magic of her gaze upon my soul. I speak the word of the hour. She shall be mine—or I will die!"

Reclining in the ilex grove, Ladislas passed the remaining hours of that too short night, entranced in bliss, as if the bright form of his beloved were still shining beside him. Gradually every beauty of the wondrous and far-famed Bay of Naples impressed itself upon his attention. The broad and beamless moon sinking behind the tall elms of Posilippo; the broken starlight on the surface of the waves—their rippling sound as they broke at his feet; Sorrento's purple promontory, and the gentle wind that blew from it; the solitary grandeur of Capri's mountain-island rising out of the middle of the bay, a colossal sphinx guarding two baths of azure light; Vesuvius breathing its smoke, and flame, and sparks, in the cloudless ether;—all became mingled in inexplicable harmony with his newborn passion, and were indelibly associated with his recollection of that night.

The next morning Idalie was sketching in the Villa Reale. She had seated herself on the outside of a shady alley. Two persons passed behind her, and the childish petulant voice of one of them drew her attention. That voice, so sweet even in its impatience, certainly belonged to her fugitive sister. "It is she!" exclaimed Idalie, gliding swift as thought between the trees, and folding the speaker to her bosom. "Marietta—my dear little Marietta! at last you are come back again. *Cattivella!* now promise to stay with me. You know not how miserable I have been about you."

"No! I cannot promise anything of the kind," replied Marietta, playing with the ribands of her guitar. "I choose to have my liberty."

Idalie's arms sunk, and her eyes were cast upon the ground when she heard the cold and decided tone in which this refusal was pronounced. On raising the latter, they glanced upon the companion of her sister, and were filled with unconquerable emotion at discovering Ladislas, the elected of her heart.

"I met your sister here a few minutes ago," explained he, partaking her feelings; "and having been so fortunate the other day as to render her a slight service"—

"Oh yes," interrupted Marietta; "I sung for him a whole evening at Gaeta. It was a curious adventure. His carriage was overturned close to the inn. I had arrived there half an hour before, and was walking in an orange grove near the spot, and saw the accident happen, and heard him speak in Polish to his servant. My heart beat with joy. He looked wondrous melancholy. I thought it must be about his country, so I crept as softly as a mouse among the trees under his balcony, and sung him a salve-song in Polish. I improvised it on the spur of the moment. I do not very well recollect it, but it was about azure heavens, southern winds, myrtle and lemon blossoms, and the illustrious unfortunate: and it ought to have pleased him.

"Just as I had finished, out starts our blessed brother, Giorgio, from the inn, and began one of his most terrific bothers. Imagine how frightened I was, for I thought he was gone to Sicily with his regiment. However, they got him away, and I followed this stranger into his room, and sang to him the rest of the evening. All my best songs,—the '*Mio ben quando verra,*' '*Nina pazza per Amore,*' the '*All' armi*' of *Generali*; the '*Dolce cara patria,*' from *Tancredi*; the '*Deh calma,*' from *Otello*, all my whole stock I assure you." Thus rattled on Marietta; and then, as if her quick eye had already discovered the secret of their attachment, she added, with an arch smile, "but don't be frightened, Idalie, though his eyes filled with tears whilst I sung, as yours often do, not a word of praise did the Sarmatian bestow on me."

"Then return and live with me, dear Marietta, and I will praise you as much, and more than you desire."

"*Santa Maria del Piê di Grotto*! What a tiresome person you are, Idalie. When you have got an idea into your head, an earthquake would not get it out again. Have I not told you that I will not. If you knew the motive you would approve my resolution. I said I liked my liberty, and so forth; but that was not the reason of my flight. I do not choose to have anything to do with Giorgio and the Princess; for, believe me, dearest Idalie, disgraceful as my present mode of life seems to you, it is innocence itself compared with the crimes they were leading me into."

"Some suspicion of this did once cross my mind," her sister replied with a sigh, "but I rejected it as too horrible. Dear child, think no more about them. Do you not know that I have left the Princess house, and am living by myself in a little pavilion far up on the Strada Nuova. There you need not fear their molestations."

"Is not Giorgio then with you?"

"No; I have not seen him for some time. I doubt if he be in Naples."

"So Messer Giorgio, you have deceived me again. But I might have known that, for he never speaks a word of truth. Be assured, however, he is in Naples, for I caught a glimpse of him this morning, mounting the hill that leads to the barracks at Pizzofalcone, and he is as intimate with the Princess as ever, though she pretends to disown him. As for me, I am engaged at San Carlos; the writing is signed and sealed, and cannot be broken without forfeiting a heavy sum of money; otherwise I should be happy to live peacefully with you; for you know not, Idalie, all I have had to suffer; how sad and ill-treated I have been! how often pinched with want and hunger; and worse than that, when Giorgio takes it into his head to pursue me, and plants himself in the pit, fixing his horrible looks upon me as I sing! how many times I have rushed out of the theatre, and spent the nights in the great wide Maremma, beset by robbers, buffaloes, and wild boars, till I was almost mad with fear and bewilderment.

"There is a curse upon our family, I think. Did not our father once live in a splendid castle of his own, with a hundred retainers to wait upon him; and do you remember the miserable garret in which he died? But I cannot stay any longer. I am wanted at the rehearsal: so, farewell, dearest Idalie. Be you at least happy, and leave me to fulfil the evil destiny that hangs over our race."

"No! no!" exclaimed Ladislas, "that must not be—the writ-

454

ing must be cancelled,"—and then, with the affection and unreserve of a brother, he entered into their sentiments; with sweet and persuasive arguments over came their scruples of receiving a pecuniary obligation from him; and finally, taking Marietta by the hand, led her away to San Carlos, in order to cancel her engagement.

And in another hour it was cancelled. Marietta was once more free and joyful; and, affectionate as old friends, the three met again in the little pavilion, which was Idalie's home. It stood alone in a myrtle wood on the last of the green promontories which form the Strada Nuova, and separate the Bay of Naples from the Bay of Baia,—a lonely hermitage secluded from the noise and turmoil of the city, whose only visitors were the faint winds of morning and evening, the smiles of the fair Italian heaven, its wandering clouds, and, perchance, a solitary bird. From every part of the building you could see the Baian Ocean sparkling breathlessly beneath the sun; through the windows and the columns of the *portico* you beheld the mountains of the distant coast shining on, hour after hour, like amethysts in a thrilling vapour of purple transparent light, so ardent yet halcyon, so bright and unreal, a poet would have chosen it to emblem the radiant atmosphere that glows around elysian isles of eternal peace and joy.

Marietta soon left the building to join some fisher boys who were dancing the *tarantella* upon the beach below. Idalie took her drawing, which was her daily employment, and furnished her the means of subsistence, and Ladislas sat by her side. There was no sound of rolling carriages, no tramp of men and horse, no distant singing, no one speaking near; the wind awoke no rustling amid the leaves of the myrtle wood, and the wave died without a murmur on the shore. Ladislas deep but melodious voice alone broke the crystal silence of the noonday air.

Italy was around him, robed in two splendours of blue and green; but he was an exile, and the recollections of his native land thronged into his memory. During the three months it had taken him to effect his escape from Warsaw to Naples, his lips had been closed in silence, whilst his mind had been wrapt in the gloom of the dreadful images that haunted it. In Idalie's countenance there was that expression of innocence and sublimity of soul, of purity and strength, that excited the warmest admiration, and inspired sudden and deep confidence. She looked like some supernatural being that walks through the world, untouched by its corruptions; like one that unconsciously, yet with delight, confers pleasure and peace; and Ladislas felt that, in speaking to her of the dark sorrows of his country, they would lose their mortal weight and be resolved into beauty, by her sympathy.

In glowing terms he described the heroic struggle of Poland for liberty; the triumph and exultation that had filled every bosom during the few months they were free; the hardships and privations they had endured, the deeds of daring bravery of the men, the heroism it had awakened in the women; and then its fall—the return of the Russians; the horrible character of Russian despotism, its sternness and deceit, its pride and selfish ignorance; the loss of public and private integrity, the disbelief of good, the blighted, hopeless, joyless life endured by those whom it crushes beneath its servitude.

Thus passed the hours of the forenoon. Then Ladislas fixing his eyes upon the coast of Baia, and expressing at the same time his impatience to visit that ancient resort of heroes and of emperors, Idalie led the way by a small path down the hill to the beach. There they found a skiff, and, unmooring it from its rocky haven, embarked in it. It had been sweet to mark the passage of that light bark freighted with these happy lovers, when borne by its sails it swept through the little ocean-channel that lies between the beaked promontories of the mainland and the closing cliffs of the island of Nisida; and when with gentler motion it glided into the open expanse of the Bay of Baia, and cut its way through the translucent water, above the ruins of temples and palaces overgrown by seaweed, on which the rays of the sun were playing, creating a thousand rainbow hues, that varied with every wave that flowed over them.

In all that plane of blue light it was the only moving thing;

and as if it had been the child of the ocean that bore it, and the sun that looked down on it, it sped gaily along in their smiles past the fortress where Brutus and Cassius sought shelter after the death of Caesar; past the temples of Jupiter and Neptune; by the ruins of that castle in which three Romans once portioned out the world between them, to the Cumean hill that enshadows the beloved Linternum of Scipio Africanus, and in which he died.

The whole of this coast is a paradise of natural beauty, investing with its own loveliness the time-eaten wrecks with which it is strewn; the mouldering past is mingled with the vivid present; ruin and grey annihilation are decked in eternal spring. The woody windings of the shore reveal, in their deep recesses, the gleaming marble fragments of the abodes of ancient heroes; the *verdurous* hues of the promontories mingle with the upright columns of shattered temples, or clothe, with nature's voluptuous bloom, the pale funereal urns of departed gods; whilst the foliage and the inland fountains, and the breaking waves upon the shore, were murmuring around their woven minstrelsy of love and joy.

Earth, sea, and sky blazed like three gods, with tranquil but animated loveliness; with a splendour that did not dazzle—with a richness that could not satiate. The air on that beautiful warm coast was as a field of fragrance; the refreshing sea-breeze seemed to blow from Paradise, quickening the senses, and bringing to them the odour of a thousand unknown blossoms.

"What world is this?" exclaimed Ladislas in a tone of rapture that nearly answered its own question. "I could imagine I had entered an enchanted garden; four heavens surround me,—the one above; the pure element beneath me with its waves that shine and tremble as stars; the adorned earth that hangs over it; and the heaven of delight they create within my breast. 'Morning is here a rose, day a tulip, night a lily; evening is, like morning, again a rose, and life seems a choral-hymn of beautiful and glowing sentiments, that I go singing to myself as I wander along this perpetual path of flowers.'"

It was night ere they again reached the pavilion. It stood dark and deserted in the clear moonshine; the door was locked. After calling and knocking repeatedly without obtaining any answer, it became evident that Marietta had quitted the dwelling. In the first moment of surprise which this occurrence occasioned, they had not observed a written sheet of paper, of a large size, which lay unfolded and placed directly before the door, as if to attract attention. Idalie took it up and read the following lines, traced by Marietta:

> Oh, Idalie! but a few hours ago, how calm and secure we were in happiness—now danger and perhaps destruction is our portion. One chance yet remains; the moment you get this, persuade—not only persuade—but compel that adorable stranger to fly instantly from Naples. He is not safe here an instant longer. Do not doubt what I say, or his life may be the forfeit. How can I impress this on your mind. I would not willingly betray any one, but how else can I save him?
>
> Giorgio has been here. Oh! the frightful violence of that man. He raved like an insane person, and let fall such dark and bloody hints as opened worlds of horror to me. I am gone to discover what I can. I know his haunts, and his associates, and shall soon find out if there be any truth in what he threatens. I could not await your return, neither dare I leave the pavilion open. Who knows if, in the interval between my departure and your return, an assassin might not conceal himself within; and your first welcome be, to see the stranger fall lifeless at your feet. His every step is watched by spies armed for his destruction. I know not what to do—and yet it seems to me that my going may possibly avert the catastrophe.
>
> Marietta.

Ladislas listened to these lines unmoved; but the effect they produced on Idalie was dreadful. She gave implicit credence to them, and every word sounded as a knell. She lost all presence of mind; every reflection that might have taught her to avert the stroke she so much dreaded, was swallowed up in anguish, as if the deed that was to be consummated were already done. What task can be more difficult than to describe the overwhelming agony which heavy and unexpected misery produces. To have lived the day that Idalie had just lived—a day in which all the beauty of existence had been unveiled to its very depths; to have dreamt, as she had done, a dream of love that steeped her soul in divine and almost uncommunicable joy; and now to sink from this pinnacle of happiness into a black and lampless cavern, the habitation of death, whose spectral form and chilling spirit was felt through all the air!

This is but a feeble metaphor of the sudden transition from rapture to misery which Idalie experienced. She looked upon Ladislas, and beheld him bright and full of life; the roseate hues of health upon his cheek, his eyes beaming with peaceful joy, his noble countenance varying not in the least from that imperturbable self-possession which was its habitual expression. And as her imagination made present to her the fatal moment, when beneath the dagger of the assassin this adored being should sink bleeding, wounded, and then be forever lost in death, her blood rushed to her heart, a deadly pause ensued, from which she awoke in a bewildering mist of horror. Ladislas beheld her excess of emotion with pain, in which, however, all was not pain, for it was blended with that triumphant exultation that a lover ever feels when he for the first time becomes assured that he is beloved by the object of his love with an affection tender and intense as his own.

As soon as Idalie recovered some presence of mind, with passionate supplications she entreated Ladislas to leave her, to fly this solitary spot, and to seek safety amid the crowded streets of Naples. He would not hear of this; he gently remonstrated with her upon the unreasonableness of her terrors, urging how little probable it was that his passing *rencontre* with Giorgio at Gaeta could have awakened in him such a deadly spirit of revenge as Marietta represented. He viewed the whole thing lightly, attributing it either to the vivacity of Marietta's imagination, which had made her attach a monstrous import to some angry expressions of her brother, or looking upon it as a merry device which she had contrived in order to frighten them; and tranquillized Idalie by assurances that they would shortly see her wild sister return laughing, and full of glee at the success of her plot.

In this expectation two hours passed away, but still no Marietta appeared, and it had grown too late to seek another shelter without exposing Idalie to the slander of evil-minded people. They passed the rest of the night therefore in the *portico*, Idalie sometimes pale and breathless, with recurring fears, and sometimes calm and happy, as Ladislas poured forth his tale of passionate love. His feelings, on the contrary, were pure and unalloyed.

Where Idalio was, there was the whole universe to him; where she was not, there was only a formless void. He had an insatiable thirst for her presence, which only grew intenser with the enjoyment of its own desire; and he blessed the fortunate occurrence that prolonged his bliss during hours which otherwise would have been spent pining in absence from her. No other considerations intruded. Blessings kindled within his eyes as he gazed upon that lovely countenance and faultless form, and angels might have envied his happiness.

Morning came, bright and serene; the sun arose, the ocean and the mountains again resumed their magic splendour; the myrtle woods and every minuter bloom of the garden shone out beneath the sun, and the whole earth was a happy form made perfect by the power of light. They recollected that they had promised to join the Princess Dashkhoff, and a large party of her friends, at eight o'clock, in an excursion to Pæstum. The point of meeting was the shore of the Villa Reale, where the numerous guests were to embark in a steamer which had been engaged for the occasion. In Idalie's present homeless and uncertain condition, this plan offered some advantages.

It would enable them to pass the day in each other's society under the auspices of the Princess, and it was to be hoped that on their return the mystery of Marietta's disappearance would be unravelled, and Idalie find her home once more open to her. They had scarcely settled to go, ere one of those horse *calessini* which ply in the streets of Naples was seen coming towards them. Its driver, a ragged boy, sat on the shaft, singing as he drove; another urchin, all in tatters, stood as lacquey behind, and between them sat Marietta; the paleness of fear was on her cheeks, and her eyes had the staggered, affrighted look of one who has gazed upon some appalling horror. She hastily descended, and bade the *calessino* retire to some distance, and await further orders.

"Why is he yet here?" said she to her sister. "You foolish, blind Idalie, why did you not mind my letter?—too proud, I suppose, to obey any but yourself; but mark, you would not hear my warnings we shall lose him, and you will feel them in your heart's core."

She then, with all the violent gesticulation of an Italian, threw herself at the feet of Ladislas, and with a countenance that expressed her own full conviction in what she said, besought him to fly instantly, not only from Naples, but from Italy, for his life would never be safe in that land of assassins and traitors. With entreaties almost as violent as her own, Ladislas and Idalie urged her to explain, but this only threw her into a new frenzy; she declared the peril was too urgent to admit of explanation—every moment was precious—another hour's stay in Naples would be his death.

The situation of Ladislas was a curious one. He had served in the Russian campaigns against Persia and Turkey, and had been there daily exposed to the chances of destruction; in the late struggle between Poland and Russia, he had performed actions of such determined and daring bravery as had made his name a glory to his countrymen, and a terror to their enemies. In all these exploits he had devoted himself so unreservedly to death, that his escape was considered as a miraculous inter position of Heaven.

It was not to be expected that this Mars in a human form, this Achilles who had braved death in a thousand shapes, should now consent to fly before the uplifted ringer and visionary warnings of a dream-sick girl; for such Marietta appeared to him to be. He pitied her sufferings, endeavoured to soothe her, but asserted he had seen no reason that could induce him to quit Naples.

A full quarter of an hour elapsed before an explanation could be wrung from Marietta. The chaos that reigned in her mind may easily be imagined. She had become possessed of a secret which involved the life of two persons. Ladislas refused to save himself unless she revealed what might place her brother's life in jeopardy. Whichever way she looked, destruction closed the view. Nature had bestowed on her a heart exquisitely alive to the sufferings of others; a mind quick in perceiving the nicest lines of moral rectitude, and strenuous in endeavouring to act up to its perceptions.

Any deviations in her conduct from these principles had been the work of a fate that, strong and fierce as a tempest, had bent down her weak youth like a reed beneath its force. She had once loved Giorgio; he had played with and caressed her in infancy—with the fond patronage of an elder brother had procured her the only indulgences her orphaned childhood had ever known. Fraternal love called loudly on her not to endanger his life; gratitude as loudly called on her not to allow her bene-factor to become his victim. This last idea was too horrible to be endured. The present moment is ever all-powerful with the young, and Marietta related what she knew.

Well might the poor child be wild and disordered. She had passed the night in the catacombs of San Gennaro, under Capo di Monte. In these subterranean galleries were held the nightly meetings of the band of desperate *bravi* of whom Giorgio was in secret the chief. The entrance to the catacombs is in a deserted vineyard, and is overgrown by huge aloes; rooted in stones and sharp rocks, they lift their thorny leaves above the opening, and conceal it effectually. A solitary fig-tree that grows near renders the spot easily recognisable by those already acquainted with the secret.

The catacombs themselves are wide winding caves, the buri-al-place of the dead of past ages. Piles of human bones, white and bleached by time, are heaped along the rocky sides of these caverns. In one of these walks, whilst they were friends, Giorgio had shown the place to Marietta. In those days he feared not to entrust his mysterious way of life to her; for although in all common concerns she was wild and untractable, yet in all that touched the interests of those few whom she loved, Marietta was silent and reserved as Epicharis herself. The menaces Giorgio let fall in his visit on the preceding forenoon had excited her highest alarm, and she determined, at any risk, to learn the extent of the danger that hung over the stranger.

After waiting in vain for Idalie's return till the close of evening, she had hastened to Capo di Monte, entered the catacombs alone, and, concealed behind a pile of bones, had awaited the arrival of the confederates. They assembled at midnight. Their first subject of consultation was the stranger. Giorgio acquainted them with his history, which he told them had been communicated to him that very morning by a Russian lady of high rank, who had likewise charged him with the business he had to unfold to them. He described Ladislas as a fugitive, unprotected by any Government; he bore about his person certain papers which had been found in the palace of Warsaw, and were the confidential communications of the Russian Autocrat to his brother the Viceroy of Poland, and were of such a nature as to rouse all Europe against their writer.

These papers had been entrusted to Ladislas, whose intention was to proceed to Paris and publish them there. Private business, however, of the greatest importance, had forced him to visit Naples first. The Russian Government had traced him to Naples, and had empowered a certain Russian lady to take any step, or go any lengths, in order to obtain these papers from Ladislas. This lady had made Giorgio her emissary; her name he carefully concealed, but Marietta averred, from his description, that it could be no other than the Princess Dashkhoff.

After much consulting among the band, the assassination of the Pole had been decided upon. This seemed to be the only sure method; for he carried the papers ever about his person, was distinguished for his bravery, and if openly attacked would resist to the last. Giorgio was no stickler in the means he employed, and told his companions he had the less reason to be so in this case, as he had received assurances from the highest quarter that his crime should go unpunished, and the reward be enormous. Ladislas was almost unknown in Naples; the Government would not interest itself for a fugitive, without passport, country or name; and what friends had he here to inquire into the circumstances of his destruction, or to interest themselves to avenge it?

Such was Marietta's tale, and Ladislas instantly acknowledged the necessity of flight. He was too well acquainted with Russian perfidy to doubt that even a lady of a rank so distinguished as the Princess Dashkhoif might be induced to undertake as foul a task as that attributed to her by Marietta. The worldly and artificial manners of this lady, in an Italian or a Frenchwoman, would only have resulted from habits of intrigue; but a Russian, unaccustomed to look on human life as sacred, taught by the Government of her own country that cruelty and treachery are venial offences, wholly destitute of a sense of honour, concealed, under such an exterior, vices the most odious, and a callousness to guilt unknown in more civilised lands. Ladislas knew this; and he knew that the badness of the Neapolitan Government afforded scope for crime, which could not exist elsewhere; and he felt that on every account it were better to withdraw himself immediately from the scene of danger.

While musing on these things, Idalie's beseeching eyes were eloquent in imploring him to fly. He consented; but a condition was annexed to his consent, that Idalie should share his flight. He urged his suit with fervour. It were easy for them on a very brief notice to seek the young lady's confessor, induce him to bestow on them the nuptial benediction, and thus to sanctify their departure together. Marietta seconded the lover's entreaties, and Idalie, blushing and confused, could only reply,—

"My accompanying you would but increase your danger, and facilitate the *bravo's* means of tracing you. How could I get a passport? How leave this place?"

"I have a plan for all," replied Ladislas; and he then related that the *Sully* steam-packet lay in the harbour of Naples, ready to sail on the shortest notice; he would engage that for their conveyance, and so speedily bid *adieu* to the shores of Naples, and all its perils.

"But that boat," exclaimed Idalie, "is the very one engaged by the Princess for the excursion to Pæstum."

This, for a time, seemed to disarrange their schemes, but they considered that no danger could happen to Ladislas while one of a party of pleasure with the Princess, who from this act of his would be quite unsuspicious of his intended departure. At night, upon their return from Pæstum, when the rest of the party should have disembarked at Naples, Ladislas and Idalie would remain on board, and the vessel immediately commence its voyage for France.

This plan thus assumed a very feasible appearance, while Ladislas, in accents of fond reproach, asked Idalie wherefore she refused to share his fortunes, and accompany him in his journey; and Marietta, clapping her hands exclaimed, "She consents! she consents! Do not ask any more, she has already yielded. We will all return to Naples. Ladislas shall go immediately to seek out the captain of the *Sully*, and arrange all with him; while, without loss of time, we will proceed to the convent of Father Basil, and get everything ready by the time Ladislas shall join us, which must be with as much speed as he can contrive."

Idalie silently acquiesced in this arrangement, and Ladislas kissed her hand with warm and overflowing gratitude. They now contrived to stow themselves in the little *calessino*, and as they proceeded on their way, Ladislas said: "We seem to have forgotten the future destiny of our dear Marietta all this time. The friendless condition in which we shall leave her fills me with anxiety. She is the preserver of my life, and we are both under the deepest obligations to her. What shall you do, Marietta, when we are gone? "

"Fear not for me," exclaimed the wild girl; "it is necessary

I should remain behind to arrange those things which Idalie's sudden departure will leave in sad disorder; but you will see me soon in Paris, for how can I exist apart from my sister?"

When near to Naples, Ladislas alighted from the *calessino*, and directed his steps towards the port, while the fair girls proceeded on their way to the convent. What the bashful, conscious Idalie would have done without her sister's help, it is difficult to guess. Marietta busied herself about all; won over the priest to the sudden marriage, contrived to put up articles of dress for the fair bride's journey, and thinking of everything, seemed the guardian angel of the lovers. Ladislas arrived at the convent; he had been successful with the master of the steam-packet, and all was prepared.

Marietta heard this from his own lips, and carried the happy news to Idalie. He did not see her till they met at the altar, where, kneeling before the venerable priest, they were united forever. And now time, as it sped on, gave them no moment to indulge their various and overpowering feelings. Idalie embraced her sister again and again, and entreating her to join them speedily in Paris, made her promise to write, and then, escorted by her husband, proceeded to the *Sully*, on board of which most of the party were already assembled.

The steamer proceeded on its course. Farewell to Naples!- that elysian city, as the poet justly calls it; that favourite of sea and land and sky. The hills that surround it smooth their rugged summits, and descend into gentle slopes and opening denies, to receive its buildings and habitations. Temples, domes, and marble palaces are ranged round the crescent form of the bay, and above them arise dark masses, and wooded clefts, and fair gardens, whose trees are ever vernal. Before it the mighty sea binds its wild streams, and smoothes them into gentlest waves, as they kiss the silver, pebbly shore, and linger with dulcet murmur around the deep-based promontories. The sky—who has not heard of the Italian sky?—one intense diffusion, one serene omnipresence, forever smiling above the boundless sea, and forever bending in azure mirth over the flowing outlines of the distant mountains.

They first passed Castel-a-Mare, and then the abrupt promontories on which Sorrento and ancient Amalfi are situated. The sublimity and intense loveliness of the scene wrapt in delight each bosom. The hills, covered with ilex, dark laurel, and bright-leaved myrtle, were mirrored in the pellucid waves, which the lower branches caressed and kissed as the winds waved them. Behind arose other hills, also covered with wood; and, more distant, forming the grand background, was sketched the huge ridge of lofty Apennines. Still proceeding on their way to Pæstum, they exchanged the rocky beach for a low and dreary shore.

The dusky mountains retired inland, and leaving a waste—the abode of malaria, and the haunt of robbers—the landscape assumed a gloomy magnificence, in place of the romantic and picturesque loveliness which had before charmed their eyes. Ladislas leaned from the side of the vessel, and gazed upon the beauty of nature with sentiments too disturbed for happiness. He was annoyed by the unpropitious presence of the idle and the gay. He saw Idalie in the midst of them, and did not even wish to join her while thus situated. He shrank into himself, and tried, forgetting the immediate discomforts of his position, to think only of that paradise into which love had led him, to compensate for his patriotic sorrows. He strove patiently to endure the tedious hours of this never-ending day, during which he must play a false part, and see his bride engaged by others.

While his attention was thus occupied, the voice of the Princess Dashkhoff startled him, and, looking up, he wondered how a face that seemed so bland, and a voice that spoke so fair, could hide so much wickedness and deceit. As the hours passed on, his situation became irksome in the extreme. Once or twice he drew near Idalie, and tried to disengage her from the crowd; but each time he saw the Princess watching him stealthily, while his young bride, with feminine prudence, avoided every opportunity of conversing apart with him.

Ladislas could ill endure this. He began to fancy that he had a thousand things to say, and that their mutual safety depended on his being able to communicate them to her. He wrote a few lines hastily on the back of a letter with a pencil, conjuring her to find some means of affording him a few minutes conversation, and telling her that if this could not be done before, he should take occasion, while the rest of the company were otherwise occupied, to steal from them that evening to the larger temple, and there await her joining him, for that everything depended on his being able to speak to her. He scarcely knew what he meant as he wrote this; but, driven by contradiction and impatience, and desirous of learning exactly how she meant to conduct herself on the Princess's disembarking at Naples, it seemed to him of the last importance that his request should be complied with. He was folding the paper when the Princess was at his side, and addressed him.

"A sonnet, Count Ladislas; surely a poetic imagination inspires you; may I not see it?"

And she held out her hand. Taken unaware, Ladislas darted at her a look which made her step back trembling and in surprise. Was she discovered? The idea was fraught with terror. But Ladislas, perceiving the indiscretion of his conduct, masked his sensations with a smile, and replied: "They are words of a Polish song, which I wish Idalie to translate for the amusement of your friends;" and, stepping forward, he gave Idalie the paper, and made his request. All pressed to know what the song was. Idalie glanced at the writing, and, changing colour, was scarcely able to command her voice to make such an excuse as was rendered necessary. She said that it required time and thought, and that she could not at that moment comply; then crushing the paper between her trembling fingers, began confusedly to talk of something else. The company interchanged smiles, but even the Princess only suspected some lover-like compliment to her protégée.

"Nay," she said, "we must at least know the subject of these verses. What is it? tell us, I entreat you."

"Treachery," said Ladislas, unable to control his feelings. The Princess became ashy pale; all her self-possession fled, and she turned from the searching glance of the Pole with sickness of heart.

They were now drawing near their destination. Idalie, grasping the paper, longed to read it before they should reach the shore. She tried to recede from the party, and Ladislas, watching her movements, in order to facilitate her designs, entered into conversation with the Princess. He had effectually roused her fears and her curiosity; and she eagerly seized the opportunity which he offered her of conversing with him, endeavouring to find out whether he indeed suspected anything, or whether her own guilty conscience suggested the alarm with which his strange expression had filled her.

Ladislas thus contrived to engross her entire attention, and led her insensibly towards the stern of the vessel; and as they leant over its side, and gazed on the waters beneath, Idalie was effectually relieved from all observation. She now disengaged herself from the rest of the party, and, walking forward, read the lines pencilled by Ladislas. Then, terrified by the secret they contained, she tore the paper, as if fearful that its contents might be guessed, and was about to throw the fragments into the sea, when she perceived the position of the Princess and Ladislas, and was aware that the lady's quick eye would soon discern the floating scraps as the boat passed on.

Idalie feared the least shadow of danger, so she retreated from the vessel's side, but still anxious to get rid of the perilous papers, she determined to throw them into the hold. She approached it, and looked down. Had the form of a serpent met her eye, she had not been more horror-struck. A shriek hovered on her lips, but with a strong effort she repressed it, and, staggering on, leant against the mast, trembling and aghast.

She could not be deceived; it was Giorgio's dark and scowling eye that she had encountered—his sinister countenance, upturned, could not be mistaken. Was danger, then, so near, so pressing, or so inevitable? How could she convey the fatal intelligence to her husband, and put him on his guard? She remembered his written request, with which she had previously determined in prudence not to comply. But it would now afford her an opportunity, should no other offer, of informing him whom she had seen.

Thus perfidy, hate, and fear possessed the hearts of these human beings, who, had a cursory observer seen them as they glided over that sea of beauty, beneath the azure heaven, along that enchanted shore, attended by every luxury, waited on by every obvious blessing of life—he would have imagined that they had been selected from the world for the enjoyment of perfect happiness. But sunny sky and laughing sea appeared to Idalie only as the haunt and resort of tigers and serpents; a dark mist seemed to blot the splendour of the sky, as the guilty souls of her fellow-creatures cast their deforming shadows over its brightness.

They had now arrived close on the low shore, and horses and two or three light open carriages were at the water's edge to convey them to the temples. They landed. Ladislas presented himself to hand Idalie across the plank from the vessel to the beach. "Yes?"—he asked her in a voice of entreaty, as he pressed her hand. She softly returned the pressure, and the word "Beware" trembled on her lips, when the young Englishman who had before admired her, and had endeavoured to engross her attention the whole day, was again at her side, to tell her that the Princess was waiting for her in her carriage, and entreated her not to delay.

The party proceeded to where those glorious relics stand, between the mountains and the sea, rising from the waste and barren soil, alone on the wide and dusky shore. A few sheep grazed at the base of the columns, and two or three wild-eyed men, clothed in garments of undressed sheepskin, loitered about. Exclamations of wonder and delight burst from all, while Ladislas, stealing away to the more distant ruin, gladly escaped from the crowd, to indulge in lonely reverie.

"What is man in his highest glory?" he thought. "Had we burst the bonds of Poland; and had she, in her freedom, emulated the magical achievements of Greece; nevertheless when time, with insidious serpent windings, had dragged its length through a few more centuries, the monuments we had erected would have fallen like these, and our monuments a new Pæstum have existed merely to excite idle wonder and frivolous curiosity!"

Ladislas was certainly in no good humour while he thus vented his spleen; but was annoyed by two circumstances, sufficient to irritate a young philosopher: he beheld a scene, whose majestic beauty filled his soul with sensibility and awe, in the midst of a crowd of pretenders, more intent on the prospect of their picnic dinner, than on regarding the glories of art; and he saw his bride, surrounded by strangers, engrossed by their conversation and flattery, and unable to interchange one word or look of confidence with him. He sighed for the hours passed under the *portico* of Idalie's solitary pavilion, and the near prospect of their voyage did not reconcile him to the present; for his soul was disturbed by the necessity of interchanging courtesies with his enemy, and haunted by images of treacherous attempts, from which his valour could not protect him.

It had been arranged that the party should dine at the archbishop's palace, and not embark again until ten o clock, when the moon would rise. After a couple of hours spent among the ruins, the servants informed them that their repast was ready; it was now nearly six o clock, and after they had dined, more than two hours must elapse before they could depart. Night had fallen on the landscape, and the darkness did not invite even the most romantic to wander again among the ruins; the Princess, eager to provide for the amusement of her guests, contrived to discover a violin, a flute, and a pipe, and with the assistance of this music, which in the hands of Italian rustics was as true to time and expression as if Weippert himself had presided, they commenced dancing.

Idalie's hand was sought by the Englishman; she looked round the room, Ladislas was not there; he had doubtless repaired to the temple to wait for her, and ignorant of the presence of Giorgio, wholly unsuspicious, and off his guard, to what dangers might he not be exposed? Her blood ran cold at the thought; she decidedly refused to dance, and perceiving the Princess whirling round in a waltz, she hastily quitted the house, and hurried along over the grass towards the ruins. When she first emerged into the night, the scene seemed wrapped in impenetrable darkness, but the stars shed their faint rays, and in a few moments she began to distinguish objects, and as she drew near the temple, she saw a man's form moving slowly among the columns; she did not doubt that it was her husband, wrapped in his cloak, awaiting her.

She was hurrying towards him, when, leaning against one of the pillars, she saw Ladislas himself, and the other, at the same moment, exchanging his stealthy pace for a tiger-like spring. She saw a dagger flashing in his hand; she darted forward to arrest his arm, and the blow descended on her. With a faint shriek, she fell on the earth, when Ladislas turned and closed with the assassin; a mortal struggle ensued; already had Ladislas wrested the *poignard* from his grasp, when the villain drew another knife. Ladislas warded off the blow, and plunged his own stiletto in the *bravo's* breast; he fell to earth with a heavy groan, and then the silence of the tomb rested on the scene; the white robe of Idalie, who lay fainting on the ground, directed Ladislas to her side. He raised her up in speechless agony, as he beheld the blood which stained her dress; but by this time she had recovered from her swoon; she assured him her wound was slight, that it was nothing; but again sank into his arms insensible.

In a moment his plan was formed; ever eager and impetuous, he executed it ere any second thought could change it. He had before resolved not to rejoin the party in the archbishop's palace, but after his interview with Idalie, to hasten on board the steamboat; he had therefore ordered his horse to be saddled, had led it to the temple, and fastened it to one of the columns. He lifted the senseless Idalie carefully in his arms, mounted his horse, and turning his steps from the lighted and noisy palace, wound his way to the lonely shore, where he found the captain and his crew already preparing for their homeward voyage.

With their help Idalie was taken on board, and Ladislas gave orders for the instant heaving of the anchor, and their immediate departure. The captain asked for the rest of the company. "They return by land," said Ladislas. As he spoke the words, he felt a slight sensation of remorse, remembering the difficulty they would have to get there; and how, during the darkness of night, they might fear to proceed on their journey on a tract of country infested by *banditti*; but the senseless and pale form of Idalie dissipated these thoughts: to arrive at Naples, to procure assistance for her, and then if, as he hoped, her wound was slight, to continue their voyage before the Princess Dashkhoif's return, were motives too paramount to allow him to hesitate.

The captain of the *Sully* asked no more questions; the anchor was weighed; and in the silver light of the moon, they stood off from the shore, and made their swift way back to Naples. They had not gone far before the care of Ladislas revived his fair bride. Her wound was in her arm, and had merely grazed the skin. Terror for her husband, horror for the mortal strife which had endangered his life, had caused her to faint more than pain or loss of blood. She bound up her own arm; and then, as there appeared no necessity for medical aid, Ladislas revoked his orders for returning to Naples, but stretching out at once to sea, they began their voyage to Marseilles.

Meanwhile, during a pause in the dance, the absence of Ladislas and Idalie was observed by the feasters in the archbishop's palace. It excited some few sarcasms, which as it continued grew more bitter. The Princess Dashkhoff joined in these, and yet she could not repress the disquietude of her heart. Had Ladislas alone been absent, her knowledge of the presence of Giorgio, and his designs, had sufficiently explained its cause and its duration to her; but that Idalie also should not be found might bring a witness to the crime committed, and discover her own guilty share in the deed of blood perpetrated at her instigation. At length the rising of the moon announced the hour when they were to repair to the shore. The horses and carriages were brought to the door, and then it was found that the steed of Ladislas was missing.

"But the Signora Idalie, had she not provided herself with a palfrey?" asked the Englishman, sneering. They were now about to mount, when it was proposed to take a last look of the temples by moonlight. The Princess opposed this, but vainly; her conscience made her voice faint, and took from her the usual decision of her manner; so she walked on silently, half fearful that her foot might strike against some object of terror, and at every word spoken by the party, anticipating an exclamation of horror; the fitful moonbeams seemed to disclose here and there ghastly countenances and mangled limbs, and the dew of night appeared to her excited imagination as the slippery moisture of the life-blood of her victim.

They had scarcely entered the temple, when a peasant brought the news that the steamboat was gone; he led Ladislas horse, who had put the bridle into the man's hands on embarking; and the fellow declared that the fainting Idalie was his companion. Terror at the prospect of their dark ride, indignation at the selfish proceeding of the lovers, raised every voice against them; and the Princess, whom conscience had before made the most silent, hearing that the Pole was alive and safe, was now loudest and most bitter in her remarks.

As they were thus all gathered together in dismay, debating what was to be done, and the Princess Dashkhoff in no gentle terms railing at the impropriety and ingratitude of Idalie's behaviour, and declaring that Poles alone could conduct themselves with such mingled deceit and baseness, a figure all bloody arose from the ground at her feet, and as the moon cast its pale rays on his yet paler countenance, she recognised Giorgio. The ladies shrieked, the men rushed towards him, while the Princess, desiring the earth to open and swallow her, stood transfixed, as by a spell, gazing on the dying man in terror and despair.

"He has escaped, lady," said Giorgio; "Ladislas has escaped your plots, and I am become their victim." He fell as he spoke these words, and when the Englishman drew near to raise, and if possible assist him, he found that life had entirely flown.

Thus ended the adventures of the Pole at Naples. The Princess returned in her *calèche* alone, for none would bear her com-

474

pany; the next day she left Naples, and was on her way to Russia, where her crime was unknown, except to those who had been accomplices in it. Marietta spread the intelligence of her sister's marriage, and thus entirely cleared Idalie's fair fame; and quitting Italy soon after, joined the happy Ladislas and his bride at Paris.

On Ghosts

I look for ghosts—but none will force
Their way to me; 'tis falsely said
That there was ever intercourse
Between the living and the dead.
> —Wordsworth

What a different earth do we inhabit from that on which our forefathers dwelt! The *antediluvian* world, strode over by mammoths, preyed upon by the *megatherion*, and peopled by the offspring of the Sons of God, is a better type of the earth of Homer, Herodotus, and Plato, than the hedged-in cornfields and measured hills of the present day. The globe was then encircled by a wall which paled in the bodies of men, whilst their feathered thoughts soared over the boundary; it had a brink, and in the deep profound which it overhung, men's imaginations, eagle-winged, dived and flew, and brought home strange tales to their believing auditors.

Deep caverns harboured giants; cloud-like birds cast their shadows upon the plains; while far out at sea lay islands of bliss, the fair paradise of Atlantis or El Dorado sparkling with untold jewels. Where are they now? The Fortunate Isles have lost the glory that spread a halo round them; for who deems himself nearer to the golden age, because he touches at the Canaries on his voyage to India? Our only riddle is the rise of the Niger; the interior of New Holland, our only *terra incognita;* and our sole mare *incognitum*, the north-west passage.

But these are tame wonders, lions in leash; we do not invest

476

Mungo Park, or the Captain of the Hecla, with divine attributes; no one fancies that the waters of the unknown river bubble up from hell's fountains, no strange and weird power is supposed to guide the iceberg, nor do we fable that a stray pickpocket from Botany Bay has found the gardens of the Hesperides within the circuit of the Blue Mountains.

What have we left to dream about? The clouds are no longer the charioted servants of the sun, nor does he any more bathe his glowing brow in the bath of Thetis; the rainbow has ceased to be the messenger of the Gods, and thunder longer their awful voice, warning man of that which is to come. We have the sun which has been weighed and measured, but not understood; we have the assemblage of the planets, the congregation of the stars, and the yet unshackled ministration of the winds:—such is the list of our ignorance.

Nor is the empire of the imagination less bounded in its own proper creations, than in those which were bestowed on it by the poor blind eyes of our ancestors. What has become of enchantresses with their palaces of crystal and dungeons of palpable darkness? What of fairies and their wands? What of witches and their familiars? and, last, what of ghosts, with beckoning hands and fleeting shapes, which quelled the soldier's brave heart, and made the murderer disclose to the astonished noon the veiled work of midnight? These which were realities to our forefathers, in our wiser age—

—*Characterless are grated*
To dusty nothing.

Yet is it true that we do not believe in ghosts? There used to be several traditionary tales repeated, with their authorities, enough to stagger us when we consigned them to that place where that is which "is as though it had never been." But these are gone out of fashion. Brutus's dream has become a deception of his over-heated brain, Lord Lyttleton's vision is called a cheat; and one by one these inhabitants of deserted houses, moonlight glades, misty mountain tops, and midnight churchyards, have been ejected from their immemorial seats, and small thrill is felt when the dead majesty of Denmark blanches the cheek and unsettles the reason of his philosophic son.

But do none of us believe in ghosts? If this question be read at noonday, when—

Every little corner, nook, and hole,
Is penetrated with the insolent light—

at such a time derision is seated on the features of my reader. But let it be twelve at night in a lone house; take up, I beseech you, the story of the Bleeding Nun; or of the Statue, to which the bridegroom gave the wedding ring, and she came in the dead of night to claim him, tall, and cold; or of the Grandsire, who with shadowy form and breathless lips stood over the couch and kissed the foreheads of his sleeping grandchildren, and thus doomed them to their fated death; and let all these details be assisted by solitude, flapping curtains, rushing wind, a long and dusky passage, an half open door—O, then truly, another answer may be given, and many will request leave to sleep upon it, before they decide whether there be such a thing as a ghost in the world, or out of the world, if that phraseology be more spiritual. What is the meaning of this feeling?

For my own part, I never saw a ghost except once in a dream. I feared it in my sleep; I awoke trembling, and lights and the speech of others could hardly dissipate my fear. Some years ago I lost a friend, and a few months afterwards visited the house where I had last seen him. It was deserted, and though in the midst of a city, its vast halls and spacious apartments occasioned the same sense of loneliness as if it had been situated on an uninhabited heath. I walked through the vacant chambers by twilight, and none save I awakened the echoes of their pavement.

The far mountains (visible from the upper windows) had lost their tinge of sunset; the tranquil atmosphere grew leaden coloured as the golden stars appeared in the firmament; no wind ruffled the shrunk-up river which crawled lazily through the deepest channel of its wide and empty bed; the chimes of the

Ave Maria had ceased, and the bell hung moveless in the open belfry: beauty invested a reposing world, and awe was inspired by beauty only. I walked through the rooms filled with sensations of the most poignant grief. He had been there; his living frame had been caged by those walls, his breath had mingled with that atmosphere, his step had been on those stones, I thought:—the earth is a tomb, the gaudy sky a vault, we but walking corpses. The wind rising in the east rushed through the open casements, making them shake;—methought, I heard, I felt—I know not what—but I trembled.

To have seen him but for a moment, I would have knelt until the stones had been worn by the impress, so I told myself, and so I knew a moment after, but then I trembled, awestruck and fearful. Wherefore? There is something beyond us of which we are ignorant. The sun drawing up the vaporous air makes a void, and the wind rushes in to fill it,—thus beyond our soul's ken there is an empty space; and our hopes and fears, in gentle gales or terrific whirlwinds, occupy the vacuum; and if it does no more, it bestows on the feeling heart a belief that influences do exist to watch and guard us, though they be impalpable to the coarser faculties.

I have heard that when Coleridge was asked if he believed in ghosts,—he replied that he had seen too many to put any trust in their reality; and the person of the most lively imagination that I ever knew echoed this reply. But these were not real ghosts (pardon, unbelievers, my mode of speech) that they saw; they were shadows, phantoms unreal; that while they appalled the senses, yet carried no other feeling to the mind of others than delusion, and were viewed as we might view an optical deception which we see to be true with our eyes, and know to be false with our understandings.

I speak of other shapes. The returning bride, who claims the fidelity of her betrothed; the murdered man who shakes to remorse the murderer's heart; ghosts that lift the curtains at the foot of your bed as the clock chimes one; who rise all pale and ghastly from the churchyard and haunt their ancient abodes;

who, spoken to, reply; and whose cold unearthly touch makes the hair stand stark upon the head; the true old-fashioned, fore-telling, flitting, gliding ghost,—who has seen such a one?

I have known two persons who at broad daylight have owned that they believed in ghosts, for that they had seen one. One of these was an Englishman, and the other an Italian. The former had lost a friend he dearly loved, who for awhile appeared to him nightly, gently stroking his cheek and spreading a serene calm over his mind. He did not fear the appearance, although he was somewhat awestricken as each night it glided into his chamber, and,

Ponsi del letto insula sponda manca.
[placed itself on the left side of the bed]

This visitation continued for several weeks, when by some accident he altered his residence, and then he saw it no more. Such a tale may easily be explained away;—but several years had passed, and he, a man of strong and virile intellect, said that "he had seen a ghost."

The Italian was a noble, a soldier, and by no means addicted to superstition: he had served in Napoleon's armies from early youth, and had been to Russia, had fought and bled, and been rewarded, and he unhesitatingly, and with deep relief, recounted his story.

This Chevalier, a young, and (somewhat a miraculous incident) a gallant Italian, was engaged in a duel with a brother officer, and wounded him in the arm. The subject of the duel was frivolous; and distressed therefore at its consequences he attended on his youthful adversary during his consequent illness, so that when the latter recovered they became firm and dear friends. They were quartered together at Milan, where the youth fell desperately in love with the wife of a musician, who disdained his passion, so that it preyed on his spirits and his health; he absented himself from all amusements, avoided all his brother officers, and his only consolation was to pour his love-sick plaints into the ear of the Chevalier, who strove in vain to inspire him either with indifference towards the fair disdainer, or to inculcate lessons of fortitude and heroism.

As a last resource he urged him to ask leave of absence; and to seek, either in change of scene, or the amusement of hunting, some diversion to his passion. One evening the youth came to the Chevalier, and said, "Well, I have asked leave of absence, and am to have it early tomorrow morning, so lend me your fowling-piece and cartridges, for I shall go to hunt for a fortnight."

The Chevalier gave him what he asked; among the shot there were a few bullets. "I will take these also," said the youth, "to secure myself against the attack of any wolf, for I mean to bury myself in the woods."

Although he had obtained that for which he came, the youth still lingered. He talked of the cruelty of his lady, lamented that she would not even permit him a hopeless attendance, but that she inexorably banished him from her sight, "so that," said he, "I have no hope but in oblivion." At length he rose to depart. He took the Chevalier's hand and said, "You will see her tomorrow, you will speak to her, and hear her speak; tell her, I entreat you, that our conversation tonight has been concerning her, and that her name was the last that I spoke."

"Yes, yes," cried the Chevalier, "I will say anything you please; but you must not talk of her any more, you must forget her." The youth embraced his friend with warmth, but the latter saw nothing more in it than the effects of his affection, combined with his melancholy at absenting himself from his mistress, whose name, joined to a tender farewell, was the last sound that he uttered.

When the Chevalier was on guard that night, he heard the report of a gun. He was at first troubled and agitated by it, but afterwards thought no more of it, and when relieved from guard went to bed, although he passed a restless, sleepless night.

Early in the morning someone knocked at his door. It was a soldier, who said that he had got the young officer's leave of absence, and had taken it to his house; a servant had admitted him, and he had gone up stairs, but the room door of the officer was locked, and no one answered to his knocking, but something oozed through from under the door that looked like blood. The Chevalier, agitated and frightened at this account, hurried to his friend's house, burst open the door, and found him stretched on the ground—he had blown out his brains, and the body lay a headless trunk, cold, and stiff.

The shock and grief which the Chevalier experienced in consequence of this catastrophe produced a fever which lasted for some days. When he got well, he obtained leave of absence, and went into the country to try to divert his mind. One evening at moonlight, he was returning home from a walk, and passed through a lane with a hedge on both sides, so high that he could not see over them. The night was balmy; the bushes gleamed with fireflies, brighter than the stars which the moon had veiled with her silver light.

Suddenly he heard a rustling near him, and the figure of his friend issued from the hedge and stood before him, mutilated as he had seen him after his death. This figure he saw several times, always in the same place. It was impalpable to the touch, motionless, except in its advance, and made no sign when it was addressed. Once the Chevalier took a friend with him to the spot. The same rustling was heard, the same shadow slept forth, his companion fled in horror, but the Chevalier staid, vainly endeavouring to discover what called his friend from his quiet tomb, and if any act of his might give repose to the restless shade.

Such are my two stories, and I record them the more willingly, since they occurred to men, and to individuals distinguished the one for courage and the other for sagacity. I will conclude my "modern instances," with a story told by M. G. Lewis, not probably so authentic as these, but perhaps more amusing. I relate it as nearly as possible in his own words:

A gentleman journeying towards the house of a friend, who lived on the skirts of an extensive forest, in the east of Germany, lost his way. He wandered for some time among the trees, when he saw a light at a distance. On approaching it he was surprised to observe that it proceeded from the interior of a ruined monastery. Before he knocked at the gate he thought it proper to look through the window. He saw a number of cats assembled round a small grave, four of whom were at that moment letting down a coffin with a crown upon it.

The gentleman startled at this unusual sight, and, imagining that he had arrived at the retreats of fiends or witches, mounted his horse and rode away with the utmost precipitation. He arrived at his friend's house at a late hour, who sate up waiting for him. On his arrival his friend questioned him as to the cause of the traces of agitation visible in his face. He began to recount his adventures after much hesitation, knowing that it was scarcely possible that his friend should give faith to his relation.

No sooner had he mentioned the coffin with the crown upon it, than his friend's cat, who seemed to have been lying asleep before the fire, leaped up, crying out, 'Then I am king of the cats;' and then scrambled up the chimney, and was never seen more.

LEONAUR

ALSO FROM LEONAUR

AVAILABLE IN SOFTCOVER OR HARDCOVER WITH DUST JACKET

THE FIRST BOOK OF AYESHA *by H. Rider Haggard*—Contains *She & Ayesha: the Return of She.*

THE SECOND BOOK OF AYESHA *by H. Rider Haggard*—Contains *She and Allan & Wisdom's Daughter.*

QUATERMAIN: THE COMPLETE ADVENTURES—1 *by H. Rider Haggard*—Contains *King Solomon's Mines & Allan Quatermain.*

QUATERMAIN: THE COMPLETE ADVENTURES—2 *by H. Rider Haggard*—Contains *Allan's Wife, Maiwa's Revenge & Marie.*

QUATERMAIN: THE COMPLETE ADVENTURES—3 *by H. Rider Haggard*—Contains *Child of Storm & Allan and the Holy Flower.*

QUATERMAIN: THE COMPLETE ADVENTURES—4 *by H. Rider Haggard*—Contains *Finished & The Ivory Child.*

QUATERMAIN: THE COMPLETE ADVENTURES—5 *by H. Rider Haggard*—Contains *The Ancient Allan & She and Allan.*

QUATERMAIN: THE COMPLETE ADVENTURES—6 *by H. Rider Haggard*—Contains *Heu-Heu or, the Monster & The Treasure of the Lake.*

QUATERMAIN: THE COMPLETE ADVENTURES—7 *by H. Rider Haggard*—Contains *Allan and the Ice Gods, Four Short Adventures & Nada the Lily.*

TROS OF SAMOTHRACE 1: WOLVES OF THE TIBER *by Talbot Mundy*—55 B.C.--an adventurer set during the Roman invasion of Britain.

TROS OF SAMOTHRACE 2: DRAGONS OF THE NORTH *by Talbot Mundy*—55 B.C. —Caesar plots, Britons war among themselves and the Vikings are coming.

TROS OF SAMOTHRACE 3: SERPENT OF THE WAVES *by Talbot Mundy*—55 B.C.--Caesar is poised to invade Britain—only a grand strategy can foil him!.

TROS OF SAMOTHRACE 4: CITY OF THE EAGLES *by Talbot Mundy*—54 B.C.—Rome—Tros treads in the streets of his sworn enemies!.

TROS OF SAMOTHRACE 5: CLEOPATRA *by Talbot Mundy*—Tros and the Roman Empire turn to the Egypt of the Pharaohs.

TROS OF SAMOTHRACE 6: THE PURPLE PIRATE *by Talbot Mundy*—The epic saga of the ancient world—Tros of Samothrace—draws to a conclusion in this sixth—and final—volume.

LEONAUR

ALSO FROM LEONAUR
AVAILABLE IN SOFTCOVER OR HARDCOVER WITH DUST JACKET

THE PRISONER OF ZENDA & ITS SEQUEL RUPERT OF HENTZAU by *Anthony Hope*—Two famous novels of high adventure in one volume.

THE GLADIATORS by *G. J. Whyte Melville*—A Classic Novel of Ancient Rome—Three Volumes in One Special Edition.

THE COMPLETE CAPTAIN DANGEROUS by *George Augustus Sala*—The Adventures of a Soldier, Sailor, Merchant, Spy, Slave and Bashaw of the Grand Turk.

ORTHERIS, LEAROYD & MULVANEY by *Rudyard Kipling*—The Complete Soldiers Three stories.

SIR NIGEL & THE WHITE COMPANY by *Arthur Conan Doyle*—Two Classic Novels of the 100 Years' War.

THE ILLUSTRATED & COMPLETE BRIGADIER GERARD by *Arthur Conan Doyle*—All 18 Stories with the Original Strand Magazine Illustrations by Wollen and Paget.

THE OHIO RIVER TRILOGY 1: BETTY ZANE by *Zane Grey*—The land along the Ohio River is newly settled. Indomitable men and women—Col. Zane and his family, the McCollochs, Wetzel, the "Death Wind" Indian killer, among them—have hewn a life out of the frontier wilderness.

THE OHIO RIVER TRILOGY 2: THE SPIRIT OF THE BORDER by *Zane Grey*—Fort Henry still stands as a bastion for the settlers on the frontier along the Ohio River. More pioneers are now moving west to carve new lives out of the wilderness.

THE OHIO RIVER TRILOGY 3: THE LAST TRAIL by *Zane Grey*—This final volume of Zane Grey's Ohio River Trilogy is a gripping finale to a great series—another thrilling story of life and death on the early American frontier and a classic in the tradition of Drums Along the Mohawk.

THE NAPOLEONIC NOVELS: VOLUME 1 by *Erckmann-Chatrian*—This book comprises two linked novels—*The Conscript* & *Waterloo*—about the adventures a young conscript in the French Army. during the Napoleonic wars.

THE NAPOLEONIC NOVELS: VOLUME 2 by *Erckmann-Chatrian*—*The Blockade of Phalsburg* & *The Invasion of France in 1814*—the events portrayed in these two novels of the Napoleonic period properly fit in time between those of the first volume. They appear together here since each—unlike the other two in this series—is a stand alone work.

LEONAUR

ALSO FROM LEONAUR
AVAILABLE IN SOFTCOVER OR HARDCOVER WITH DUST JACKET

THE CIVIL WAR NOVELS: 1 *by Joseph A. Altsheler*—*The Guns of Bull Run &* *The Guns of Shiloh*—the first and second novels of a series of eight adventures which follow the momentous events, campaigns and battles of the great American Civil War between the Northern and Southern states.

THE CIVIL WAR NOVELS: 2 *by Joseph A. Altsheler*—*The Scouts of Stonewall* & *The Sword of Antietam*—the third and fourth novels of a series of nine adventures which follow the momentous events, campaigns and battles of the great American Civil War between the Northern and Southern states.

THE CIVIL WAR NOVELS: 3 *by Joseph A. Altsheler*—*The Star of Gettysburg* & *The Rock of Chickamauga*—the fifth and sixth novels of a series of nine adventures which follow the momentous events, campaigns and battles of the great American Civil War between the Northern and Southern states.

THE CIVIL WAR NOVELS: 4 *by Joseph A. Altsheler*—*The Shades of the Wilderness* & *The Tree of Appomattox*—the seventh and eighth novels of a series of nine adventures which follow the momentous events, campaigns and battles of the great American Civil War between the Northern and Southern states.

THE CIVIL WAR NOVELS: 5 *by Joseph A. Altsheler*—*Before the Dawn: a Story of the Fall of Richmond*—the last of a series of nine adventures which follow the momentous events, campaigns and battles of the great American Civil War between the Northern and Southern states.

THE FRENCH & INDIAN WAR NOVELS: 1 *by Joseph A. Altsheler*—*The Hunters of the Hills* & *The Shadow of the North*—In this three volume, six novel set the story of the war, with many of its real life characters, is told through the adventures of its principal characters, Robert Lennox, the hunter Willet and his Indian companion Tayoga.

THE FRENCH & INDIAN WAR NOVELS: 2 *by Joseph A. Altsheler*—*The Rulers of the Lakes* & *The Masters of the Peaks*—In this three volume, six novel set the story of the war, with many of its real life characters, is told through the adventures of its principal characters, Robert Lennox, the hunter Willet and his Indian companion Tayoga.

THE FRENCH & INDIAN WAR NOVELS: 1 *by Joseph A. Altsheler*—*The Lords of the Wild & The Sun of Quebec*—In this three volume, six novel set the story of the war, with many of its real life characters, is told through the adventures of its principal characters, Robert Lennox, the hunter Willet and his Indian companion Tayoga.

ALSO FROM LEONAUR

AVAILABLE IN SOFTCOVER OR HARDCOVER WITH DUST JACKET

THE LONG PATROL *by George Berrie*—A Novel of Light Horsemen from Gallipoli to the Palestine campaign of the First World War.

NAPOLEONIC WAR STORIES *by Arthur Quiller-Couch*—Tales of soldiers, spies, battles & sieges from the Peninsular & Waterloo campaingns.

THE FIRST DETECTIVE *by Edgar Allan Poe*—The Complete Auguste Dupin Stories—The Murders in the Rue Morgue, The Mystery of Marie Rogêt & The Purloined Letter.

THE COMPLETE DR NIKOLA—MAN OF MYSTERY: 1 *by Guy Boothby*—*A Bid for Fortune & Dr Nikola Returns*—Guy Boothby's Dr.Nikola adventures continue to fascinate readers and enthusiasts of crime and mystery fiction because—in the manner of Raffles, the gentleman cracksman—here is character far removed from the uncompromising goodness of Holmes and Watson or the uncompromising evil of Professor Moriarty.

THE COMPLETE DR NIKOLA—MAN OF MYSTERY: 2 *by Guy Boothby*—*The Lust of Hate, Dr Nikola's Experiment & Farewell, Nikola*—Guy Boothby's Dr.Nikola adventures continue to fascinate readers and enthusiasts of crime and mystery fiction because—in the manner of Raffles, the gentleman cracksman—here is character far removed from the uncompromising goodness of Holmes and Watson or the uncompromising evil of Professor Moriarty.

THE CASEBOOKS OF MR J. G. REEDER: BOOK 1 *by Edgar Wallace*—*Room 13, The Mind of Mr J. G. Reeder* and *Terror Keep*—Edgar Wallace's sleuth—whose territory is the London of the 1920s—is an unlikely figure, more bank clerk than detective in appearance, ever wearing his square topped bowler, frock coat, cravat and muffler, Mr Reeder is usually inseparable from his umbrella.

THE CASEBOOKS OF MR J. G. REEDER: BOOK 2 *by Edgar Wallace*—*Red Aces, Mr J. G. Reeder Returns, The Guv'nor* and *The Man Who Passed*—Edgar Wallace's sleuth—whose territory is the London of the 1920s—is an unlikely figure, more bank clerk than detective in appearance, ever wearing his square topped bowler, frock coat, cravat and muffler, Mr Reeder is usually inseparable from his umbrella.

THE COMPLETE FOUR JUST MEN: VOLUME 1 *by Edgar Wallace*—*The Four Just Men, The Council of Justice & The Just Men of Cordova*—disillusioned with a world where the wicked and the abusers of power perpetually go unpunished, the Just Men set about to rectify matters according to their own standards, and retribution is dispensed on swift and deadly wings.

LEONAUR

ALSO FROM LEONAUR
AVAILABLE IN SOFTCOVER OR HARDCOVER WITH DUST JACKET

THE COMPLETE FOUR JUST MEN: VOLUME 2 *by Edgar Wallace*—*The Law of the Four Just Men & The Three Just Men*—disillusioned with a world where the wicked and the abusers of power perpetually go unpunished, the Just Men set about to rectify matters according to their own standards, and retribution is dispensed on swift and deadly wings.

THE COMPLETE RAFFLES: 1 *by E. W. Hornung*—*The Amateur Cracksman & The Black Mask*—By turns urbane gentleman about town and accomplished cricketer, life is just too ordinary for Raffles and that sets him on a series of adventures that have long been treasured as a real antidote to the 'white knights' who are the usual heroes of the crime fiction of this period.

THE COMPLETE RAFFLES: 2 *by E. W. Hornung*—*A Thief in the Night & Mr Justice Raffles*—By turns urbane gentleman about town and accomplished cricketer, life is just too ordinary for Raffles and that sets him on a series of adventures that have long been treasured as a real antidote to the 'white knights' who are the usual heroes of the crime fiction of this period.

THE COLLECTED SUPERNATURAL AND WEIRD FICTION OF WILKIE COLLINS: VOLUME 1 *by Wilkie Collins*—Contains one novel 'The Haunted Hotel', one novella 'Mad Monkton', three novelettes 'Mr Percy and the Prophet', 'The Biter Bit' and 'The Dead Alive' and eight short stories to chill the blood.

THE COLLECTED SUPERNATURAL AND WEIRD FICTION OF WILKIE COLLINS: VOLUME 2 *by Wilkie Collins*—Contains one novel 'The Two Destinies', three novellas 'The Frozen deep', 'Sister Rose' and 'The Yellow Mask' and two short stories to chill the blood.

THE COLLECTED SUPERNATURAL AND WEIRD FICTION OF WILKIE COLLINS: VOLUME 3 *by Wilkie Collins*—Contains one novel 'Dead Secret,' two novelettes 'Mrs Zant and the Ghost' and 'The Nun's Story of Gabriel's Marriage' and five short stories to chill the blood.

FUNNY BONES *selected by Dorothy Scarborough*—An Anthology of Humorous Ghost Stories.

MONTEZUMA'S CASTLE AND OTHER WEIRD TALES *by Charles B. Cory*—Cory has written a superb collection of eighteen ghostly and weird stories to chill and thrill the avid enthusiast of supernatural fiction.

SUPERNATURAL BUCHAN *by John Buchan*—Stories of Ancient Spirits, Uncanny Places & Strange Creatures.

www.ingramcontent.com/pod-product-compliance
Lightning Source LLC
Chambersburg PA
CBHW030747030726
47497CB00001B/168